TOYER

Plays by Gardner McKay

Sea Marks
Me.
Toyer
In Order of Appearance
Masters of the Sea
This Fortunate Island

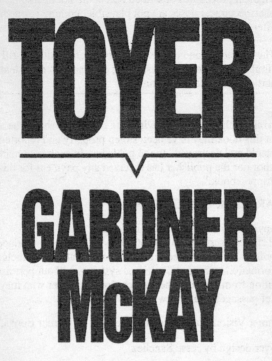

TOYER

GARDNER McKAY

WARNER
VISION
BOOKS

A Time Warner Company

WARNER BOOKS EDITION

Copyright © 1998 by Gardner McKay
All rights reserved. No part of this book may be reproduced in any form or by any electronic or mechanical means, including information storage and retrieval systems, without permission in writing from the publisher, except by a reviewer who may quote brief passages in a review.

Warner Vision is a registered trademark of Warner Books, Inc.

Cover design by Jesse Sanchez

Warner Books, Inc.
1271 Avenue of the Americas
New York, NY 10020

Visit our Web site at
www.twbookmark.com

W A Time Warner Company

Printed in the United States of America

Originally published in hardcover by Little, Brown and Company
First Paperback Printing: December 1999

10 9 8 7 6 5 4 3 2 1

Madeleine

The real crime is not the crime.
The real crime is that we turn the page.

———————

Never order a Margarita in a Chinese restaurant.

TOYER

PRELUDE
LOS ANGELES

The primary color, pearl gray, a whitish blue sky. At night, the purple loom of the city, an all-night dusk.

Here, the wind never blows, it hardly ever rains. Los Angeles does not look well in the rain; its stucco houses change color like a runner's sweatshirt. No building is well-worn, nothing is burnished, there is no rust, there are no weathered houses, no forgotten graveyards.

Los Angeles has no history, no monuments, no statues, no comment. It exists because its water was once stolen from Inyo County to the north.

Its land was stolen from the Chumash Indians by the Spanish, then stolen from the Spanish by the Americans. Now, the Indians are dead, the Spanish have returned, and Los Angeles is waiting for revenge from the ruined county to the north, the county that no longer has water, which is now dead. It is ripe for retribution.

There is Beverly Hills. Everything here is new. Cars fresh as eggs, consortiums built on lunches, recent clothes designed in ancient cities, iridescent paintings nearly dry, wafer-soled shoes that never walk stab German accelerators, bright snappy credit cards, young hair. Nothing said yesterday is remembered today. Only the new is trusted, admired. It is all famously temporary. Haunted by ghosts of its late celebratti, those who traded up, house to house, some only renting, then died. Roots equal stagnation. Timeworn equals poverty. Realtors equal beau monde. Oranges lie in gutters beside furry tennis balls. There are no poor.

The Sunset Strip. A tribute to democratic free enterprise, seen by a cartoonist. Its billboards sell vanities, set in place above the low buildings to divert the sky, the stained air. Outdoor cafés abound close to sealed cars driven in anger. Strollers are intruders.

Hollywood. The hills are legally green, a green without death. Dusk colors seen in noon gloaming. Palms in still-life, crematorium ash on their fronds. The landscape ages in the manner of a vinyl sofa. The silence is eerie.

There are two seasons, day and night.

Downtown. Packing crates stand around, half-opened; a cluster of shiny buildings that will not be allowed to age.

Los Angeles is not a city, it is a wide town. A town without a history; it does not want one. It is incomplete, possibly hiding. It is made up of dozens of districts, some with their own city hall, each with its own police precinct, its own complacency, its own anger.

It has no memory, no center. It is waiting to become. Anything. Created by water theft. A done deal.

Toyer. He is a masterpiece. A natural response to this neighborhood. He is perfect. The fresh curse. There has never been anything like Toyer, but of course, each time there never is. Each time, the newest cutting-edge-serial-lunatic has the same refreshing aspect; he is unimaginable.

He has it all. He is a reservoir of all those who have preceded him. Of Ted Bundy, because he has the charisma of a would-be congressman. The Nightstalker, as a beautiful Satan. The steadfast Hillside Strangler, with his plodding self-expressionism. The pathetic Son of Sam who took orders from a dog's voice. The misguided Zodiac. The expressionless Iceman. Tod.

Toyer's domain is Los Angeles. And to the north, the San Fernando Valley, a vast, dry flatland that aspires to be Los Angeles when it grows up. He uses the wide town without opinion, as though he were playing tennis on a court too large, its base lines out of sight. The map of his conquests bewilders the police. Investigators connect colored pins hoping to see pentacles, to discover constellations. He gives them no clue except: he is new and he is unimaginable.

THE BEGINNING

LYDIA SNOW LAVIN

BUT THE MOVIE was far longer than Lydia wanted it to be. When she stood up, it had been over for her a long time. An endless anecdote. Would the lovers die badly? No, of course they wouldn't, she no longer cared, she had seen the trailer. Still, she had stayed on for the final terrorist explosion, waiting it out.

The FBI agent who'd assigned them to work together knew how much they disliked each other, which meant they'd fall in love. But when they did, Lydia could see that the actors still disliked each other. Horrible kisses.

When the lights came up, dimly raising the theater to its fetid grandeur, she noticed that she was nearly alone. Half-a-dozen couples rose, brushing crumbs. She slipped her movie glasses off, tucked them into her purse. One by one, she had clicked off the moments from the trailer. *Whoever makes the trailer sure doesn't make the movie. Trailers are so much better, it's always a breathless filmlet guided by a spiritual baritone who begins, "In a world where . . ."*

You can't return a movie. Return a dress, a steak, wine, but never a movie. It's a blind date from Hollywood and your evening's shot. What about an evening of two-minute movies?

In protest, she dropped her Diet Pepsi cup with a *clack* on the cement floor.

Six rows down, a man looked over at her, a black-haired man wearing a white shirt, sleeves rolled up a bit, two buttons open, he was with a much shorter girl. He turned away down the aisle and looked back, smiled directly at Lydia, shrugged. About the movie? She intuitively looked down. *He could be in sales, he could be in advertising.* Lydia's set dream: the care and feeding of a rising professional who drives away to work every morning smelling of soap, wearing shined shoes.

The lush heat of the parking lot surrounded her ears and neck. Used air. She followed the black-haired man and his much shorter date, a couple no longer speaking, as they passed between atmospheres from theater lobby to night to car.

But her car would not start. Lydia sat, key turned, pumping the gas pedal. It almost started, but it just would not. And the air conditioner would not work without the motor, she wondered why. She saw her black-haired executive get into a small new car *with his midget girlfriend.* Now they were arguing. Of course they would, *they were so mismatched.* Lydia signaled to him, waving. *I'll bet he can start my car,* but only the *dwarf* saw her wave, the rising professional had turned the other way and they drove off.

Lydia tried the starter again. The battery worked, she heard the fierce whine under the hood, determined. The lights came on, the radio played. But the air conditioner would not. *Where the hell is Rick?*

Now she smelled gas. *Great. The thing is flooded.* Whenever you smell gas, according to Rick, it's flooded.

Rick isn't available. If he was, she would not need to call him, he would be here with her. She had telephoned him from the lobby, he had not answered. *He's home with his ratty bimbo.* She listened again to his male hunter-gatherer message, *I'm-out-your-call-is-important-to-me-maybe*. She left a message so loud they both could hear it in the bedroom, telling him to go fuck himself.

She looked back at the theater, probably built in the 1940s, a shabby temple created to dignify bad movies. Whatever palatial magic it once held was gone. She stayed in her car ten minutes as Rick had told her to do, waiting for whatever needed to happen to a flooded motor. *Drain, I guess.*

Lydia stared at the hood. The lights on the theater's marquee snapped off. Now in the black, she could see the moon faintly reflected on the hood. Once, when she was six and plump, she stood up in class and answered that she would love to live on the moon but what would she eat there? Even her teacher had laughed. *That comes back to me at the strangest times.*

Lydia got out of the car, looked directly up at the moon, a tough little shard, a wintry moon on a sultry night. *Winter up there, maybe.* Strangely clear. Jupiter and Orion and Mars. *Everything is in order. Life goes on. Without Rick.*

She knocked on the glass door of the theater, rattling it. The staff had slipped away, only the popcorn machine stood watch, glowing, loaded with puffed kibble for tomorrow's audience.

She sat again in the locked car, holding the wheel with both hands, head down, waiting for something to happen.

A man, maybe twenty-five or so, in a dark jacket and white rubber-soled shoes, was using the pay telephone, lit at the corner of the parking lot, leaning on a bronze car the size of an aircraft carrier. One hip out. Jeans. She watched him. *If he ever gets through talking, I'll call Rick and say I'm sorry.*

When he hung up she waved to him. "Excuse me?" she called out. "Sir?" He got into his car and drove over to her.

Her hood was up. He had raised it effortlessly, blindly pressing the release hook with insolent skill. He stood between their cars, slouched, thinking with his face. *Good skin.* He was about her age and she could not tell in the overhead light exactly what he looked like, whether he was cute or not, but he seemed uncomplicated, a familiar type. Shy. His jacket had a large orange H on it. *I don't know anyone who still wears their letter jacket.*

He had not turned off his engine and it churned beside them with the bass grumbling of proud carburetors, storming the night. Gleaming wheels, the hood's polished whorls, both ends jacked up an extra foot off the ground. His car's interior looked tidy and she felt lucky.

A shy, boy-man devoted to cars. Why shouldn't she ask him for help? She had always gotten along well with simple men and here was a simple man. She wasn't too complicated herself, she thought, why shouldn't she get along? Anyway, he wore a letter jacket and called her transmission a *tranny* and she thought that was cute.

He connected his work-light from his battery and hung it under her hood. She gave him a coat hanger from the back seat of her car and he sculpted it into a long o-o and installed it under her hood. She thanked him before he fixed it, as he was fixing it, and when he had fixed it. She started her car. A classic nice guy. *All you hear are warnings.*

Driving. Even at night, barely seen, the barren main streets of the Valley were without redemption. Above the closed stores on the scathing signs, the merchants' pleadings: *SALE!* A visitor to the San Fernando Valley would sense sweeping fear of bankruptcy. Tension lingered along blocks of dark stores. *Sell. Sell.* There was no restraint. The number .99 figured in all appeals, a nagging tribute to buyers' mindlessness.

In her rearview mirror, Lydia watched his headlights several car lengths behind her. He was driving in the inside lane so his lights would not irritate her. He had offered to follow her home to make sure the wire coat hanger held.

Now the flat, billboard boulevards began to curve, rising gently toward the hills. The Valley changed as she drove, the drastic store-fronts became firm New England dwellings, Spanish haciendas. Narrow streets named by Realtors, ending in *dale* and *crest* and *view*. They passed Multiview Drive. Now, occasional streetlights through the area named Warren Oak Crest.

Into the hills, known to be the Santa Monica Mountains, that ran the breadth of the Valley to the south. Mounds made of decomposing granite that rose maybe two hundred and fifty feet. Houses that resembled Lego toys clung to steep miniature lots where no houses belonged and only animals were able walk among abrupt inclines. Some were built in air, standing on stilts. Below, the slopes were covered by growths of sage and sumac, already dried by summer, ready to burn.

He drove behind her at the same measured distance. *Good guys. Where do they come from? Where are they going?* He parked with fierce speed half a block behind her on the slanted street. *He may never have finished school and he's nicer than almost anyone at work.*

The porch light was on, surrounded by flights of moths who believed they had found the sun. Dimly lit was the small stoop by the front door, space for only a straight wood bench.

The cottage was built in the tradition of appliances never intended to outlast their guarantee, maybe fifty years ago in the 1940s or the 1950s, no one knew when. But it had lasted, and in the 1960s a laundry room had been added to the kitchen and, later, a spindly carport. There were no standard stains of age because there was no real weather, only infectious air. The small house looked wizened.

He stood in the doorway. The lighting in the living room never seemed to matter to Lydia. There was the original ceiling light, exhausted, that gave the room a masculine etch. There were two small lamps, bought used, one with an amber shade, the other with a red shade. There was a suite of white wicker furniture and a defeated sofa. On the walls were framed posters. The bathroom door was open, displaying dark plastic bottles.

"Pliers?" He opened and closed his hand. *School for the deaf.* "You have pliers, miss?" *Miss? He's forgotten my name.*

"Yes. I'll get them." *Rick left a pair.*

"I'd like to finish the job up so you could get to work tomorrow, and a screwdriver, please. And a rag."

She found a rag but no screwdriver and she handed him an iced tea spoon taken from a café. "You love cars, right?"

"I guess." When she handed him the spoon, he almost smiled. "This is a spoon."

She wanted to laugh. "It's as close to a screwdriver as you get here."

"No problem." She saw him now, a doer of good deeds. Not entirely unattractive to her. Taller. Slightly older. Still, he seemed mindless, and she knew she would never be even slightly interested in a mindless man, no matter how good he was. He might lie under cars all day and watch baseball in the evenings and aspire to golf. *Like Dad.*

His bronze aircraft carrier idled down the block by the curb. He switched the great drumbling motor off, leaving the night unstartled. In a moment, delicate sounds of rushing insects joined them.

She brought him a cup of coffee.

"I don't drink coffee, but thank you, miss."

"Oh, come on in." She had forgotten his name, if she ever knew it at all. "I'm not going to hurt you." She wanted to get him talking, maybe learn just a little more about why her car stopped running.

By the time he came to the door again she was dipping two tea bags into a white china teapot, vapor rising. "It works," he said, grinning.

"Great." *Everyone else I know is so damned complicated.* For all her freedom, Lydia was unfree.

"Well, I've got to be driving back up to Northridge." *Nice guys live in Northridge.*

"Come on in for a minute. I mean, I wish I could pay you something but I know you wouldn't accept it. After all, you rode by like a knight on horseback and rescued me." *He isn't getting the part about the knight.* "I've just made a pot of tea."

"Hot tea?"

"Yeah, believe it or not, it's good on hot nights."

"What time is it?"

He doesn't even have a watch. Everyone has a watch.

"Well, let's see, what time did the movie start? Eight twenty?"

"Yeah, so it's got to be . . ." he moved his fingers along his thigh without knowing it, counting, "probably eleven thirty or so. I better go."

"Oh, have a cup. Hot tea's better than iced tea on summer nights, makes you hotter inside than out, keeps you from sweating."

"Oh, yeah?" He sat on the sofa with a clump. "Good movie, huh?" he said.

"You saw it?" *He was there?* "I didn't know you saw it."

"Yeah, most of it. Cool plane crash." *Where was he sitting?*

"I hated it, quite honestly." *So did my executive.* She handed him the cup and saucer. "Did you really believe those two belonged together?"

"Yeah, why not?" *God, isn't he something?*

"I don't know, just two movie stars. Love is . . ." She stopped, too personal.

"No rules, I guess."

No rules? Where did that come from? "No, I guess maybe not." *No rules in love.* "Maybe you're right. Maybe anyone belongs with anyone." *Was that him in the back row? Someone came in late.*

He was looking around the room. "Nice place you've got here." *Well, he's not an architect, anyway.* "Very quiet."

"It gets on my nerves sometimes, frankly."

Deep thought. "Yeah. I guess." *My knight, unhorsed, is really boring.*

He put the cup aside, embarrassed. "Hey, I'm sorry. It's too hot for me."

"It's just as well. We have to get up."

"Who's we?"

"Well, you know, I have . . . a roommate coming home anytime." *What made me say that?* "She sleeps right where you're sitting as a matter of fact, it's a sofa bed." *I don't have a roommate coming home and it's not a sofa bed. Why am I lying?*

He half rose. Sat. Stood. Maybe embarrassed that she had so obviously put a border on the evening. *Mom told me never to tell a man you live alone unless you're prepared to spend the night with him.*

They looked away from each other in silence, listening to the absolute soundlessness of the night. Lydia had not heard a car pass the house for ten minutes. The gap of silence widened. He had nothing left to say. Neither did she.

"Lydia . . ." He stopped. There was something wrong, *Lydia was too familiar, too sure. He knows my name after all.* Her name hung in the room as though she had been accused.

"Your roommate's not coming home. I don't think." He said it simply, as if to set the record straight.

"What do you mean?"

"She's moved." He added, "Carol," as if he liked the name. *He knows our names. He knows she stayed here last month.*

"I was in here earlier," he said.

"But what do you mean?" She was feeling dizzy.

"Here." His eyes scanned the room aimlessly. "I cut your phone line." He pointed to the window. "Outside." He sat with his arms spread across the back of the sofa.

She barely heard him and when she did, hearing him say it again in her mind, she did not think she really had. She wanted to ask him how he knew Carol's name but she could not shape the words.

"Now don't go getting upset."

"I'm not." The first wave of fear. *Oh, dear Christ, what's going on? Be cool.* "It's just that it's late and I want some more tea."

He reached his untouched cup of tea to her without standing and looked at her with a surprisingly weary look. "Have mine, please. Your throat's a little dry, isn't it?"

It is dry. Lydia looked down at her hands reaching for the cup, they looked small and bleached.

He was standing above her.

"My boyfriend . . ."

"Rick?"

Jesus.

"You're not seeing Rick anymore." Condolences.

What a strange thing was happening to Lydia.

"I've been picking up your phone messages recently."

No no no no no no. Could she run out the door? Throw herself through the window? She was not sure her legs would work.

"Why?" She said it too weakly to be heard. She raised her head, looked up at his waist. "Why me? Why do you want me?" She sat forward on the white wicker chair, her legs bent like spring levers under her, trying to be ready.

He was here earlier. He saw I lived alone. He followed me to the movie. He came back here. He cut my phone line. He went back to the theater. He broke my car. He saw part of the movie. He was waiting for me in the parking lot. Why did I stay to the end of that stupid movie?

He sat. He stared at her face. Pale, steady, simple, he stared at her sweetly, a suitor come with flowers. When he spoke, he spoke kindly. "I love you," he said.

The words slugged her. Plain, everyday, greeting card words. She looked at his face for further meaning, for something to come from him that would help her, to tell her, "*I only wanted you to know that I love you. I'm not going to harm you. I'm really not a lunatic.*" But he did not say that.

She realized her mouth was open. He turned his head to the kitchen for an instant. *Push up jump run. Run. Run. Door.* She was on her feet, running for the front door. *Door. Door. Door. Please be open.* Reaching for the knob. He was there waiting for her, between her and the door. Waiting. She had not even heard him move. *He's liquid.*

He walked her back to her chair, holding the cord of her neck locked between his thumb and index finger. If she hesitated, the pain became abrupt.

"Don't. Please," he whispered. His voice, tired but still kind. An apology was there. "I'm just so quick." Then, with a helpless respect for something he could not control, "God, I'm quick." As though he possessed a sort of terrible excellence he barely understood. "Don't be afraid, Lydia."

She was, very. She began to hear a wide hollowness echo in her ears, then a busy clamor of voices that she had to speak above to be heard.

"I'm not afraid of you." Her voice drifted away toward the ceiling, lighter than the thick air.

What if he really does love me? If he does, he won't hurt me. He's not going to rape me, is he? Rapists are violent and he's so shy and quiet. I've got to let him know, tell him that it'll be okay, if that's what he wants, I'll give it to him. He's cute. I don't want him to rape me. He won't have to. He has to know what I'll do or he'll be scared and hurt me. His fingers are too strong.

Lydia was giving way, feeling younger than she had since school, knowing that what was happening now was going to be over soon, that it would come out all right, that Rick would realize his mistake and feel remorse and come looking for her and burst through the door at any second.

But there is no Rick anymore. I told him to go fuck himself and everyone else is asleep and I'm alone in the world.

He came over to her. He did not touch her. He stood. He seemed adrift in the room.

He won't ever leave until he gets what he wants. "What do you want me to do?"

"Don't cry."

"I won't."

I want it to be over. I want it to be an hour from now, I want it to be tomorrow morning.

"You don't know what's going on, do you?"

Lydia stopped breathing. "Can you *please* tell me what you want?" *I can hear my body trembling.*

"Don't you know who I am?"

Please, no.

"You must have heard of me." He spoke so quietly. *This is him.* "Have you? Do you have any idea how famous I am?"

She no longer could feel her face. She had the impression that her insides were not there anymore and that the rest of her was falling a long way down in front of her.

Six years old. Caught. Coat pockets in the locker room. Hairpins. Silver coins. Thief. Waiting for the principal. Down in the big sticky chair, my panties stuck to the leather. Phone call to Mom. The electric clock, 10:10. Snow. Everyone in school knows. Dismissed. Sent home. Punishment. Everyone on earth knows.

For a few moments, Lydia did not know how long, she drifted away above the room with the stupid swap meet lamps that she always hated and watched the two of them from an enlightened place. He was talking, she was listening. She heard the word *moon* once and then again. She vaguely realized he had stopped talking and was staring at her, waiting for something, maybe for her to speak. He had said something about the moon and it came back to her the way church bells come back into your sleep and you know exactly what time it is. "The night is a memory of night. No one knows the night anymore. No one looks at the sky. No one knows what to look for. Light is too important," was what he had said. "Have you ever looked at the moon?"

"Of course, yes, I love the moon." *What does he mean?* "I used to want to live there." *He's a lunatic.*

"Dead as the moon. The saddest words I ever heard." He was staring at her, imploring her. "The moon is dead but she goes on being beautiful, doesn't she? Rising and setting, on and on."

This is what he looks like. Toyer. I've read every word they've written about him. Everyone has. The women are always drugged.

"Am I drugged?"

He nodded once.

The tea. Yes.

"Just think, you won't see tomorrow and I will."

Beyond the room, the Valley slept. Across the vast basin, the twitching of edgy televisions lit its ceilings.

Please rape me. Do it to me. But don't do the other thing. He sat forward, concerned. "What were you going to do tomorrow?"

I'm going to run through the window. It'll cut me. I'll cover my face. Now. Through the window. Out.

Her legs straightened and she leaped toward the window. He caught her arm. She fell against him and jerked herself back and swung her fists at him but she did not feel them hitting him. She was screaming or thought she was screaming. Maybe she hit him a dozen times, she tried to bite him. She stopped.

Empty, she lowered herself without muscle back into the white wicker armchair. She remembered the decorative pattern of the protective bars outside the window. *There are never any goddamn open windows in a woman's house.*

He stood above her again, breathing evenly. "Don't scream again." The way he said it, bone dry, without apology, was different from anything else he had said. He prompted her, as though he needed to know her plans, "What were you going to do tomorrow?"

"Work. Lunch with a girlfriend . . ."

"Who?"

"Katrina." *Why does he want to know her name?* "She's Swedish. She's getting married. Cash my paycheck. Pay for a dress." She pulled the pillow around from behind her and pressed it into her face, smothering herself, so she could bite into it, jolted by her sobs, sobbing helplessly, without strength, without knowing where she was, a step out from the world she was standing on, almost falling, free, almost falling, dead, her world remembered as a place she once knew, a place she could not imagine how she got to or why she was leaving. He seemed disappointed in her as though he had relied on her and she had let him down.

Good faces cannot be measured. Pretty, comely faces. In Lydia's there was an imbalance between the alertness of her eyes, a lightness, a playful maliciousness; and the spread of her mouth, a serious, grave mouth. Her eyes, somehow even now, seemed optimistic, her mouth dark with fear as if she deserved grief.

This is what dead is like. But he won't kill me. He never does. All those girls, living on wheels, wheeled around. Who'll wheel me around? I'll be in Pennsylvania with my folks again. They'll look after me. They'll read to me. I'll watch television. People will love me. It'll make them sad about me. They love victims. I'll be able to see it in their faces. Thank God I've got a big family.

He was speaking. "I may never stop." So poised. "But then I may. If something goes wrong, I think they'll take good care of me, they'll give me their very best." *This is Toyer telling me about Toyer's agenda.*

"Listen to me." She could not hear him. Sound was rushing past her ears. She felt him touch her shoulder and jerked away with the pillow held tight to her face as if it alone would keep her safe.

"Listen to me. Can you hear me? I've got a present for you. You're going to do those things tomorrow. You're going to be all right."

Lydia peered at him above the pillow. He was standing in the middle of the room. He was smiling.

"I live down the street. I see you drive by every day. I just followed you to the movies." He talked to Lydia as if he were talking to a parakeet.

Say it again.

"It's all right. Please, I didn't mean to go all the way. I'm sorry. I didn't mean to scare you."

What.

Now he brought his hands from behind his head and leaned close to her face. He waited until her eyes opened. He was so close that his face blurred into a single owl's eye. He said in an easy, trained voice, "I'm an actor."

He spoke with such ease, such trueness, he might have been royalty handing her his crested calling card.

"An actor?" *God, I hate actors.*

"Well, an unemployed actor." He pulled a black comb from his back pocket. "Haven't had a good part since I came here. Not in this town anyway." He took a moment. "Except this. I was playing a part, understand? I just wanted to make some total stranger believe me. I try to build a character and when I think it's all there I . . ." He interrupted himself to comb his hair. "Then I sort of cut it down a bit, try to make it work." She could see he was enjoying the moment, that it *had* worked for him.

He smiled and stood, filled a glass of water, drank. He was smiling for himself and standing for effect. She watched him carefully. Not his face but his arms and shoulders which were a pleasing blur. He opened the front door and gathered in some air, closed it before the mosquitoes found out. She had thought of him as her age but now he seemed less than her age. He had slung his letterman's jacket onto the back of the sofa.

From its pocket, he was bringing out two pages, stapled, folded twice, quartered. Marked notes. The scene they had just played out had been in his back pocket all evening. He smoothed it flat on the coffee table between them. On the top it said *Toyer* and then, *two characters*, as if it were a play.

Lydia's eyes came stinging back to her and she covered her face again and felt herself slip away and so held her temples and forced her eyes away from him to the poster of an over-dressed 1900s woman on a bicycle holding a protest sign.

"Mind if I get myself a drink?" She did not answer. He had just finished one. When he came back from the kitchen he handed her a glass of ice water.

When she took her hands down from her temples, they shook. "What do you mean, you made it up? Why'd you want to do that?" *Don't call him crazy. They don't like to be called crazy if they are and he probably is.* But she did not care. What she did care about was the difference between who he said he was and who he was, and what time he was leaving.

"Why would you pretend . . ." But she could not say the word *Toyer.*

"It's important to me. To my development. To invent a character and make someone believe my character."

His easy voice sickened her. "Would you stop talking, please? Thanks."

Anyway, life looks good again. I'd been feeling sorry for myself about losing Rick. If I can't do better than Rick, I deserve to die. But what a way to find out. Suddenly she remembered that her parents were not going to see her picture in the newspaper and she laughed.

"I can't figure why anyone would want to do what you just did. I don't even know who you are."

He laughed nicely for the first time all evening. "Well, I don't know who you are either."

"Sure you do."

"No I don't. What's your name?"

"I told you, Lydia."

"No, your last name." He stood framed in the doorway.

"You really don't know?"

"I really don't know. I swear."

"Well, you never will know it. I'll never tell you. Leave it at that. I'm just curious, how did you know Carol doesn't live here?"

"When I was fixing your car I saw her name scratched off your mailbox. Carol . . ." He looked blank.

"Miller."

more

"Yeah."

"What about Rick?"

"I know Rick."

"He never mentioned you."

"Just kidding. I heard you tell him to go stuff himself. I was standing right there listening by the rest rooms."

"Am I drugged?"

"*No.*" He smiled. "Tell people they're drugged and they feel drugged."

But I do feel drugged. "Just go."

"I'm going, I'm going, but for your own peace of mind I want to show you I'm an actor and a neighbor. My ID's in my car. That's all. Excuse me." He opened the door, slipped out, closed it. He was gone.

The door opened and he leaned inside again.

"You forgot about your phone. I told you I cut your phone line, remember? Try it. See if it works." He was gone again, clomping down the three wood steps. A late night stirring of air turned the paper flower hung from the ceiling by a thread, first one way then the other.

Lydia glanced at the telephone, the darkest object in the room. *Why did I get a black phone?* It had its own small swap meet table, an eccentric telephone table from the twenties.

She stared at it. *I'm sure it works. Why should I let him see me trying it? That means I'm still scared.* Seconds passed. *I've got to.* She crossed the room quickly and yanked the telephone to her ear.

Waiting for the dial tone, the wide hollowness rang again in her ears. *Dead.* Her fingers flashed down, jamming the receiver. One two three four. Dead. One two three four. Dead. Dead. Dead. Dead. Dead. As the moon.

She stared at the telephone until it blurred. Her insides were slipping away from her. *He's watching me from the doorway.* She didn't turn, holding the moment. *I know he's standing there.*

She turned.

He was.

Just inside the door. Smiling. Head canted. Caught-boy smile. Lips pressed together. He nodded once, twice. Sweet. Sorry. Something shiny she could not quite see, an icicle, held just behind his leg.

He spoke. So quietly she could barely hear him. She watched his lips move. Felt the third wave of sleep, deeper than the other waves crashing ashore in her drugged night, felt her legs leaving her, being drawn away from her in the wave's undertow, being drawn out to sea.

"I love you," he said.

MAUDE GARANCE

NIGHT. A small house in a canyon above Los Angeles. A woman enters.

Her name is Maude Garance. She is thirty-six years old. Tonight her skin is papery, her face complicated by woven scars of fatigue. They highlight her eyes, smart eyes cowled by the pain of the ordeal at the hospital that has been going on now for nearly a year. Nurses who follow her on rounds watch her carefully, worry about her, regard her as a mythical creature; some imitate her. She regards most of them as unskilled.

Maude Garance lives alone now, in this rented house that was never air-conditioned. Maybe if she owned it, it would be, but these airless nights are rare up on Tigertail Road. And tonight, the day's heat clings to the arms of the trees, the walls of her rooms. For maybe one month each year, sweat-heat rises through the tangled arroyos from the Los Angeles basin below, where miles away downtown, lamppost lights shine in Silverlake Park, families too hot to stay home sit on benches waiting for the night to cool the pavements. It is April 30, a hot night, too soon, even in the canyons above Los Angeles.

It is nearly ten. The telephone answering machine blinks once. One call. She switches it on, listens to the soft silence of telephone static. A male voice, Ed Tredescant, without irony, calm, paternal.

"You needn't be upset at yourself or at me, Maude, we none of us are perfect. We just don't know why these things are happening. They are, that's all."

"Yup," she says. "They certainly are, Doctor T." She can see him telephoning. He sits in an office chair, a size too small for him, his polished brogans side-by-side. He wears grainy tweeds and earth tones, looks as if he dressed in health foods. The chief-of-service at the Kipness, clumsy, loyal. In love with Maude, still unexpressed.

"Our task has always been to cure, hasn't it?"

"Yup," Maude says to the taped voice. "Best of my knowledge." She stands, steps around the counter to the kitchen, and sets a kettle on the stove.

"If not cure, to help. We're on the sidelines, the damage is simply irreversible."

"Yup."

". . . your task now is to prepare them for their new lives, their many years ahead. . . ."

"They're too young."

". . . but please don't let anger blur your vision." She hears him take in his breath. "I'm sorry this is happening to you. But, you know you can take a leave any time. . . ." *If the strain becomes too much.* The tape turns in silence.

He coughs. "Please come by before rounds. You can find me on Six." He pauses. "Goodnight, Maude, get some sleep." Dial tone. He is not able to tell Maude that he loves her. She drops her skirt around her ankles. Unbuttons her silk blouse. Maude has come home defeated; she is losing Karen Beck after a month of therapy. Karen, her patient, will remain on earth as a flower, a pretty, pale flower, forever.

She pulls a metal loop and rolls back the top of a small can marked Feline Feast, causing a pale ginger cat to appear from the windowsill behind a curtain. It is Jimmy G.

A creak, not of a cricket, outside the window behind the sofa. A small human sound, a scrape?, in the bushes. Maude stands in her underpants and green silk blouse without moving. She listens to the white hum of the city come up through the canyons miles away.

She listens to the black hillside. Silence. The faraway yelp of a young dog or maybe a coyote. Jimmy G's right ear twitches, nettled. He is afraid of coyotes, their strange cries.

Maude opens the refrigerator, squats easily, takes three ice cubes in her palm, crosses the room and pushes the *play* button on her CD player, sits in her chair, legs wide. She cools herself, moving the ice cubes on her neck, arms and shoulders, between her knees, wherever her body requires it, feeling the melt cross her limbs. Jimmy G flattens on his side just below her fingers. The disk spins, male voices sing far too loudly; she makes no move to turn it down, she absorbs it. Their strength reaffirms something she needs to hear. *The Pearl Fishers* duet between two brothers in love with the same woman, both trying to decide the right thing to do, which turns out to be abandoning her. *Stupid.* Maude settles and submits, trying to let the music enter her and her the music. Before the duet ends, she is asleep.

The *peep-peep-peep* shock of her beeper wakes Jimmy G beside her, who raises his head and watches her reach the telephone and tap in the hospital's numbers. His eyes Chinese, nearly closed, he lowers his ruff down onto his paw. Ed Tredescant comes on the telephone.

"Me again."

"Yes, Elias?" Maude is the only one who calls him by his middle name.

"Maude, it kills me to ask you," the paternal voice says, "but could you get back down here?"

Not a fair question. "What can I do for you tonight, Elias?"

She knows before he tells her. "An *invalid*, Maude. Just in." He uses the word *invalid* only when he describes her patients. The victims.

"How old is she, Elias?" She does not know why she asks.

"Young, I don't know, Maude."

"What do you think?" *Is there hope for her?*

They have had this conversation before. He pauses. "I'm not sure, Doctor."

He calls me Doctor when he needs me. "Stop anyone from testing her 'til I get down there."

Doctor Tredescant is also careful never to mention the name *Toyer* to Maude. Neither he nor any of her nurses. It is absolutely forbidden. They remember her fury when she examined her first patient, Virginia Sapen. A nurse, Chleo, called Maude borderline, not to her face.

"What's her name, Elias?"

She hears him turn a page while he looks. "Lydia Snow Lavin."

"Ask Chleo to prep her for an MRI. I'll leave in five minutes." Tonight; Toyer's ninth, Maude's ninth.

LYDIA

THE KIPNESS Memorial Neurological Center for Advanced Research, seen as an ocean liner at anchor under a lover's moon.

Maude drives up an incline then to a stop in the painted rectangle marked GARANCE. Most upper floor lights are out. The Kipness, above Malibu, set on its own twelve acres among low hills, overlooks the Pacific Ocean from an earthquake-free eminence.

Maude can see Doctor Tredescant waiting just inside the air-conditioned Emergency entrance. He is holding two paper cups of black coffee, one for her. *Drainage from the gutters of abattoirs.*

There are five in motion, walking toward the elevators. The drill is familiar. Maude is followed by a small swarm of respect. Maude is a known victim, a recent widow.

A new nurse says, "Serum sodium is off the chart, Doctor." Maude nods. *Of course.*

"It'll take a full ten days to bring it up," Nurse Chleo says.

"She's got the ten days, Chleo," Maude says. *She's got ten thousand days.*

A thin woman Maude has never seen says, "I can't find her medical."

"No card?"

"Nothing. Do I put her on the crime fund?"

Maude is thrown for a moment, billing is not her concern. "Well, if she can't pay . . ." *She'd have to be an heiress to afford this one.*

Doctor Tredescant says, "Go ahead, Andrea, bill the police for the time being."

Everyone nods slightly, *Just so,* the woman concerned with billing drops away. Maude says, "Have you monitored her breathing?"

"Yes, well, it's clustered," Chleo says.

Yeah, it would be.

Lydia Snow Lavin lies under a large hospital tunic. Another pale pretty flower. A skin-toned bandage is centered across the nape of her neck. White gauze covers abrasions on two of her fingers. Maybe she has fallen. Or fought.

Three people in white watch her without speaking: Doctor T, Maude, the new nurse, new enough to be aghast. Maria.

Maude: "Is she drugged?"

"As before," Ed says.

It is Xylazene, the wild animal tranquilizer.

"She looks stable."

"She is."

"Yes. When ——?"

"Almost five hours ago."

Maude nods blankly. Doctor Soong from the city has just joined them and stands against the wall.

"Bring me the disk, please, nurse," Maude says.

The new nurse stands, immobile.

"Nurse. The disk, please." The nurse nods *yes* and goes.

"Let's begin the tests," Maude says to the floor, no longer regarding the patient. "Give me the ice-water caloric." Chleo moves.

She adds, "I want some blood."

Doctor Tredescant says, "Uhm . . ."

"I want an AIDS test, Elias."

"Why?"

"Why not? This is a sociopath, maybe he wants to share."

"Is there proof of sex?"

"Assume there is. *Blood*, okay? Thank you." Chleo goes.

Maude runs smelling salts under the patient's nose. Again. Nothing. She whips out a tiny flashlight, rolls up an eyelid on a stick, probes her pupils for response. Nothing.

The new nurse comes back with a small CD player. Maude sets it by Lydia, turns it on. A female voice is singing.

"Ready for the calorics, Doctor."

Lydia Snow Lavin has the unblemished face of a twelve-year-old girl; pale skinned, pale haired, light eyebrowed, lovely. Straw fields in sun. Eyes are pale and show absolutely no response to the music. Apparently, she has been spinally cordotomized.

Chleo turns her head on the pillow, surrounds it with a towel. From a syringe, she squirts small shots of ice water into her ear. Lydia's eyes reveal nothing.

"That's it, Chleo." Chleo wipes Lydia's cheek, straightens her head on the pillow, closes her eyes.

Maude stares at her new patient. She stands absolutely still moments too long. She feels sick, her stomach has turned upside down. This happened with the last patient. She feels her fiber starting to give way and cannot show it. Doctor Tredescant reaches his hand out and touches her shoulder.

"Never mind," Maude says. *Forget the test.* Nurse Maria folds her arms, looks away at nothing.

"Want me to set up the tangent screen?" Chleo says.

Maude shakes her head *no*.

"You want a Glascow Coma Scale?"

"Set her up for an angiography in five minutes."

In the furthest silence, Lydia Snow Lavin sees: *White lines. Now whiter. Gradually forming clouded perimeter. A blurred too-white room. Figures moving in cloud banks, unfamiliar, altered voices. Vague forms dressed in white, shifting in jolts. Untouchable reality. New bright sounds . . . Nonsense, sounds jumble. Space is silent again. A female voice is singing. Lone white-gowned form remains. Cool. Water falling dashed on rocks, purling downstream, womanly.*

"The Shepherd's Song" from the Auvergne. A Basque folk aria. The superb beauty of the rich soprano voice, supremely feminine. As soon as possible, Maude will obtain the actual disks and tapes that Lydia last listened to in her car and at home.

Eyes. Hair. Face, a woman's face, pale, close, young-eyed. Materializes out of blinding white light, gradually forming exact features. *Lean, short-haired, attractive, thirties, nononsense.*

Maude is close, looking for light in Lydia's eyes, a sign. She moves a vase. *Simple flowers, good flowers.* Pale blue and lavender wildflowers, thin stalks.

"Will she regain basic functions, Doctor?" The new nurse has reentered. Maude does not answer her. At this stage she believes that there exists the possibility of reclaiming some neurological loss.

The soprano voice twists into scales of intense notes close

to screams. The nurse's eyes widen, she looks irritated, Lydia's remain fixed.

The soprano continues singing the shepherd's *aires*. Maude whispers to Lydia, to herself, "Please. Please. Lydia. Please. Try. You've got to try. We'll try together."

Blurred words. Maude calmly pleads for response. Looks closely, eye to eye. The black fog bank rolls toward Lydia and enshrouds her.

No one is closer to these unique victims than Maude Garance is. She is the first doctor called in to examine each victim and make the preliminary prognosis. That is, to discover if there is a telling light in their eyes that might indicate the possibility of partial recovery. She is a physiatrist.

It was accidental. From the start, when the first victim of Toyer was admitted to the Kipness for a series of tests under the direct supervision of Maude Garance, it was to determine whether rehabilitation was possible. And, as always, the hope of the police is that the victim may be made well enough to reveal a description of her destructor.

Maude sits for a long time staring at Lydia. *Nothing*. The singing shepherdess does not register in her dead eyes. In Lydia, Maude sees a perfect universe of atoms and molecules rushing together without hope. *Like ours*, she thinks, *but in perfect asymmetry*. She will try again tomorrow.

She cuts off the *aire* with a tough snap, sending the CD player and disk clattering to the floor. The new nurse scrambles to gather up the rolling batteries.

Embarrassment. Helplessness. Irrational behavior. She has just broken the CD player. Is Doctor T troubled by the imbalance?

Maude looks away to the night-black window, contains her fury. She picks up the clipboard, marks her comment and the time, hands it to the nurse and exits.

A woman no one knows has been standing in the hallway outside the room pretending to be occupied. She is in her thirties but has a surprisingly young face, alert, as though she has been protected from common troubles.

"Doctor Garance, I'm an admirer of yours."

"Who are you?" *It's just not a good time to meet new people.* Maude dislikes her on sight, she does not know why.

"Sara Smith."

Sara Smith. Maude knows the name. "From the *Herald?*"

A month ago, it was Sara Smith who wrote a piece portraying Maude as a noble heroine magnificently trained, yet only acting as a physiatrist who is unable to cure these patients. She interviewed nurses at the Kipness without Maude's knowledge. Maude was appalled.

"How did you get in here?"

Sara Smith pauses, professionally, she is a reporter after all. "Police call came in on my beeper."

"Well you can beep yourself the fuck back out of here."

The F word. Sara Smith is in shock. *Never before.* She looks for support to Luis Alvarez, a security man who has strayed over to them. Luis seems comfortable with Maude's suggestion, riding the moment.

"Doctor, please let me have just five minutes. I'm doing a story."

"We are not a story."

"It's a very important story."

"Stories are fiction."

"Well, we refer to them as stories."

"Maybe that's what's wrong, stories are for storybooks. Maybe you're storytellers. This is real, this is really happening."

Maude pushes Lydia's door open. The reporter hesitates reverentially. Her face is white, empty.

"See the story of the girl in the coma?"

Lydia Snow Lavin is asleep for life.

MAUDE

SHE DRIVES HOME, unlocks the door of her wooden house in Randall Canyon. The darkness is rising, it is getting light, May first, already hot.

She, too, has been scoured. She has just been introduced to Lydia Snow Lavin. Rage, frustration.

One telephone message. She switches on the tape, sits, listens to it rewind, clasps her hands, they are trembling. Surprisingly, it is from Sara Smith of the *Herald*. She erases all of Smith's telephone numbers, there are four, taps seven familiar numbers, waits three rings. The calm taped voice. She waits for the long *squeee* to end.

"I'm scared, Elias," she says into it. "Am I losing it? I looked into the eyes of one more dead girl tonight. But she's alive. But she's not. Why, in this *putrid* world, would anyone want to do that to women? And keep doing it. I ought to know by now but I just don't. *Fuck it.*"

If Doctor T had been home, he would have cut in, told her that street language is unbecoming to her position.

"I met a reporter tonight who thinks this whole thing is a perfect story." *Give me the story.* "I threw her out. But you know something? Bad as she is, she's the only one out there who seems half-awake. The police haven't a clue, you know? No one's doing *anything.*"

Doctor T's tape turns, recording her silence.

"Maybe I will."

She waits for him to object. "I've got no right to call you this late. Sorry . . . oh, God, I'm getting weepy. Thanks for listening." Sixty seconds, another *squeee* cuts her off. She sighs briskly. She wanted to add: "This call does not require an answer."

Maude kneels, gazes into the dry bathtub, its hollowness intrigues her, it seems infinite, she turns both faucets three times to the left, on full, staring into the flat water until she can feel its heat rise warmer than the air.

She snaps open the CD player, slides in a disk. *The Pearl Fishers*. She sits in the deep Timmons chair and runs an ice cube on her neck and shoulders waiting for the tub to fill. In a few moments the overture has engulfed her.

Maude's father loved his operas, he listened to one every weekend on the radio. He was brutal to her, growing up. This raw man who'd clawed his way to the top of the foundry world in Elcott, Pennsylvania, wept when he heard "Core n'gao." Her mother hoped that he died while he was listening to "E lucevan le stelle" on the radio. He believed in his own invincibility, a man of heroic ego, a tyrant's ambience, no man greater than he. James Garance.

Now his daughter allows the grand maleness of the voices to swarm over her, enter through her pores, fill her with male vibrato, the earthborn beauty of her gender, her inner song, her culture. Up from the floor, the music suffuses her like new blood, rushing out her limbs to her drooping fingertips, drowning out the whispers of her inner voice.

James Garance never stopped dreaming. Maude remembers, *One day we'll move to California*, he would tell her mother, long after they knew it was impossible. They had met in Madigan's, a Dublin pub, when he was twenty-one and raw and her mother was a student traveling from Maine. They had married and she brought him home on her passport. All of his life he had refused to become an American citizen, and despite his great will to thrive, he never got the hang of America, he died full of questions. Maude remembers the explicit power of his old ways. The rudeness of his old manners.

He was admitted to the hospital for a broken kneecap, he died of complications, clotting to the heart. James Garance, alone in his room, listening to the radio in that hospital, a special broadcast from Rome. He did not expect to die. Maude's mother hopes he died listening to a human voice greater than his own. It makes her happy to think so, anyway, for his surprised soul. *All of our destinations end in bed.*

Jimmy G finds that he has finished his Feline Feast, drifts over to her, tail high, to her limp fingertips extended from the chair, touches them with his globed forehead, *Thanks, missus.* He senses nothing untoward and he is probably right. Jimmy G stands square-legged looking up at her. Maude has never known another cat who could do this, stand like a small fur table and, neck back, look straight up, giving her the full flat of his face. He is the calmest cat she has ever known, a pale, pale orange, not quite absent stripes, a lean cat with cheeks who purrs at her glance. Who almost never opens his claws, who cannot be stealthy, who wakes Maude each morning at just the right time by stomping back and forth across the sheet that covers her body, to save her from the jolt of her alarm clock.

Whenever she comes home this late, her ordeal at the hospital leaves her neck and lower body muscles taut. Now that there is no husband, no more Mason to knead her muscles, her habit is to stand in the middle of her living room and perform gentle yoga movements to ease the strain in her lower back and legs. Each morning, she feels her body grow opulent, by midday it begins its decline, by evening it aches, her lower back buzzes, no matter what shoes she wears. Stretching its cords helps put her in the most direct descent pattern for sleep.

She drops her skirt and stands within its rumpled circle in the center of the living room. She begins by stretching her tender calf muscles.

Last year, Maude apologized to Jimmy G before she drove him to the veterinarian's to have him fixed. *He might forgive me, he might think emasculation is a natural human act.* Later, Jimmy G remained unchanged; retiring, mature, as he was before. Young and calm, unusual in any species. He had had no agenda other than to stay with her, he never wanted to explore her neighborhood, maybe still afraid of coyotes.

She is looking at him now. *Emasculation may be a natural human act, but spinal cordotomy is not.*

In the bathroom, she slips out of her panties, glimpses them as they drop into the hamper. The finest she has; *Mason*, happier times. Beige. Their shade has been named *Champagne*, though champagne, if it has turned beige, has spoiled.

SARA SMITH

IN THE MORNING, the *Los Angeles Herald*, bottom of page three, Local News, Tuesday, May 1:

Ninth Victim Similar to First Eight
Pattern Leaves No Doubt: Toyer Again

Lydia Snow Lavin is Toyer's ninth victim. She is twenty-six, and until yesterday, was employed at Boeing Aircraft in Santa Monica as a research assistant. Today Ms. Lavin remains in a coma at the Kipness Memorial Neurological Center under the care of Doctor Maude Garance, resident physiatrist in charge.

In a related article also on page three:

The scar is hardly noticeable, the result is the same as always. The victim was intelligent and pretty. Though police decline to comment, this reporter has learned that evidence was found at Ms. Lavin's apartment to indicate that she entertained her visitor earlier in the evening, shared a cup of tea with him, possibly played backgammon, his board game of preference. Doctor Garance told me that she will impose a news blackout on the victim's condition pending completion of her tests. "At this point, it is a matter of privacy be-

tween my patient and her family," she told me last night at
the Kipness.

— Sara Smith

The *Los Angeles Herald* is the city's second newspaper.
Thin and loud. Sara Smith likes working at the *Herald*, its stories are refreshingly brief, like friendly slaps. She dislikes the
Los Angeles Times. She says that it has the incontinence of an
old person and for some reason it is unable to control, dribbles
on and on, until everyone has left the room.

MAUDE

TUESDAY. It is eleven. The day has already wilted. Sara
Smith stands facing Maude's front door. The gardenia
plants are crisp, they need water. Sara sucks in her courage,
knocks, *rap-rap-rap*, waking Jimmy G at once. Maude peers
between the bedroom curtains, recognizes her. *How did she get
my address?* She speaks through the front door.

"You. Leave me alone."

She stands fast. "Sara Smith. Doctor, I think I can help
you."

"You want to help yourself."

"I'm sorry, Doctor, am I being pushy, coming to your
house?"

"I think most definitely."

"Please, I apologize. And for the other night."

Silence.

"You call what I try to do a *story*. You want me to play a
part in it, the powerless but noble heroine."

"I didn't come to write a story."

Silence.

"Mind if I water these?" The gardenia, the ficus.

"As long as you've driven over here."

Sara goes to her car, brings a plastic bottle of well water from France. Maude goes back into her bedroom.

"Doctor, I think we can help each other bring Toyer in." *Is she still here?*

"Go away."

"I have an idea."

"Really."

"Please hear me out, please tell me if it's a bad one. I'll leave it up to you." *Atta girl.* "If I could please come in for just a couple of minutes."

"I have a problem with you."

"Yes?"

"I have a problem knowing if you want to help, apologize, or are simply trying to get another story. Why don't you just tell me what you want."

"I don't feel comfortable talking to a door."

"I do. Go away."

Sara is stung. *I can accept that.*

She leaves.

MR. AND MRS. LAVIN

WEDNESDAY. It is always the same.

There they are, Maude knows them on sight, Mr. and Mrs. Lavin, the parents of Lydia, they could be no one else.

The clock behind them on the wall reads 10:06. They are sitting in the public reception room downstairs at the Kipness waiting for Maude, who is six minutes late. A small suitcase between them. She watches them for a moment before going over to meet them. They sit bewildered, like dogs in coats. When she smiles at them they stand, she is taller than he is. Because the victims have all been young their parents are never old, though the strangeness of the grieving flight has made them seem aged. They expect nothing, ready to be grateful.

Maude is their hostess, these are her guests. She knows them, it is always the same: They will have flown all night from someplace where the bed has been left unmade. They will be reverential. One of them will say "Tell me, Doctor . . ." and then ask what is impossible to answer. They will be stunned, deeply hurt.

It is worse because the morning outside, seen through the twelve-foot deco glass doors, is superb, a bright perfect sky, high scudding clouds.

"Shall we go up?" The word *up* goes up by itself and Maude hears herself sounding foolish, optimistic.

The three in the elevator. It climbs much too slowly. The Lavins stand in a brief coma. One cannot talk in this elevator. Finally, the third floor.

The door is ajar, a nurse is leaving, Lydia has been made pretty, and she is. The horror lies in her stillness.

When they see her there is no restraint. "Who hurt my little girl? Who hurt my little girl?" she cries. Mr. Lavin can only moan, "My God, my God, my God . . ." They hold on to each other, braced, using their four legs well.

Do you have a faith? Maude always asks here, now, it is not a room for agnostics. When they say they are both Catholic she feels some relief, there are so many things a Catholic can do during the next days and weeks to keep busy.

How long will they stay with their daughter? Virginia's parents refused to go, they could not leave their daughter and spent the night in the other bed. Maude had it removed the night Gwyneth Freeman was brought in, the second victim.

Maude excuses herself, makes her rounds. When she comes

back to the room they are seated. Mrs. Lavin has found a way
to perch on Lydia's bed, the toes of her shoes miss the floor by
a foot.

Whether they had written regularly to their daughter, or
telephoned her occasionally, or were not speaking to her can
be resolved now. Maude warns them that it is still too soon but
Lydia might be able to hear them, there is a chance. That fac-
ulty will certainly develop, she tells them.

"I hate to ask this, Doctor, but Grammy, her grandmother,
asked for a picture. Am I allowed to take just one?" In his
palm, a common flash camera that can make anyone look vi-
vacious.

Maude nods. "Of course you may, Mr. Lavin." *Take a still
life of her.*

Mrs. Lavin, a small woman, Maude can barely hear her say,
"Do you think they will they ever catch him, Doctor?"

"Oh, my, yes, Mrs. Lavin." Maude has never doubted it.
Suddenly she realizes how strange that is.

"When they do," her voice is faint, her daughter might be
listening, "what will they do to him? This . . . creature?"

Was she going to say, "This Satan"?

"I don't know, Mrs. Lavin."

"Well, they ought to do the same to him as what he did to
Lydia."

An eye for an eye. Well done, Mrs. Lavin.

It is the people his victims leave behind who are incarcerated.

"Oh, no, Mrs. Lavin, he's a psychopath. But they'll certainly punish him." She hears herself docked by her profes-
sionalism. *But what will they do?* Strange that no one had ever
asked her that.

Mr. and Mrs. Lavin stare at Lydia. They will take her to
Whites Valley, Pennsylvania. It will be different talking to
Lydia than talking to a gravestone but Maude has never once
said to any of them, mother, father, lover, brother, sister, *Think
of it as a blessing that she's still alive.*

MASON

MAUDE ONCE SAT for hours sifting her fingers
through her dead husband's ashes following a professional service for him that did not remind her of anyone she
had ever known. Mason. She sat alone with his ashes in a
room that they had formed, painted, and sewn, on the window
seat of a wide arced window that had once looked out over the
Pacific Ocean, but no longer did because of hotel construction. She sifted through the ashes, feeling their gross weight,
wanting Mason's strength to enter her just once more for the
years ahead. Without him, she too was gone. She waited for a
sign from her fingertips, but no sign came, so she carried the
copper urn in a brown market bag to the flat umber beach a
few blocks away, and waited under the gaseous sky for the last
chilled people to leave, waited to be alone, for a breeze to
blow his ashes into the sea. A weatherless late afternoon, the
sky white-rimmed the way old people's pupils are sometimes
white-rimmed.

She left her shoes on the sand, waded out onto the hard-
bottomed shallows and spread his ashes as if she were sowing
grass seed into the sea. She watched the ashes float gray, then
blacken and drown. The breeze came and took the rest of him
from her.

Much later, while she was undressing, she found his dust in
her brassiere and smiled back at him.

It has been good and now he was not here. Everything she
knew of him was empty: his shoes, his chair, his trousers, his
coffee cup, his hat. Their bed. She moved to Randall Canyon,
tried to come back to life.

She is a widow. Widowed at the zenith of a young marriage.
She had lived with Mason in another country with its own climate, rules, values, truths.

Maude has a darkness about her. Her dreams are important, they are her horoscope. Pure unedited longings, the wren bones of reality. Now, if only she and Mason could drive away from the hospital just once, through flashing tunnels of trees, stop at an inn and after a late lunch climb the stairs, sleep together through the afternoon for days, until she is reported missing, then everything would be all right again. Once.

She learned to be alone. *We all end up in small rooms, alone.* At first, her woman's facade had become a distraction to her concentrated work at the hospital, her taut, good legs, her clear-cut nose, her fine forehead, the flamboyance of her hair the color of horse chestnuts, she had attracted men who were attracted to leggy, long-haired, strong women. She began wearing slacks, cut her hair cropped close to her head, in the way pigeons wear their feathers.

She began to understand that she was destined to live alone, that her life was more than leftover time. But from the first night she realized that working with Toyer's victims, being unable to rehabilitate them in any way, coming home to the small house atop Randall Canyon would be an ordeal she would soon learn to dread.

Moving to Randall Canyon was a small adventure for Maude, Tigertail Road still has unpaved stretches, no sidewalks. She has lived there a year, long enough to identify the animal sounds she hears outside her bedroom, sounds that occasional guests are not aware of.

Almost every night as Maude drives home, her headlights pick up a coyote's dancing trot, the low tail, the rounded haunch, heading up a driveway for garbage or maybe a cat. She is still surprised by coyotes. She thinks it is nicely balancing that a city as rude and wide as Los Angeles can be a sanctuary for possums, deer, raccoons, foxes, hawks, coyotes. And that they are left to live in peace at the pleasure of the inhabitants. They are not competition.

Last night she heard her nightingale for the first time this spring and tonight feels honored that he has come back and taken up his old position on the same branch of the olive tree outside her bedroom window. She is glad to donate some of her sleep to him. She detects frantic loneliness within the beauty of the trills and riffs he lavishes on the night sky to find a nightingale who feels the way he does. Maude hears the familiar frustration. She will put a tape recorder on the windowsill and record his ariettas so that he can continue to sing her to sleep long after he has found his mate.

One morning early, when she had first moved to Tigertail Road, a pale ginger cat with a direct stare, maybe frightened, appeared at the window with a severe cut on top of his head, maybe from a coyote. He was pale ginger, humble, and she loved him on sight. When she opened the front door to him, he passed by her into the house, his tail definitely skimming her knee. She felt he was a savior in cat's clothing and named him on the spot, Jimmy G, she had no idea why. He had come to stay.

MAUDE

A WHITE THURSDAY MORNING, the Santa Monica Freeway, nine o'clock. Traffic is sparse, Maude has driven the Lavins from the hospital to a motel in Santa Monica and now is driving home, holding a cup of coffee, the *Herald* on the seat beside her.

Without knowing that she is crying, she feels tears streaming down her cheeks, dripping into her cup. She slows, looks for an exit, drops her cup onto the freeway, turns off on the ramp, drives as far as she is able to see and parks. With her head against the steering wheel, she sobs without relief, parked on the busy street until a woman taps on her window. Maude smiles, waves her away. The woman nods as if she knew nothing and, with the expression of a deaf mute, walks off.

Cars glint in the street. She pulls the sun visor down, sees herself in the small mirror. Her blouse is stained, a button is gone, her hair is crisp, there are crumbs, her face is splotched, wet. There was a time when she committed women who looked like this.

No one is close to stopping him. No one is doing anything. Except him and that smart-ass reporter.

She spins the car around and drives home, gripping the steering wheel much too tightly.

Maude can see from the front door that the answering machine is blinking its red eye, three telephone messages, one from Sara Smith. "Please call me, Doctor, I need to speak to you." Two hang-ups, probably both from Smith.

Maude lies down on her bed, takes her pulse. It is racing. *One sign of a breakdown.* She tries to breathe, slowly, twenty times a minute, then fifteen. She lies with Jimmy G beside her until she is able to breathe ten times a minute.

After an hour, calm, she calls the *Herald*, asks for Sara Smith. She waits. What will she say? By the time she comes on the telephone, Maude has hung up.

She calls Doctor T, leaves him a taped message. "I'm calling the D.A. I'm going to see him tomorrow." *Try and stop me.* She imagines Elias objecting.

She dials City Hall. "Can you please connect me to Ray Yellen's office?"

No comment from the operator. Click, ring. A secretarial voice.

"District Attorney Yellen's office."

"This is Doctor Garance over at the Kipness? I have a question that involves sentencing."

"Can you be more specific? I need to direct your call."

"It concerns the person the press is calling Toyer."

"He is unapprehended, correct?"

"Correct."

"I'll transfer you to Assistant District Attorney Meyerson."
Click. Ring.

"Assistant District Attorney Meyerson's office."

She asks the secretary if she can find out the sentence for
Toyer's conviction.

"Who?" the secretary says.

Maude describes Toyer.

"I haven't the faintest idea."

"Of the sentence, or if you can find out?"

"I told you, miss, I haven't the faintest idea."

"May I speak with Mr. Meyerson?"

"He's in conference."

"Can you ask him?"

"He'll tell you the same thing I just did."

"Can you give me an appointment to see him?"

"I'm afraid that's impossible, miss."

"Doctor."

"Doctor." Click.

Maude can practically hear the word *nutcase*.

BOB MEYERSON

DAY. The wide city panorama seen from Assistant District
Attorney Bob Meyerson's twenty-sixth-floor office. His
controlled hemisphere. Maude enters, a middle-aged secretary
close behind her.

Meyerson rises. "It's all right, Ciel."

Maude ignores the chair he offers facing his desk, crosses
the room to the window. A man who resembles a bouncer
stands behind Meyerson's desk, eyes like mothballs, legs
wide, hands cupped over his pelvis, which is thrust forward.

Meyerson answers his buzzer, listens, hangs up, looks at his intruder. Both smile charmlessly. *Pretty doctor with attitude.* The aide looks blank, makes his mouth smaller.

It is a plain office compared to the gala view seen beyond its vast window: distant city hills stained by the surrounding air. An award stands on a table with a tiny electroplated statue of a man aiming a handgun, there are photographs, reminders in cheap frames of women and children left at home.

"Seriously, Doctor, what can we do for you?" He has been elected by the people.

She stays at the window. *You can catch Toyer.* "Well, I am concerned about the sentencing in this case."

"And you are . . . ?"

"I am the doctor who evaluates and treats his victims."

"Toyer."

"Yes. I mentioned that to your receptionist."

"Yes. If he is apprehended." They nod. They are in accord. The assistant district attorney is no longer interested. He smiles, on familiar ground, turns to his aide. "You reach me that guideline, Carl?"

Carl pulls a floppy paperback from a shelf of unappetizing books.

"What sentence will we ask?" He breaks a seal, opens the book for the first time, thumbs through it. "Certainly. Penetration cannot be proved, correct?"

"Only of the medulla cerebrum."

"Right. But what I mean is . . . anything of a sexual nature." He continues thumbing through the index, as if anything she will say matters.

"Lord, no, Mr. Meyerson." *Physically dead for the rest of their lives, sir, but we cannot prove sex.* The aide is not 100-percent certain if Maude is showing disrespect. She looks edgy, ready to come apart.

"Okay, here we are." Meyerson finds the page, the paragraph. He reads from a pulpit, " 'Any person who maliciously deprives another person of the use of his body, disables or disfigures it, is guilty of mayhem.' "

Maude intones the word.

"Yes, mayhem. Unusual word. My guess is it comes from old English, the Middle Ages, from the root *to maim*."

"Fascinating. What's the rap?"

"The sentence for mayhem is . . . two to eight years, state prison."

"That seems comfortable."

"We would ask the maximum."

"What is the rap for stealing a new car?"

"New or old, same sentence." He turns pages. "Here we are. Grand theft auto. Not as bad, two-to-five. Funny."

"Funny?"

"I mean it's funny that it's a relatively similar sentence."

"It's a car, Mr. Meyerson."

"Yes, I know."

"It might not even run that well."

The aide shifts, looks at Maude's breasts.

"Those women are my patients, they were perfect before he got to them. You protect your cars better than these women."

"We treat these crimes under the law. That's all we can do until the law changes."

"If he is apprehended and somehow survives the court system and is convicted of mayhem by a jury of his peers, and you give him a light sentence, there will be a public response that could end your career."

Meyerson blinks quickly several times. "You're a psychiatrist, right?"

"*Physiatrist*, yes."

"Well, you seem awfully young to be putting all this stress into your attractive head. May I call you Maude?"

"Please don't. As a matter of fact, I am able to put this stress into my attractive head, Mr. Meyerson. When I got my M.D. degree, I was able to squeeze four years of psychopathology into it, then I managed to slip a psychiatric residency into it, then I jammed five years of neuropsychology into it, and somehow it was also able to handle neurological rehabilitation, and now psychotherapy. I just don't know how my attractive head did it. And here I am, God knows why, sitting in your office asking you simple questions and getting dumb answers."

Meyerson is still absorbing what she has said. He looks as if he has been pumped full of antiemetic drugs for seasickness. He will call Mrs. Kipness this afternoon.

"Well, Doctor, I'm just a simple assistant district attorney for Los Angeles County, so will you forgive my stupidity?"

"No."

Now the aide is positive Maude has insulted Meyerson. He has gone to the door, turned the knob, stands staring stupidly at her. His mouth forms an *0*. Meyerson has risen. "Is there anything this office can do for you?"

"Catch Toyer, Mr. Meyerson."

Meyerson looks at his watch. "We're making every effort."

"And he seems to be enjoying every single one of them."

"Trust me, Doctor Garance," he smiles warmly.

"Whenever someone says *Trust me* I usually call a cop. But, well, here I am."

"I'm late, Doctor, I'll call you the minute we hear anything. Carl?" Carl opens the door. Meyerson is passing through the doorway, still smiling warmly. He has decided to dictate a fax to Mrs. Kipness, she should be warned about this doctor, who is obviously off her rocker.

"Why don't you just let us do our job?" he says.

"Because you're not doing it?"

Meyerson stops, stands in the open doorway. He sucks in his breath. He will be facing reelection in four months.

"When we apprehend this individual, Doctor, we're all going to feel a hell of a lot better, just as happy as you feel when you cure one of his victims."

"You don't get it, do you? I don't cure them. I only try to make them comfortable for the rest of their lives."

Meyerson escapes.

The aide, Carl, is left holding the door open for Maude.

Carl has decided she is one of these women who is losing her mind, possibly menstruating.

DOCTOR TREDESCANT

THAT EVENING Maude is seated in the dark, alone in her windowless office, head down, on the telephone. Ed Tredescant opens the door, sees her, starts to slip away politely, she motions him in. She turns on the desk lamp. Files in stacked marked cartons. Tredescant waits awkwardly, a gentleman caller. His hands are too big, his brown shoes look hobnailed. Head down, she continues listening to the voice coming from the receiver. Her caller, an Armani psychiatrist, has just told her that she lacks a necessary passion.

"Passion? I don't need a sex act with you to define myself," she says into the telephone then listens briefly. "I can always run your semen count by some of my nurses. Can you get a smear over to me in the morning?" She puts the telephone down without a *goodbye*. Brushes invisible crumbs onto the floor.

"Elias." She smiles and stands.

Elias hesitates. "Do you still feel like fetuccini vongole?"

"Why wouldn't I? I feel great about fetuccini vongole."

He indicates the telephone call.

"Oh, that." Maude shrugs. "Some playboy shrink is suggesting a release for my id. His moist, hairy body."

Later, when they've had two glasses of chianti reserva and ordered dinner, he says, "Maude I got a call from the Woman today." The *Woman* is Mrs. Kipness, chairman of the board of Kipness Memorial Neurological Center.

"Oh?"

"Maude, you really can't barge into the D.A.'s office telling him he's not doing his job."

"I can't?"

"That's crazy." He says it nicely. "He sent this to her." He's pulled out a fax on Assistant District Attorney stationery. Maude scans it. It describes her erratic behavior in his office this morning.

"Is that asking a lot of you? It hurts the Kipness."

"A psychopath is destroying the brightest women around, my beautiful patients, and the D.A.'s sending the Woman my report card with a D-minus for comportment?"

"Quick temper's a mark of stupidity."

"Maybe. But patience is sure no mark of wisdom."

"Maybe, but she's still taking it hard, Maude. It's a county hospital, we depend on county money and city council can press to relieve you, believe it or not." He pauses. "No matter how fine your work is."

"Do you agree?"

He is chief-of-service, her boss, he admires her. More than that, he dreams about her.

"I don't, of course, but Maude, are you some kind of terrorist? No, you're a physiatrist."

"I was beginning to forget."

"I don't like the sound of that."

"Hell, I don't know, Elias." She lays her hand limp on his arm, he quickly covers her hand with his. "I'm just not going to turn the page on this one, you know what I mean?"

"That we can't *assume* these crimes."

Maude nods. "Ever know that feeling?" Suddenly they are close. He is older, slow-talking, sure. He moves around her life, barely grazing her, wanting to invade. He holds her psyche like a cracked vase, concerned, as if it might topple and break into fragments.

"But we heal patients, Maude, we don't rearrange the world."

It is his nose. A nose of wealth, intelligence, a splendid nose. It is the first thing you see when you meet this man. It is formal, it is permanent. It is shaped like a shark's fin, a macaw's beak, but more decent. Maude has decided that it is a family nose, she has never asked. One day. People listen to a man with such a nose. It has proved him to be right, it has opened doors. There is no small talk, tables appear for it in crowded restaurants, taxis wait.

"Don't you ever have the urge to follow the trocar back to its source?"

"Let the police do that."

"If they ever run across him, by an expired car registration or something, he'll get expert testimony, plead insanity, and enjoy his stay at Camarillo until he feels well enough to go apartment hunting and get on with his life."

He truly wants to save her. She is the woman he could never have, she is the answer. She keeps something fierce, hidden, an understanding sometimes too quick. He feels a vague danger.

While he is holding her hand he lays his other hand across her bare knee gripping it gently. It is not a fatherly gesture, he needs to feel the smooth muscle of her thigh, her warmth, to have his hand within a whim of her vagina.

"I don't have any answers, just please look after yourself."

"Everyone does that, look after themselves. He's still out there, tonight. And he's not tired of what he's doing and he's marvelous at it. He's even getting better. I watch his progress. He's what I'd call in full bloom . . . expressing his id fully. He knows and they know."

"She wants you to take a week or two off. She thinks she's being generous."

"I'll quit when he quits."

"Humor her, Maude." He is aware of his own faults, all he can do is love her.

MEYERSON

THERE IS A LARGE ENVELOPE on his desk, no return address. He opens it as if it were a letter bomb. Inside are 8x10 glossy photographs.

"What the hell is this?"

Nine black-and-white photographs, portraits of pale women, in many ways similar, all attractive and all apparently fast asleep.

Ciel says, "There's a note to you inside the envelope, sir."

A handwritten note in ink:

Bob Meyerson
Assistant District Attorney
Los Angeles County

Dear Mr. Meyerson,

I've decided to share some photographs with you that I have taken over the past year. These women are my patients. They are not dead, Mr. Meyerson, they only act dead. You see, whoever is doing this to them avoids your strict homicide sentencing and is only subject to your car-theft sentencing. That is, if he were ever to be caught. It certainly seems to have worked for him so far, don't you agree?

Dr. Maude Garance
Attending Physiatrist
Kipness Memorial Hospital

He slides the portraits out of sight, back into the envelope.

"This is that psychiatrist woman who was in here the other

day, right? I don't think she's the full taco, Ciel, what do you think?"

Ciel looks out the window, she could go either way on this one. On close calls, she tends to agree with her boss.

TOYER

*W*HO THE HELL *is this wonderful woman?*
Her persona has excited him since Sara Smith first printed her name in the *Herald. It sounds like Sara Smith resents her. She's so protective of my girls.*

Maude Garance. *The name. What does she look like? Is she fifty? Is she tall? Fat? Pretty? Married? Is she sexual? Asexual? Lesbian?* He decides that he must visit the Kipness. He needs to see her face, see her body, her arms. Why Sara Smith resents her.

It is afternoon, midweek, past the heat of the day. He drives to Malibu, the Kipness. It is set on a high place inland, among groves of eucalyptus, beyond the trees, the sea. He parks in VISITOR PARKING, walks through STAFF PARKING, a covered area.

She is somewhere close. A nameless car is parked in a slip marked GARANCE. He enters the hospital through a side door by a delivery port marked EMERGENCY.

The hospital is busy, it is the end of the day, the watch is changing, he hurries through Emergency; towels are being stacked, gurneys lined up, preparations for tonight's company. He wears a slightly spattered white coat, carries a clipboard, pen and stethoscope, nods to visitors, rides the elevator to the sixth floor.

He walks the hallway on Six, reads door tags, passes Paula's door, Gwyneth's, Lydia's, looks in on Lydia without entering, watches for Dr. Garance to pass. She does not. He asks a man holding a mop about her hours. She is around somewhere.

He enters Lydia's room. There are two beds, one empty. A small reading lamp unlit. It is Lydia, unchanged, calm, eyes nearly closed, the sad mouth. He sits on a chair behind the empty bed, in the gloom.

Five minutes pass. He is seated in the corner, leaning against a wall. A woman nearly as tall as he is enters quickly, pulls a chair to the bedside. There is the scent of rose soap on her breeze. *It's her.* Maybe ten years older than he is. She is wearing an open white blouse, tan trousers. She does not notice him, or if she does, he does not matter to her. She sits turned away from him. It is dim. He is surprised by the curtness of her hair, her youngness. Her day begins and ends with death.

He has come to see her. She has elegant posture, she is tall, unused, available, cool. There is no dullness about her. She displays no authority, but he senses control, she may turn and discipline him.

Her face electrifies him. She has an aura. He glimpses it, her forehead, her fine nose. Her beauty comes from her countenance, not from a light within, as though she were at odds with it, an accident.

She sits with her back to him, now, concentrated, maybe whispering. He wants to hear her words, he wants to talk to her. He only needs minutes.

He watches the two, Lydia and Maude, victim and healer. Direct, concentrated. He is responsible, he has given Lydia to her.

He stands, it is time to go.

She is unmarried, she may live with a cat. He cannot imagine her friends. *No cosmetics. Her hair clings to her, parted like a little boy's. She looks parched. She would laugh beautifully if she had the reason. Maybe she doesn't sleep well.* One would look to her for approval.

Does she have a middle name? Is she still able to smile?
He stands by the door. He feels very young, maybe fourteen. Where would he touch her first? He has the impulse to manipulate her neck, her back, her buttocks, lie beside her in the dark, near an open window to suck the life out of her. Someday.

VIRGINIA SAPEN

A YEAR AGO NO ONE KNEW, no one had ever heard of such a thing. At first nothing made sense.

When Virginia Sapen had been brought in to the Kipness, it was simply because she had been found at an apartment nearby in Malibu. The Kipness was the closest hospital and Maude happened to be on duty. The accident of time and place.

A homicide detective had accompanied the victim. He had found a bullet's entry point, had assumed that it was attempted murder. He kept asking about the bullet so that he could determine the weapon used.

He was told to wait. "We have what appears to be a small-gauge gunshot wound. Possible paralysis. Base of brain stem. Neurological arrest. Brain trauma." So far, so good.

But the patient was making no response, nothing was making sense to Maude. After two hours, Chleo, the duty nurse, came in to see Maude and found her wanly staring at the patient.

"Doctor, that homicide detective keeps asking is there a bullet."

"Tell him we're working on it."

But by 2:00 A.M., the only thing Maude was able to tell the

detective was: *Entry point found. No exit point. No bullet in skull. The weapon is not a gun. Go away, this may take a while.*

She had found traces of animal tranquilizer in the victim's blood and had learned that its effects were not long-term.

Heartbeat, blood pressure, breathing, all intact. The patient remained stable. Maude, exhausted, lay down on a cot beside the bed and slept.

By morning she had clipped four small highly colored transparencies of Virginia's brain to a light box and was studying them, wearing magnifying goggles, sipping coffee. Then she saw it, the near invisible wavy purple strokes. She reexamined the wound at the base of Virginia Sapen's skull. The opening might have been made by a carpet needle. "Ah, God. Jesus."

Chleo, dozing in a chair, "What is it, Doctor?"

"Where's Doctor Tredescant?"

"He's gone home hours ago."

"Call him."

Chleo tapped the call number, waited. A bed-warm male voice answered, not asleep: "Doctor Tredescant."

"Elias, you won't believe this. Virginia Sapen. Her arcuate fibers have been cut."

"Huh?"

"All her nerve fibers have been scoured in the cerebrum. Expertly, exactly. It's a clean sweep."

"Maude, I'm surprised at you. Lobotomy's been obsolete since the nineteen thirties,"

"Not entirely."

"Apparently." Then he said, "If you're right, Maude, it's a one-time deal, you'll never see lobotomy again as long as you live."

"Not lobotomy, Elias, it's a cervical cordotomy. She's been spinally cordotomized." Maude can still remember using the words for the first time since school and not liking them at all. She listened to the empty telephone line while they imagined this woman, pierced above her brain stem, purged of all her upper-brain functions.

"Is she breathing normally?"

"Yes. Heartbeat, blood pressure, normal."

"Then I disagree, Doctor." He speaks carefully. "It is not spinal cordotomy, I think what we may have is a surgical disconnection, something called posterior cingulectomy. Whoever's done this has managed to keep her spinal cord intact."

She stood holding the telephone, waiting.

"I'll be in."

"No. Thanks, Elias, nothing to do about it. Go back to sleep. She's stable." The conversation was over, Chleo removed the telephone from her hand. "Can I say something, Doctor?"

Maude didn't speak.

"If it ain't rape and it ain't robbery and it ain't drugs, what is it? Who'd do this shit to her head?"

"Maybe a surgeon." Maude was not thinking clearly.

"He's got to be pretty upset at her, right?"

"Bring me a trocar, nurse."

"Say what?"

"T-r-o-c-a-r," Maude spelled the new word. "Ask Willis."

Alone with the victim, Virginia, in silence. Maude spoke quietly into her ear. "This was not normal anger, was it, Virginia? This was highly controlled psychotic behavior. You knew him. You'd been playing gin rummy with him. This was personal."

Another nurse, Paula, brought the trocar wrapped in a cloth and handed it to Maude. She pulled it away from the cloth. A gleaming, three-bladed icicle six inches long. No matter how Maude held it, its chromed facets snared the light. As if it demanded to be seen.

Paula marveled at the victim. "Is this an isolated case?"

"One in a billion. Call in the detective and tell him we've found the weapon."

Alone again, Maude looked at the victim, spoke to her in her deep silence, without hope of hearing an answer.

"Tell me who was trying so hard not to kill you, Virginia. Please." Maude took the abandoned hand in both of hers, it was like glass. "Who wanted to keep you alive?"

MAUDE

MAUDE CANNOT SLEEP. She is waiting.

Now, tonight, it is a year and a week since she first beheld Virginia Sapen.

She lies in the dark, eyes open, pupils black, listening to the night, the small animal sounds, she has learned which is which, the human baby cry of a nightingale, a raccoon chattering under the house, the yip of a coyote puppy maybe wrestling its plastic garbage bag to the ground, the sham hurt whimpering of a male coyote trying to lure a dog away from the safety of his yard. So close to the city.

1:20 A.M. She is haunted by the stringless marionettes she sits with every day, they are at her window now, their calm faces. She knows she will meet a new victim, wheeled before her. She is waiting. She feels boneless, she has lost any hope of helping any new patient. It will be a very long night. She forces her mind to drift.

She remembers. More than ten years ago, during a pathology exam for surgical procedure, she had accidentally punctured a cadaver's large intestine. The escaping gas whistled so shrilly it sounded to the other students like an expiring party balloon, and the cadaver itself seemed to come back to life for one final tap-dancing shuffle step. Maude continued the exam without looking up, but the watching students reacted idiotically, dissolving into laughter, clowning, and retching elaborately.

The examining doctor, impressed by Maude's cool concentration, wrote her a high grade. Yet, no cadaver she had ever opened, no slashed and dying victim she had recklessly tried to save in Emergency, nothing she had experienced in her years had prepared her for what Toyer did to women.

She sits up with a start. Black anxiety. Her mind is churning. The night is still. She is waiting. She listens for the permanent sigh of Los Angeles, like the sea, hoping to hear it, but she cannot. She feels the bottomless anxiety of waiting.

There will be another victim. Between her wish to see the victim made well and the victim's wellness lies a void too strange to cross. Because of Mason, Maude shares with her patients a deep bond of grief. But she knows that the grief she feels for Mason's dying is a token to theirs.

She snaps on the light. Abruptly, she realizes she has been waiting for the telephone to ring. Jimmy G wakes, balanced on the windowsill, hops to the bed. Stiffly. *Churr?* He butts her chin with his forehead, pleased with Maude's presence in his night.

"Oh, Jimmy G, I *adore* you." She runs her fingernails through his fur in places he cannot reach. She cannot take another sedative. Together, they purr.

She stands, moves through the dark living room toward the refrigerator, divides a glass of milk with Jimmy G. She can no longer endure sleeping in her bedroom with the living dead women who have been left behind for her to live with, their drained faces pass through her window, come into her bedroom, sleep on the pillow beside her head.

The telephone rings.

MARLA

A WOMAN FAR TOO YOUNG, a teenager, torn, on a gurney is moving at six miles an hour through a bright corridor. Facial cuts, slits, her mouth agape, blood-matted black hair in disarray. It is too soon, it is too soon.

Trotting medical people, serious faces, Doctor Tredescant uncombed and unbuttoned, an Hispanic police officer holding an aluminum notepad, an exchange internist from Rome, well groomed. Maude walks with surprising vigor, hand on gurney. No one speaks. They enter the elevator.

"What's her name? Oh here it is, Marla. Full name?"

The police officer says, "We don't know yet."

"Blood loss three pints, Doctor, but she's stable."

"Too messy, Ed, I get frenzy here."

Chleo looks at her. "Say what?"

"Psychokinesia."

Just outside the swarm, Sara Smith hears the new word, writes *psycho kinesia* in her oblong reporter's notebook. She wears her *Herald* press tag as if it were a sapphire brooch. This is what reporting is all about. *The dare, the challenge.* She lurks, pretending not to be present, waiting for the decisive moment to talk to Maude. Just above a whisper, she asks the security man, Alvarez, "How old . . . ?" She nods her head toward Marla.

"No idea, miss, very young, fourteen."

"Fourteen, my God."

"Maybe less. They grow up now, so fast it's hard to tell." Alvarez is the father of three girls.

Where I come from, she would have been grounded.

Marla is wheeled in one smooth turn into her own clean white coma room. Gwyneth Freeman's first room, Karen Beck's.

Only Marla's face can be seen above the monogrammed

HOSPITAL sheet. Her pure features have been calmed, she might have dozed off in a hammock. It is a pretty face interrupted by tiny yellow metal hoops, one through her upper lip, another through her eyebrow.

Maude scans her pupils with a flashlight, tries to startle her with smelling salts, holds her hand. She was born the year Maude entered medical school.

"Marla?"

Her underpants are gone. There is proof of sex. Anal bleeding. Rage.

"I want an ice-water caloric and set up the tangent screen."

Her mouth will not stay closed. Possible motor dysphasia.

There are clefts cut cleanly through the fine bones outside her eyes, just above. Clefts no larger than would be made by a stiletto.

"What do you think, Doctor T?"

Ed Tredescant smiles, shrugs, *All this testing is too optimistic.* "His other procedures have been so . . . controlled. He never once cut muscle tissue." The Roman internist, pallid, nods.

In her mind, Maude has been hearing the phrase *orbital lobotomy*, over and over. She will not say it aloud. Not yet. *Not possible.*

"Take blood, test her for Xylazene, AIDS, take vaginal and anal smears."

"Want me to set her up for an angiography, Doctor?"

"No, no. I want to see her in intensive rehab in five minutes. Move her oh so carefully." She washes her hands.

"Do we lose the hoops, Doctor?" The tiny yellow metal hoops that punctuate Marla's face.

"God, no, Chleo, she wants them there."

Alert, precocious Sara Smith stands waiting in the corridor. Ex-apprentice to Time Inc. Still dressed as she was the day she arrived at Ethel Walker's School for Girls, age twelve. Natural ocher hair, her dad's, combed flat. Eastern girl-college rules. Stables her horse, Cricket, at a riding club. A story, *any story,* is sent from God. Tonight, God has sent her one and she is the only reporter on earth aware of it.

The Hispanic police officer notices Sara, comes over to her. They read each other's name tags, she writes down his name, M. Alvarez. "You're going to have to wait awhile, Miss Smith, 'til the doctor comes out."

"Toyer, right?"

He nods sagely, importantly.

"What's the victim's name, officer?" *No one knows about her but me.* She is close to shivering.

"Marla."

"Marla what?"

"That's all we know."

"Is she a black woman?"

"Yeah, black."

Sahara tan, when she was wheeled past Sara Smith at six miles an hour, the color of too much milk in black coffee. *Black? Fundamentally black, if you will.*

Suddenly Sara Smith is standing in front of Maude.

"Doctor Garance, I'm with the *Herald:* Sara Smith." *Too weak.* She winces. "You told me to go . . . fuck myself?"

Just last week. Maude remembers her. "And how was it?"

Sara reddens, smiles a muscular smile. Maude realizes why she dislikes her. She is an East Coast debutante got up as a feminist in a man's world, nothing more.

"Don't you have a home with a nice bed, or are you a homeless person?"

In the momentary silence, seared by insults, Sara Smith hears a car horn so faint, so far away that it sounds like a loon's cry.

"Doctor Garance, you deserve to be written about. You and your hospital. The finest neurological trauma rehab center west of Chicago."

"New York."

Doesn't the public have a right to know? Aren't I their messenger?

"I'm on a deadline. We're going to press. I'd like your comments." She holds her reporter's notebook like a dance card. *Give me the story, give me the story.*

"When you publish anything about my patients, you do it against my policy. You are creating a star out of him, don't you see that? It's what he wants, reading about himself and the effect he's had." She starts to walk away, Sara Smith balances her weight evenly on her feet.

"I need your comment for our bulldog edition."

"You wouldn't want to print it."

"You've already been too generous, Doctor Garance, you've given me more than enough."

Clever girl, Maude thinks, *maybe there's something to her.* She nods to Officer Alvarez. "Officer, please escort Miz Smith to her car in the parking lot." Smith starts walking away, led by Officer Alvarez. Maude turns. "And make sure you actually see her drive away."

SARA

TUESDAY, IT IS SARA. She stands at Maude's front door watering the beige gardenia plant from a liter bottle of spring water from Colorado.

Maude is at home, in bed. She has agreed to Doctor T's suggestion, a two-week leave of absence. Sara knocks.

"It's Sara Smith from the *Herald,* are you busy?"

Yes, I'm studying the horrors of morning television. Maude peers out between the bedroom curtains, sees the young woman watering a dead plant. She feels tears well up. She goes to the front door. Speaks through it.

"Yes?"

"I apologize for last night. Please, Doctor, can we speak?"

"You said you had an idea, a way to apprehend Toyer. What is it?"

"Through the door?"

"I can hear you clearly, Miz Smith, tell me your idea."

She pauses. "Doctor. I want you to analyze Toyer."

"*That's* your idea?"

"Yes."

Jesus God save us from amateurs. "He'd break his first appointment."

Sara smiles, Doctor Garance has made a joke. "No, Doctor, you'd analyze him for the *Herald*."

"In your newspaper?"

"Yes, on the op-ed page."

"What's that?"

"Opposite the editorial page. Op-ed."

"One word: unethical."

Sara is prepared. "Is there an *ethical* here? Why don't we drop that word, Doctor. He has."

"No, there certainly is an ethical here, Miz Smith, one doesn't become psychopathic to treat psychopathy."

"Please, Doctor, think about it. I believe he'd be susceptible to your influence. You yourself said he'd like to read about himself, maybe he cares what you think."

A thinking pause. "Sorry, no."

"Don't you have free time now?" *Just guessing wildly.*

"How did you know I was on leave?"

I heard suspension. "Shouldn't we do what we can even if it's slightly fishy? Can't you even consider it?"

Silence from within.

"I truly believe you're the only one who can reach him, Doctor."

Sara waits.

Maybe if I hosed Miz Smith down. Through the door: "Number one, I don't want to lose my license to practice medicine."

"Someone has to do something."

"I agree."

"You went to see Bob Meyerson."

"I did, and he's what's wrong."

"An absolute clown."

They are in agreement on Meyerson. Sara smiles.

"By the way, he hasn't even assigned a detective to the case."

"Miz Smith, I simply cannot practice mail-order therapy."

"It won't be therapy, Doctor, think of it as a series of educational articles in print every Monday morning."

Silence.

"We can provide you with a forum."

A forum? Maude doesn't answer.

"Let's talk again."

Maude is in very real pain. Soon, she will receive the eleventh telephone call from the Kipness. She can see no hope of ending the flow at ten victims. This forum that Sara Smith is asking her to create sounds plausible, who knows? It may only be a way to pressure Meyerson.

"May I give you my card?"

"Please slide it under the door."

She does.

She's bulletproof.

That morning, bottom of page three, the *Los Angeles Herald*:

Toyer's Tenth Victim Critical
Unlike Previous Nine Women

By Sara Smith

In his tenth in a series of brutal assaults, Toyer has incapacitated a young woman known only as Marla, pending further identification. Last night's assault victim is quite different from his previous nine. First, Marla is young, perhaps as young as fourteen; his previous victims have all been in their twenties. Marla is black; his previous victims have all been white. Marla may have been raped and violently mistreated, perhaps fatally. "Her life hangs in the balance," according to a nurse close to the patient. Today, she remains unstable, in critical condition in the crisis ward at the Kipness Memorial Hospital where she was brought last night just after midnight.

The extent of her injuries remains a mystery. Dr. Maude Garance, resident physiatrist, would not comment to this reporter, refusing to divulge any information as to Marla's condition or to the specific details of her assault. In fact, for the past two months, Dr. Garance has become increasingly protective of her patients' privacy, effectively stonewalling the press on their behalf. Last night during a brief interview, Dr. Garance went so far as to imply to this reporter that the public does not have a right to know. The *Herald* disagrees. We believe that the public does indeed have a right to know and we will continue to provide our readers with all aspects of the news.

TOYER

NIGHT. IT IS HER. He glimpses Maude leaving the Kipness, crossing the parking lot. Tall, tonight she is wearing a baggy cotton dress. The brow, the jaw, the high straight nose. Close-cropped hair.

He follows her home, a long drive, he measures seventeen miles driving far behind her, sometimes without headlights.

On Tigertail Road, a blacktop road with grassy patches running alongside, no paved sidewalk up Randall Canyon, he parks, walks the last few hundred yards to her house.

He is dressed like a jogger, a hallmark of innocence, a stopwatch dangles from his neck, he can go anywhere in the name of health.

There are few houses on Tigertail Road, none of them large.

Well named, it meanders, it seems foreign to the brusque streets below, the all-night Chinese lanterns of the city's streets.

He identifies her car again by the license plate, pallid and square, a car like any other. It is parked in a spindly carport built to shield the sun. He likes her for her car, it is not her alter ego.

He watches her house, for minutes, a cottage, one story, maybe gray, fireproof composite roof. A tiny farmhouse without a farm. There seem to be half-a-dozen ways to enter it without a key.

He stands still, leaning against a thin eucalyptus tree, in ten minutes the night sounds resume, the nightingale relaxes and begins singing. Inside, Doctor Garance, the sound of opera repeating a certain duet between two men again and again. *Is she alone?*

Step by step, in slow motion, he moves toward the house, pausing half a minute between steps, stepping firmly on the rattling leaves. Finally he leans forward over a dead bush, peers into the living room. At first he cannot see her, she is lying on the floor. An arm flashes by. There she is, now cross-legged on the floor, arms over her head. She is wearing a flesh-colored brassiere and matching panties, the material is invisible. Her body is pale, lithe, her breasts unexaggerated, her waist fine, defined by hips that flare slightly. She is limber.

She stands, her posture erect, he could watch her walk for hours, he watches her pass several times from the kitchen area to the bedroom, with a bowl, a glass, a book, her small well-turned buttocks, the panties too high. She moves through the house like a woman who lives alone.

After a while she goes to bed.

MAUDE

PALE, DRY MORNINGS. Maude dozes long after waking up, trying not to dream, lying abed, dazed by breakfast talk shows, people delighted with their quirks. Gleefully exposed, sharing their traumas with Maude for a flight to New York, a slab dinner at Kelly's Beef Factory, a room at the Essex House. *What about Psychotic Physiatrists?*

She has been sent away, a two-week vacation, laid off. There is a stack of library books she means to read but will not finish. Jean Rhys, Isak Dinesen, Edna O'Brien. She is reading *Out of Africa* for the first time. She has memorized its first sentence, "I had a farm in Africa, at the foot of the Ngong Hills."

Midday. She cannot function far from her house. At Food King Market she leans against an empty cart under dress-store lighting, staring at military formations of produce standing at attention. She forms each decision to buy produce slowly.

Every day she telephones the Kipness when she wakes up, searching for clues, reasons, speaks to Chleo in a whisper, meets Doctor T for lunch, sometimes for dinner. Her girls remain as she left them, deeply inert. She is not responsible to anyone, only to them.

A message blinks on the machine. Sara Smith again. *You can't embarrass this woman.* She leaves her four telephone numbers. *Can't she understand an insult? She will pay Toyer homage forever unless someone stops her.*

TOYER

HE HAS CHOSEN THE BATHROOM WINDOW. The room is white, immaculate, the medicine cabinet orderly, the gleaming sink, one could perform surgery. It is a bright still morning, the day not yet warm. He has seen her drive away.

In the living room, there is a windowful of sun. He is impressed by the inventions of glass, stone, chrome. Horizontal and vertical lines, no clutter, less rather than more. A New Mexican cross, wind-pitted, lifted from someone's grave. An architectural drawing of the Louvre. Pristine. The brutal self-consciousness of the Parisian. The coolness of the place. The effect is certainly more masculine than feminine.

He looks for the telephones, there are two. *Blank. If it's not on the phone it isn't anywhere.* He presses double 0. After a taped *thank-you* message by a trained voice, a living operator comes on.

"Pacific Bell, how may I help you?"

His voice is barely able to speak above the ravages of old age, in a cracked whisper, the daily emergency of the dying.

"What is your name, dear?"

"Tricia."

"Tricia, can you please tell me . . . what my telephone number is? I . . . I can't remember it."

"Certainly, madam."

He writes the number down on the telephone pad, tears away the page.

What to see? The medicine cabinet, of course. Secrets abound. The closets, blouses, skirts, slacks, in the bureau drawers necklaces, bracelets, more blouses. Her underwear is fine, it smells of women's hallways, scents nearly invisible. Her privacy. Is there a medical bag?

On a cabinet back in the living room there are framed photographs, one in silver signed "*Thine, Mason.*" A man made of wood and rock with more hair than she, slightly bearded, pants rolled, barefoot on a beach standing in a sea wind. If Maude Garance is a sloop, Mason is a schooner. He can find no other sign of him in her house, wonders where he is.

In the kitchen, he finds a key that fits the back door, he removes it from a ring of several hung on a hook by the refrigerator.

There is a tentative knocking. Someone is at the front door. He stops, stands motionless.

"Maude? Are you there?" A young female voice.

After a minute or two, a note is slipped under the door. He stands in place until he hears a car drive away.

> Maude, I must talk to you about T please call me.
> Urgent.

It is signed *Sara.*

He goes back into the bedroom, stretches out on the wildly unmade bed and amid her books and underwear, imagines her asleep.

JIM O'LAND

A GED GLOOM, the executive editor's office of the *Los Angeles Herald*. No view, not from his second-story window, its pane partially obscured by 1900s residue of street fires, newspaper strikes, urban malignancy. On the table, two glass ashtrays, one closed over the other, shells to form a nasty clam.

Lanky Jim O'Land, the benchmark, done-it-all newspaper

editor who looks strong wincing over a cigarette pinched in his lips, busy with a fat Berol crayon marking printouts, a cliché in his own time. Always an amused aspect about him, always ready to jab-and-parry; logically superior to the passage of idiots, helpfully rude, just this side of pompous. He insists on being called Jim, even by Sara who has trouble with the informality. A man easily followed, his face is well made, he is iron-haired, permanently stooped from a plane crash. Years of street reporting for the *Boston Globe* and the *Baltimore Sun* have left cracks in his facade, the nearly invisible lines on the face of fine old china, cracks not yet seen by Sara Smith.

She stands, facing him, across the glass-topped wood table. He cannot see them, but her knees are trembling. She holds a letter.

To him, Sara Smith is a foil, a bright girl, but an eager reporter with unchecked sources. He hazes her for wearing barrettes, sensible shoes, minor eastern schoolgirl regimen.

He decides he will take a breather from his printout to play with her. He reaches for his dismal espresso and milk, too long in its Styrofoam.

"What have you got there, Sara Smith?"

She holds the single typed page out to him, she is trying not to seem overwhelmed by its implications.

"It's a letter from the person who's been disabling all those women." She says it quietly so she will not stammer, her bowels are cool from excitement.

O'Land nicely masks his disbelief.

"That would be Toyer, wouldn't it, Sara?"

She nods.

"Say *Toyer*, Sara. Not *the person who's been disabling all those women*."

"Toyer, Mr. O'Land, Jim. Okay? I hate that name. I never liked it."

"You made it up."

"Yes, I did, but now, it doesn't fit the deed."

"It fits the headline."

She shifts her weight. "Well, anyway, this letter is from him." She says it firmly.

"Good. I'm glad he wrote to you, I've been wondering when he'd get around to it."

"Aren't you ever surprised by anything at all, Jim?"

"Surprised? Why, no, what's on his mind this morning?"

She sighs. She is not going to play. "He simply claims that he's not responsible for Marla Booth. He wrote here, directly to the *Herald*, attention, me."

She reaches the letter out to him. Jim O'Land does not take it, sips the cooled café machiatto. He lets her stand dripping in front of him a moment longer.

"That letter isn't from Toyer, Sara. It's from someone else, someone who sleeps at the foot of his mother's bed, someone who dates inflatable girls, you know, a psycho."

"You're dead wrong this time, *Mister* O'Land, it's the real thing." She is frowning, sighing.

"*Mister O'Land?*" O'Land is happy to see her dander up. He grins. "Sara, Los Angeles has more psychos than you've had bubble baths."

"I know that. And for your files, I shower."

For an instant he sees her nude, slim, wet as a seal. She wins.

"Now if I thought for one second that you showered entirely in the nude, that remark would qualify me for a handsome sexual harassment settlement. Our union would be very kind to me." He smiles, drops his Styrofoam cup, still with coffee, into the wastebasket, turns back to the full-size photocopy of the front page. "Now please go away."

Sara does not move. She holds the letter away from her, toward him, as if it might hit its flash point, burst into flames.

"He read my piece, he's demanding a retraction."

O'Land is still having fun, but he will only allot her another minute.

"Retract what?"

"Retract Marla Booth. She wasn't his. She was different.

Look, I was there. I overheard all sorts of things off the record. They were all acting strange."

"So he wrote you a letter to clear things up."

"*Yes.*"

"Watch my mouth, Sara: wanted felons do not write letters to newspapers demanding retractions, that's just something I couldn't help noticing over the years editing newspapers in Washington, Boston, London, and now here. Go." He turns his back on her and picks up his crayon, absolutely indicating dismissal.

"*He* does. He writes letters to me."

Chilly silence. *Joke's over.* O'Land turns, looks up at her, not angry. "No he doesn't."

She is suddenly inflamed. "You fucking haven't even read it."

His mouth drops open, she sees gold glint. He has never heard her utter the F-word.

"Sara, for your files, one would never say *fucking* haven't; it's either *fucking* even, or *fucking* read, or *fucking* letter, but never *fucking* haven't." He is about to rise.

Her body burns, feels naked. She wants to apologize. "He gives proof right here that he's Toyer. He knew his letter would be doubted, so he says . . ." She reads: " '*I always leave my handprint at the scene.*' "

"His handprint? That's great. How come no one's ever found it?"

She continues reading, " 'It's always in the highest place in the room, on the top of a window where no one would ever think to look for prints. See for yourself.' "

O'Land rises, speaks carefully, "Has he done this with all his victims?"

"Yes, and he's embarrassed by this Marla Booth. So what he's saying —"

"Is that he didn't leave a handprint." O'Land feels a small firecracker go off inside him. "What do we look for?"

She clenches her fist, shows O'Land the exact area of the

imprint described in the letter, between her pinky and wrist, presses it on the glass-topped table and rolls it. It leaves a print. "That's the mark he's been leaving."

She can hear him exhale. "So he's telling us that this Marla is not his victim. That she's the first Toyer copycat." Sara nods. She is aware that this moment is a black-and-white photograph she will always keep.

He sits, not wanting to break anything. *If this is true, if Toyer has written to us and not the* Times, *our early edition will be over the million mark tomorrow. Four press runs.*

"If this checks out," he tells her, "if I can get one site confirmed, I'm running it in the bulldog." He punches the district attorney's number onto the telephone. "Write me forty inches." He holds the letter as he would a parchment anatomy pen-and-ink drawing by Michelangelo. "Remember, by denying the Marla Booth crime, he's confessing to nine others. Nice working with you, Sara Smith, front-page byline. What do you plan to do for the rest of your life?"

She smiles, looking precocious. *Dad, I scooped the* Times.

As she leaves his office, O'Land is smiling, he is waiting to speak to the D.A. She turns. Their eyes catch, cleanly.

"Just imagine his ego," she whispers.

RAY YELLEN

DISTRICT ATTORNEY RAY YELLEN calls Jim O'-Land back at six that evening. Yes. Their criminologist has found that the windows at Paula Straub's apartment have been cleaned but there remains the ghostly imprint of a fist mark, though it has been wiped, it is there. At Gwyneth Freeman's apartment and Lydia Lavin's house, *yes*, the crime lab has found pale prints, alone and firm, on window glass near the ceiling, exactly where Toyer said they would be. Sara's letter is valid.

Yellen asks O'Land to proceed carefully, to please stay in touch with the assistant district attorney, Bob Meyerson. He can help, he says.

While O'Land was waiting to hear from Yellen, he told Sara to call Maude Garance and get a reaction comment to Toyer's letter, its meaning, any clues, its authenticity, any character description. She reached her at home, read her the letter. Maude was appalled by it, asked Sara not to run it.

When Sara called O'Land back with Maude's reaction, he told her that the letter's authenticity had just been confirmed by the D.A.'s office and that the *Herald* would have no choice but to run it tomorrow.

He tells her to move a local story and to set the Toyer story up on the front page below the fold to read:

TOYER EXONERATED

A drop-head for those *Herald* readers who don't understand what the word *exonerated* means:

Not Guilty in Marla's Death

Jim wants the headline to read, "*Toyer Off the Hook*"; Sara fights him for "*Not Guilty*." She wins. Either way, the *Times* is once again a day late and half-a-million readers short. Either way, the wronged Toyer is absolved.

TOYER

THE FOLLOWING MORNING, a Wednesday, the lower half of the front page of the *Herald* explodes with Toyer. *It's irresistible,* O'Land says. *It's reader-proof.* Toyer's name crosses all lines, social, racial, economic, cultural, it is household. The text of his letter, he is embarrassed by whomever imitated him, apologizes to the victim. A chillingly humane letter. *Newspaper magic.*

TOYER TALKS

CLAIMS CRITICAL TENTH VICTIM
NOT LINKED TO PREVIOUS NINE

But Kipness Cautious
on Preliminary Tests

The text of Toyer's letter:

Dear Sara Smith,

I did not kill Marla Booth. I couldn't possibly have. I'll tell you why—I don't kill. I can't.

I hope someone does find Marla's killer. It is not me. Killing is the worst sin of all. I have read the Bible. I feel sorry for the poor woman and also the person who could do those things to her. Anal sex, jabbing her in the face with a knife, letting her bleed without calling the paramedics. Anyone who knows me will tell you that's not my way of doing things. I may be capable of a great many things but not murder.

It is signed *Toyer.*

An amazing document. O'Land says it is unprecedented in journalism. A first. For weeks throughout the United States, Toyer's note remains pressed by magnets to refrigerators for visitors to marvel at, saved for descendants. As O'Land had hoped, the *Herald* sells out four press runs totaling 1,115,500 and passes the *Times* for the first time since Franklin Roosevelt's reelection, November 1936. It is accomplished. Victory.

"Sara, go ask Doctor Garance, now does she want to comment? Yes or no. Tell her that the paper will certainly make room for whatever thoughts she cares to write on Toyer."

Once again, Maude won't speak to her.

Sara reports this encounter to O'Land, that Maude says running the letter will reactivate Toyer's psychosis, that psychotics become more dangerous when they become less confused, when they are reaffirmed. She has told Sara that if they turn the *Herald* into a pulpit for Toyer, they will make him more active. Beatified, as the *Herald* will be doing. O'Land smiles at the word *beatified.*

"These are the risks," he says.

Until now, nothing but dreadful news of Toyer's activities has been reported by the responsible newspapers, the papers that carry gold prices, theater reviews, wire services, five-day weather forecasts.

Now the *Los Angeles Times*, a responsible newspaper, cannot disregard Toyer's note printed in this morning's *Herald*, it must print its text, quote Sara Smith, credit the *Herald* and continue competing with it.

Less responsible publications across the country pick up the *Herald*'s copyrighted letter, one is *Hell Magazine* (paid circulation 400) of the East Village, New York. Pirated reprints. In its campy column, *Toyer Watch*, readers are encouraged to report Toyer sightings, describe him, what he was wearing and doing, what sort of contact they had with him. Fun stuff. One named him the country's top performance artist, nonpareil. Toyer has proved he can fly, he can sell. He is major.

"Let's hope Toyer stays in touch with you," Jim tells Sara. "Your career depends on it."

What if it's true? What if he never writes me again?

Thursday morning O'Land passes Sara's desk, stops. "By the way, Miz Smith, I need forty inches on Toyer for tomorrow and a think piece on him for Sunday."

Because she has nothing left to say about him, she is forced to create a more dramatic style without texture that readers learn to respond to. It is filled with a childlike wonder:

In the one-seat theaters of our minds, we have imagined him, we have read his words, he walks on our stages. He is real. He has a persona. What does he eat? What kind of socks does he wear? We want to know and we may never unravel these mysteries, but we do know that if Toyer lacks a face, he no longer lacks a voice. He cares what we think. We hadn't thought he would. We are believers.

"Lighter than gravity, quicker than the speed of sound, dumber than a box of rocks," Jim O'Land says, the four television networks, two cable production companies, two studios, seven independent filmmakers, announce plans for Toyer-driven projects. Sara is flanked. She has given him a life. Does he eat Chinese? Thai? Italian? Does he drink beer, vodka, Diet Coke? Smoke Winstons, grass? Do cocaine? Heroin? Is he liberal? Conservative? Dogs or cats?

Sara's Toyer generates a feel-bad-feel-good media pageant; the news is bad, the entertainment is good. It is a familiar story, it must be familiar to work for the public. She has known it all along.

A number of these film projects will fall away, of course, smothered by the competition, but it is the muscle behind their spontaneous vigor that startles even Jim O'Land.

She asks him why her piece is buried inside on page three instead of on the front page. He tells her that he wants readers to actually purchase the paper and open it up, not just read it off the front page at newsstands.

"This must have been brewing for a long time," he tells Sara. He welcomes the explosion of public interest, it is welcome, the fine cracks in his ceramic are visible to her.

MEYERSON

OH, HELLO THERE, Jim, it's Bob Meyerson."

"Yes, hello, Mr. Meyerson.

"No, Jim, it's Bob, we met."

"We met . . ."

"We met at the Alzheimer's Follies, big charity thing." O'-Land thinks of *Almayer's Folly*. "I met you with Mrs. O'Land."

The ex–Mrs. O'Land. That makes it over a year.

"Yeah, okay, I remember, Bob."

"Hate those things but you know, they must do some good after expenses, I guess."

"Yeah." *Not a clue.*

"Anyway, Ray Yellen asked me to touch base with you. I'm his assistant D.A." *The clouds clear.*

"You've got an election coming up."

"Don't I know it? Kissing butts all over the place."

Jim makes an agreeable sound.

"Jim, I wonder if you'd let the city buy you lunch today." *And now, my butt.*

"Sorry, Bob, always eat here at my desk unless I'm firing someone."

"That's when you take them out to lunch?"

"Sort of a tradition. We take 'em to the Lion's Head."

An editor has come into his office, remains in front of his desk, shifting his weight.

"Is this about the election?"

"No way!" He chuckles over the idea, but it *is* about the election. "It's that Toyer piece in yesterday's paper."

O'Land is still glowing from it, he has gotten nothing but compliments. David versus Goliath. The figures are still warm; the *Herald* has beaten the *Times*, which he calls *the heaviest void on earth*. It is a good win. Across town but less than a mile away, the *Times*'s offices are entirely carpeted. Every square inch, three-ply Brussels, taupe. O'Land has been in journalism all his life and he has never seen such a phenomenon.

Bob is talking. "It's been nagging Ray all morning. He's telling me that for what it's worth, he asked me to call you to tell you that kind of hype isn't going to do anyone a whole lot of good downtown here. We've got our butts full." *The word again.*

"He's a pretty bad character, Bob."

"I *know* that, Jim, Ray knows it, too, he must be, I had a visit from a wacko psychiatrist who's giving me all kinds of grief. Let me tell you how Ray puts it."

"Can you hold on one minute, I've got someone here." Meyerson can hear O'Land telling a Rick to get right over to Burbank for the high school arson and to find Tracy and tell her that she's got to be at UCLA by noon or she's not going to get anything.

"Yeah, Bob." O'Land is back.

"Okay. So we agree this is a bad dude and all that crap, but can I please read you something that Ray had sent up to me by the chief of police?"

"By all means."

Paper sounds. "Uuuhm. Okay, here we are. Fourteen homicides, one serial killer, one serial rapist, God knows how many other rapists . . ."

"We get the same printouts."

"These are this morning's, Jim."

"I know, Bob, I get it."

"So I can't do much for your Toyer. And hey, I want to do more, but I've got just so many detectives out there and bad as he is, your guy's only a class C felon."

"Thanks for telling me."

"You're positive you don't want to take a break and have lunch on the city?"

Small silence. "Uh, no, thanks."

"Anyway, Jim, thanks for listening. I tell you, Ray's unhappy and he wanted me to convey this to you. He suggested maybe you're making a little bit too much out of this guy and you're starting to make us look bad down here."

"Uh-huh."

"And him look good."

"Uh-huh." *You cannot insult a politician.*

"Let's talk again."

Click.

MAUDE

SHE IS AWARE OF HIS TEETH. In her dream she tries to make out his face, he is amorphous. First he is Mason then his face dissolves, he melts into another being. He has no features, or if he does, they constantly erase themselves.

It is an ancient walk-up tenement, a slum building inhabited by calm women who never speak. Maude has come here looking for Mason. Someone said he was living here now. But she is standing close to the other man in the slim hallway. The thin walls murmur as if the foundation they are standing on objects to their being there. There is only poverty. The rooms are dark. The dreadful boardinghouse stands alone, close to a swamp, strange for a city. He is the landlord. He is charming.

He whispers in her ear. What is he saying? She feels her

sweat run down inside her arms from having stood too close to him. He wants her to live here as a tenant. One of his women. She tries to lead him outdoors where she can talk to him above a whisper, make a bargain. He anchors her with his arms, her dress vaporizes. He presses her back to the wall. Her thighs up, held in his hands, her feet high against the stair railing. What he does to her is accurate, stunning.

Following deeply satisfying sex, walking down the narrow stairs, she slashes at him from behind with a scalpel. She kills him easily, without urgency, with finesse, as though it were expected. Without leaving a mark.

Toyer is in her bedroom, he is standing at the foot of her bed looking down at her, watching her dream. He is *there*. He has slowed his breathing to match hers. He is quite comfortable watching Maude.

Outside, it is getting light. She has not been able to move, sees his blood on her nightgown. She feels a *frisson*. She opens her eyes, sickened. The skin is still risen on her arms, as it rose once when she locked eyes with a Siberian tiger in a zoo.

When she wakes, he is no longer in the room. Gone. She realizes she has dreamed of killing him, not healing him. She has killed him with a scalpel. She wakes clenched, churned, damp. She can smell his presence. It is her cologne that she smells, worn on his body.

The telephone does not ring, she hears the answering machine click-click, she has turned the ringer off. In half sleep she hears the voice. It is Sara Smith, breathless, as if she has found a great dress at half price for the country club dance.

"Doctor Garance, this is Sara Smith, I *really need* to speak to you, it's important . . . will you please take my call."

Again she leaves her four telephone numbers. There is not a moment during Sara Smith's days and nights that she cannot be intruded upon.

Eyes closed, Maude reaches out and presses the ERASE but-

ton. When she opens them, she sees the digital clock, *07:01.*
Unusual.

Lying half-awake she tries to remember his face but Sara
Smith has dissolved him, she is still aware of his teeth, his
calm voice, an unnerving charm. And that he was holding a
silver instrument in his right hand, a shiny skewer hanging
against his thigh, bright as an icicle.

SARA

SATURDAY AFTERNOON. Sara is all but alone in the
vast second floor of the *Herald.* Except for sports, there is
no news on Saturday, the Sunday pages carry stories on geol-
ogy, historic events, civic leaders, water rights, lives of stars,
syndicated pickups. Think pieces.

Silence. A whisper-level drone emanates from air-
conditioning, telex machines, TV monitors, blood in veins.
The open-wall atmosphere of a metro newspaper, the *Herald,*
L.A.'s Number Two Morning Newspaper. The outspoken one,
the one that talks your language, the one with the great sports
section, the lean one, *the one that's fun to read.*

Sara Smith's desk is one of twenty in the news section set in
tile patterns, in pairs or fours, never one desk standing alone.
At the far end she sees Kit Menninger, food editor, describing
last night's dinner out. In the near distance, behind a low par-
tition, is Irv Kupchak, sports editor, Pulitzer Prize. He is huge,
watching several baseball games simultaneously on TV monitors. *How does he tell them apart?* Sara smiles, to her, Irv resembles a long-haired tennis ball with head and arms. He
looks so unathletic, and Kit looks so athletic. *Why don't they
switch jobs?* She imagines that, dawdling while she wills her-

self to write another 'graph about Toyer. It is as if she were under contract to him, not a nice thought.

All desks are open, one locked drawer in each. But there is absolute privacy to her file bank. Each reporter has his own secret entry password, known only to the reporter and the managing editor.

Sara taps in *C-R-I-C-K-E-T*, the name of her beloved chestnut horse, a birthday present, being kept alive at the Wee Burn Stables in Darien, Connecticut, and looked after by Keene, her little sister. Her telephone rings. *Please, be Doctor Garance.* She picks it up.

"Sara Smith." She tries to sound older, busy, and bored but cannot. It is not in her. For a few moments she hears a woman's voice in the background reporting the news. It is radio, not television. Sara repeats her name. Then as if to test her patience the voice says, "Is this Sara Smith?"

She has said her name twice, clearly. It is a moment for sarcasm. But wait, she stops, she says again, "This is Sara Smith." Plain and controlled. There is a pause, as if the caller were shy.

"Thank you, Sara Smith," the voice says.

After a moment, while she can hear radio news in his background, he hangs up. Gone. She holds the telephone, staring across the distance to the human tennis ball, sitting glazed, facing his monitors, until he becomes a blur. *That was. His voice.*

Jesus. He thanked me. For telling a million people locally, God knows how many nationally, that he was not responsible for Marla Booth. He is touchy about what he will and will not do. She feels singled out, alone in the world, special, she wants her parents standing there beside her at her desk. She has just been personally thanked by Toyer. *Dad, I'm the only reporter in the world who's had contact with this diabolic monster.* The police have heard his voice, of course, but absolutely no one has ever heard his voice *so intimately.* Her arms are no longer hers. She puts the telephone down at a great distance.

Sara needs a witness. The tennis ball with a head will not do, nor will Kit Menninger. She looks around to see who else is there, there are no witnesses. The news desk editor, *a kid of twenty with dreadful skin*, is in the hall by the elevators, smoking. *Why isn't Franny down here today?* She is training an apprentice, Francesca Jackson.

What Sara has allowed Toyer to say to her readers is that there is a wrong way to mess up a girl and a right way. He does it the right way. It is *how* you mess her up not *that* you mess her up. She has been badly used, she had not realized.

Toyer has telephoned me, he has called me by my first name, we know each other.

But he will follow her home.

The parking lot of the *Herald*. The steel exit door is pushed open by the guard, it is Sara, walking to her car. She has a good walk, nicely beveled legs, parted hair. Her manila folder falls onto the grim surface, papers scatter, she squats like a bird, one knee lower than the other. He starts over to her, he wants to help her. She is too far away, he cannot reach her without running. *It would have been perfect, a cute meeting.* He knows her car, watches her get into it from the right angle.

He has been waiting since five, watches her drive away. In a few moments he is driving behind her then ahead of her. It is easy for him, he knows Sara's address, he has been there before, he knows the way in.

He likes her apartment, it is light, simple, clean, underfurnished. One bedroom, one living room, one kitchen area, a patio with a glass door that can be opened from outside with a sturdy blade. Inside, an Italian screen, a few chairs, love seat, dining table. A stage set for farce. The main piece of furniture is a presidential desk, standing like a hippo, centrally located, shipped here from her father's office. Once a month Sara sits down and works through the night, clearing its baskets of their papers. It is more important to her than the bed.

It is early evening, still light outside, the long summer twilight. When she enters her apartment, he is behind the Italian screen. He has locked the sliding door. She locks the front door, he hears her clip on the four-inch chain. It is for protection from suspicious visitors.

She's locked us in together.

The sack is over her head, tied loosely, a soft magician's sack meant for white doves. The tape is over her mouth. She is throwing punches. She kicks girlishly but it is too black, she is overwhelmed by his accuracy, his sureness. She is down on the carpet, he tapes her ankles, her wrists behind her back.

"You breathe okay?"

She nods. She is liquid with fear.

"You wanna fight me, go ahead, I don' recommend it."

She shakes her head. *He's got an accent. What is it?*

"You wanna give it t'me or you wan' me to take it? Your call."

Sara believes she nods. She is floating. She feels her trembling excite him.

He frees her ankles. She will be raped. She is led by the arm. The scent of her own bedroom surrounds her.

"Stan' still." She does. He must be sitting on the bed either in front of her or behind her. She feels his hands moving up under her skirt, she feels her panties drawn down her legs. Without thinking she steps out of them. Realizes she is cooperating. His touch is smooth, he may be wearing surgical gloves thin as condoms.

She tries to say something to him through the tape.

"Yeah?"

She tries again. *Bphoom.* She is saying bathroom. She needs to pee.

Somehow he interprets the word, leads her into the bathroom, she backs against the sink, positions herself, he lifts her skirt, lowers her onto the toilet seat. She feels him above her, looming. A minute passes, another. She hears him leave the bathroom. He is watching her. She pees. He comes back in. She stands, he wipes her, flushes the toilet, leads her back into the bedroom. The rape can begin.

"Stan' still."

She catches the scent of something that does not belong to her, leather.

He pushes her shoulders, she falls backward at the knees, the bed catches her. He is not rough. He has not touched her breasts. She feels her dress being raised again. Squirming is all she can do, squirming is not enough.

He spreads her legs, she has no choice. She lies exposed to the evening. She wills herself to submit to him without giving up. She thinks of her parents, of Cricket. She waits. Legs spread without secrets. The telephone rings. Nobody. She wants the mattress to fold around her, close her into a safe pocket where no one can find her. Waiting, waiting. Several times she hears him say the name *Elaine*.

Five minutes pass. She remains nude from the waist down, legs wide. He has left her, gone into the living room. The velvet bag over her head forces sweat to run out of her hair down her cheeks, settle behind her neck.

He is through with her, she senses that it is over.

The refrigerator door opens and closes. There is nothing for him in there, cantaloupe, endive, asparagus, fizzy water, sour cream, champagne.

She hears the front door click shut. It is finished.

Sara has no way of knowing, she imagines that it takes her an hour to free her right wrist taped to the leg of the bed below the innerspring. It is after dark when she removes the hood. It is a soft piece of blackout cloth stapled into a magician's bag.

She will not call the police, she will not mention it to Jim O'Land, nor will she report it in the *Herald*. Sara has no one to tell.

"I'm coming over, Doctor, you've got to let me in." Her voice has a frightened urgency. She hangs up.

She drives over to Maude's, sobbing dryly from the trauma of being led close to death. The humiliation of being exposed. She is devastated, confused, she feels elation from filthy survival, of not being raped, not being incapacitated, of being touched by Toyer. She is disgusted by his power. Making preparations to rape her then choosing not to.

Maude opens the door, lets Sara in without questioning her. She senses how serious it is. As Sara enters the small house, she is trembling, she sits in the deep chair without speaking. Maude brings her a fine-stemmed glass of wine, a pinot noir. She senses he may have come closer to her.

"Don't talk 'til you've had a big gulp, then start at the beginning."

Sara sits back, drinks, swallows, closes her eyes, drinks.

"Has this something to do with Toyer?" Sara cannot speak. "What did he do to you?"

"*Why?*" Sara exasperated, spills her drink. "Why would he do it?"

"Toyer."

Sara nods. "He'd just called me an hour earlier to thank me for God's sake for doing him a favor."

"What did he do?"

"Everything. Nothing. He started to —" Maude can barely hear her. "He didn't rape me." Eyes still closed, Sara describes the evening in detail, his power, finesse, accuracy, restraint. "I didn't even see him." Maude listens, watching Sara's mouth. "Why?"

"It's what he does, Sara. These girls all think he's their best friend."

"But he didn't rape me. Everything but."

"That's because he likes you." Maude mops up Sara's spilled drink with a kitchen towel. "No police?"

"I've been thinking about it but what's the point? I'm sure he wore latex gloves, all I'd end up with is a piece in the *Star.*"

"What about your own paper?"

Sara shakes her head, waves her hand. "It's what he wants."

"You need to lie down?"

She shakes her head. "Isn't that his ultimate power? To stretch me out, tie me up, spread my legs, I mean open me to the heavens, and then not screw me?"

"What do you think, really? Was it him?"

"It's him. It's just too big a coincidence. *A*, no psychopath has ever tied me to my bed, and, *B*, a psychopath called me two hours before it happened. I think he was waiting for me all that time. It's him, it's toying. I ought to know, I gave him the name."

"You did?" Maude did not know. "The *Herald* started that name?"

"Yup. After they found he'd beaten Gwyneth Freeman at backgammon. God knows what stakes *they* were playing for."

"I have always disliked that name."

"Me too. But it fits."

Maude nods. "Remember, this might not even be him, Sara."

"I wonder if he's black, Maude."

Maude is surprised. The question of race, nationality. She has never thought of Toyer as Italian, Jewish, Mexican. To her he has always been a white, middle-class college graduate, pre-med.

"Always a remote possibility. His psychosis is so unique it could come from anyone."

Maude makes them both big serious drinks instead of more pinot noir or dinner, double gins with small doses of tonic and bitters.

Sara has relaxed a notch or two. When she entered the house she chose to sit in the deep Timmons chair. She feels ingenuous, fine-boned. She is able to look around, see where she is. Surprisingly, to her, it is a cold modern interior, black and gray, stone and glass, nothing like the distempered exterior of the house. The oil-painted screen of monolithic columns, steps, paving, arches, the stones of Venice.

The deep chair, the gin. Sara tries to stop trembling especially when Maude is looking at her, she is ashamed of her weakness. She has been humiliated, made to feel absurdly young. Maude sees traumatic shock in Sara. She cannot cast her out into the night, she cannot send her home, Sara has nowhere to go. Maude asks her to stay over.

Jimmy G regards Sara, postponing his decision. She is slightly drunk. Maude feels that they could never be friends, their values lie at opposite poles. She feels close to her tonight only through Toyer.

In the night, Sara tries to sleep on Maude's sofa, the deep silence of the canyon roaring in her ears. She cannot get the ordeal out of her mind. She is unable to stop trembling. The total exposure, enslavement, humiliation, where anything might have happened but nothing did. Her body aches from imaginary scars. But in the night, the ache grows from fear into rage, a fierce personal hatred for Toyer that she has seen in Maude but not understood. The feeling is still too strong for Sara to grasp, it is unfamiliar.

In the morning she remembers, he called her by a name, not hers, he called her Elaine. She tells Maude, "Do you think I just walked in on him burglarizing the wrong apartment?"

"No," Maude says, "he meant to be there and he meant to call you Elaine."

Sara calls a locksmith, drives back to her apartment. The locksmith changes the lock on the front door, installs a dead bolt, he does not disturb the catch on the sliding glass door that Toyer flicked open to enter.

MAUDE

THE FOLLOWING NIGHT Maude dreams again. She is aware of his teeth, as always. There is no longer the dreadful tenement house, there are no silent women. There is no Mason. They are now standing outdoors, apart. He is alone, naked, facing her across a field of tall grass. Daffodils, bluebells, cowslips. He is walking toward her. He is tall, lean, fair-skinned light-haired. His motions are vague. He walks toward her through the waist-high grass. Maybe he has an erection. She wakes on the verge of orgasm, feeling sickened. She is horrified by what she sees in herself, feels contaminated by a poison she cannot isolate.

Awake, she cannot remember his face. She has never been in this field, a field of tall grass that is no longer there, outside of Dublin, that her mother has told her about many times. A field of tall grass and, each May, marigolds and bluebells, that is now gone, covered with houses that have identical roofs. She can only remember his voice, his virility. She feels herself slipping badly, she cannot stop herself from wondering what it must have been like to be blindfolded and seduced.

Her telephone rings. Maude's images are corrupted. In her sleep she picks up the receiver. She has left the ringer on in case Sara needs to call her. It is a male voice, sonorous.

"She tell you what happened?" the voice says. It seems to be part of her dream.

"Who is this?"

"She tell you?" *This is him?* She snaps awake. Tries to clear her voice.

"Nothing happened." He is still in her dream.

"Not true, Doc, I gave her the tour."

She tries to tell him that she wants to meet him but she cannot speak. Outside, it is black.

"Don' you think I been a good boy, Doc?"

In the numbing silence Maude can hear traffic sounds behind him. He hangs up silently, with his finger, then it is the dial tone. *Yes,* she says.

She sits up on the side of the bed, her feet on the floor, stunned as if she were a bird gripped by a boa constrictor during the pause before it raises its coil to crush the breath out of it. The clock reads 03:10.

The house is silent. She is half-asleep. She has had three gin and tonics, all of them strong. The walls are clamoring with voices trying to get out. She is experiencing what it must be like to become one of her own patients.

Change my number. Maude is fully awake, holding the telephone in the air between her ear and the cradle. *I've got to change my number.* She punches in 00. Waits.

"How may I help you?" The operator sounds alert, Maude sounds sick.

"Uhm. I'd like to change my phone number as soon as possible please, I have a crank caller annoying me."

"I'm so sorry. Are you speaking from your current number?"

"Yes, I am." She confirms the number. The operator repeats it. Abruptly Maude catches herself, realizes. *It's my only link with him. I can't cut it, he'll think that I've rejected him.*

"I'm sorry, operator, I forgot something, may I call you back tomorrow, please? I'll let you know."

"I'll make a note of your number and pass it along to our business office and a representative will call you in the morning."

"No, no, operator, please, my mistake, I forgot, someone's supposed to call me at this number, someone I can't reach, thanks for your trouble."

The operator continues, "If it's urgent, dial six one one after eight A.M. and they'll assign you a new listing. For tonight I can only suggest that you turn your instrument off and try to get a good night's sleep."

"Thank you so much for your trouble." Mumble mumble, hangup.

She gets out of bed, takes a long shower, first too hot, then too cold.

Now it begins. This is what I've been waiting for. If I can't handle him nobody can.

SARA

IT IS THREE DAYS since Toyer has not raped Sara.

Sara continues to feel anger, she is taking prescription tranquilizers for trembling that erupts spontaneously, she has told no one, not her doctor, not Jim O'Land, only Maude, and Maude realizes that she finds herself wishing it had happened to her. Even Maude does not realize that what he did to Sara, he did to intrigue Maude.

Unbelievable to Sara, Toyer writes to her again. He has used a pink birthday envelope, it is not her birthday. Holding the pink envelope, Sara jogs through the news department to O'Land's office, signals him out of a meeting with two reporters. When she reads it to him he is overwhelmed, more than she could imagine him being, she has never seen him ecstatic.

As if in payment, Toyer writes Sara that he will mail to her accounts of his encounter with each of his women, beginning with Lydia Snow Lavin, his ninth victim, and going back to Virginia Sapen, his first, last year. In passing he mentions Maude.

Standing in front of O'Land after reading him the letter, Sara feels naked and bound. She sits quickly. It is too soon. Toyer forced her to undress in front of him spread her legs wide on her own bed and now he has written a personal letter to her in a pink envelope.

"Why aren't you smiling, Sara Smith?"

"I'm a little tired." She will never be able to tell him.

Of course she is being badly used, she knows that, she is being tied up again by him, but if not her, who? *I can't let him write for the* Times. *No, this is my story. Any reporter would kill for it and it's mine.* She feels ill.

"Excuse me, Jim, I'll be right back." She walks quickly to the ladies' room, tries to vomit but cannot.

When she comes back she tells Jim that she hopes Toyer will drop clues in his accounts without knowing it. There are so many keen readers, maybe some of them will be intrigued enough to play detective and come forward with solutions.

O'Land agrees. "One of our readers solves this thing the Bob and Ray Show will go crazy."

Sara shrugs. *Who?*

"Bob Meyerson and Ray Yellen."

Back at her desk, she telephones Maude. No answer.

Here we go again, Maude. I'm writing another article about this prick and including his letter. Am I immortalizing him? Sure. So you're right, Maude, we're perpetuating his career, but I think it's his ego talking, and his ego is the only thing that'll bring him down. But more than I ever thought possible, I want his head on my platter. And, yes, the Herald will sell more papers.

When she has written her piece and is ready to leave, she calls Maude again. No answer.

MASON

MAUDE IS NOT ANSWERING her telephone today. She has been trying to remember Mason, but she cannot. She believes he will stabilize her. She has been trying to taste their two years together. When it was all good, they scoured each other and came away from their bed purified, odorless. At night she has been trying to dream about Mason but she dreams about Toyer, instead. She stares into his photographs. She can barely remember their days. Isolated days when Mason was without a job and she was changing hers.

Lavish time when they stayed home free to make love without deadline. They had saved a little money and put it into a savings account, *the fat,* they called it, and they could live off it if they needed to for months. Empty time to fill while their telephone stood upside down under cushions, the clock lost on the floor, when they knew no one and could lie together without end, waking messy-eyed from lovemaking, on a bed so vast Mason had charted a northeast territory and a southwest territory. Maude kept its sheets fresh with the raspberry smell of spring. And in these memories, white cotton curtains are always blowing.

She remembers.

Once. A summer afternoon. Mason wet from the shower, baby naked, standing in the bathroom doorway, watching her undress. It never grew familiar to him. She drops her skirt in a pool on the floor, picks it up and lays it across his cock, then her blouse, then her bra, then her panties, until everything except her wide straw hat is hung on his peg. Finally, her wide straw hat. The next time he came out of the shower erect, she reached for the wicker stool. He fell on the floor, laughing.

She had never felt so beautiful as she had with Mason, so deeply beautiful. So perfectly nude.

She remembers, too.

Mason dead in a lacquered casket, embalmed. *Mason is dead. Dead Mason.* Odd, in that foreign gallery of used music, music for dead people to lie down to. The soaring dead displayed to busy living people. One by one. The sob truer than the smile. Maude's last impression of Mason so wildly different from her first.

Black-and-white vision of Mason lying at attention in that silly box, legs together, shoes polished, his best dining-out suit, cheeks made up in silent screen makeup, powdered lips pursed, a pout I never saw him make. Lips I have never kissed. Is his cock hard? Oh, why can't they just let him lie curled up on his side the way he used to sleep wearing his old pajama bottoms,

*his arm under his head, his head on a pillow? Who wants to
face eternity sleeping at attention?*

*How many hilarious embalmers do I know? Is the embalming more important than the embalmed? It is an interpretive
art, telling me, "This is what Mason ought to look like."*

Ever to dream of Mason, to remember breezy afternoons
and nights, their adoration, their lightness of being, Maude
must kill the surreal vision that protocol has forced her to haul
around with her for the rest of her lifetime. Her pale vampire
lying in that bloodless room.

MAUDE

I T IS LATE THAT NIGHT, later than midnight, maybe later
than one. Maude is driving from the Kipness in North Malibu to the Herald Building in downtown Los Angeles, thirty
miles, the length and width of the town. The Herald Building;
she did not expect to see a wide two-story building, a 1900
wedding cake. It is empty, half lit, silent. She buzzes loudly at
a dented steel door, the back entrance from the parking lot.
The guard, who reminds her of sticky chocolate, is surprised
to see any visitor, especially Maude, trying to enter the building this late.

The guard says that he thinks Mr. O'Land is leaving, coming down at any moment. "Let me call up, miss." He presses a
button on the telephone. She waits. She hears him repeat her
name.

"He says to come on up." He apologizes before he runs an
aluminum wand, a metal detector squeaking at her purse, up
and down her body as if it were a sex toy. She is not carrying
tools of destruction under her summer dress.

"Use those stairs, it's on the second floor."

She climbs marble stairs that have been worn out and re-placed only where it was needed. The guard watches her from behind step by step, as if they had just had sex. She feels him thinking that she is there to see Jim O'Land for a late-night li-aison with the chief.

She knows O'Land right away, who else could he be? The unconscious authority. He is slightly taller than she imagined him, with a good head, caterpillar brows. He stands, stooped, outside the long nearly empty newsroom, by the elevator, waiting for her, as if he has come from a battle where someone he knows has been killed. His hands are empty.

They nod as if they know each other.

"Mr. O'Land? I'm Doctor Garance of the Kipness. I phoned."

"Thanks for coming, Doctor, you caught me leaving for the day." *Proud of his long hours.*

The climate in the abandoned newsroom is worn out, old, closer to death than birth.

"Mr. O'Land, your reporter Sara Smith tells me that you in-tend to print Toyer's diaries."

"That's right, Doctor. And we wanted your comments but she tells me you were unavailable."

"No, I was available. I would like to beg you not to print them."

"I feel the public's got a right to read what he has to say."

"Why? Why does the public have a right to read the work-ings of his mind? The public hasn't crawled out of its sleeping bag for fifty years."

O'Land chuckles nicely. "I've got to go along with you there, Doctor, you're absolutely right. Not since World War Two, to be exact."

"So, why do they?"

"They have a right."

"Even if they're backward?"

"Yup. They get a front-row seat."

"Front-row seat? It's a show?"

"More or less."

"Then put his diaries in your movie section."

O'Land is weary, maybe not ready for a fight. He turns toward the stairs, holding his arm out to Maude. *Let's walk and talk.* She chooses the iron railing.

"You'll make him feel like a star, don't you see what you're doing? You're giving him credibility. You can't do that."

"Why not?" He asks to learn.

"For one thing, he's got an *id.*" She holds her hands out, shaping a watermelon.

"Pardon?"

"*Id.* His uncontrolled subconscious drive."

"Right." O'Land walks with a slight limp.

"The worst thing we can do is take a psychotic's actions seriously. We reinforce his behavior, he'll feel that what he's doing is acceptable."

Maude feels exhausted, as if losing this argument will damage her permanently. "Bad news makes good copy, doesn't it."

"It certainly does."

Maude stops on the stairs. O'Land turns and waits, looking up at her.

"Look, Doctor, you're entitled to speak. If you'd care to advise him in any way, I'll give you twenty inches on tomorrow's op-ed page."

"Advise him?"

"Anything you'd like to write that might cause him to screw up. There's got to be something you can do that would be debilitating to his progress."

"You sound serious."

"I am." O'Land could be acting but probably is not. "I can hold as much space as you need."

"He seems to have some sort of ethics, a streak that worries me. He actually seems to care about what happens to his victims."

"Why should that be a worry?"

"Because then he's doing what he does in good conscience."

"Well, if you can analyze him, maybe we can kick ass. I'm definitely interested in getting him off the street as soon as possible."

"Psychiatry's a gradual process."

"The *Herald* will be here for you should you consider it. Any day you tell me to, I'll print exactly what you say, unedited. A lively discussion between the two of you would do nothing but good."

"For your circulation."

"Give it a shot, Doctor, I already like your style."

They are in the parking lot.

"Go fuck yourself, Mr. O'Land."

He chuckles again, delightedly. "Last time a woman told me to do that, I married her."

"Try to keep your neuroses out of this."

"Aha," O'Land laughs at the parking lot moon. "Spirited women, what can I tell you?"

"Please, it's *spirited horses*."

"Right, *headstrong* women." He laughs again, he does not see her smile. "I'll go a step further, Doctor, I'll hire you to write analytical responses to his crimes, whatever he does. Maybe you can bring him to his knees, who knows? I can give you three hundred dollars for each piece. It's not A.M.A. money, but it's Hollywood script money in the newspaper world. We can run your weekly piece coming off the weekend, say Monday morning." She has made his night.

"As I said before, don't print that letter."

A subterranean series of whines grows into a grand steady moan, an otherworldly din. O'Land checks his watch.

"You hear that rumbling sound? I'm sorry, Doctor, the letter is in, the presses are rolling."

O'LAND

THIS TIME Jim O'Land has printed a box on page one:

TOYER'S NINTH VICTIM
HIS OWN ACCOUNT

Los Angeles. May 23. Special to the *Los Angeles Herald*. The following account is the complete text of a letter received by the *Herald* yesterday. It is written by the unapprehended felon known as Toyer.

This is his own account of the evening he spent with Lydia Snow Lavin on April 30. Lavin was found in her Los Angeles apartment early Thursday morning, following brief telephone notification by Toyer to the Los Angeles Police. She is his ninth victim, and similar to his eight previous female victims, had been cervically cordotomized.

Then, on page three:

MY OWN ACCOUNT
Toyer

The moment Lydia opened the front door for me I felt at home. Her little house is an eclectic combination of everything she likes and I knew right away we'd get along. I already *liked* her. She'd hung a paper cow from the ceiling on a string. That made me laugh. I asked her where she got it and she told me Tijuana. Personal objects were everywhere in plain sight. I think she was making an effort to reveal herself to whoever visited her. Her place was really clean but she had an untidiness I liked. Anyway, after she made me a hot cup of tea, we sat around her new coffee table talking. She was so pretty. And she still is. Very pale which is unusual in Los Angeles. She told me she didn't want to be tan. Pretty and pale and *smart,* not that you need to be smart to beat me at backgammon. But we didn't play. The D.A. was wrong. I set the pieces on the board later. It was almost midnight when I stood up and told her I'd have to be going. She seemed surprised. Women are always surprised when you don't come on to them at full speed, head-on. They *expect* a bit of a struggle, they like to be forced into the position of saying NO very clearly. If you don't give them that chance, they think something's wrong with them and they go out the next day and buy makeup. Later when Lydia realized what was happening and who I was etc., she asked about her photograph. She said that her best one was being enlarged and she begged me not to let them use her yearbook picture in the newspapers. She wrote down the name of the photo lab and left it for the LAPD, but they used the yearbook one she doesn't like. Lydia told me about her parents in Pennsylvania and how much they miss her so I know she's going to be well looked after. That makes a big difference. I'm afraid not everyone has nice parents like hers. We more or less said goodbye to each other. Lydia is different. She has special traits you don't see every day.

It is signed *Toyer.*

There is nothing there, it is an empty sack. But to judge from the overnight response, Toyer has star quality. Readers who look for the good in people have been touched by his openness, the response is 75–25 favorable, by telephone and then by mail.

When O'Land gives Sara the figures, he is elated, surprised that she is not. For the first time she has an inkling of what Maude has been telling her, that they have created a dummy news-hero and that the *Herald* is presenting him to the soiled-fingered world as a chatty host on his own talk show. This was Sara's story from the beginning, after all. And it feels bad.

MAUDE

MAUDE DOES NOT HAVE an appointment to see Assistant District Attorney Meyerson. She has just slammed in, the receptionist calling after her, dialing in her wake.

"It's all right, Ciel, let her in." A weary male voice on the intercom. *The running of the bulls.*

Maude has located her dark tailored suit last worn at Mason's funeral, not cleaned since then. She has forgotten to look at herself in the mirror this morning, forgotten to wash, to brush her hair, badges of a madwoman.

"I'm at your disposal, Doctor Garance."

"Don't say that, Mr. Meyerson, I might."

"Might what?"

"Might dispose of you." She glances out the morning window. *Too early for humor.*

He is not alone, a woman is with him, standing by his desk, looking down over his shoulder. *Is she carrying a shoulder bag or a dead beaver?*

"Excuse me for barging in, Mr. Meyerson, but this unapprehended psychopath is now writing a newspaper column. NBC and Fox are planning to shoot movies."

"I don't control the entertainment industry, Doctor."

"Well, he's certainly entertaining us, isn't he? Oh, and, by the way, you're entertaining him. What does it take to embarrass you?"

"Believe me, I am embarrassed. Oh, this is my associate from our public affairs department, Ruth Sakamoto." *Her married name, obviously,* she is a stout redheaded woman. She greets Maude with a searing smile. Maude looks unwell.

"Why can't Homicide nail him? All the clues he leaves lying around?" Maude is back at her window.

"You're not comparing these crimes to homicides are you, Doctor?" The smiling public affairs lady is surprisingly harsh for someone in public affairs.

"Yes, I am," Maude says.

"Well, they're not, Doctor. There's a fine line there," Bob Meyerson says.

Ruth Sakamoto adds, "We're dedicated to prosecuting those who deny us life." Maude hears diabolic primness in her voice.

"Life is soul, isn't it?" Maude says. "These girls have had their souls surgically removed."

A bit grand but true enough. It causes Meyerson to pause. Ruth Sakamoto, standing behind him, speaks.

"His crimes may be diabolic, Doctor, but they are simply not homicides."

Maude feels herself getting dizzy again, she does not want to cry. "He's effectively denying them life."

Ruth Sakamoto touches Meyerson's shoulder. "How many homicides last week, Bob? Was it twenty?"

"Almost."

"And only one cordotomy, is that what you're saying?"

"Sorry, Doctor," the woman says, soothingly, "homicide's as bad as it gets."

Meyerson chimes in, "Yeah, what's worse than death?"

"Waking up."

"Any life is better than no life, Doctor, I'm surprised you don't know that."

By now the room is turning full swing around Maude, making revolutions. Last night she swallowed 200 milligrams of meperidine to make her sleep. She is losing her grip.

There is the trophy with the small brass-plated man gripping a tiny pistol, *first prize for pissing straight.* "What's this for, Meyerson?"

"Small arms, target."

"I've seen junk like this in joke stores." She picks it up. The woman raises her chin, *en garde.*

"Catch."

The woman freezes.

Maude throws the trophy overhand toward Meyerson, shattering the glass carafe behind him. They duck. By the time they open their eyes, they are alone again.

Meyerson calls the Kipness, speaks to Mrs. Kipness personally.

"I have just been assaulted with a deadly weapon by your Doctor Garance. I will press charges if I ever see this person in my office again."

Mrs. Kipness, dowager empress to her late husband's endowment, the Kipness Memorial Neurological Center for Advanced Research, personally telephones her chief-of-service, Doctor Edward Tredescant. He is in surgery. She takes an unusual step and leaves a voice message on his tape. She repeats what Meyerson has told her then adds, *Ed, suspend her.*

DOCTOR T

THEY ARE DRIVING, looking for Che Italia. Doctor T has been unable to tell Maude that she is to be suspended from the Kipness for six more weeks.

The year behind us has caused her unseen damage. Her colleagues notice changes in her but aren't sure what to think, and in the absence of opinion, opinion forms. None of them can see it, except me, probably, that it is more serious, that she is ripe for breakdown.

"Where is this place?"

"What did you throw?"

"Some kind of toy."

"Did you toss it or did you throw it?"

"What do you think? Overhand. I'm playing hardball."

"He's threatening to file assault-with-deadly-weapon charges. The Woman is livid."

"Where is this place?"

"Is all you can think of, *pesto?*"

"No, there's always *pollaio alla saltimbocca.*"

"Maude, what happened?"

She is changing lanes, driving badly.

"You went back. I *told* you."

"The D.A.'s sorry, but downtown you gotta die to get any attention."

"Stop, stop. Turn here."

They have a superb, surprisingly easygoing dinner at Che Italia, a restaurant that is rundown for all the right reasons.

He tells her.

"The Woman wants you to take a sabbatical. Stay at home, give it a rest. I can't say I disagree."

"Are you suspending me, Elias?"

"Of course not."

Maude understands, what she does not say is that she agrees.

He is always aware of his own shortcomings. He was married too long to the wrong wife. All he can do is to love Maude, without mentioning it.

It is a long slow dinner, full of brash tastes, dark wine, they are old friends. Plates and silverware clash behind them. They smile at each other over their forks, she takes his hand, holds it without pressure. He wishes there was more to it than this.

When they come out onto the street, the wall of night-heat pushes itself against them, into their faces. The thick air feels as if it might give rain, but it will not tonight.

"I'll miss my girls, Elias, can I come see them?"

"After visiting hours. Keep your head down and wear a hard hat."

She will lean heavily on him, everything will turn out all right. *I am the only man in her life.* He smiles at her, and ready to fly, kisses her goodnight gently, on the mouth. They are old friends.

MAUDE

THE *HERALD*, PAGE ONE, lies on the front seat of Maude's car. When she gets home from the hospital, she calls Sara back at one of her several numbers, on the second try reaches her at home. She does not mind Sara Smith, they may never become friends, it is not important that they do, still, she worries about her, the trauma from the experience with Toyer is not leaving her. It is far too late to call.

She hears Sara's voice surfacing from the deep. It is a ridiculous hour, maybe three, she has not looked.

"Hello, did I wake you?" *Of course I woke you.*

"Yes, who is this?"

"Maude. I'm sorry, Sara, I lost track of the time. Are you better?"

"I'll know when I wake up. What time is it?"

"I'll call in the morning."

"No, no. What is it, Maude?"

"Were you planning to visit me tomorrow and ask me to write articles for your paper?"

"I was."

"You don't need to. I'll do it. I know he'll just love that. But at the same time it'll embarrass the D.A.'s office into doing something. *Capisce*, Sara?"

"*Capisce*." She's awake, delighted. It is 2:10 A.M.

"I know we've got a hell of a conflict, Maude, we'll probably make him a bigger star before we bring him down. I bet you we'll see the question-mark-faced Toyer *Time* magazine cover. But let's try anything, I want what you want only I don't care if he's alive or dead and I'd prefer the latter."

"I almost agree."

"Can you come into the paper tomorrow? Meet Jim O'-Land, my boss?"

"I already have."

"Funny, he forgot to mention you."

It is Sara Smith's persistence. Maude feels an abstract respect for her. *In spite of the fact that he's actually laid hands on her and humiliated her and that she's escaped with her life intact, her dogged pain-in-the-ass persistence in the face of it all including my rejection of her. It is a quality that I do not have. I may be losing some marbles from my sack, but I can't dismiss my training.*

She understands Sara's anger. Of course she does, she has trouble dispersing her own rage on a daily basis. She knows it is unethical to write psychiatric evaluations publicly about a patient she has not met. She understands why Sara Smith does what she does as a journalist, why people require her to do it. The public cannot enjoy Peter Pan without seeing the wires connected to the ceiling that make him fly. They need to see how Toyer toys.

SARA

THE FOLLOWING DAY at the bottom of the op-ed page, just above Letters, Sara inserts a box:

Doctor Maude Garance, resident physiatrist on leave
from the Kipness Memorial Hospital, will probe into
Toyer's psyche in a weekly series of articles beginning
next Monday morning in Section A.

It is all that Maude can do.

Sara has grown years this past month, she feels this is
something more than scoop, story, exclusive, acceptance.
What is it? For the first time she feels something in her run
stronger, deeper, a controlled frenzy, it feels dangerous, in her
short life's experience, it is the difference between being
kissed on the cheek at her father's front door in Greenwich,
and getting fucked by the Swedish crewman aboard the
Winslow yacht on Long Island Sound.

MAUDE

NOW THEY ARE SITTING on the sofa. Sara Smith has
brought over supper, steamed *shóyu* chicken in soy sauce
with ginger, scallions. They have had excellent black tea.
Maude has not had a drink all evening. She is reading her
notes aloud without conviction.

*"You are a psychopath. A sociopath. You create nothing but
pain . . ."*

"In the ass," Sara says.

"I sense your anger, Sara."

"Oh?" She laughs. It is the first time she has loosened her
grip. Maude likes her more each time she comes over.

*"You may or may not have a moral streak; you claim you
cannot kill. But it may be that you only fear the death sentence
that murder carries."*

Sara says nothing.

"You are a performer, an impersonator. You use your ability as an instrument of destruction. The proximity of duality is necessary, but you are only one player in a city of players, the kind of player that this city above all others strives to create and perfect. You are in pain. You create victims to relieve yourself of this pain. It may, but not for long. I pity you."

She puts the page down.

"That's a start." She is trying to be diplomatic.

"Do you think he'll read it?"

"Yes, Maude, I'm sure he'll try to get through it. I don't know about our other readers. It may put them to sleep."

"Seriously?"

"Seriously, Jim's not going to run that, it's just a description of the conditions. Keep working, you'll find your way in. Just focus on what he did to your patients. Even what he did to me. And try to change his life, try to make him see himself in our light. Wouldn't it be something if you could cut him off at ten victims? If tomorrow he just quit?"

"That would be a problem."

"Why? He'd be cured."

"Yeah, and he vanishes. He moves to a town in Mexico or Canada and we never hear from him again."

"And we celebrate."

"No."

"You want his head?"

"That had crossed my mind."

"And his balls."

Later, after Sara has left, Maude slips out of bed, clears her dining table. Alone, she sits, the page is blank.

How can I treat a patient who hasn't come to me for treatment? Elias T will tell me it's a gimmick, that I'm a palm-reader with beaded curtains. God knows what Toyer will think.

Jimmy G is awake, frozen at the window, staring out into the night at small ghosts. She writes in a fine hand with a black ball-point pen:

"Dear Toyer," she begins. She crosses out the *Dear.*

By dawn, and with Jimmy G soft asleep on her pages, Maude puts down her pen and straightens her fingers. The nightingale has gone to sleep. She reads her notes, folds them. She calls Sara Smith at home, waking her again. It is Sunday.

SARA

SARA IS DELIGHTED, she tells Maude it is perfect; brief, uncomplicated, anyone can understand it, and that it has basic human appeal newspaper editors crave. Sara drives over to Maude's house later in the morning, finds the letter in the mailbox where Maude has left it for her. That night it goes to press.

Los Angeles. June 4. Special to the *Los Angeles Herald.* Beginning in today's edition, Doctor Maude Garance, M.D., attending physiatrist at the Kipness Memorial Hospital, will be writing a weekly column voicing her in-depth concerns as regards the unapprehended felon known as Toyer.

Toyer,

We get the psychotics we deserve. Hasn't it always been that way? We ordered you. Ironically, you fill a gap in the balance of nature.

In reviewing your possible motivations, naturally I am helpless to guess. But I would speculate that you may be in the aftermath of an experience so devastating that you feel you must avenge it.

All of us at some time in our lives have been deeply disturbed by tragedy. But we have many ways to dissolve our pain.

Don't you periodically feel the familiar rage rising in you

as you strive to right the wrong that was done to you? By choosing revenge to balance your state of mind you will aggravate it, never satisfy it. You attack this pain of yours with each victim. As your pain vanishes, a feeling of well-being ensues. Sadly, it only lasts a short time.

Do you agree that the revenge you have taken on the innocent women is far worse than its cause?

Catharsis is unattainable. You suffer from a repetition compulsion. You have become an actor in your own psychodramas; assuming a second identity requires a mild psychosis, the facility of a chameleon to change color with every leaf it stands on.

> Maude Garance, M.D.
> Attending Physiatrist
> The Kipness Memorial Hospital

It has a certain human interest appeal that newspaper readers look for. Throughout Tuesday, telephone calls come in regarding it.

A science teacher calls on behalf of chameleons everywhere, their elegance, their fantastic history, their ancient origins. They have been badly used by Doctor Garance.

The president of the Screen Actors Guild warns that he will write a letter in the name of all actors, demanding a retraction, that by comparing Toyer to an actor Doctor Garance has maligned a profession as important as her own. A hundred and twenty-six telephone calls, divided pro and con, most of them difficult to understand, are logged on the *Herald*'s switchboard. Among the pro-Toyer calls, there is one, possibly from him.

TOYER

THREE DAYS LATER, Friday, June 8, O'Land prints Toyer's response to Maude's first analysis. Everyone is excited, even Maude is surprised, she did not think he would write a letter.

O'Land formally tells Sara, "This is unprecedented in the annals of journalism."

"Jim, get a grip."

Toyer's note is brief and colorful:

Los Angeles. June 8. Special to the *Los Angeles Herald*. The following account is the complete text of a letter received by the *Herald* today. It is written by the unapprehended felon known as Toyer. This is his response to a letter published in last Monday's *Herald* by Doctor Maude Garance, attending physiatrist, Kipness Memorial Hospital, Los Angeles.

Dear Dr. Garance,
You called me chameleon in Monday's paper? Sorry, Doc, no sale. Chameleons are dull, slow-moving ugly critters. They eat flies—ugh. I learned that in school. So here's the big difference between us. A chameleon changes his color to the color of the leaf he's standing on, okay?—I change the color of the leaf I'm standing on to my color.

As before it is signed *Toyer.*
Sara finds Jim O'Land at his desk, chuckling away. "Now we've got 'em corresponding."

DOCTOR T

IT IS NEARLY LIGHT. 5:45 A.M. Maude has driven home late from the hospital where she spent the last hours of the night with Gwyneth, Lydia. Only the night nurse, Chleo, has seen her moving from room to room. She has had a glass of excellent gin and gone to bed.

Toyer, I have dreamt of you. I have killed you in my dreams. The rapist who rapes minds and leaves bodies. I'll dream of you again tonight.

The telephone rings, jolting her. She hesitates.

"Are you still up?" It is Doctor T.

"Yes, Elias. It's all right."

"May I come over?"

"What's wrong?"

"Nothing wrong at the hospital, I need to talk to you."

"The *Herald*."

"Maude, you're committing suicide."

"Am I?"

"I think most definitely."

"I need to do it, Elias."

"You'll lose your career."

"I can beat him."

"It's not your duty to beat him, it's flagrantly unethical."

"I might not be able to stop myself."

"May I come over?"

"No, Elias, thanks, I'm exhausted."

"Are you going to do it again?"

"It's necessary."

"I wouldn't. Once is very risky, but twice, I don't think so. I might not be able to save you."

"Save me?"

"Your license."

"It's that serious."

"It is. Please use that attractive little head of yours as the D.A. would say." He laughs weakly, she likes his laugh.

"May I stop by for a cup of coffee? I'm going in early this morning."

"Yes, come over."

Elias really does care.

She slips out of bed. His insight is accurate, she will lose everything. Maude sits staring at nothing, unable to doze off. It has grown light outside, still too early for coffee, she may be able to fall asleep after he leaves.

He arrives polished, fresh for the day. He is a big man who wears large gleaming cordovan shoes. Doctor T has no one. Neither has Maude. *Is anyone necessary?*

Maude has never seen the interior of Elias's apartment and Elias hopes she never will. He lives in a well-appointed museum of artifacts exhumed from the ancient evenings of a dead marriage; long dead.

He has always tried to regard Maude as a gifted niece rather than a woman and now feels pleasantly incestuous wanting to make love to her. *Of course she knows, isn't it a hidden obvious?*

She is still in her robe standing in the kitchen area among the details of coffee, cups, filters. Maude sees him at the door as a courting male. She understands. A gush passes through her.

She wants to allow her robe to fall open, just once, just for him to see her. She wants him to remove those massive shoes, to burrow that great nose of his into her neck and breasts. She wants him to join her in bed this morning, now, even though she knows it would be a transference from her erotic dreams, her dreaded dreams. But she cannot let her robe fall open to him. Her mind is elsewhere.

He sits in the kitchen. By the time the water for his coffee boils she has come out of the bedroom dressed and brushed, a clear sign that they will only drink coffee this morning.

She assumed her position at the hospital one month after

Mason died. Her eyes were dead with grief, she worked substitute hours, she had nowhere to go. Doctor T has felt all along that the light has never fully come back into her eyes, the light that must have been there before.

The coffee is fragrant, hot, she has dripped near-boiling water onto coarse grains of French roast beans through a paper towel. He sips the coffee black then asks for milk. He senses something extraordinary in the air, a scent that she is giving off.

"How are you, Maude?" It is not a question of mental or physical health. She knows. She is a widow.

"About Mason."

"Why, yes." He seems unsurprised, he expects her to know what he is thinking. It is time to ask.

"What about Mason, Elias?"

"Do you feel any closure?"

"Closure."

"Yes."

"I dislike that word, Elias, I never use it with my cases. It means put it behind you, get over it. Go out on dates, find another one-and-only great love of your life. It's a new word for fast mourning."

He is sorry he used the word and does not mention his reason for coming over; to talk her out of counseling Toyer in the *Herald*. It is light outside when he draws her to her feet to kiss her goodbye, she responds fully. Their mouths connect nicely. When they separate, it is he, not she, who moves away. She goes into the bedroom, closes the door without slamming it. He sits, finishes his coffee, leaves the house fully dressed, shoes tied, at six-thirty, as if he lived there. He feels a surge he has not felt for years, it is strong enough to drive him to the hospital and a long way farther.

NINA VOELKER

WEST HOLLYWOOD Station Police Officer Nina Voelker is clairvoyant. Every year since she was fourteen, she has had her fortune told on her birthday. She believes in prophecy. She believes that she will one day meet Toyer, that she will be the one who brings him to justice. Her secret special assignment is a personal one; keep an eye out twenty-four hours a day for clues. Any clue, move on it, check it out, anything suspicious. Three weeks ago on her twenty-sixth birthday a Mexican fortune teller told her that she will meet a most evil man and that her life will change dramatically for the better. That can only mean one thing. Promotion, respect, possibly love. She feels this prophecy daily.

Her station has been on alert like most stations in Los Angeles and the Valley. Nina has lectured other officers on theories, developments, psychology, clues. This has been going on for nine months. But still, she does not know, no one does, what race Toyer is, what age, what height, what weight. It is only presumed Toyer's victims have had sex with him, no semen has ever been detected, no condom has ever been found. Some still dispute his gender.

For Nina it is personal. More than a prophecy, now, a vendetta. Last fall she had been invited to a Sunday afternoon baby shower for a friend of hers who had gone to school with Luisa Cooke. Cooke had accepted of course, but was not able to come because the night before she had become Toyer's third victim. Nina never met Luisa Cooke. That was nine months ago, but the memory is fresh. She *knows* she will be the one who meets Toyer and brings him in.

She imagines him. She imagines his physique, his facelessness. She has heard the tapes of his voice. She imagines her attack, her retaliation, her superiority, complete to his final castration. She imagines her citation, her promotion. Finally, she dreams of a flattering picture with her hair down engulfing her face, on the front page, above the fold, of the *Los Angeles Herald*. She always keeps a glazier's knife, pressed to her skin, held flat by her bra strap.

Her recurrent premonition: She will be alone in a room with him. She has told her mother about the premonition, about the razor knife, that she is keeping her hair long for that frontpage picture in the *Herald*, the woman-to-woman piece by Sara Smith, the inevitable flight to New York, *Good Morning America*, the picture story in *People* magazine, maybe the cover. She knows she will be the one to apprehend him and bring him down.

Nina sleeps late Sunday morning, it is her treat. She works the third watch and always goes for coffee after midnight. At Sizzler's over her Sunday breakfast, she spots a Personal ad in the *L.A. Weekly*:

HELP! New in town. White slim single straight male late twenties seeks love and more from same age clever bright pretty brunette. Love rules. Absolutely no fatties. Mark. Call Box 88970

Nina smiles, she is definitely no fatty, not anymore anyway, not since she joined the force. She reads the ad again and again, each time she feels a chill. In her mind she hears choral music, she can actually hear the theme from "Unchained Melody." There is something to this.

MEYERSON

"HELLO, JIM, I think it's time we sat down, don't you?"

"I am sitting down, Bob."

"Jim, please. We ought to sit down together. We gotta talk about this Doctor Garance. She's the wacko lady who paid me a visit. Told me to shove it."

And did you?

"In front of my secretary, can you believe it? I reported her to her boss at the hospital."

"How can I help you?"

"You've got her writing letters to this guy. Come on, Jim, it's very bad for us."

"How so?"

"Hurts our office, Jim, it's in an uproar. She's like an amateur crime stopper."

"I can't chop her column, Bob, she's on a weekly retainer."

"A written contract?"

Jim does not answer, waits. *D.A.s are lawyers.*

"My honest opinion? She's doing you more harm than good."

"I think she's doing a hell of a job and judging by her first piece I'd say she'll do you more good than harm."

Sara stands listening. When she gets back to her desk, she calls Maude.

MARK TAYLOR

A BLAZING MORNING, June 10, West Hollywood.
Leanna Esteban enters Ruben's at 9:50 A.M., scans the room as an immigration agent would, settles for a booth by the cash register. On the table in front of her, the *L.A. Weekly* lies open to the Personals section, an ad that begins *HELP! New in town. White slim single straight male* is circled. A clear mating call. Leanna Esteban is nervous, orders coffee, opens her novel about a woman lost in California who succeeds in meeting and marrying a movie star. Mark Taylor, seated in a back booth, exits.

Farther down Melrose Avenue, within five minutes, Mark enters the Bell Coffee Shop, sits down with the wrong girl and introduces himself. Her boyfriend enters and taps him on the shoulder. Mark exits.

At 10:10, Lynne Trainer walks into Tops Pizza, catches Mark's eye as she passes through the restaurant on her way to the ladies' room, smoothing the creases in her dress over her waist and hips. When she comes out, Mark has gone.

At 10:20, five blocks east of Tops Pizza, Nina Voelker enters the Camellia Street Cafe with the *L.A. Weekly* in her purse and, without looking around, takes a booth by the window. Mark Taylor stands outside, across the street, looking in. She is knifed by a diagonal of sunlight that bisects the window, her image misted by the hazy glass, the sunlight burnishes her amber hair. She sits without moving, withdrawn, staring onto the sidewalk, gazing at nothing, resembling a worn-out photograph. She touches a chord Mark cannot trace. He crosses the street.

As he springs up onto the curb, he catches her eye through the glass and smiles. She pulls back and turns away, looking for a waitress. This is new for Nina.

"I didn't mean to startle you," Mark says.

"You didn't." Then, "Oh, don't mind me, I'm not awake yet. You're Mark, aren't you?" They exchange names.

Across the table she gives him a small hard handshake. Mark Taylor, meet Nina Voelker.

"I've never done this before," she says.

"Neither have I, Nina."

"You look like a Mark Taylor," she says. *He's better looking than he sounded in the ad.*

They talk about their jobs, Mark hates his, says he is a teacher. Nina loves hers, will not tell him what it is. *Baseball,* she loves it, he does not. *Music,* he likes less structured classics and the opera, she has never really heard an opera clear through to the end but likes several rock operas. *Cars,* she loves them, he does not. *Clothes,* she thinks they are vital to a man's character and confidence and sex appeal. Mark tells her that a man can get through life with one linen suit, four shoes and four T-shirts. *Toyer,* he is a diabolic maniac who should be hung from a burning tree by his tongue. They agree at last.

Neither can adequately explain Mark's need to create an ad or Nina's need to answer it, two so obvious cries for help. They simply tell each other that they were tired of the people they knew and wanted to try something entirely different.

Brunch? They decide *yes.* They are pleased with each other. It is early. Mark can take his time. A Sunday morning in summer. They are both adults, able to make decisions, steer their lives. There is no cause for alarm. Mark likes being Mark.

Nina realizes she was wrong about the ad, Mark cannot be Toyer. How does she know? Mark is a level, privileged cute guy who simply does not know his way around town; *end of story.* Why would he be Toyer? He does not fit any known police profile. You look for problems: drugs, poverty, fears, tensions, mental illness. *No problems.* The rage required to be Toyer would have no source in someone this pulled together, attractive and obviously casual as Mark is. Anyway, she likes him, wonders what it would feel like to have her breasts squeezed against the hairs of his chest.

She is a cop, she says. Just like that. *A bit close.* Mark laughs. *I wonder what it's like to go to bed with a peace officer.* But he does not say that. He asks her if she is working today, what time she gets off.

She is on the third watch, she says. Midnight.

"What's open at midnight?" he says, then smiles. "Me?"

He likes her. *Why not? I've got nothing against her.* Though he can never be sure how he will feel about her later on in the evening, or toward morning when Nina gets off her watch.

She has not told him of her recurrent premonition, seeing her picture on the front page of the *Herald* just below the headline *POLICEWOMAN APPREHENDS TOYER.*

She will share her premonition with Mark later, in bed.

TOYER

THE NAME *Nina* reminds him of tissue paper.

Her apartment is unexpectedly feminine. Especially for a law enforcement officer, he thinks. *What did I expect?* So many frills, little china dolls, china sugar and creamer sets. Acrylic pictures of any available paradise. She shares the apartment with her *mom,* who is away for the week.

He tells her he can fix the refrigerator door so that it swings shut by itself. She is comfortable with him at once.

While she is in the bedroom changing, Mark thumbs through a thousand-page Norton Lit paperback he has found on the bookshelf. She looks out, watches him snoop, "That's from high school." The pages are still marked with green ballpoint ink, in squat schoolgirl handwriting. Written above *A Piece of String* is "sympathy toward Life." In the margin of *A*

Tree of Night she has written, "Symbolism." The word *metaphor* appears. By the title of T. S. Eliot's *Prufrock* she has written, "images of Death and Dying."

Just like that.

In a plastic market bag, he has brought a cold bottle of sweet sparkling wine. He pours two sorbet glasses to the brim, lightly doses hers with Seconal to relax her mind and muscles for the hours ahead.

Sitting on the bed, they talk. He runs his fingers over her like flowers. He lays her on her back.

"Don't."

Touching her ear, he whispers: "Nina, we are poor people, between us we have two minds, two bodies, two mouths, two breasts."

"Stop. Don't." She giggles, she is high on cheap bubbles and Seconal.

His fingers approach her crevices. "Let us make the most of our few gifts, between us we have only one penis, one vagina." Key words. She giggles again, flushed. Penis, vagina; no man has ever spoken these words to her at this stage, a grave psychological moment. She feels a rush, a nice hopelessness. The words make her ready. He lifts her skirt and lightly scans the inside of her thighs with his tongue. This is also new to her.

Still, she pushes him away, exhales her demureness, wraps her legs around his waist and says, "Please don't make love to me, Mark."

"All right." He is strong but does not exhibit muscles. A convict's strength. He pins her in place like a bug, pulls away what clothing he does not require, enters her with his tongue. She responds with open relief, it is what she wants after all. She stretches her back and legs, bends them and even kicks out, arching her back, making sure that Mark's motions touch her entirely. Only then does she release herself to him in freedom built of loneliness. When she comes she says *Bingo*.

Much later, after what seems hours, because she whimpers

in a childlike voice, he says wet words to her, that might embarrass him at breakfast, but it excites him when she finds them beautiful. And he is anxious to hear her say *Bingo* again.

They wake up thirsty. They finish the bottle of formula champagne-noise, cool, flat. He wants to say he has been improvising a scene, trying to play Toyer, but he cannot. Instead, tells her about his hobby, and an acting exercise that he recently did. He feels chatty.

She tells him about a man she had been dating for months. He wanted her to put him under arrest, handcuff him and then force him to make love to her while she was wearing her full uniform and he was in her custody.

"Were you wearing your gun and holster?" he asks.

"Funny, he asked me to. He thought it made sex a felony."

When he comes back from the kitchen he asks if she wore the gun and holster for him. She says she laughed at him and did not.

He does not ask her why, but instead says, solemnly, "I'd be embarrassed to ask you to do a thing like that."

"I would do anything with someone if I was in love with them." Her breasts are pale, unused, tender.

She arrested him, frisked him, cuffed him, held her gun on him until he could get it up then forced him to fuck her and they both loved it.

She lets him finger her service revolver. She has never let anyone do that either, she says. *You tell that to all the guys*, he says. *No, it's true.* She is ready to cry. *I believe you*, he says. He does. Then he cleans the gun carefully, like a spent penis. In the alley below the kitchen window two men are arguing, maybe about a car.

Lying on his back on clean sheets, he finally tells her his plan, that he took out the ad to meet a "victim" for his improvisation. She is intrigued, unsure. *It's so close.* He tells her that he needed to come on to someone as Toyer, to play a dumb acting exercise, a game. The Personal ads are free in the *Weekly* so, why not?

She is astounded. She says "weird." She had a premonition about the ad when she read it, she felt a chill, she *knew*. She knew he was Toyer when she read it and when she met him she knew he was not. It gives her chills to think about that. She shivers. Feel my arm, she says, *chicken skin*. Mark touches her arm, it is true, her skin has risen finely along her forearm.

"What were you reading the Personal ads for?"

"Police work," she says crisply.

They talk about Toyer in low voices, like gamblers. Again she tells him her prophecy. The odds of catching Toyer this year, the chances he takes, when there is to be another victim. He is the great loner, an American folk horror-hero. It is a sport, a game. Any number can play.

From the bed, he has been studying small photographs standing on the shelf and dresser. Every face stares out at him in flash cube ecstasy, no one looks away.

He stands, holds his penis like a drawn revolver and puts Nina under arrest. "What would you do if you had him in your sights—bring him down or bring him in?"

"That one's too close to call," she says. "I'd have to be there facing him."

"You are," he tells her, "*there*," and puts his penis between her fingers. She loves it, she is trembling, it excites her playing cop-and-Toyer games in bed. It is too good.

The furniture is turning gray by the time Nina closes her eyes for the last time and falls spinning through the mattress into a starless universe, a galaxy of long-dead stars, the blackest sleep she has ever known.

NINA

THE DEADLY REEK of all-night coffee. Coffee blots into the inside walls of paper cups, flat, wood stirrers. Doughnuts shine and molt. The morning watch operator has just sat down at the dispatch desk. It is just before 8:00 A.M. in Nina Voelker's own precinct, the second watch change of the new day.

The desk telephone rings once. The operator picks it up, "West Hollywood Precinct." There is a moment's silence. Before she can speak again, she guesses. It is Toyer. The call is authentic, she knows; his first words are the international telecommunications initials for his own name: *Tango, Oscar, Yankee, Echo, Romeo.* He speaks in a surprisingly intimate, clear voice. She has been trained to listen, should he ever call. *There is a woman to be found.* Next, he gives the victim's birthdate and place of birth. Routine business. Then, her address. This is known in the precincts as Toyer's "courtesy call."

Last, he spells the victim's name. The operator knocks her coffee over when she hears it. She knows Nina by sight from roll call.

She breaks discipline, pathetically, too late, "Fuck you, motherfucker," she says to Toyer who has already hung up. All of his calls are automatically recorded, and none has ever lasted more than twenty-five seconds.

The operator buzzes the watch captain. A strict routine is set into action. The nearest ambulance is dispatched to the address given on the telephone. Doctor Soong, a surgeon from the city medical office downtown, is notified. Doctor Tredescant at the Kipness. Two detectives in an unmarked car.

When they find Nina Voelker, she is lying naked on her

huge bed, spread like a compass rose, pointing to each of the four corners of the mattress with a foot or a hand. The bed is neatly made, the sheet surrounding her is white, flat, clean. A small flesh-colored bandage neatly placed over the nape of her neck. There are no stains. Her nicely polished service revolver is snapped safe in its holster, which is hanging from the bedroom doorknob.

Not one of the first five people allowed to see her body before it is covered describes it as a gruesome scene. It suggests an Epiphanic painting never imagined by El Greco.

MAUDE

HE HAS THE NEATNESS *of a bride. He leaves behind him a tidy room, folded towels, a well-made bed, the girl comfortably positioned, at rest. No scrawls on mirrors. No messy dressing table, no broken glass in the sink. He has self-esteem, he wants my approval. He needs it. She has been driving on freeways fast in fast lanes.*

It is still early, after 3:00 A.M. It will be this morning, I know it. She enters her small house. The answering machine is flashing: five messages.

She pours a drink, turns the light out, lies on the sofa. She lies still, crying, cringing, a voice inside the walls is whispering to her. Wearing a nightgown, she sits on her bed drinking in the black.

Suddenly the telephone bursts. She cannot see, she launches herself blindly toward the kitchen telephone, knocks a glass off a table, crosses the room, reaches for a lamp, turns it on briefly, knocks it over, it falls, flashes when it explodes on the floor. The room is black again. The telephone has not stopped ringing. The bathroom door is open, Maude's face collides with the sharp edge of the door, it knocks her to the floor, opens a gash under her eye.

She reaches the telephone in the bedroom. The Kipness. Chleo.

"I jus' knew you was there, Doctor Garance. We have an invalid, they brought her in last night. Please can you come in." *I'm on suspension.*

"Does Doctor Tredescant know?"

"Yeah, he knows. An' he says you should get yourself a cell phone like everybody else in the whole wide world."

From Maude's gash, there is blood on her nightgown, on the tops of her toes.

NINA

THE NINA VOELKER STORY manages to catch the final edition of the *Herald,* set in a box cut on the front page, it is enough to sell out the run. The following morning in the bulldog, the *Herald* carries Sara Smith's more complete story with a remote-looking photograph of Nina above the fold, it sells out the family edition. A sad little picture, she seems to be staring at someone who disliked her. Her hair is not long, not nearly as long as it is now, not as long as she would wish it to be in her most glamorous moment. It was taken three years earlier at her graduation from the police academy. Nina would not have been at all happy with it.

MAUDE

DRIVING HOME NOW at 5:00 A.M., she has been sitting with Nina Voelker and has called it a night. An ache has set into the bones of her face, she can barely see to drive. Doctor T has sewn closed the skin over her cheekbone, four stitches. *His first penetration.* It may not leave a scar. She turns off the freeway, parks the car on a side street, locks the doors, cries. She does not weep, she cries jolting sobs. When she can no longer cry, the grueling sadness remains. When she can see, she drives home. There she drinks several glasses of gin over ice and falls into a deep sleep on the sofa.

The telephone rings.

"Are you all right?" Sara. It is light outside. Maude is lying on the sofa.

"I don't know, I really don't." She feels herself begin to cry again, slip into a sunless chasm, a place without life, air, she doesn't know what to do about it.

"I was permitted a couple of hours last night trying to try and contact the victim, courtesy of Doctor Tredescant."

"Is she . . ." Sara fumbles, recovers. "Without hope?"

"Yes she is," Maude says. "At the present time she is certainly without hope."

She'll never give up. "I'm so sorry."

"Thanks for calling me, Sara."

Is there anything left I can say?

"By the way, the police are taking this one very seriously. Officer Voelker is, after all, one of their own people."

"Good."

"Meyerson won't return my call."

"That's a start."

O'LAND

FRONT PAGE. O'Land scribbles the headline, Sara writes the story under it.

TOYER DISABLES POLICEWOMAN

West Hollywood Precinct Stunned
"Shameless . . . Unbelievable"
Slap in Face to LAPD, DA

By Sara Smith

Los Angeles. June 11. When Officer Nina Voelker walked home late Tuesday night after watch duty at the West Hollywood Police Station she crossed the street and entered her immaculate one-bedroom apartment on Fountain Avenue. It was almost certainly the last time she would ever be able to do this simple act. . . .

In the same issue, page fifteen, Maude writes, in part:

It is not just your victims you destroy, it is your victims' relatives and friends, all the ones that you leave behind you without a thought. You are killing a neighborhood to destroy a single person. Your vengeance is misshapen.

I feel you need the help of someone in my profession. I am available to you, awaiting your response and will help you any way you need to be helped. Our conversation will be confidential, protected by law. Call me at the Kipness.

Maude Garance, M.D.
Attending Physiatrist
The Kipness Memorial Neurological Center

She expects no change, he will go on and on. She will write him again expecting failure, unaware that he has turned her into his executioner.

MEYERSON

AN 8x11 ENVELOPE on his desk, no return address. He opens it. The face of a pale woman asleep. It is Nina Voelker. A note written in ink on the back:

Bob,

Here's a portrait to hang on your office wall. It's a recent photo I took of Officer Nina Voelker, one of your former employees. She's still alive of course—no homicide—so I guess you'd have to say she's on leave.

If you have any thoughts, please call me.

Dr. Maude Garance

He says aloud to himself, "This is definitely harassment, I gotta stop this broad."

He calls through the open door, "Ciel, run an abstract on this loopy doctor, you know how to spell her name. But before you do that, please get me Jim O'Land at the *Herald*. Thanks."

The computer "abstract" turns up no outstanding traffic violations on Maude's record. O'Land telephones him back in half an hour.

"Bob, what is it?"

"Jim, it's your loopy doctor's starting to get to me."

Loopy? "You're welcome to write us a letter, Bob, let's open this thing up. I'll give you a forum."

"Unofficially, Jim. I can't come right out here and say a word." *I am a servant of the people.* "Look, Nina Voelker has family in El Segundo." *Voters.*

"So do I, Bob."

This is not true, Jim's family does not live in El Segundo, they moved west to Montana from Chicago and live in a ranch house near Wolf Creek where Jim hopes one day to retire.

"Well. Have a good day."

"Sorry, Bob." They hang up.

"Ciel, get me the commanding officer, West Hollywood." In a few moments he picks up the telephone. "This is Meyerson downtown, who's this?"

"Sergeant Thomas."

"Hello, Billy."

"Hello, Mr. Meyerson, how can I help you?"

"Are you the watch officer?"

"I am, sir."

"Good. You're pretty busy?"

"We are, sir."

"I need a detective for a few hours a week, no big deal, can you break one loose for me?"

"I think I can, sir, what's the case?"

"This Toyer crap."

"I understand."

"Who's on the roster today, Billy?"

"Let's see, there's Fred Smollet, McCarthy, uhm, Perrino."

"Perrino." The luxury of assigning names.

Pale, meaty, awkward, able, slow-moving, Detective I. Perrino. He wears black varnished shoes that will never dull, pale short-sleeved shirts that can never wrinkle, permanent-press pants, above, the hint of stippled undershorts.

Detective I. Perrino is looking forward to lunch and afterward, a short nap. Spread before him on his desk, a paper box of spaghetti and meatballs to be washed down with thirty-two ounces of Dr Pepper that has lost its bubbles.

"Yes, sir, Mr. Meyerson. I'll get right on it." *After lunch.*

SARA

IT IS EARLY, ugly, already hot, the sun is a white disc. Maude has slipped into the Kipness to see Nina Voelker's chart and driven home. She has been there since dawn, has not slept. She has seen both articles in the *Herald*. She feels more isolated than ever this morning.

Sara stands outside Maude's front door. She has brought along two bottles of mineral water, she pours one onto the roots of the grapevine. The grapevine is colorless, the gardenia is dead, the ficus close to death. Pale dust etches the door moldings. She presses the painted doorbell button again, hears nothing, wipes the dust from her finger on her briefcase. She discovers a brittle hose and at the outlet turns it on and stands soaking the rattling plants.

She rings again, listens. *The doorbell is broken.* She knocks. She can smell freshly dripped coffee.

From inside, "Yes?"

"It's Sara Smith."

"I saw the paper."

She opens the front door. Sara passes through into the dim living room.

"Do you think it's going to do any good?"

Inside it is shaded, unexpectedly cool, keeping the night air close.

"What do *you* think, Maude?"

"I wonder, it's a bit of a shock."

"Well, I've brought you a little *après shock* offering." She sets a canvas tennis bag on the coffee table. "But first, congrats."

"For what?"

"I just got a call from a Detective I. Perrino in the West Hollywood Station. Meyerson assigned him to the case."

"At last." She is tired. "What's your little offering?"

"Oh, coffee. Greek coffee. The stuff Poseidon drank to steady his hands before he'd do an earthquake. Wouldn't touch one without it."

"Ah, a cultured broad with a sense of humor."

Maude sets a kettle of recently boiling water on the stove again. She will make Greek coffee. She stays in the kitchen area, Sara in the deep Timmons chair. She turns the boiling kettle off. "You'd better show me how to do this."

Sara goes to the kitchen and drops three spoonfuls of ground coffee into the coffeepot and pours the water.

"That's it?"

"Greek coffee. You can chew it. Or you can splash a few drops of cold water on the surface to make the grounds settle."

Maude pours the Greek coffee into cups, brings in the tray of coffee and biscotti, sets it between them on the coffee table.

"My God, Maude, you look dreadful."

"I'm sure I do. I've had four stitches. I ran full speed into that door. I was having a nightmare. I'm not drinking, by the way, I mean I am, but not that kind of drinking."

"When I met you, you looked harried, but you didn't look ill. I'm sorry but you look ill."

"Why thank you, dear."

"I'm sorry . . . I . . ."

Maude sort of laughs, touches Sara's knee. "You've caught me in the middle of a breakdown. Know any good psychiatrists?"

The iceberg is nicely broken.

"Now, not to change the subject but why don't you tell me a little bit about yourself."

"Okay, I'm from back east, from a state with tough winters. I have morals . . ."

"Which state?"

"Connecticut, born in Vermont. I apprenticed at Time Inc. I was taught that a story is a story, you know, Heaven-sent. I went along with that, my editors were the Announcing Angels who taught me to love the First Amendment as I loved my God."

"Hard to break old habits."

"Yes emphatically. I remember the very words. *Congress shall make no law abridging the freedom of speech.* I don't have a clue where the hell *the public has a right to know* came from, maybe because of Nixon. I trace a lot of crap back to him."

"Well, the *Herald* has definitely stretched the First Amendment way past the boring point."

"I agree, and this week I'm just beginning to see that we haven't been giving news, we've been selling Product Toyer to a public who thinks it's a movie."

"Bless the public."

We're bonding, for God's sake.

"From what I've seen of the man-in-the-street since I've been an interviewing reporter, if the public were a single human being, you wouldn't want it in your house. It's a thing. It's a lazy, untalented, disloyal, self-centered, slow-moving, inarticulate, barely able to read, dishonest, fickle, overweight, born follower thing." She tries to keep the Connecticut *yaw* out of her voice.

Very impressive.

"Toyer mentioned you in his letter to me. I think he likes you. Just kidding."

"Me? By name?" Maude feels a rush. "What sort of mention?"

"Say *hi* to her."

That's too intimate. "How does he know you and I know each other?"

"He assumes it, like so many other things he assumes."

"Jesus."

"My gut feeling is that if he recognizes your part in this, he must respect you. What do you think?"

"Yeah, I suppose."

Is that good? Yes. Very good for now.

In half an hour, after coffee, Maude's risen spirits have fallen again. She wants to be alone, her head is buzzing. She wonders why Sara is here, usually she arrives with an agenda.

"I'm not sleeping, Maude, I haven't slept a night through since . . . it happened."

"The nonrape."

"Yeah. Every time I come home I have my Mace atomizer cocked and hidden in my left hand. He was hiding behind my bamboo screen, so when I go in I look behind everything, in everything, under everything, and it doesn't do a damn bit of good, the apartment itself is contaminated. Luckily there's another one in the building available next month and the landlord is giving me the same rate. He understands."

"He'd better, he could be liable."

"So, next month I'm moving two flights up. I have a balcony, I can start fresh."

"Just tell me if I can help."

"You can. Will you write me a prescription? I need to sleep. Maybe something with codeine."

"Sure."

"Now let's see if we can figure out a way to talk the monster in. God how I hate him."

"You forgot to mention complacent."

"Huh?"

"For your man-in-the-street profile."

Sara laughs, "Oh, yes, very complacent."

"You've thought about this *has a right to know* business."

"I have indeed."

"So you don't want to serve them anymore."

"Really, Maude, this week I wavered, I have so much hatred for him, for the first time since I started reporting, I questioned what I was doing. I've personally seen his work and suddenly I woke up from my long nap and I didn't see why on earth the public has any right to know what a working psychopathic killer wants them to know."

"Hear, hear."

"I've decided something, I'm not printing the next account he mails me. The idea disgusts me. O'Land cannot publish it. It's my mail, it is being sent to me, he isn't sending letters to Jim O'Land."

"It's evidence, Sara."

"I know. I'll still give the original to the police and make a copy. It scares me a little, I don't know how Jim'll react. He could fire me."

"He could go either way, but I think he'll stick with you, try to resolve your problem with him. I think he's like that."

"Maybe Toyer'll fire me."

"He may, but I think he'll want to do something about you."

"Like not rape me again, only this time . . ."

"That's a cheery thought. He may feel that you've been a friend to him and now you've rejected him, he might just come looking for you." *I wish he'd come looking for me.*

Sara does not say anything.

"Have you spoken to O'Land about this?"

"Not yet. He's been acting very strange, he can do no wrong. You don't know what beating the *Times* has done for this man's ego. The *Legendary Newspaperman.* I mean I respect him but I don't like what I'm seeing."

"Would he fire you?"

"He could, but I'm the only link. Jim's always told me it's my ass if I lose Toyer."

"He'd be foolish to fire you."

"Of course, but look what I'm doing. I'm threatening to take away the only good thing that's ever happened to his newspaper." She knows she will hear from Toyer again. Not today.

TOYER

A WATCHMAN discovers the letter at 4:00 A.M. the next morning on his rounds. A blue envelope without a stamp, Sara's name misspelled. It has been slid under the battered steel parking lot door. The watchman puts it in her box, neglects to call her. *Not my job.*

It is not until late morning that she finds it in her box. Toyer. A proposition. What about publishing all ten of his accounts, his *oeuvre*, and bringing them out in a book, each chapter with extensive details. Suddenly a book. *Everyone's got a book in them. How dare he?*

As she is reading the single page, holding it between three fingers, she feels a small flash, the note comes alive in her hand, she is aware of his presence, as if he were standing somewhere in the newsroom, nearby, watching her. She senses his persona. She feels fear. Her temples throb, her hands moisten.

At the bottom of the page he writes: "I believe the profits from the book could be in the millions of dollars." She can feel his mind working. His ego. *How can this scumbag think about getting rich off what he's doing?*

As before, he has typed the note on a word processor, the impressions of the words are pale. His spelling is impeccable. Or maybe not. *How would anyone know? Maybe he uses spelling software. The only misspelled word is Sarah.*

At midday, she sits in O'Land's office waiting for him to return from the union meeting. When he does she hands him the letter. He is impressed, she can tell, his eyebrows rise, trying to leave his face. When he has read it twice he says, "Who'd buy a book by him? Me."

"Not me."

"Whoa there, Sara Smith."

"How does he expect to get paid? Even if we could pay him, the Son of Sam law states that no convicted felon can show monetary gain from his crimes."

"He's not a convicted felon, Sara."

"No, but he's out there and every time he writes me he convicts himself. What the hell do you think he means by *my women*? His movie dates?"

O'Land asks Sara to meet him at the Lion's Head across the street for a pub lunch at one. "Keep this between our heads, Sara Smith, I need to think about it."

At one, Sara joins him in a booth. They order Stilton cheese caper sardine arugula salads and highly chilled glasses of lager.

"I'm wondering how sick this guy really is or if he means it," he says. "It's short and sweet, add your comments and we'll run it tomorrow."

"You're not touching my letter."

"Hmmmm?"

"That's my letter, Jim, I just showed it to you."

"Oh, really?" He continues eating. "We're morally bound to publish it."

"Bullshit."

"Sara Smith, my word. I've got to run this letter, this is news."

"I won't show you the next one."

He smiles. "I'll have your mail delivered directly to my office and you can pick it up there."

"You can't do that."

He wipes his mouth, takes a long draft. "Get a lawyer, kid, he's writing letters to an employee of my newspaper, not to you personally." He reaches in his pocket and hands it back to her. "Tell you what, Sara Smith, let's hold off for a day and let the reader decide." O'Land makes a five-dollar bet with her. He knows he will win. He has not even bothered to get angry.

SARA

THE FOLLOWING MORNING Sara Smith's six-inch piece appears on the op-ed page stating why she may no longer be able to publish further Toyer letters. Her reasons are clear: they encourage him, it is not news. Right versus Wrong.

She sits at her desk, blanched. O'Land watches her from his office, he wonders if maybe there is something personal in her hatred, something beyond ethics. He does not call her into his office.

Late in the morning the first reader calls, by afternoon, readers' calls clog the switchboard, wait on hold minutes to speak their piece. If the *Herald* abandons Toyer's diaries, they will drop their subscriptions, one reader, a lawyer, has threatened to sue on the grounds that the *Herald* would be withholding from her what is constitutionally hers. Anger, anger, casually made threats of arson, assassination. O'Land believes Sara will crack. He wins. She goes to his office, defeated, hands him the letter with a five-dollar bill folded neatly inside. He is smiling.

An office boy leans in and tells her there is a call at her desk. She excuses herself, picks it up. "Sara Smith."

"You get my letter?" A sonorous male voice.

It's him.

"I forgot something. What if those millions of dollars of profit from my book were to be divided among my women?" *He never calls them his victims.*

He hangs up.

It is so simple. Is this penance? False humility? *What an amazing idea. Profit sharing. Is it possible?*

She goes back to tell O'Land about it, but he is on the telephone settling a union problem with the delivery trucks.

She saves it for lunch, in case things get rough. They meet

at the *Herald* cafeteria downstairs. German potato salad, iced tea, red Jell-O.

"There *is* a big goddamned book in it, Sara Smith, a huge bestseller," he says, barely aloud. "First we syndicate, sell it to a couple of hundred papers, then we get a New York publisher who'll print a million. Critical introduction by the president of Turkey or somebody but the book'll be Toyer's. His version. Bio, vision, hints, clues. All victims, their bios. Art, graphs, charts, maps. Details, details, details." O'Land is good at this, covering a story from all angles, "Might even tuck a video in the back."

"Might even get him nailed."

"Might not, might get us rich, however. Then I'd take him *and* you to lunch. Hell, it's a great story. Why wouldn't any good New York publisher want to publish his side?"

"Because he's a flesh-eating monster?"

"Flesh-eating monsters are thought-provoking."

"And commercial."

"The *Herald* would split profits down the middle with any New York publisher."

"Want to know what he told me this morning?"

"What he *told* you?"

"He called me, Jim. He'd forgotten to say something in his letter. Or maybe he hadn't thought of it when he sent it."

O'Land stops eating. "What."

"I won't tell you."

"Don't brawl with me, Sara Smith."

She tells him. O'Land is blown away.

"Okay. He's forcing my hand. This is a damned handsome gesture considering the source, and we can't ignore it. Syndication means big money and the victims' families will get the syndication. We'll get the circulation. But there's got to be a contract, there'll be scrutiny. He's trying to atone for his sins with a method frankly I could never have imagined. To stand in his way would be to go against the families of his victims."

"It's blackmail."

"Right. My kind of blackmail. It's a smart idea. I mean, it's a very, very smart idea he came up with."

"His conscience comes cheap."

"Yeah but cheap is provocative, Sara Smith. I think we may have a newspaperman out there."

"Try not to make him too warm and fuzzy."

"This changes everything."

"How?"

"We lose his profits but make new friends."

Back in his office at two, O'Land's first call is to New York, Bill Tallman, a friend at the *New York Times* Syndicate.

What is his opinion on the possibility of a pickup order for Toyer's hypothetical book. It is a confidential inquiry. His friend does not hesitate, his response is *no*.

After lunch, Sara reaches Maude at home.

"He called me, Maude, he says if we'll print his book, we can give his share of the profits to the families of his victims. It's for the good of all."

"I didn't know he was in charge."

"Well, now you do."

TOYER

SATURDAY, normally a dry day for news, there is a piece by Sara Smith along with another letter from Toyer, both appear on page three. He has won a small battle. The more-available Toyer has become chatty.

In his new casual style, he has written in response to a group of women calling themselves Women for Women that has said: "We are supposed to be above predators, rapists, and others who serve no purpose in this eco-structure of ours. Who needs them?"

His is a fulsome response, rambling. He says that transgressors, including himself, have become red warning lights, stranger than predators, stronger than laws, that tell us where we are going and how far we can go. They are as necessary as pain is necessary, to warn. "Society needs us," he writes. "A needle under my fingernail," Sara says aloud.

It may or may not be an interesting point he makes, but it is unique to him and would never be printed on page three if anyone but Toyer had written it. O'Land runs it unedited on the lower right hand of the page. There is a front-page teaser above the bannerline:

TOYER DISCUSSES HIS METHOD

In her brief accompanying article, Sara says that no matter how egregious his crimes are, they will never be treated with a small fraction of the attention that homicides get from the police. Nothing new.

Sara cannot reach Maude by telephone, she drives to her house, stands outside talking through the front door as she did last month. She is sure that Maude has seen the piece, she is right, it will be damaging.

"Go away."

"It was Jim, I can't stop him." *Too weak.* "That wasn't me, goddammit, Maude."

"Go away."

Silence.

"I don't know what to think, Sara."

"Something's happened."

Through the door: "What?"

"Bad news."

The voice through the door: "Yes?"

Sara tells her that the publisher's lawyer wrote notifying her that the mailroom is authorized to redirect all of her mail to James O'Land, Executive Editor. It is legal. Toyer's letters to her are no longer her letters, there is no protection. Anything he says will be published.

"That's how it got in," she says. She goes on, "Who in hell will stop him? His ego will flourish, thrive, bloom. We've given him his raison d'être."

"And causing us to reinforce the mystery of his identity. Yadda yadda yadda. I see the problem." The door opens.

MAUDE

SHE CAN NO LONGER find Mason anywhere in her night, she can no longer feel him in her morning. He does not exist. He is like childhood. But if it is Mason in her dream, even as a bystander, he is in Toyer's image.

She faces him once again across the Dublin meadow where daffodils, bluebells and marigolds once grew wild. She is aware of his teeth, his virility. He is walking toward her, lean, smiling, erect. Now it is standing before him, up from his groin, jolting slightly as he walks. She sees the bright silver instrument.

He is younger than Maude, strong, persuasive. He seems casual. He walks close to her through the nearly waist-high grass. She feels a rush of emotion, a tremor along her neck. Her upper thighs tighten squeezing her vagina.

Now he is standing nude, nearly against her, arms at his sides. She feels his erection graze her pelvis, feels it against her stomach.

Her hands slide over his chest up to his neck. Her thumbs, crossed like a falcon's talons, close his larynx between them. He stands without resisting, without expression, his eyes blank, then he sags, falls away.

It is morning. When she wakes, she wakes to his women, seeing them, one at a time. Reprisal. Maude has not killed him, she has wanted to. Unacceptable behavior to be noted in a distinguished psychiatrist. She feels herself slip a notch. She is deeply hungover, she has no one to tell—she is not quite certain of Sara Smith's allegiance, cannot confess to Doctor T. Whenever she closes her eyes she sees fireflies.

Jimmy G is watching her full-eyed from the window, ears high, as if she had called out. She waves him over. For a moment he watches her carefully, suddenly jumps onto the bed, then her. She feels his claws knead dough on her stomach, eyes closed, purring. She feels his happy volume.

After a while, she gets up, sits at her desk, sets out a white legal pad. It is the only method she knows. From school, she remembers lines written by Thomas Hobbes. Something like, "Life. Solitary, poor, nasty, brutish, short."

And that's only in the morning.

SARA

EVENING, the heat is lifting, it is just six.

Sara Smith is sitting in Maude's living room. Maude is at the refrigerator filling a martini shaker with ice cubes, dropping one or two on the floor. Jimmy G is draped on his back, the tip of his tail, *twitch-twitch*, maybe dreaming of cool nights and blind birds.

"I didn't want to talk to you on the phone."

"That's okay, relax, you're here."

"I can't."

The tone of her voice, Maude looks at her. "Single or double?"

"Very double." It is something her father used to say. "He really seems to be writing a fucking book. From *out there*. He intends to send us installments, one chapter per victim."

"Oh, my God." Maude stops pouring gin into the shaker, sets it by the sink. "Let me get this straight. While he's out there performing cordotomies at night, in the daytime he'll be writing his memoirs?"

"Yes."

"But two careers can be so tiring, I'll worry."

"Yeah." Sara laughs. "What a guy."

Sara glances at her. She is startled by the expression on Maude's face, the bewilderment.

"Maude?"

Maude does not answer. She is standing in the kitchen, the frosted martini shaker in her hand. She seems to be listening to a radio that does not exist.

"Maude?"

Abruptly she turns.

"Olive or onion?"

"Your call."

Maude brings the shaker from the kitchen, sets down two martini glasses on the low table, there is a tiny marinated onion in each. She fills them almost to the brim, takes hers with her, sits by the window.

"Cheers." Sara raises her glass to her.

"Cheers." They sip. The gush of icy gin.

Jimmy G wakes, a good host, greets Sara with his back high.

"I didn't know whether to have a baby or a cat, but then I met Jimmy G. He'd already done college."

"All cats have."

Sara feels Maude's presence return to the room. She has been away, anyone could have seen it.

"Well, I just wanted you to know about the book. It'll be the biggest thing in publishing since the Pope's confession. You look depressed."

"I meant to look cheery. I'm just so happy for him."

"I didn't mean to upset you."

"Nice try."

"He's a lousy writer, if that's any consolation. I'll ghost it for him, I'll use about a quarter of it in the *Herald* and hold the rest. Now that he's discovered his voice, he simply won't shut up. It's the most incredible mess of evidence. Nothing like this has ever happened, Jim keeps telling me. No one's quite sure how to act."

"Act normal. He does." Then, "You can see what's going on, can't you, Sara?"

"I'm just hoping he'll spill something."

"I don't think so."

"Look, down the line, when he's written his fucking book and, well, if the restitution comes true, why wouldn't he just quit?"

"That's what frightens me, he'll quit and he won't be well. It's not a logical sequence, quitting and getting well. He'll still be dangerous."

Sara notices Maude's odd, listening expression again, she does not recognize her for an instant, she is ashamed that she cannot mention it to her. "He'll disappear, I just know it," she says.

"He could always get run over by a pickup truck."

"And we'd never even know."

"Who he was or why he did what he did. I want him caught alive."

"You're a professional, Maude, I'm not. Never mind the gentle understanding, I want him stretched on a rack. I'm from witch-burning country, I want to turn the crank myself."

They sip, the subject is dead but unburied.

Sara says, "By the way, how's your next installment coming?"

Maude smiles. "Want another ice-cold martini?"

"I do indeed."

Maude stands. *Sara, dear, my feelings are not all that professional. I want to slit his throat and watch the liquid contents of his body drain out through his trachea.*

She takes Sara's empty glass to the kitchen.

MAUDE

MAUDE CANNOT REMEMBER the first time she heard the whisper. It was not abrupt. Maybe first it was only in dreams, when she was half awake, then from the walls if the morning was already hot. The voice is familiar. Of course it is familiar, it is her own voice. She knows the rules of madness.

Then, outside of her dream, it spoke to her in the quiet moments before sleep. Now she hears it in the daytime, at odd hours, while she is driving, waiting in line, it coaxes her, again, clearly, whispering to her, *Kill him, kill him. . . .*

When she listens to opera, the whisper goes away. The powerful tenor voices singing great arias dissolve the whisper, voice against voice, but then in the minutes before sleep, it returns. The sepulchral whisper. It tells her there is no possible cure for her patients, that the only cure is to kill Toyer. The constancy of the voice, urging, pleading, whining. It is unthinkable for a physiatrist to prescribe death as a cure. But each night it is there.

She has not told anyone. Who? Certainly not Doctor T, who could never let her resume specific duties. There are lingering rumors of her bad temper at the Kipness whenever Toyer sent her an early victim, last year, of her outbursts at nurses who remain loyal to her despite her abuse. They understand. They have stood behind Maude many times in the night when the first patients were brought in. It has taken her a year to accept the grotesque crimes as part of her days and nights. From the beginning, part of her anger has been formed from guilt she felt over her uselessness.

Recently, hearing her inner voice, she has felt herself slipping, she recognizes familiar signposts pointing to the gentle slope of uncontrollable psychosis, a descent to a place Toyer calls *madness*.

One symptom is the inner voice. The syndrome is called *command hallucination*. It is a voice that suggests psychotic behavior to its subject. The second sign is when the voice commands the subject to act.

By listening to opera each evening Maude can overcome the voice. She is, without realizing it, connecting herself to her father, a man who once in a fit of uncontrolled madness killed one of his own foundry workers.

Maude is alone. Sara has telephoned, she has noticed quirky behavior in Maude's mannerisms but has said nothing. Maude has taken a cool shower, damp, she towels herself lightly, makes herself another gin and tonic, she feels deer-footed, though her stomach is alive with sick turmoil, as if she had swallowed beetles.

DOCTOR T

THEY ARE IN HIS OFFICE. Doctor T holds an opened envelope and letter.

"The Board of Medical Examiners for the State of California wants to suspend your license to practice." He says it without conviction but she knows he is serious.

"Forever?"

He nods.

"It's the *Herald* pieces."

He shrugs *of course*. "This diagnostic letter-writing, Maude. I've spoken to the board and they're willing to cut you slack because of your excellent work and your credentials but unless you stop publishing them . . ." He regards the letter. "If you continue, starting after tomorrow's date, I can't keep them from revoking your license to practice medicine."

"Can they do that?"

"Oh, yes they can."

"Why?"

"You can't treat your patients publicly. Especially patients you haven't met."

"I'd be glad to set up a session with Toyer, but he hasn't given me his home number."

"They say it denigrates our profession."

"What do you say?"

"Of course it does, but I can see your need to do it."

"Do you like my letters?"

"They're damned good letters. It's just not the way we practice, don't you see that?"

"Why do they think I'm doing it?"

"They may think it's for publicity." He smiles. "Like defense lawyers do."

Maude flinches.

"Here's your copy of the letter. I signed for it." He hands her a sealed registered envelope. "They also say that if you continue writing letters they have the right to sue your practice."

He does not want to let her get away from him tonight, nor does she want him to go. He follows her home, brings French food, duck with fruits from La Provençal that she does not touch, a cold Muscadet, two bottles that he ices in her freezer.

The evening is over, past midnight. His jacket lies across the sofa. He finishes his coffee and sets the cup down on the glass table. The saucer shrieks. He must stay with her. It is crucial. He feels the longevity of his emotion, the biding of his passion. He imagines the two of them as flesh-bound lovers who cannot see or hear. It is not casual. Maude and Elias. They are approaching a time, it is urgent, they regard each other crucially, as though they were in grave danger.

She knows. She wants to ask him to stay for the night, to

help him off with his giant shoes, to lie beside him, feel him surround her, sweat into him. The night has not cooled the day. She wants him to make love to her gradually, accidentally. She can tell him what she wants, she can tell him anything. She feels unwashed, virginal. *Does he sense that?* She touches his nose, she has always wanted to do that.

She knows. She turns the lights off in the living room, goes into the bedroom. The light coming through the doorway from the bedroom throws the living room into a theatrical half-light, equal to the moment. She is undressing, her shadows are banging on the bedroom door.

She knows. This time she will let her robe fall open. It is a simple device. She has taken a cold shower to close her pores, she says. It is when she comes out. The wine is in the bucket, there are two candles, no other light in the living room. He has taken his jacket and tie away, his shoes wait side-by-side. He looks up at her holding his glass, waiting. She stands in the bedroom doorway. This is when she lets her robe fall open.

Now.

It has been two years since Mason died. She has never considered making love with another man until tonight. Undressing for Elias has excited her, she has swollen.

Elias feels the strength of her loneliness. He stands, guides her back into the bedroom, when he finally enters her, he feels her duality, her restraining thighs, closing, a tight pouch of hot oysters. Maude yields. Her breathing is hoarse, her need of him is fantastic.

His need of her is fantastic, he has wanted to make love with her since he met her, the first day she walked into his office and sat down. He manages lust and love together, a big man with strong hands, the nose of a Roman emperor, he can only direct the sum of his waiting power into her through his penis. It is what men can do.

He will not go home tonight. He knows that on another night years ago, a night in May 1969, near Laos, he was not killed by mortar fire for this moment.

Early in the morning, when it is getting light he drives away. Maude sits at the window watching his taillights disappear down the road. Elias is a man, she feels exuberant. She is moist, scentless.

MAUDE

BUT MAUDE FEELS HERSELF traveling in longitudinal time, with no latitude in sight, nothing has changed. That night she fills a low wide glass with ice and gin, sits like a widow at the window looking out. Eventually she begins writing a letter.

"Dear Toyer, you mind-fucker . . . ," tears it up. She realizes that she is not able to stop wanting to kill him.

Call me. Her head is swirling, it is very good gin. *Meet me, meet me.*

When he calls, I won't be angry, I'll be supportive, complaisant, open, gullible. He'll call and when he does I'll be all those things. Dead Mason told me I could get a job doing phone sex.

I must meet you, help you, then I must simply kill you.

He'll call, when he does I won't be surprised, I'll be ready for him.

I'll say I want to meet him.

He'll say—Where?

I'll say this to him. I'll say, Hello, I don't know what you want me to call you so give me a name, any name. Then I'll say the name. Do you know who I am? Of course you do. Then please call me Maude. Such an ugly name, Maude, I always wanted to be called Savanna.

I want you to know something. I feel I know you, and I feel I

understand you. I feel your loneliness the way you feel mine. To
me you are caught in a trap.

No, no, just listen to me.

I'm caught in a trap too, like everyone else. We get into these
traps we can't get out of but we stay in them, living, as if we
were living in the wrong house but we stay on in them and we
paint them and decorate them and make them livable, but they
will always be traps. Am I making sense?

Listen. I will submit to you. I can do this. I know how to do
it. I was married once. My husband is dead. One day I will tell
you what happened. I will wear my long loose silk skirt, a
blouse, nothing else. Sandals. You will know me by touch.

She is asleep. Her white legal pad lies beside her, her pen
has fallen to the floor. Jimmy G likes to bat pens, all of
Maude's pens lie out of reach under furniture unless she keeps
them in jars or drawers.

Her cry wakes her from a dream. She has been in her
mother's field of high grass. Bluebells, daffodils, cowslips.
He was there again as before, walking in the sunlight, pushing
his way through the high grass, wearing nothing. Walking
toward her, walking closer and closer. He does not look at her.
She has finally seen his face. He seemed amused

He will call me again. When he does I won't act surprised, I'll
be ready for him. I will tell him I want to meet him. Anywhere.
I no longer care about me. I am no longer afraid.

He is coming.

TOYER

SHE BELIEVES she has answered the telephone during the
first ring. It is still ringing, she locates it deep in her sleep,
picks it up, exhales *Hello*. It is the sonorous voice. *It's him.* She

is not sure where she fell asleep, she has forgotten her life. She drinks herself to sleep now. It is simpler.

Suddenly awake, she feels his weight, there is the dim sound of traffic under his voice like bed music. He does not speak for several moments.

"Hello?" She tries to add something to that, she is trembling.

Then he says, "What's your name?"

"Maude." Not *Maude Garance or Doctor Garance, Maude.*

She is still on the sofa. She puts her feet on the floor, turns on the table lamp, then in control of her voice, she tells him that she wants to meet him.

He says he likes her voice. It is an absolutely chilling sexual remark.

If he can say that, he can say anything. He can ask me what I'm wearing. If he does, I'll tell him. But he does not ask.

"Don't hang up," she says, "I need to meet you."

He has been expecting this. "Go to the corner of Wilshire and Beverly Glen, the northeast corner, and wait for me there."

"When."

"Now."

She will not inform Detective I. Perrino. This is her solution not the police's. Like an entirely original work of art, he falls into no known category. Certainly none of theirs. *A bulky presence, the police in their wool mittens don't know crystal stemware. Their surveillance of me could alert him, one mistake would alienate him and he'd withdraw from me and maybe everyone forever.*

Maude's hands are shaking while she dresses. Her choice of clothing has been ready, hung separately, but it is suddenly now. It seems too soon. She slips the loose dress over her head, her nude body. She fixes her hair twice, once down, once tousled, she decides on down.

In her medical bag under the sink, she finds Doctor T's tiny muscle scalpel, slips it out of its case. Using flesh-colored tape, she tapes it to the arch of her foot along the lateral malleolus. She has thought this through several times but never rehearsed it. If it comes loose while she walks, if she does not tape it just right, the scalpel will open a deep gash on the bottom of her foot maybe sever a tendon. *Horrible. I'd just be standing there losing blood through my sandals. He'd be bound to notice.*

The boulevards are empty at two-fifteen, she drives carefully, quickly, wearing sandals, loose beige dress.

The drive takes her fifteen minutes.

Of course there is no one waiting, it is a wide boulevard, Wilshire, no parked cars. There is a telephone booth on the northeast corner where she has been told to wait. In a few minutes, it rings.

"Where do you want to meet?"

My choice?

"You decide."

It's as if we'd met at a singles bar.

"I'll tell you where. Not now. I have someplace in mind that I think's very private. Keep driving west and when you get down to Venice Park, wait at the northeast corner, where Windward crosses Ocean Avenue."

Now that she has heard him speak sentences, she knows his voice is more than sonorous, languid. He may be black, he may not be.

In twenty-five minutes she is there on the corner, standing alone. The stores are closed. The telephone attached to the building rings.

"I know you've come here alone, Maude. Walk past all the buildings onto the beach and keep walking. That's all."

He knows I've come alone. I want to be alone. This is a safe place where I can be seen from a distance.

It is a vast area, there is no moon.

The sand is cold under her bare feet, the ocean cannot be seen or heard. She has left her sandals in the car. The scalpel stays secure along the bottom of her left foot. The beach is a mile wide, flat, permanently cratered by feet, it has nothing to do with the ocean.

A midsummer gloom hangs just past the boardwalk, not a pretty night, the close hot air. Beyond, the night is black, sightless.

A hundred feet out onto the sand Maude can no longer see ahead of her. She can only feel her feet trudging. Her eyes are not accustomed to the black, she closes them and opens them slowly. She is dragging a woven shawl behind her in the sand, something to fall back on. She is wearing one garment, her long crinkled silk dress. The muscle scalpel is still taped to the bridge of her foot. She is not carrying a purse, if she is badly hurt, her body will be found in the morning by the first man with a metal detector out looking for lost treasure. If she is killed, it will take the police a while, maybe all morning, to connect her to the plain car parked a distance away on Ocean Avenue.

She would never have been able to come here unless she had had several drinks from a bottle of gin she brought to the car. But the gin has fled her body. She is sober from trying to penetrate the pasty black air, she is edgy from listening. She has counted five hundred paces, a quarter mile.

She stops. She senses the absence of a void, a solid presence. Someone has passed close to her, someone who could have touched her but did not, she has felt the air change and stop, a scent. It may be a sea bird floating on the air, the way they do, inspecting her. *But sea birds don't fly at night.*

She is immobilized. She is very frightened, brimming with fear. She did not think she would be, she felt she had nothing left to lose. But now she wonders why she is here, she is sorry she started this. She is alone, the gin has vanished.

A long distance behind her, there are streetlights and car lights, nothing ahead between her and the phantom sea. She turns away. Looks back toward the lights in the distance. Something intercepts the lights for an instant then stops. A presence. It is there, it is close, it is not breathing.

She can see a shape. The absence of light. A man is standing not more than five feet away, watching her. Someone whose eyes are used to the dark. He has been following her.

Now is the time to submit. She will give in to him. Whatever he wants to do to her, it is nothing compared with what she will do to him. She will give in willingly then she will precisely slit his throat from left to right with a single steady gesture.

A hand touches her arm lightly. She cannot speak. It raises her arm, as if to dance at a cotillion. The fingers are taking her pulse. She knows it must be 180. Now there are two hands, one on her elbow, one holding her hand.

She is limp. She lets the hands pass over her, up her arms, her armpits, they are gentle as Sara described them, they touch the silk, the shawl, they discover that under the loose dress she is nude, that her breasts are bare, that her neck, her hair, that everything about her is bare, open, passive, pulsing. The hands will do her no harm. They are in perfect control, they brush between her legs up her thighs, pass over the fine hairs of her vagina with no interest, between her buttocks, lightly. Up from her ankles to her spine, ears, hair. The hands are searching, they have found nothing. What they are searching for is taped to the instep of her right foot.

The hands have fled. There is no one. She cannot see. She stands eyes closed, head down, available. Waiting. Her heart is booming. *How could I be here?*

A rustling sound. Without a breath, in a single motion, she is lifted from the ground in one gesture, her feet wobble, she is weightless, the air squeezed out of her. Maude does not know it, but it is not a rape, merely a chance collision, maybe a mugging. She is surrounded, rigid, she is turned, dropped to her knees, jolted, his body is on top of her, she is on her back engulfed in her own silk.

She easily peels back the tape across her instep, the muscle scalpel is so small, the blade is naked, mean, she might lose a finger if she grasps it the wrong way. It lands free in her hand, just right, the handle in her palm as she meant it to be. The fingers of her left hand dig into his back, bracing her. She moves her hands to his shoulders, the back of his neck. He does not notice. She is finding the place. The entry. With the scalpel in her right hand she tries to stab the length of the blade into the right side of his neck by the clavicle and slice across the width of his throat.

He is choking bubbling, warm blood gushes into her mouth and eyes, her breasts, her hair, she squirms but she cannot escape his pouring weight. He collapses unconscious without protest, his arms pull back, his elbows clutch his body. He drops on top of her, pinning her into the sand, his streaming mouth on hers, his open throat on hers. She cannot move. Time goes away. She is soaked with his blood, a tumult of blood. There is no other sound. Her breathing slows. She struggles in the sand to free herself, pushing her hands into its fluency. The blood and sand form a paste, gluing her eyes, joining her fingers.

Toyer kept his appointment with her. She slithers out from under his weight like a child. He joins the beach, his body will pour into the sand throughout the night.

She must leave no trace, she is not known as a killer to anyone but herself and him. If no one knows, it was not done. The scalpel is lost. She must find it. She sifts the sand carefully, she must not cut her hand. She cannot leave it behind. She must leave nothing behind but the dying Toyer for the early-morning scavengers to find, as they fan the sand with their metal detectors for bright salvages.

She hears voices, not far off, a man and woman who have been making love and are now gathering their thoughts.

Maude slips away from Toyer's body across the sand toward the lights of the boardwalk and drives home. She has never been there.

MAUDE

THE DAY IS STILL, the earth surrounding her house is arid. There are no birds. The rooms are asleep, silent. Sunlight crosses the living room floor picking up pale rose-colored smears on towels, rugs. In the bathroom there are wet soaps, washcloths. Bloody foot stains on the tiled floor, the shower. The cat box has been flipped, leaving a small beach, there is the smell of vomit.

In the bedroom Jimmy G is awake, he watches Maude sleep wrapped in clean white towels. Her scorched hands inert, half closed, soiled. There is sand on her pillow, in her ear, a smeared bottle of Tanqueray close by, empty on the bed. It is ten. She is waking, her eyes dark with fatigue.

Jesus. I did it. He's gone. A jabbing stick of pain is lodged in her intestines. Her breasts ache. Her elbow is badly bruised, it feels like a bone chip. She can remember falling in the shower on the creamy slime of blood. On the floor her silk dress is balled up tight within her woven shawl. She had brought a beach towel for the front seat of the car, bandages, expecting a mess, ready for anything.

By the time she had driven home and thrown herself under the shower without undressing, her hair had become crisp with blood, her face, arms, breasts varnished with blood and sand. She passed out briefly on the living room rug, somehow later found herself in bed wrapped in fresh white bath towels. She has washed herself continuously, cleansing herself of the gushed blood. She is beginning to recall a night of gin and washing.

She has killed. *Forever no more no more. I killed him and no one will ever know.* Beyond her good reasons, she has killed, she has stopped a life in a detestable way. She feels sick exuberance, she knows that a part of her life has ended, will always be over.

She half wakes. She wants to call everyone and tell them that Toyer's gone. If she could, surprisingly, Chleo would be the first, the veteran of all ten victims, at her side for two years. No more patients. She would call Doctor T, then Sara.

There are pale smears on the front doorframe near the keyhole. When she opens it, the daylight blinds her, the morning paper has been thrown in the naked hedge, naturally there is nothing in it about the killing. It is five hours too early. *The presses were rolling when I was still at the beach.* She sees blood on the car door, the steering wheel.

She knows there will never be anything written about Toyer's murder. *His death is secret, he will disappear, only I will ever know what happened to him.* There will always be an intriguing suspense. Gradually they will decide that he quit.

Maude imagines police in black shoes on the sand, the yellow DO NOT CROSS bands blowing, the awful gawking.

Unless she tells them to, the police will not have any reason to match this morning's palm print with Toyer's *mark*, why should they? The file will stay open.

The afternoon papers will say, not on page one,

BODY FOUND SAVAGELY MURDERED.

An ill feeling cools her viscera.

Tomorrow, if anything, less. It will never be more than that. Another killing. No one will ever know it was him. End of book.

One day when everything is calm, when I have been reinstated, I will tell you, Doctor T, what I did last night. Maybe I will send Sara a one-sentence, unsigned letter to the Herald and tell you that the body found on Venice Beach, June 20, was the body of Toyer. The police will match the body's handprint. You may have the scoop.

GEOFF

AFTERNOON. Maude is catatonic. There is no report of a murder on the radio, it is too small a killing. She scans the television channels. She feels high, sick. She has no strength, no appetite. At two o'clock there is news of an incident at a beach. It is something else, a fire, it is not on Venice Beach, it is Manhattan Beach. How could they not have found Toyer? She drives to the market for a bottle of Tanqueray, sits in the parking lot, the short neck of the zinc green bottle sticking up out of a paper bag. *An attractive look.*

Then late, after she has gone to bed, she hears the words *Venice Beach* from the radio she has left on in the living room.

Toyer has been discovered by a couple who are credited with saving his life. He is now hospitalized in I.C.U. A black wave sweeps over her, Toyer is alive. She feels faint. It is incredible, the woman who discovered him once studied medicine. He is critical.

Maude decides to contact Detective I. Perrino. She cannot telephone a police station from her house. But in the morning an anonymous caller will tell Perrino that Toyer is the unidentified Venice Beach stabbing victim now at St. John's Hospital and the voice will suggest that he take a palm-heel print from his right hand.

In the morning she drives to the market to make the telephone call to Perrino. The car radio is on.

"The victim in Wednesday night's bizarre Venice Beach attack has been identified. . . ." It appears that she has assaulted what appears to be a homeless man, still without a last name. Nothing more than that.

She faints in the front seat of her car in the market's parking lot.

She goes back to Food King Market, buys the early editions of the *Times* and *Herald*. On page seven of the *Herald:*

Bizarre Beach Assault

A homeless man has been discovered brutally attacked on Venice Beach not far from his sleeping mat. He is between thirty and thirty-five. Based on a tattoo, his name appears to be Geoff, no one questioned seemed to know his last name. Geoff is a known beach personality, a familiar face. He owned a surfboard that he kept under a house. Occasionally people gave him food. He is believed to be from Ohio or Illinois.

He is pleasant looking, simple, popular. Some call him a beach creature, others call him a free spirit. The *Herald* reporter Rick Nize, who writes a small piece, asks anyone who might have known Geoff's last name to step forward, he gives the newspaper's telephone number, his extension. There is no photograph.

Along the beach there is less astonishment at this assault. He was a homeless man after all. It is a nature conservancy out there. *Thinning the herd.*

Today or tomorrow, someone will say who Geoff really is. An ex-wife, a mother will claim him as her own. If he survives.

Please, God.

Instead of killing Toyer, Maude has wounded someone else, a sunburned residue, one of God's own. Not even a rapist. *A simple man asleep who woke up to a blind chance that came to him in a dream. A simple man who she prays will survive. No one will ever know I tried to kill him.*

At three, Sara calls, leaves a message, asks if she can stop by for a drink at five. Maude is at home, hears her voice asking. She does not pick up the telephone. *Not yet. Not quite yet.*

At four, Maude hears on the radio that a scalpel with dried

blood has been found buried in the sand, picked up by some-one's metal detector. It is a Swedish muscle scalpel, the best.

At five-thirty or so, Sara takes a chance, stops by, she is worried about Maude, her absence, her voice. When she gets out of her car, she sees white smoke rising behind the small house, something is burning, she smells damp cloth on fire. She walks around behind the house. There is Maude, her nearly naked body, back to her, standing in front of the barbe-cue, squirting charcoal lighting fluid on a bath towel and what could be a dress. Sara backs away, it is too private.

At six-thirty she calls Maude. She answers. Sara asks again if she can stop by for a drink, Maude refuses politely, they talk briefly, Sara asks if she is free for lunch tomorrow. Maude agrees. Sara will ask her tomorrow.

TOYER

FIVE A.M. Maude's telephone rings. *Doesn't anybody sleep anymore?* She picks it up, does not speak, listens, ready for crisis.

"Maude?" *It's him.*

"Yes."

"My word. What have we done?"

Maude does not speak.

"Ain't we been bad? My my my. I don't know *what* to think about you anymore, am I angry or flattered?"

"I still want to meet you."

"And I still want to meet you but look how you behave. I thought you was a healer. Now I'm confused."

"Tell me where to meet you."

Click. Hmmmmmmmmmmmmmmmm.

He is at the top of his game. He is having a marvelous time.

In the morning she continues washing, scrubbing. The radio is on in the living room, tuned to the news on Public Radio, loud enough to be heard wherever she is. Listening, she continues washing. Rugs, curtains, pots, pans, floors, windows, rags, Jimmy G, the car. She has burned her silk dress and her favorite shawl.

Then she hears it. Geoff has been identified. He is Geoff Wates. Born in St. Paul, played football at a Catholic high school, he did not show promise in any known career. His father remains in a small militia that believes the government is evil. Nine years ago, Geoff Wates hitchhiked to California to find himself and that was the last his father heard of him. He tells a reporter that Geoff was always good with dogs and cats. He remains in critical condition.

When he recovers he will always remember the night he was attacked by a woman with a knife who kept calling him Toyer.

DOCTOR T

DOCTOR T stands toweling himself in the bathroom doorway. He is on his way to work. He is tall, there are rubbery areas.

Over the past two weeks, he has spent four nights in Maude's small house on the undeveloped road above the canyon. He senses that she needs him now more than ever, he feels he knows her, that is enough, he does not need details. For the first time he has felt her body join his.

Abruptly she sobs, choking, her head bucks with sobbing. "Don't worry, it'll be fine." She goes to him. She is limp, he is supporting her.

Why she is crying. *If I could only tell you why.* She sobs.

She cannot stop. On his arm, he leads her back to bed, lowers her. She is weak.

"Maude, please, I am always here."

Between sobs, all she can say is, "Oh, Elias, if you only knew why." She wants to tell him that she has borrowed one of his scalpels, she has nearly murdered a stranger, someone called Geoff. She wants him to understand. Has he noticed a small one missing? Surgeons have favorites. She imagines he will understand, maybe one day but not now. Now it is impossible. It is too new, she can still smell the blood.

It is his perspective. She sees herself, sees him. She sees them together. He is stationary.

That night Maude cooks pasta for him, it is *puttanesca*, the quick mix developed for convenience in Italian brothels, capers, tomatoes, anchovies, olives, oregano, red pepper, in olive oil and linguini. Doctor T moans happily.

She touches his shoulders from behind, "When was the last time you were fed by someone who adored you?"

"Never."

It is an excellent time to make love.

TELEN GACEY

Ms. Sara Smith
The Los Angeles Herald
Herald Square, L.A. 90019

Dear Sara Smith,

I am distantly related to you by marriage. If you speak to your father, please tell him that Madeleine Haussman's daughter got in touch with you and see what he says. He was married to my mother's older sister Ghiseline one summer long before you were born so that makes me your ex-cousin. I think.

I came out here last year from Wisconsin, after my father died suddenly ice fishing (my mother's fine) and I'm trying to become a writer, I guess. I'm in the Actors Group studying acting and learning to write dialogue for movie scripts.

Anyway, I'd love to have you come and see my first one-act play. Or maybe we can just meet?

Telen Gacey

P.S. I admire your reporting very much, and would love to know you. We've all read every word you've written on Toyer—you've really brought that story to life. Please try to come to the Group. We meet every Saturday morning.

THE MIDDLE

THE MIDDLE

HOLLYWOOD

THE LEAN MAN flips the quarter. Catches it.

"Heads or tails."

The woman on the sofa stares up at him, she sits, knees high, paralyzed. She is in her twenties, colorless from fear.

He flips the coin again and catches it.

"Call it."

She cannot speak.

"Last chance," the man smiles. He flips the coin and catches it. *"Heads or tails. Choose."*

"I can't," she sobs, she feels her life depends on her choice. "Please." She can barely be heard.

"You know what I'm going to do, don't you?"

The girl looks faint. "Please just give me one chance."

"Heads or tails."

She stretches away from him on the sofa, whispers without looking.

"Heads."

"Tails." He says without glancing at the coin. He puts it back in his pants pocket.

"Just tell me what you want. I'll do it." She wipes her eyes. "That's the best way, isn't it?"

"It's the only way." He smiles and changes the long knife to his right hand. "We'll do what I want, whatever you say."

"It's what we both want."

The knife glints nicely in the overhead track light.

In a split instant, the dark-haired man jams the knife-blade into the tabletop. The girl looks up, startled, caught by its rapid metronomic beat. Her eyes glaze. She buries her face in a cushion and sobs in full body action, completely.

Quietly, from somewhere beyond a black imaginary wall, a woman's voice commands, "Tell her to undress for you, Billy."

The dark-haired man hesitates. "Go on," the woman's voice urges, "tell her."

He has not taken his eyes from his victim, "Undress." He says it without conviction.

The girl looks up at him, holding the pillow like a lover. Still crying.

"Stand up," the man says. Stronger.

She does.

"All right, undress."

The girl, clearly trapped, hesitates.

"Go on, Telen," the woman's voice says from the dark.

Obviously embarrassed, and staring at her tormentor's feet, the girl unfastens her skirt from the side. Luckily, she remembers, she has put on a slip that morning. In a few moments she is standing in front of the man in a half-slip and brassiere. Her fingers are poised behind her, about to unclip her brassiere. Her angled limbs look especially lithe. She flicks the clasp. The loosened brassiere droops over her breasts, her sudden nipples.

The woman's voice is calm. "Thank you, Telen, thank you, Billy." The clapping of a dozen actors breaks the silence.

Telen reclips her brassiere, immediately reaches for her skirt and T-shirt and slips into them. The dark-haired man turns his back to her and faces the black glare of the track lights. The woman's voice says, "That wasn't so bad, was it, Telen?"

It is over. "Horrible," she mouths to herself. The girl raises her head and pushes her hair away from her eyes, dazed, hoping for praise. She looks as if she had been rescued from drowning. She is busy concealing what she has just revealed. She shakes her head several times, half smiles. Alert, she squints into the audience below hot pools of light, shielding her eyes with one hand and with the other wiping them with a tissue. She is wildly attractive in her exposed disarray, haggard from mourning her own loss.

"That was good work, Telen," the woman says. "Who wants to go first?" She is holding a clipboard where she has written notes.

Anna Blouse, a large somehow radiant woman in a pale muumuu. Telen has never seen a face like hers, it seems to be constructed of disappointments, her body grown large from abandonment. Behind her back they call her Granny Blouse. Still, there is a radiance about her.

The dark-haired man left standing without the compliment is Billy Waterland, not his real name. He yanks his knife from the table, sits down heavily across a chair dangling a leg, pushing a tense sigh up through his body, "*Feeeeooooooo.*"

"Who wants to go first?" Anna Blouse repeats. Neither actor speaks.

"Okay, Telen, you go."

Telen blows her nose. Her closed mouth always seems to be smiling. Her father was a drunk.

"You okay?"

Telen nods.

"Okay, what were you using for fear?"

Telen draws herself up on the sofa. She can barely see the large woman in the gloom, seated in the front row of the box theater. She squints at the area where she knows she is sitting. "Well, the knife, of course."

"Something internal, please," the voice is richly patient.

"I was using an old nightmare of mine."

"Do you want to tell us about it?"

Sometimes Telen's father would come home late and fall into bed with her wearing only an undershirt.

"I'd rather not, Anna, it's just always there."

"And it worked for you."

"Yes, Anna, he really frightened me."

"I believed you, Telen." High praise.

When Telen first walked into the Actors Group and beheld Anna Blouse, she appeared to be hungover. Ten in the morning, the first session of the Group, nineteen actors assembled in forty seats facing a low stage furnished with veteran chairs, tables, sofa, all ripe with memories. Anna Blouse opened a supermarket shopping bag and unwrapped from newspapers four parcels. The first was the Oscar she had won for *In Extremis,* the other three were the Tonys she had won for *Valstrice, The Generosity of Fire,* and *Bring on the Day.* Without ever referring to them, she set them on the grubby stage, the Oscar stage right, the Tonys stage left. Whatever she said to the actors that day was heard, possibly always remembered.

Now, this morning, Anna turns the discussion on Billy.

"Did you think about who Toyer is, where he slept last night? How he shaves? What he eats?"

"*Who* he ate last night," a voice behind her in the dark whispers. No one laughs.

"Yes," Billy says, "I did."

"I wasn't frightened at all, Billy," she says cheerily.

Billy nods, eyes closed to indicate understanding and removal, ready to receive the blow he has paid for.

"Toyer is nonviolent, Billy, everyone knows that. He doesn't hurl women around the way you threw Telen on the sofa. He doesn't do that. He's very careful not to. I bet he's the *only* one who doesn't. He doesn't punch and he doesn't kill. He doesn't like guns. He probably makes love to his victims, yes? I think he would. He's sensitive. In a strange way he's very respectful of his victims, yes? He's certainly the only practicing sociopath who keeps a diary and publishes it."

Billy listens, smart enough not to disagree. He can sense her pale muumuu shift in the dark. "Now I didn't see any of that respect for his victims today. I'm sorry, Billy, you were playing the familiar diabolic killer. You did everything but roll your eyes and twirl your moustache." She pauses for climax. "But are we unshockable? Yes I think we are. We've seen it all and experienced nothing and so we feel nothing. Your Toyer needs enough of an inner life for us to understand him. Why do they call him Toyer? Because he toys with people. Backgammon, gin rummy? Who knows what else, for Christ's sake. *Think,* Billy. He plays games with them, he drinks with them, dances, fucks, then when he feels it, he simply lobotomizes them and says goodnight to them. Why you chose him I don't know, but you forgot to get into his head. You don't understand him."

She has cut Billy fairly, her rapier through the neck, leaving the brain alive.

"And you do?" Billy stares at her. His eyes are wet. He goes to bed late. It is difficult for him to make his head by 10:00 A.M., to organize thoughts, reach emotional climaxes.

"Billy, don't get angry with me, yes? Get angry with your character." She does not wait for him to answer, turns around and faces the dozen or so actors.

"What do we know about him?"

They exude. Hands are up. Deer-faced women, wolf-faced men; actresses for hysterics, actors for machismo. It is a catacomb of jawbones and cheekbones.

"Yes, Jed."

"He's very neat. I'd say he has a tidiness fixation."

"Yes," Anna says.

"He respects his victims," a mouselike actress says.

Anna nods, "Uh-huh."

Sitting here are replicas of successful actors. A Jack Nicholson without irony, an Italian James Dean from Brooklyn, a

Katharine Hepburn from Toluca Lake, a youngish Marlon Brando with none of his resources. Beethoven's deafness everywhere, without his greatness.

"Yes?"

"Well," a Sigourney Weaver girl says, "there are no signs of force. No robbery. Just a brief telephone message. A few words, we don't know what they are."

"Yes, Shelly."

"There's no rape. There's consent, maybe even love," the Jack Nicholson personage says.

"Love?" Anna picks it up. "That's right, he must have *something* going for him. Maybe it's consensual. Please don't roll your eyes, Billy."

"He's a monster, Anna, I tried to play a monster." Billy sounds like a defense lawyer.

"Sure he's a monster, Billy, but he's got charm. Our monsters walk around in plain sight. To create a real monster you create a character with a desperate need, yes? An innocent person with a problem. A quirk. Anyone can turn. You're safer with leopards."

What Anna is saying, Billy thinks, is that it would be better, more *dramatic* if the wrong person would play Toyer.

What Anna is saying indirectly is something Billy already knows. He tends to miscolor onstage, not a promising trait for an actor who dreams of becoming a star.

"I can't imagine why you chose to do him, Billy."

"Peter suggested it." He looks out bleakly into the small audience for proof. "He follows his adventures like Prince Valiant, he's his number one fan. He cuts his articles out of the paper."

Anna turns to Peter. "Why, Peter?"

"It was the biggest challenge I could think of for him."

"The biggest challenge for him would be a simpler reality. To have someone he's never met believe that he's Toyer or a door-to-door salesman. Someone out there." She sweeps her hand across the prairies of Los Angeles. "Some poor soul you can hold only with your character choices."

"A stranger?"

"Why not? Acting is human-to-human between strangers, isn't that all we do? Isn't it all politicians do? Car salesmen? Agents? Aren't you introducing new ideas to a girl you've just met when you take her out on a date?"

Sara Smith has been sitting in the last row. There are six rows of fiberglass chairs. She received Telen's note yesterday and tried to call her. This morning she left a telephone message at Telen's apartment but she had already gone. *This is a totally different world. It's all so foreign. This is where actors come from.*

An hour later, the discussion ends of its own fatigue, house lights are switched on in the unpleasant room, drab walls, chairs on worn plywood risers, the actors stand and stretch. It is just after midday. The class has run more than three hours.

Sara Smith stands. *Actors are molded in these grubby crucibles, every Hollywood actor has been colored and sharpened and buffed here in these caves. This woman, Anna, her appetite for truth, her ear for language, her eye for beauty, her nose for fraud, she creates their false realism.*

Sara half waves to Telen but of course is not recognized. She walks down to the stage riser, step by plywood step, "Telen, *surprise*, it's Sara Smith."

"Oh, my God."

"I left you a message this morning."

Telen is shocked, tries to remember what she did onstage in the scene.

"O-ooh, I'm so embarrassed." Her unexpected breasts in the glare.

"Don't be, it was wonderful, it was very real." Telen accepts the compliment. "You told me what, when, and where, I had the time and here I am. It's very exciting, I had no idea."

Peter comes over, then Billy. Introductions.

"You're the Sara Smith that writes about Toyer," Billy says. "Oh, my God this is fabulous, you're great."

"You are read and admired," Peter says with a slight bow.

"Thanks very much, it's nice to know you're being read." Telen is not that much younger, maybe six or seven years.

She says to Telen, "We should get together for dinner sometime."

"Well, how about now?" She glances at the boys, "Can you have coffee with us at Ruben's? We just walk there."

"Well." Wristwatch. "Sure."

"The three of us hang out there after Group."

"We'll make it four today." She agrees.

She's so nice.

Together, they walk to Ruben's, the two boys walking ahead of them, Telen says, "It's true, they read you and discuss you." Billy has the *Herald* in his back pocket. "It's an honor for them, believe it or not."

"I'm flattered." *In a city of cheap stardom, one million stars.*

The boys, like everyone in the Group, dress in amorphous clothes, trendy mufti, outside all fashion, their clothes are like their skins, available for any decade. They blend. Sara does not blend. She is dressed entirely in simple Connecticut. She has moved to California, her clothes have not. Tan slacks, a white cotton shirt with a rounded collar, small gold pin, wise walking shoes, low heels.

As Sara and Telen walk to Ruben's, Sara nods toward the boys walking ahead. The nod is the familiar woman's question asked of another woman. It means *Anything serious?*

Telen shrugs. "They're really nice, you know." *Really nice,* the other word for death. It is a devastating coup, the entrails. The shrug. The shrug has caused duels.

"Are they gay?"

"No! No, I don't think so."

Telen does not want to be involved with a man, not now.

To Sara it is a strange world, Hollywood acting, and one that she knows nothing and has cared nothing about. *Acting is done in New York.* Acting here seems perfunctory, minor, based on personality. Yet she remains fascinated by the morning's session.

Actors are boys and girls, there is a youngness to what they do no matter how old they are, they are dressing up in their parents' clothes, playing someone who isn't them. Anyone who isn't them. How strange that is. Yet they create our guidelines for human response, because we watch them for clues to our limits, our anger, laughter, our pain and fear.

DOCTOR T

SATURDAY MORNING, a day of rest. Dr. T is shiny from the shower, he is making toast and coffee. Maude lies on the bed in her sweat, nude without a sheet, she plummeted back into sleep while Doctor T was in the bathroom.

For a few moments she wishes she was able to stuff mushrooms, set out a plank of cheeses and grapes, pour wine for his friends under the trees on Saturday afternoons.

"I had a strange phone call," he says, "you can't imagine."

"I won't even try."

Suddenly she's awake. *It's him.*

"Some guy called and asked if one of my scalpels was missing, he identified it as a Siva, a Swedish muscle scalpel. I have one. I looked for it and it's missing. It's a very good one."

"Strange." She is lying on her side, a sculpture of a cyclist, turned away from him. He cannot see her face. He cannot see her reaction.

"Why would he call me?"

She is feigning drowsiness.

"Maybe it's someone who works for you."

"Could be, you think? Someone stole it and someone else is turning him in."

"Hmmmm."

"But it's a mystery."

When he calls you again, he'll solve it for you.

THE UNCASTABLES

THEY CALL THEMSELVES THE UNCASTABLES, Billy, Peter, Telen. They cherish that name. Every Saturday, following the Actors Group workshop, the three Uncastables have walked over to Ruben's. They do not see each other away from the Group but are friends because they are clever, detached, uncastable. Sara is delighted to be included, she is onto something that she knows nothing about, *this is Hollywood's hidden life.*

If the Uncastables appear unhurried, time is on their side, they stroll easily into Ruben's, Peter with his drowsy competence, Billy with his coiled energy, Telen, chin high, her defensive aplomb, leading Sara Smith. They take their usual booth with *droits des vedettes*, the women on the inside, Sara beside Billy. Telen has nearly recovered from the devastating Toyer scene. Peter seems ready for bed. Sara wipes the Formica tabletop in front of her, *How many sticky elbows today?*

Today Billy will order lunch from the lined, white-haired waitress named Brandi. It is his turn. "Ve vill haff matzo ball chicken soup," he says in a German accent, an odd choice. Last time it was Peter's choice, the dank wonderful meatball sandwiches, the week before it was Telen's pastrami with mustard and sauerkraut. The choice is on a rotation basis. They order iced teas, free refills.

Peter has grabbed Billy's *Herald*, it is flopped on the Formica tabletop open to page one:

TOYER DISCUSSES METHOD, TENTH VICTIM HIS OWN ACCOUNT

By Sara Smith

Sara is royalty. The boys agree not to discuss Toyer. Instead, there will be showing off today at Ruben's for her.

Peter caresses his chin and cheek, facing an imaginary mirror. He is in rehearsal for his first TV commercial audition. He repeats his mantra, *"Women don't mind stubble on Wayne Hartig's cheeks, but on mine? Forget-about-it."* He smiles ruefully at his plight into the plate-glass window. A jocose wag of his head. Billy's eyes watch him as a Lexington trainer would watch a colt trot.

"Who is Wayne Hartig?" he says.

"Hockey."

Sara is watching. *What fun, unemployed Hollywood actors in bloom, orchids in a vivarium, a genus of flora unknown anywhere else in the world. It's not London or New York, Hollywood actors only need to be themselves, be whoever they are, don't need to raise their voices, there's no audience, always a microphone, but the camera must love them.*

Sara realizes that all four of them are from elsewhere and will go elsewhere when they are through with Los Angeles. *It draws you in and you stay until you're finished and you can't stay anymore.*

By the time the matzo ball soups arrive, the table's support for Peter's commercial has crumbled, after all, neither Billy nor Telen has ever auditioned for a TV commercial.

Telen has a boyish look, slim-hipped, small, surprisingly fine breasted, onstage she seemed overtly vulnerable, female.

Billy is funny, sort of a stand-up comic, he seems secure, he carries himself like a gymnast. Leaning forward. Maybe he's too eager to explain himself.

Peter calls Billy's stance his *Why-don't-you-jump?* stance. He was a gymnast in high school. Billy thinks about death every day.

Peter is more elusive. Blond, vain. He seems detached from acting as though the profession were beneath him. One would think to ask him, "What made you want to become an actor?" Whereas with Billy the question answers itself. They both seem more interesting than the characters they want to play.

Billy looks up at Sara. As commander of the booth, he will show off for her. He points to the article. "Now this guy's got standards, he's read his Bible, I like his style, his voice."

"What did you think of his work?" Peter says to Sara.

"Meaning Billy or Toyer?"

"Billy."

"I liked it." *What can I say?*

"And what Anna said?"

"Good criticism."

During the short silence, Sara Smith, a near contemporary, says to them, "Why do you all want to become actors?" She says it nicely, to be informed, it is not a challenge.

Telen says she is observing acting so that she can write screenplays for actors. *Cool.* Billy says it is because he trusts poverty. *Cool.* Peter says he doesn't give a damn. *Cool.*

It's true. Peter doesn't. He is not an *actor:* he cannot speak words he has not thought of himself.

Billy says to him, "Why don't you give it a try?"

"Why don't I give what a try?"

"Giving a fuck."

Telen says to Sara, "Please excuse him, Billy has Tourette's syndrome." It is the word *fuck. So unnecessary.*

"Can I quote Anna? She says you caricature onstage."

Peter shrugs. "I don't know, is she right?"

Billy is ready. "Anna says you disappear onstage, okay? You're tall and you're blond and we can't fucking *see* you.

You wanna know why? You don't fucking *care*. This is her talking, not me."

Is it an argument? Sara cannot tell what is for the visitor or what is real. Telen touches Sara's shoe with hers, catches her eye. This is fun, not serious, she loves their *mano a mano*. It is performance.

Billy continues. "You wanna try Toyer? Be my guest, you heard her, Anna, make an outsider buy into it. Someone entirely out there."

Peter is waking. It will be *mano a mano* for Sara. He cracks his knuckles, a dreadful warning.

"Let me show you acting. Watch me very carefully," he says to Billy, "I want to avoid any confusion here."

Telen is wrong, Peter is very angry. His face is sharply marked, his features definite, there is a tiny vein Telen has not seen before standing out, a pink blotch between his eye and his ear. But Sara has missed it, it is still all light, combed, barely visible.

The four have "not been noticing" two men in the booth just behind theirs. While they have been talking, they have been hearing almost every word. It is obvious, one of them has a severe speech disorder.

The larger of the two has his back to them, arms draped widely over the top of the booth. His head is the hairless dome of a newborn marine. His neck and arms resemble cuts of prime meat. The other man, facing him, probably his younger brother, can hardly utter a word but never gives up trying to. He looks as if he will, but instead, he gags or retches into his soft drink, sometimes snorting. He stutters on every consonant. The Uncastables, who do not stutter, are fascinated. *What a role*, Billy thinks.

"Give me a moment," Peter whispers to the three. He leans toward the weaker brother, stares at him, stuttering. Studies him briefly, amazed, his head cocked like a robin's. The shaved marine is not aware of Peter.

"Okay," Peter whispers to Sara, Billy and Telen. "Watch."

He buttons the top button on his shirt, takes a breath, lets it out. He leans over and taps the shaved marine on the shoulder. Alert to touch as a guard dog would be, the shaved marine spins and faces Peter, who points to the stutterer. Peter laughs.

The marine looks blank at first, without opinion, then realizes the enormity of Peter's affront and shoots him with an evil eye. Peter nods, points his thumb at the little brother, laughs again.

The marine continues to glare at Peter. And the more he does, the more Peter loves it, finally losing control, and falling back, doubled with laughter. The stutterer seems to be the funniest thing he has ever seen.

The three do not know where to look.

The marine turns away. "Let's get outta here, guy." He puts a bill on the table. They stand, leave, without looking back.

"That's it?" Billy says, "Thanks for the acting lesson. He wanted to kill you."

"God, you're so crazy," Telen says. *What a rush.*

"I was truly frightened, frankly," Sara says. Now that they have gone she is embarrassed for Peter.

"He'll be back," Peter says quietly. "That's the part I want to show you." And so he will be. Billy sees him coming back through the door. Suddenly the marine is above them, swaying like a giant derrick. His surprisingly clean fingernail is one inch below Peter's nose as if it could lift him by one nostril. Peter has stopped laughing.

"You. Faggot. You think that's funny how my kid brother talks?"

Peter looks puzzled, nods *yes.*

"It's an affliction."

Peter smiles charmingly, nods, then crumples with laughter.

Telen shrinks away. Sara is paralyzed.

Billy says quickly, "Hey, buddy, he does not mean it, I swear to you, he's mentally ill, right, Peter?"

The marine only hears the name.

"Peter. Come on, Peter, it's *Go* time, let me show you the parking lot out back. It's got a nice blacktop surface, Peter."

The marine reaches down and lifts Peter by one armpit. Peter, his face twisted, his eyes clear, his body half out of the booth, looks oddly relaxed.

"Please put him down," Sara says.

Telen says, "He's having tremendous emotional problems, sir, like stress." She points to her own head. "Everyone died in his family."

Billy says, "This morning."

The shaved marine turns to Billy, still holding Peter like a strand of kelp. "What a coincidence."

"Don't take him away," Sara says.

"Okay, you want me to punish him here, miss? I gotta warn you, shit splatters."

No one has been watching Peter. He has fruited his lips like a tuba player. All this time he has been attempting to speak, but nothing has come out of his mouth except spitting noises. He appears to be trying to peck seeds. A consonant emerges.

Still holding Peter by the armpit, halfway to his feet, the shaved marine stares at him trying to form a word, trying to overcome an affliction so full, so pathetically real that the four are now working hard to understand him.

Fascinated, wary, the shaved marine's eyes narrow, his mouth opens, listening. It takes him a few moments to see that Peter is a serious invalid, a tour de force stutterer fit to be institutionalized, more pathetic than his own brother. Carefully the marine lowers Peter back onto his seat.

"Awesome," he says to Sara. "He always been this bad?"

Billy nods. "Oh, yeah, for years."

They all nod. The marine pats Peter's arm, "He's trying too hard, that's what's wrong." His great mutton face relaxes, cut by relief.

"Hey, man, forget what I said." He extends his palms like twin catcher's mitts, offering Peter a low five.

Peter gently slaps the mitts and extends his own for the return. The shaved marine gives Sara, Billy and Telen a private *believe-me-I-been-there* look. He turns back to Peter. "Let me buy you breakfast, whatever." He flattens out a ten-dollar bill on the table in front of Peter.

While Peter is still hammering out the *th* in thanks, the shaved marine interrupts, "Have a good day," turns and leaves.

The three wait until the door swings shut. He is gone.

Peter says, "Fuck you, Billy."

Billy is the clear loser here. "That was nice."

"God, how did you *do* that?" Telen is regaining her color. "He was going to kill you for sure."

"Life and death?"

Telen grips his arm, her fingers are hot. "Yes, Peter, I definitely sensed we were in the presence of death," she says.

"Okay." The defeated Billy stands. "I gotta go." He has a new job, parking cars for Voiture Valet. He puts two dollars and sixty-five cents on the tough plastic tabletop.

Peter shoves the money aside. "Your money's no good here." He holds the ten-dollar bill up to the light, it may be counterfeit. "When they pay you to act, you're a professional." It is the first money he has ever earned as an actor.

Sara is impressed with his performance, but what Billy says is true, he is not an actor, what she saw was something else, Peter may be able to play his own lines, he cannot give meaning to the meaningless.

Sara makes her goodbyes. *Maybe I should write a Sunday piece about all this crazy stuff.*

After Sara leaves, Telen wraps two dinner rolls in a paper napkin, harvests her possessions, sunglasses, mints, a pen, and pushes them into a brightly decorated sack from India. There are tiny mirrors like eyes. She stands. But Ruben's customers only notice her when she passes by them wearing her little red dress with spaghetti straps.

That afternoon at his shaving audition, a tiny woman, who reminds Peter of an otter pulled from an oil spill, tells him that

he has not gotten the part of Shaver because he is better looking than Wayne Hartig, which is not true, but casting people
need to be loved.

Peter never seems right for any part, which is something
else.

SARA

SHE IS SITTING WITH MAUDE, she tells her that there
is another world lying beneath Los Angeles, it is the world
made of actors' lives.

"They're odd. They're very serious about imagining
they're someone else. They feel important. There's something
to it, I know there's an article in this. But what is it? Maybe if
I write it I can put my finger on it."

"Why am I interested in this?"

"Because they did a scene about Toyer today, this guy Billy
and my distant cousin, Telen."

"Telen."

"T-e-l-e-i-n-e, actually, but she shortened it. It's from her
parents' names, Madeleine and Ted. Anyway, they sat there on
the stage and actually pretended the whole near-death experience. You would have vomited."

"Why?"

"It seemed so—"

"Sick."

"I was going to say real. Do you have any idea how many
of them there are?"

"How many actors?"

"Guess."

"Where, here?"

"Yes."

"Five thousand? That seems like too many, doesn't it."

"Ninety."

"Ninety thousand?"

Sara nods. "Union actors, that doesn't even include my cousin or any of them. They can't join because they've never worked."

"Huh. So why am I learning this?"

"Because they scare the hell out of me."

Sara tells her about the stutterer at the coffee shop.

"What am I doing in this conversation?"

"Don't you hear what I'm saying?"

"Not really."

"Toyer is an actor."

"A union actor?"

"Maude, please. I saw it in action. It works. They can suspend someone's belief one-on-one, they don't need a stage. I was scared, let me tell you."

"Sounds dangerous."

"It is, they're oblivious to the world, they don't know where China is. I mean this is their life and they're not even allowed to work in it, they're frustrated, their days are empty, they don't think, the system supports them."

"Paradise," says Doctor T. He has been reading a book by the window. "I envy them their ignorance."

"It's such an island."

"Or an asylum," he says.

"They all sound borderline to me," Maude says.

"And Toyer doesn't?"

"I see."

TELEN

Ms. Sara Smith
The Los Angeles Herald
1 Herald Square, L.A. 90019

Dear Sara,

I've called a couple of times and I guess you've been busy. I hope you still want to come to my play. We'll put on four performances, minimum sets. Two weekends, July 13–14 and 20–21 at the Actors Group Theater in Hollywood. Three short plays, mine's the middle one. Tell me if you want me to hold your "usual seat." Remember, no air conditioning.

Telen

DOCTOR T

THE BED TABLE LIGHT is finally off, they lie in the dark, their eyes familiar with the wall shadows, the pleasant ceiling. Their bodies do not touch. Now he can ask her.

"Maude, help me with a problem."

"Yeah, of course."

"Well, you know that call I got last week? He called again. I don't know what to think."

Maude feels a bolt of illness, it is better to lie in the dark for this.

"Okay, what?"

"In a sentence, he told me that you stole my scalpel."

Maude exhales loudly.

"He said my scalpel was the one turned in at the beach. The one that was reported in the newspapers. Why he would say this I have no idea. Crazy, huh. So what I did was, I got in touch with the police and told them one of my scalpels was missing. I described it. A detective very kindly brought it in today for me to see. I believe it's mine. The murder weapon."

"No one was killed."

It is too quick, Maude hears her own voice. Elias sucks in air, sighs. The bedroom is quiet, she feels him waiting. It is an important moment, it is their life. *How much do you want to know? Do you want to know everything?*

The silence is too long.

"Is there anything you want to tell me?" Then he adds, "Maude, darling, you can tell me anything and it'll be safe forever."

"Do you think that was me who tried to kill that homeless man?"

"Maude, I'm sorry, I don't know what to think."

Maude and Doctor T twist in the dark.

She feels his fingers on her face, they brush imaginary hair away from her eyes. His arm comes around her, its weight lies across her breasts. It is too hot but tonight it is welcome. She forms words, almost speaks. His fingers touch her lips, seal them as if her mouth were a change purse. Doctor T nods in the dark. He is a man in love, it is all he can do.

TELEN

S ARA CALLS TELEN. She sounds rushed.

"I'm hard to reach sometimes, sorry. So you've written a play? What's it about?"

"It's a scene really, a doctor and his patient. The doctor's transplanted a heart that he acquired from a death row donor. This guy Roy Slayton who cannibalized kids, and so forth, really a monster, just before he died donated it to science. But the doctor never told the recipient who's in his seventies. He just thought, you know. So the patient finds out and is very upset at him. We're rehearsing it now. I'm directing."

"Sounds promising, do you have a title?"

"Untold Damage."

"Are Peter and Billy doing it?"

"Good guess, Peter gets to wear makeup to make him old."

"Interesting."

Telen takes this as faint praise. "It's about a lot of things, you know, how one feels about genetics, I mean how would you like to have Toyer's heart beating in *your* chest?"

"I'd rather have it spinning in my garbage disposal."

Telen laughs. *I like her.*

"Tell me where to be and at what time."

"Okay, two weekends, July thirteenth and July twentieth."

"Can I bring a friend?"

"Sure, and dress lightly, remember. No admission charge."

THE REHEARSAL

THE WIND NEVER BLOWS in Los Angeles. And because there is no wind, carbon monoxide dust settles on leaves, palm fronds, and succulents such as jade plants. Sometimes in Silverlake, where Peter lives, he walks by neighbors standing outside, wiping their plants.

On July 9, a Monday, at midday it grows dark as twilight. As though there will be an act of God. A tidal wave. Rain. The low pressure gets caught in the basin between the sea and the low hills and cannot get out. The dark sky rolls over and over, stays upside down and lets the rain come down. The storm takes everyone by surprise as it always does. The rain falls vertically, smoking from sour pavements, the wind does not blow.

The rehearsal for Telen's play will be at Peter's. He lives just under the roof in an apartment of many steep slants, on the top floor of a worn 1920 house in Silverlake, almost down-town, a soiled neighborhood where people walk on sidewalks because they must go somewhere, the way they walk in real towns.

Telen and Sara climb the stairs to the top floor. Peter will be late, he has given Telen a key. Sara has come to watch a re-hearsal, she has decided to do a light Sunday piece about the trials of non-union actors. She will write about their work-shops, their inconveniences, their dreams, their eating habits, their annual incomes, even though she finds their trials un-troubling, their lives jejune. She may call her article "The Others," but she isn't sure.

It is an old place, everything is poor, it reminds Sara of an apartment over a stable near home that used to smell of var-nished wood. The tiny bedroom, one wall plug, wires everywhere, the kitchen alcove. There is a table with nothing on it, no computer.

Peter lives like a squirrel, neat, as though he had run away from home. It is all temporary, he could pack in twenty min-utes. *But this is his entire life isn't it? He is not young, Rupert Brooke had already died at his age.*

Outside the old-fashioned windows, the rain builds, smack-ing the roof just above Sara, wood shingles are bent like seashells, looking up she can see them glisten. Arid roofs leak.

Billy arrives. He bends to kiss them, barely grazing Telen's cheek, lingering on Sara's, touching her arm. *Why is he so in-timate with me?* The scent of leather. He crosses the room like a gymnast, opens the two windows, snaps on the fans, dumps ice from the refrigerator into a pitcher. Sara watches his hips. The word *energized* comes to her, he is electric, she realizes he is performing for her, not for Telen. Sara is, after all, the Press.

He brings them glasses of ice water. He will do what is needed.

Billy calls his message service. It is a short respectful call, his appointment has been canceled.

"I'll probably end up producing."

"No more acting?" Sara says.

"Whaddaya got, I'm listening."

A small tight laugh. Billy is capable of standard ethnic delivery, labeled simply: Irish, Jewish, Brooklyn, Russian, Chinese, British.

The rain drums the house, holds them prisoners. It rains so rarely that it rains without knowing how. Flat streets flood, canyon mud slides. The water does not know where to go. Sara misses seasons, she misses crackling summer cloudbursts that cool the grass, she misses autumn light swelling up in the windows on dark afternoons, granite winter skies that foretell snow. She misses snow.

Waiting for Peter, Telen and Billy improvise. They are showing Sara their craft. Embarrassed, she watches as a voyeur, feeling herself too close to a scene of anger that is not true. Billy is graceful with Telen, he is probably graceful with all women. She notices his fingertips, they are quite beautiful. Telen's neck drips, Billy's shirt is wet, Sara can see hair through it.

They sit by the windows, waiting for Peter, they watch people walk by in the rain, they wince as though it stings their faces, they squint upward at the sky to verify its source. It is getting dark, the town is stained. Unevenly as litmus paper, pink stucco houses turn brown, chartreuse houses to khaki, gray houses to black.

Peter never arrives. At five-thirty, Sara goes into the bathroom and dabs her face with cold water. She excuses herself, it is time to go. Billy stands and kisses her hand as if he were a royal guardsman, to impress her or Telen, she cannot tell which.

SARA

"WANNA SEE A PLAY?"

"What do you mean?"

"A play, remember plays?"

"Yes, I do."

"How long has it been?"

"Forever."

"Is that a yes?"

"Why would I want to see a play?"

"Because for one thing it's been written by my long-lost cousin who's a sweetie but I can't vouch for her writing."

"So why me?"

"I think one of the actors might be quite good."

"Oh, dear."

"No, no, no, it's not like that."

"Yes, it is."

"Maybe it is. Anyhow, wanna come? It'll be a goof."

"What's it about?"

"It's just a one-act. A medical play about a heart transplant from a serial killer on death row, which ought to suit you just fine."

"I'll check with Elias, he may want to come."

"No, he won't, I'll pick you up at seven-thirty Saturday, we can eat later."

"Oh, no you don't, I'm not tagging along with you and your actor, thanks anyway."

When Sara comes to pick her up, she wears a loose black dress and heavy black shoes. Maude says, "What on earth have you got on?"

"Oh, this. Telen advised me when I come to the Group not to wear my foreign clothes. I stand out too much, they think I'm an imposter."

"You are, baby."

"Yes of course. So, why don't *you* change so no one'll recognize you, we'll sit in the back, don't worry."

Maude takes off her dress, puts on a T-shirt and jeans.

"Want an ice-cold martini for the road?"

"I do indeed."

"May I have one, too?" It is Doctor T. He has come out of the bedroom pinked from a long shower, a sharp creamy shave, he is wearing an open white shirt, tan slacks, black socks. A rolled magazine is in his hand.

"Yes, you may, Elias."

"Hello, Sara."

"Hello, Elias." He winces. Sara is the other person on earth who calls him by his middle name. It is a private endearment of Maude's. He has learned to accept Sara on her terms, not his. He believes it is Sara who has led Maude astray, to the brink of disaster. He goes to the kitchen area, drops ice cubes into the stainless steel shaker.

"It'll be fun," Sara calls out to Maude, "I swear to God, no worries tonight, Maude. Can we have fun?"

UNTOLD DAMAGE

IT IS IMPOSSIBLE to make the Actors Group Theater look gala. It will always be a converted auto body shop. Above the stage a dozen lighting instruments in plain sight are hung a couple of feet above the actors' heads. There is thrown-away furniture. Wherever a scene is set, a penthouse, a beach, the furniture screams *low rent!*

Maude and Sara take their contoured fiberglass seats in the back row, out of the lights. They want to watch the actors, they do not want to be watched by them.

Telen's play is the second of three. Sara is pleasantly surprised. Maude survives. The scene is well written. But it is anecdotal, lacks depth, "I've got good news and bad news. The heart transplant is a success, the heart is from a monster."

Maude smiles, the actor who plays Doctor Paulus is attractive, dynamic, energized. He talks to his patient too loudly, uses his stethoscope as a prop. But he is the more believable of the two, he is dynamic, ruthless, brilliant. The other actor has gone too far into his old-man makeup, he wears a gray wig and a gray moustache, resembles an English comedy buffoon. *But never mind, it's her first.* Sara congratulates Telen. "So good to have a relative in the theater, darling." She mimics an East Coast hostess.

It is a celebration. Telen has asked the Uncastables to supper and to listen to music somewhere. Telen invites Sara along, she calls her *cousine.* Sara feels good about sticking with them, learning about another side of town, a younger side, though she's not much past thirty herself. Maude is meeting Doctor T at ten for dinner and takes Sara's car. Billy will drive Sara home.

Outdoor cafés are everywhere, too close to speeding cars. The only pedestrians seen are homeless people.

It is also a celebration for Billy's first paid acting job, it came without warning, no audition, in and out, the part of roofer watching a house across the street being painted. A commercial, he has no lines, he cannot join the Screen Actors Guild. Art imitates life, Telen tells him. Billy and Peter work as part-time roofers for one of the actors at the Group.

Their waiter at Palms has stayed close to them since they entered the café and sat down, close as a cow-fly. He has introduced himself by his given name, Brice, with the promise of loyalty, possible friendship. He has gently removed Telen's napkin from her fingers and spread it across her knees. He has brought them citrus-smelling washcloths to make their hands smell like public toilets, he has recited the names of pastas. He has tried to shake their hands. Later he will come to them with the giant pepper mill.

"If the pepper mill is taller than you are, the food has gotta suck," Billy says. He knows, he was a waiter in a family Tuscan restaurant, freshly milled pepper on each table.

Sara laughs, *it's all so foreign*. She is glad she tagged along.

Brice is consulting Telen on the importance of ordering the Grand Marnier dessert soufflé now, so that it will be ready in time for dessert. He will shepherd them through this meal, he will be there for them, he seems to have the requirements of a true friend.

The obligation is too much for Billy, the debt to Brice.

"Let's get out of here," he says. "When it's this precious it's a boutique." They put the huge menus down and get to their feet.

"Tell me what you want," says the unending Brice.

"We want to go," Peter says.

Brice looks past them. Lasting friendship is no longer possible, out of the question. It is over. There will be no oversized pepper mill, no conglomerate pasta, no wine chat, no forty-five-minute soufflé. Brice has relied on their trust and they have violated it. He turns his head, averts his face, he has spoken his last word to them. What he does is delicate work, like nothing else. He will get over this but it will take time. If only one of them had dropped a few bills on the table it would not hurt quite so much. They will never meet again, if they do, Brice will cut them dead.

In the street they laugh him off like confetti.

"Wasn't he beautiful?"

"I can still feel the pressure."

"Will he be okay?"

"I feel awful, shouldn't we have left him something?"

"Yeah, you can tip a waiter forever but he'll never tip you back," Billy says.

But nothing is open except fast food labs and they do not

count so instead of eating dinner they eat chili rellenos and navy blue tortilla chips at Taxco's.

"All Mexican food is fast," Billy says. He is the emcee of the party, the evening depends on him for guidance. Telen and Peter would have submitted to Brice, Sara would have settled for a cab.

Later on at Picaroon's, Billy and Sara watch Peter and Telen dance slow on the small dance floor. They dance with clear plastic cups of wine held at arm's length on a dance floor at sea. They dance as if they were aboard a ship crossing the Atlantic in a gale, Peter rocking her slowly, bracing himself against the ship's roll, sometimes losing his balance. *Is the S.S.* Hollywood *sinking?*

All evening, Peter has advanced toward Telen, who is in slow retreat. Billy watches, outwardly content. He wonders if he really cares.

Sara dances with Billy. She is an older woman, maybe thirty-two or -three to his twenty-six. Dancing to the soft concussion and slap of the music, wine in their heads, Billy pressing against her, Sara feels his heat, his restive muscle. His jut. Her breathing deepens, her hands hold Billy's surprising shoulders up his back from behind. She wonders what Maude is doing.

Sara. Around her turn sunny, streaked blondes, the stealthy starving women dressed just in time, wearing whatever works for them right now. The men with good cars and heavy watches who dress like little boys.

It is wine-drunk out all night long. Celebratory. Sara drinks and worries about Maude, who is becoming strange. Peter has no friends except Billy. Together they watch Telen and Sara walk the walk to the ladies' room. From across the room the women emit radiance. Peter watches Telen: *Could I ever really love her?* Billy watches Sara: *Good ass.*

Finally, at two, the music thickens and stops. The four dancers dance out of Picaroon's like hooved animals on marble.

Peter and Telen drive back to her swirling apartment, she

senses possibilities, they are high and have everything. They lie down on her bed under the purple loom of the city. Peter is on his back, she opens his trousers pulls them down his length, kisses his penis. He never wakes up, he passes out on her closed bed.

Billy drives Sara home, parks under her building. She asks him up, they ride the grinding elevator to the third floor. He is the first man to enter her apartment since the trauma, Sara wonders if she will be all right. The wine has helped. From the refrigerator she brings out a chilled bottle of Bordeaux already open. Billy uncorks it with his teeth, blows the cork into a potted gardenia, pours wine into two very thin glasses. Without turning on lights, they dance to the songs of Cesare Evora, Sara's favorite, she sings in Portuguese, it does not matter what she says. It is whatever they want. Sara feels a deep gouging rush but in the crucial moments when she can feel every inch of his topography hard against her, suddenly she senses the blindfold on her face, Toyer somewhere in the room, his hands gently pulling her panties down her legs. Billy notices nothing. She will ask him to leave, she will say that it is too soon, that she does not know him well enough to go any further. She withdraws delicately to the kitchen area, switches on the white light. The evening is over. She will kiss him lightly, there will be an unspoken promise in it. In Connecticut and New York, this tacit agreement young men from eastern schools understand, they do not force their wills, they withdraw. But Sara has moved here from Connecticut and Connecticut game rules do not apply in Los Angeles. Billy is not from Connecticut or any eastern school, he has not heard of these rules, he is standing in the kitchen behind her, amazingly through her dress she feels his bare penis against her buttocks, the light is off again, he turns her to face him, presses her against the counter.

"Don't, Billy."

It is not the word *don't*, but how it is spoken. Billy enjoys hearing it spoken this way. *Don't*. As an entreaty, an understanding. To him it is a word like *maybe*, less used but slightly stronger. It is part of the evening. *Without the word* don't *there can be no seduction.*

Sara knows the old words, too: *don't, we shouldn't, please stop.* According to the shape of the night, they can mean *don't stop, we shouldn't stop, please don't stop.* Because she knows. By understanding tyranny she is controlling it. She is a woman in charge of her life and so she can enjoy being over-whelmed by a man. *Who else is there to do it to us?* It is nature, it is not for everyone. *The current gatekeepers of my species are bewildered, innocent, afraid, dead wrong.*

He swings her around and up in his arms, sets her on the kitchen counter, spreads her around him, enters her easily, she feels the wet heat of her vagina welcome him.

"Don't, Billy, please." *Don't stop, Billy, please.*

She is moving with him fully. She says *don't* rhythmically while he is doing it to her, it is a wonderfully young feeling.

Don't Billy don't Billy don't Billy, she moans through her bucking orgasm. It is Connecticut saying *don't* and Los Ange-les saying *yes.* It is good sex.

TOYER

HIS RESPONSE to Maude's public reproach finally comes on Tuesday, there is a letter for Sara Smith waiting in her box. It has been opened and taped closed. It was mailed from the post office near the Herald Building, which indicates he might have wanted to drop it off at the paper but decided not to take a chance. It is urgent. It catches O'Land and Sara Smith completely off guard.

Toyer writes her in strict confidence, *off the record;* he will do what he can to stop. He writes that he hates himself for doing what he has been doing. Maude is mentioned through-out, nine times. He calls her a lovely woman and a great force, he thanks her for giving over so much of her time and thought to him. He has hated causing her worry and hardship. He has been busy, he says, trying to write his book. It is personal. He signs it "*T.*" Intimate as an old friend. It may be true, Sara does not think so.

There is nothing in the letter that O'Land can use, it is off the record, out of respect for the future continuity he will only include it in the book when this is all over.

"All bets are on," O'Land says, whether he believes it or not. He calls Sara into his office, holds up a full-sized photo-copy of the front page at arm's length, the headline in 124-point boldface:

TOYER QUITS! CLAIMS HE'S CURED
CREDITS *HERALD* COUNSELING

Says Kipness Doctor
Altered His Perceptions

Could Leave Los Angeles Area—
Ten Victims Remain Unconscious

"You can't run that, Jim—"

"Thanks, Sara, I'm not. I'm just going to hold it for good luck."

When she reads it to Maude over the telephone, she tells her, "Whatever magic you were trying on him seems to be working."

"Bullshit. Off the record of course." Maude is shocked by his toadying. She says it doesn't make sense, she wonders what he is really saying. "If he gets past the next full moon without taking another victim, we might have done some-thing. And if we have, it'll be one for the textbooks."

BILLY WATERLAND

THE NEXT EVENING, parking cars, Billy meets his earliest demigod, Robert Hobbs, the star he has revered above all others since he was a boy, when he's told to park Hobbs's Rolls-Royce convertible at Lily Calloway's Bastille Day bash in Bel Aire. Hobbs, a bona fide movie star (*Wellington, Death Is Not Enough, Clarendon, Jake's Word*), has arrived with a long-sparred date wearing a teeny dress made of what appear to be mackerel scales. She is named Melissa Crewe and possesses a beauty so profound, so remote to Billy that he cannot place her chimera in any known category and imagines her descended from an endangered species of exotic antelope he's seen on television grazing the veldts of Africa.

He adjusts the driver's seat back an inch or two, *hmmm-m-m-m.* Melissa's arousing scent marks certain zones where her lovely hide has pressed into the car's dark blue leather seat beside him. Billy is aroused.

The metallic French blue hood reflects the stars. He cannot hear the motor. He drives the perfect car down Chalon Drive to the designated parking area, but instead of slowing and parking it, he cannot stop, gripped by a higher force, he keeps driving, driving down to Sunset Boulevard then right, along the miles of Sunset Boulevard to its terminus at the mild flat sea fifteen miles west. He hasn't examined his motive, it is simply a cool rush that feels right, a growing need to be alone with this car.

Whenever he slows to a stop, he is observed, he feels the explicit looks that gleaming women save for those few men they really want to look at. He feels the respect of men driving lesser cars who give way to him as he passes them on Sunset, lesser men who have not attained what Billy has. Men he has always resented, he now feels rapport with, compassion for.

Dire men. They stare at him as he drives by with the *who's that?* stare he himself has stared so many times. It is unimaginable to Billy that adoration can be thrown to him in so many different bouquets.

Billy parks on Pacific Coast Highway and stares out where the Pacific ought to be, the area without streetlights, his head a jumble of dreams brought on by the drive. He knows that it is temporary delusory insanity and that it feels fabulous. *I am a star.*

He longs for the distant love of headwaiters. To fall asleep in the arms of a rising starlet to the gurgling melody of his own pool filter. He imagines the special fear he imbues in his own sycophants. *My people.* The hidden resentment of have-nots. The awe of fans. *Fans must make great lovers,* Billy thinks. *Even bad room service must be good.* He wants the world to tongue his fundament in the name of love.

Billy is Robert Hobbs. It is so easy.

Driving back toward Beverly Hills, he takes a slower route, down the coast through a canyon, toward Santa Monica, he stops at a light and gives a girl in shorts a ride. Her name is Aurora. She asks him who he is. He gives her the name of a producer he held a car door open for earlier that evening, and he names a current film playing everywhere. They talk. He looks away and smiles successfully, tells her that with greed you know where you stand. She asks him to stop on a shaded street without overhead lamps not far from where she lives and when he parks the car, Aurora makes no move to open the door. Instead, she puts her hand high on Billy's leg.

"May I?"

"What?"

"Hold it."

Billy has not been aware that such a request can be made.

"Please," she says. "I just want to thank you, that's all."

Blinded, Billy looks away toward the moon, slim as a lemon's zest.

"For the ride," she says. "You don't have to let me if you don't want to."

"Of course," he is able to whisper, "of course." He permits himself a smile.

She opens the front of his pants with wonder, cradles what she finds within as if she has saved a baby bird fallen from a nest. She puts her cheek against his penis. It is as if this were the only known method to express thanks used by women too inexperienced to have developed other skills.

Billy stretches his stiffened legs against the pedals as she continues to thank him for giving her a ride. To reaffirm that he is not imagining what is happening to him, he glances down at Aurora's dancing hair with a dull stare of ecstasy.

The car-phone chirps, startling them both.

"I'm not taking calls," Billy says without opening his eyes. Above all he is an actor. Aurora does not lose her rhythm.

Before she leaves him, she writes her telephone number, on a crumpled paper napkin she finds in her purse, folds it and tucks it in his pocket. "Don't forget me," she says. She will come to him, anytime anywhere. She caresses the car door's dark veneer as she holds it open. She is a flake of ash, she does not exist, her life means nothing compared to his.

"I'll call, trust me."

Billy assumed that Robert Hobbs would linger at the party for at least two hours. He assumed wrong. As Hobbs entered Lily Calloway's Bastille Day party, he spotted his recent ex-wife, turned and immediately exited hand-in-hand with his creature. His Rolls-Royce was missing, could not be found, the stunned *maître* of Voiture Valet, Pancho, could offer no explanation except that one of his trusted employees was also missing.

Robert Hobbs made a scene that included the police. They reported his car stolen. For nearly two hours the eleven-million-plus-percentage movie star and his lady were stationed in the Lily Calloway parking lot, waiting for the police to locate his lacquered French blue convertible somewhere in the thousands of square miles that are Los Angeles, a county the size of Delaware.

At ten past eleven, Billy, in the stardust haze of borrowed splendor, drives into Lily Calloway's driveway. Parks, opens the car door, sees Melissa Crewe posed by a stand of rhododendrons. A well-groomed police officer in midnight-blue jodhpurs and black riding boots hails him, politely helps him with the car door, then at high speed slams him face down onto the pavement, locks his arms to his lower spine, frisks him for weaponry, clips handcuffs on his wrists. The ride is over.

The awesome Melissa Crewe stands close by gazing down upon Billy's vilification, her expression darting between resentment and amusement. Her hair has been cut to boot camp length, which makes her eyes appear massive. With his cheek pressed on the concrete, he is able to gaze up her antelope legs toward a pantyless heaven. She shifts her weight so exquisitely, he believes he can hear her thighs graze each other.

Now, while the handcuffed Billy lies pinned to the tiled parking area awaiting his fate, Robert Hobbs emerges from the house, he glances at Billy as if he were an extra who has ruined a scene, he inspects the car's twenty-four-coat lacquered surface for lacerations, as the impossible Melissa seats herself in the front seat chatting languidly, eyes nearly closed. From where he lies, Billy can smell her deeply placed scents.

The officer asks Hobbs if he wants to press charges.

Don't keep Melissa waiting, Robert, imagine the tensile strength in those slim thighs.

In a better mood following the inspection, Hobbs tells the officer to forget about it, he does not want to go down to the Beverly Hills Police Station, he has wasted enough of his time.

As he gets into his Rolls, he slams the door, Billy's boyhood idol looks directly at him, lying on the tiled driveway.

"As for jou, *bandito*, nes' time jou steal ma horse, I hang your *cojones* on a cactus."

Melissa laughs. It is a line from *O'Brien's Men*.

Suddenly, Billy is free to go. The handcuffs come off. Dirty and humiliated, he tosses his red valet jacket toward Pancho, who doesn't look at him, formally banishing Billy forever from Voiture Valet.

A few moments later Melissa Crewe has an idea. "Robert, please call Lily, stop that boy, have them press charges. Please. I'll be quick, just one photo for the *Times*." Hobbs calls the Calloway house just in time to have Billy detained. Lily calls her own press agent, it is the least she can do, and arranges to have a photographer meet them at the police precinct. It is a story.

Around 3:00 A.M., Billy reaches Peter in Silverlake, tells him where he is. The bail is a hundred and twenty dollars. On the drive home, Billy tells Peter about Robert Hobbs whom he describes with pained generosity and awe. Then in great detail, the celestial Melissa Crewe, who only wore one garment beside her heels, the tiny dress made of mackerel scales. Peter asks how Billy knew this. He is fascinated, he asks about her height, her lips, her breasts, her legs, her scent, her hair. Billy says he will have a chart made, he is entertaining. It is almost a routine.

About his outing, he comments, "You are definitely what you drive."

O'LAND

IN TOYER'S GOOD NAME, O'Land is now able to write to six New York book publishers whom he has chosen suggesting that they jointly publish a book of Toyer's crimes. En-

counters, as he now introduces the project to them, is to be narrated by Toyer, an autobiography edited by himself, one chapter devoted to each victim, now ten, including art, graphics, charts, maps. In each letter, he suggests that the six might need to form a consortium to publish a single book under a new banner, to remove any stigma from their houses.

The prime incentive for this project, he tells them, and the sole touch of dignity will be at Toyer's suggestion, that all net profits be transferred to the ten victims. The gross profits, O'-Land says, may tally in eight figures. They listen. "This is a proposal of a highly confidential nature. Please respect that confidentiality until that time when and if we may make a joint announcement." He adds that it is possible that this project could cause Toyer to reveal certain details about his life that might lead to his arrest.

The editors are incensed, O'Land's letter is shredded by one, balled up and tossed by another; what editor with self-esteem would agree to touch a manuscript by this grotesque creature?

When rumors of O'Land's proposal drift upward to various chairmen's offices, meetings are rescheduled, the matter is revived, seriously discussed, without O'Land's knowledge. When the initial outrage has expired, what is left standing is the framework of a sensible venture. The publishing houses, after all, are owned by vast corporations, and Toyer's offer is sound business. There is now real interest.

O'Land has provoked a second meeting by mid-July. In a week, O'Land flies to New York to meet with the editors in chief of the six publishing houses. Still, two publishers refuse to continue discussions and fall away. The four surviving publishers agree to his suggestion and form a consortium among themselves, to be named, simply, The Publishers' Consortium, risking no unnecessary public contempt.

The next day, the four publishers but not the *Herald* each agree to put up an even million-dollar advance payment guaranteeing that the book royalties will go toward the victims' medical expenses, a windfall for the victims' families. And one that the publishers are proud to give, in "true public spirit-edness," as their joint public relations representative tells the press. There is an additional paragraph appended to the contract, suggested by O'Land: subsequent film rights.

TELEN

Dear Mom,

Well here's my annual report. Sorry! I promise, I promise, I promise to write every month.

Well I am officially a playwright at last. I'm still with the Group I told you about and we put it on there. It went very well, full house. It's 25 minutes long. Enclosed is a copy. I'm writing two screenplays now but I need a job.

Remember that man Ghiseline married for about half an hour in the sixties? He married someone else later and had a daughter. She's a "famous" reporter because of Toyer. She named him!!! I wrote her a note and she called me back. Her name is Sara, she couldn't be nicer. I'd guess she's 35 or so. And I've enclosed one of her articles. She's thinking of doing a "Sunday piece" on our Group.

One of the guys in my play is called Peter Matson. I think I like him but it's all very innocent (!?!) between us. If you don't believe that, neither do I, but it's true. Didn't you tell me a good man is hard to find? I'm changing that to a good man might not even exist, and no, thank you very much, he's not gay. Stay tuned.

Love,
Telen

MELISSA CREWE

TEN FORTY-FIVE P.M., the outdoor parking lot of the Marina Shopping Mall.

As she is backing her new car out, she feels a slight thump, something unfamiliar, hears someone behind her car shout, thud the rear fender of her car. Immediately she brakes, cuts the motor, jumps out, faces the victim of her negligence. She is already devastated. There he is, a man lying on his side, his foot and calf on the pavement under her car, his other leg strangely warped. An ugly rip in his Blah-Blah labeled jeans and an abrasion on his palm give the calamity just the right tone. The word *lawsuit* whisks through her mind which is blank as she stands above the fallen, still partly attached to her car under her rear bumper.

"Hi," he says pleasantly. "Would you drive forward a few feet please, let me get myself up?"

"Oh, sure, sure, of course."

"Remember: Forward."

She does and gets out, comes to him again.

"Is that better?"

"I'm okay, I think, don't worry about me. Just my leg, I got another one." He smiles at his joke, she smiles.

She is frightened, of course, of looming claims; vengeance will come from her own insurance company. And the vast possibilities for the handicraft of his lawyers. But her legal fears are not all, she is sickened by her own carelessness. "Oh God, what have . . . are you all right, sir?"

Sir?

"I didn't even *see* you, honestly."

And I believe you, great wondrous creature, you were never meant to see me crouched behind your car, lying on the ground one leg slipped under your bumper, gently wedged against your tire.

He smiles up at her.

"What can I do?" She is radiant with uncertainty.

What a moment. Sexual in distress. Do?

He holds out his hand. *Oh, look, a self-inflicted abrasion here on my palm. Oooh.* She helps him up with a strong pull. He notices her thighs slightly tighten her skirt as she pulls, her half-visible breasts are taut. Tall, her height from long thighs and calves.

When he stands, his slicked down hair reminds her of someone. He smiles, she smiles. With one finger, he dusts his wound. His dark blue contact lenses itch. Tonight his hair is greasy, in sticky curls, trendy wetback, combed to the shape of his head. He leans against her car.

"May I see your driver's license? D'you mind?" A thrilling conversation starter. He sees her smile dissolve, a vague line appears above her eyes.

"You want my license number, don't you?"

"No. Not especially. You hardly hurt me at all."

"It's okay, you should have it."

He smiles nicely. "Look, I've fallen down before, but let me see it anyway. I think it's the law."

A small chained purse that costs more than his rent. She hands him her license.

"Nothing wrong with my leg I don't think, but I'll know better tomorrow." *Leave the hook in her mouth for tonight.*

Her license smells of good things created for women in labs. The photograph, unblemished by makeup, she was caught cleanly in the flash at the Department of Motor Vehicles, her face swept, her sheer beauty.

"Ooh, I *hate* that picture."

Will there ever be better ones for me to see?

"I just wanted to see how they photographed you." *He smiles up again. My age. Oh, my God, five-eleven.*

He smiles, returns it. "It's all my fault."

She wants to hug him.

Finding Melissa has been simple. She was a dancer with L.A. Danceworks, interpretive dance. Now she supports herself modeling, acting in TV commercials. He knows her agency, her union, her Social Security number. She owes big credit card money. In a pinch she borrows money from certain men she dates. He knows her address, the Capistrano at the Marina. A single woman with a biography of sentences in gossip columns where sometimes her name is not the one in bold print. Famous for entering galas on the arm of fame. Melissa Crewe, a one-night stand to the gods.

Easy.

"I *will* let you buy me a cup of coffee if they have a decent one at that café over there."

"Of course, I'd love to," she says. *Is he hitting on me or is he gay?*

She is exhilarated from her narrow escape, the shock of running him over has passed, it is in the aftershock, the consequence, that she begins to wonder about.

They cross the parking lot, he limps a simple limp. *Do not touch her.*

His story is told in his boneless posture, his loose clothes, his trendy hair shiny as street-rain, his 1920s-style glasses. *His voice is easy to take. A nice guy.*

It is a one-room espresso/pastry café with two tables outside lit like a drugstore called Forget-About-It. They sit alone under an umbrella, facing the dangerous parking lot. The counter girl comes out, she is young, haggard, she says, "I'm Allison. I can make you guys a great mozzarella and Gorgonzola burger."

"No, thanks," they say it nearly together, "no meat." They laugh. She touches his arm to corroborate, looks at him.

"I truly believe my body is my temple."

And I have come to worship in it.

She looks up at Allison, "No food, but thanks." She wants the waitress not to hate her. Women hate her on sight, it is so easy for women to hate Melissa's category, she tries to control it. Allison has no attitude.

"What do you guys want to drink?" *Melissa is not a guy.*

Allison shifts her weight, she is from Portland, Oregon. *I have nothing but talent, I've played fucking* Elektra, *the entire fucking* Doll's House, *I am rehearsing* Threepenny, *and I am actually standing here serving this bimbo. I am Allison Anders, who the fuck are you?*

"Decaf cappuccino, please."

"And you, sir?"

He sighs, hands her the menu. "Café Americano, I guess." *It is not on the menu.*

"You mean American coffee," Allison corrects.

"No, Allison, café Americano," he says patiently. "It's an entirely different thing. But never mind, no problemo."

Melissa admires refinements she has never heard of.

"Please tell me, I'll try to make it, okay?"

He smiles, trying to remember, "Espresso steamed milk brandy triple-sec white crème de cacao with a mantle of chilled cream." *He says it too quickly, victory is his.*

Allison looks stunned, now she hates both of them. *Impressing his no-talent date, the beauty contest winner.*

"No, wait." Melissa smiles up at Allison. "Why not just have what I'm having?" *The thread that binds women against men draws tight for an instant.*

"Why not?" he says. "Just make me a plain old cappuccino loaded with caffeine, thanks."

"Pastry?" *She is playing the part of Rude Waitress.*

"No pastry."

Allison is gone. They are alone.

"I'm Melissa Crewe."

"Beautiful name. I'm Mark Cunard." *Mark or Scott.*

"Oh, is that like the ship line?"

"That's what my father tells me."

Melissa relaxes noticeably.

"Haven't I seen your picture someplace?"

Melissa glows. "I'm in *Us* magazine, they did something on me last month."

"What?"

"Stockings." She pooches her lips.

Do not touch her leg under the table.

"I know what you're thinking," he says.

"What am I thinking?"

"You're thinking: Is Mark Cunard going to go home tonight and discover that he's seriously injured his leg and call his lawyer tomorrow?"

"Wrong." She pauses prettily. "Well . . . are you?"

"No, he's my father's lawyer and I'd never call him about anything, I'm sick of being told that I'm stupid for doing the right thing."

"Which is—?"

"Which is admitting you're wrong when you're wrong. It was a dumb place for me to be standing, I saw your backing lights. You back up real fast, by the way."

He studies her eyes. Neither notices that Allison has brought them glasses of ice water.

"Sure, my leg hurts a little."

She looks at his leg. *Touch it.* She notices the rip in his pants. "Where did you get those jeans?"

"Carrol's." A Beverly Hills store he has never entered. "Why?"

"Because I want to replace them, if you'll let me. I'll need your size, Mark."

I'll give you my size.

Usually Mark is not attracted to women whose hair is shorter than his. But it is her neat English schoolboy part that makes her antelope eyes seem huge. He stares into them, falling forward.

"Thirty-four, long."

Her eyes are wide-set, the way prey animals' eyes are wide-set, the eyes of animals who must always notice who is sneaking up behind them. As he looks into them he becomes aware that no one seems to be driving Melissa tonight. *Have they been looked at so much they no longer see?*

"Thirty-four long," she repeats. *An erotic size.*

Mark's eyes are set closer together, aiming straight ahead. Predator eyes, seen on animals who don't give a damn who's sneaking up behind them.

"I like your hair," he says. *What's left of it.*

She thanks him, "Everyone told me I was an idiot of course." She touches the back of his hand briefly.

Do not touch her.

He does not know what to add, so he tells her about last month traveling aboard *Queen Elizabeth 2*, the gala night, the Captain's Ball, days at sea, star-crowded nights. Her thighs sigh keenly as she crosses them under the table again and again, listening.

He asks about her ambitions. She tells him that someone has promised her an audition test for an **eight**-hour cable movie version of *Justine*.

"Isn't that a famous book?"

"Yes, Lawrence Durrell, I've been *reading* it. I'm up for the part of Melissa. Nice coincidence."

She tells him that if her career doesn't work out she can always become a Scientologist.

"Why would you . . ."

"Protection."

He doesn't know what to say to that.

After sitting with her for half an hour, listening to her thighs being recrossed eight times, he remains overwhelmed, even though he has seen the entire contents of her head spill out into the espresso spoon beside his cup.

Almost time.

Again he feels the friendly movement in his groin. He wants to guide her long-fingered hand under the table inside his jeans while he tells her about his investments. He leaves her hand where it is. He has not located her sense of humor.

"Is that going to be all? We're closing." Allison Anders is

back, her charisma revived for the tip. "Have a nice evening, I mean it." *I'm sure you'll get in there, studdo.* She places the check beside his hand, on it are two mints wrapped in foil. A procedure.

"My treat," Melissa says, her cool fingers over his. "Please, may I?" He surrenders the check.

"Let me do that." The tip. He tucks a ten-dollar bill under the check.

"Oh, no, not for her, that's too much." *She hates Allison.*

"Okay." Mark shrugs nicely, substitutes a dollar bill.

He'll give the ten to the poor. He's careless with money, a curable illness.

Melissa looks up. The overhead café lights fuse briefly, click off and on. A dizziness passes through her. It's taken twenty minutes.

"You okay, Melissa?"

"Sure, I'm okay."

She is not okay. What she feels is a cool run of nausea behind her throat. She stands, willowy, then sits.

"Allison, can you bring us a glass of soda water." To Melissa he says, "It'll help, believe me. All this excitement."

I gotta get you home and out of those pesky clothes.

"Are you well enough to drive?"

She gazes dreamily at him, chin on palms, a lover's gaze, while they wait for the soda water.

"How far do you live?"

"Not far. Capistrano."

"Well, let me drive you home?"

She nods. *She's not thinking well at all.*

"Let's take your car, leave mine here."

Finally he touches her, steadying her arm as she walks on stilts though the parking lot.

The interior of Melissa Crewe's condominium at the Capistrano: glass, leather, chrome, no loose fabric, vanity magazines, few personal objects in sight, and those seen look out of place, primitive stone sculptures. A whitened animal horn. Gifts. The pictures hung are chilly visions of herself. No mess.

Furnished in an hour by a design store expert with a close-out sale on black and silver. Death is everywhere.

A black kitchen. Shining.

Without a word, Melissa lies flat on the black sofa, her pelvis risen slightly above her thighs and stomach. One shoe falls off. "Please don't think I'm being rude." She mumbles. She closes her eyes.

The telephone chirps. She can barely reach it, so he holds it to her lips. He can hear a male voice inquiring how she has been then where she has been. She tells the male voice, *To a movie, alone.* The male voice questions her. "Well, do I have to tell you the plot?" She tells him she wants to go to bed, she is dead tired.

He continues to hold the telephone for her. She must swear again to the voice who is now Bob that she had been alone all evening. *Bob doesn't trust her.* She says goodnight, huskily. When he hangs up the telephone, he clicks the chirper onto *Off.* She closes her eyes again. He stares at her, lying blindly below him.

"I'm sorry Mark. You've been so nice, would you excuse me?" *Meaning: Leave.* "I just need to close my eyes for half a minute."

She has lain on her back again, a hand across her stomach a hand behind her head, her head on a cushion, and she turns, her legs touching the flat end of the sofa, ankles uncrossed, frankly. The other shoe drops.

He reaches down and carefully raises her skirt. He stands looking down her length for several minutes, his right hand deep inside his pants pocket, her panties are white, tiny. He takes a coin from his pocket and tosses it up and catches it. Again and again.

"Heads or tails, Melissa."

She wakes, turns her head slightly. Eyes open, half asleep, lying in a lush pink membrane crowded with pillows. Her tongue touches her lips, wetting them.

She finds him with her eyes far far above her, smiles a silly smile.

"Heads." *A game?*

"It's bedtime, Melissa."

"Is it?"

She stirs.

"I'll do what you want me to do, Mark."

"It's time to undress, Melissa," he tells her quietly.

O'LAND

ONE-OH-FOUR A.M. The detritus of journalism. Fat soft pencils. Smudges. Round metal wastebaskets stuffed with paper. The smell of rust. Sara sits in O'Land's office watching him proof the giant photocopy of the front page just before he rolls the presses. On the makeup table, national weeklies are fanned out, extinct headlines abound (*I Have Toyer's Baby*), nonsense pieces (*Schoolmate Reveals Toyer Sex Change*), jumbled fiction (*Is AIDS Toyer Gay?*). Sara watches Jim as one watches a star, waiting to see what he will do next. Tonight she is tired of anything that has to do with Toyer. He is not, his eyes dart quick as a rare bird's looking for bugs among the paragraphs. There is always the possibility of a smile. He folds the proof and drops it into the metal wastebasket. Without looking at his watch, he leans back in his chair, reaches behind him, presses a brass button on the wall. Sara waits to hear the firebell below them muffled by stone walls. There it is. He has switched the presses on under the building. The lights in the office dim briefly, the cylinders are rolling, the entire second story of the building trembles. To O'Land, this remains a thrilling ritual, however diminished by time. She watches the surface of his coffee come alive.

Below them bands of wet ink printed on paper have begun to stream by in a gray blur, a million words. Men in earmufflers stand by, adjusting the darkness of the flow, the sweet smell of printer's ink. The vast turbines resemble a massive ship's engine room in full swing from the era of great turbine-driven ocean liners.

Sara watches him enjoy the moment. They sit in his desolated office where only the walls are old. Nothing except the brass button's burnished escutcheon on the wall has remained here long enough to age. The bell that was used to roll the presses for the bannerlines WAR WITH GERMANY DECLARED, VICTORY!, and, on April 14, 1912, the day after she sank: TITANIC IS SINKING AT SEA.

They have just finished reading Maude's third article written directly to Toyer. Between them, tall as a samson post on a dock, stands a liter bottle of Paddy, the blue-collar Irish whiskey that O'Land cherishes above all others. It is a rare bottle, unobtainable in America. Sara has tinted her soda water with whiskey, O'Land savors his whiskey neat, both drink without ice. Outside the grubby window the mist has turned to rain. It is a good moment.

The *Herald*'s circulation now stands at a steady million-and-a-quarter, subscriptions have doubled, the *Times*'s circulation has not risen back over a million since Toyer started writing for the *Herald. Amazing stuff.* Jim O'Land knows that he has beaten television, too. It stands begging him for his releases, trying to film appetizers without meals, certified glibs. *How about Sara Smith? Her thoughts? No thanks.* Once again, it is a nation of journalism, the flash thrill of folding open the morning newspaper with coffee and toast, a black-and-white land of words. *Hooray! The presses are rolling again, look out!*

How can television's vast teaspoons compete with printed text? Somehow without pictures. Toyer may be its very favorite news anecdote, but television does not have a clue where to set up a camera or send a remote crew to cover his story. Because there is none. Television is pictures and there are no pictures. Toyer is internal, in people's imaginations, in their dreams, where television cannot go. He haunts them. The public has rejected television and taken an eager step backward to an earlier era.

There is a solid dark pocket of citizens who admire Toyer for the respect he gives police, women, themselves. They are awed by his finesse. He is Zorro, Robin Hood, he is a mythic character and the public cannot ever be without these characters to amuse them, to lull them to sleep. It is a wide country.

And Toyer understands the vast public's Schadenfreude, a word unique to the German language that salutes the feeling of well-being human beings get from the tragedy of others.

Jim raises his gray-shaded glass and toasts Sara. "Here's to you, Sara Smith, for keeping the story with us. That was a great piece of newspaper work."

She has finally been accepted by him. She smiles and sips, feels herself ready to cry. It is morning. They will go home now, not together.

Earlier today, Jim agreed that the Publishers' Consortium publishing plan, still secret, will be to run off an unprecedented first printing for the North American edition of Toyer's book of two million copies. Overwhelming, unprecedented. The book's list price will be twenty-five dollars, the author's royalty to be twenty percent, ten million dollars from the first press run. There will be paperback income when the first run is sold out. Translations are proposed in eleven languages. It is to be designated a double credit by the Book-of-the-Month Club. This has been planned between Jim O'Land, Sara Smith, three men, a woman, and eight assistants, all sworn to silence.

The desk telephone jolts them, Sara is closer, she picks it up. It is the news desk. *A woman has been found.*

"Okay, Richard." She puts the phone down.

O'Land knows, he says, "I can guess."

THE UNCASTABLES

BILLY HAS NOT BEEN AROUND, he was not at the Group today. Whenever Peter calls him, he makes excuses.

Saturday morning they are surprised to see him come into Ruben's. He is thin, he says his hair hurts, he looks as if he has been crying. He does not speak sentences, he poses. Peter is enjoying the performance, *The Athlete Dying Young*. "You want to talk about it?"

Billy opens the *Herald* and drops it flat on the table, the front page open, above the bannerline:

Toyer's Eleventh Victim Found
See Sara Smith Page 3

It is Melissa Crewe, Robert Hobbs's sometime escort.

Billy points. He cannot speak. Telen takes his hand, he sits, taps the newspaper. "That's her." He chokes, says it several times. "She's the one I told you about, remember?" He puts his hand on Telen's shoulder. "Gone."

"Are you running a fever, Billy?"

He wipes his face with a paper napkin, starts to say something in a whisper then stops, puts his hand over his eyes. No one speaks. He turns his palms out. *"Why?"* Now he is the man on TV, standing beside the ashes of his burnt home wherein his family has been recently cremated. His fingernails are black. He is someone who has lost everything.

"Jesus, I'm sorry, I didn't know. I didn't see the news." Peter stands, brings Billy down beside him. Peter is pale, he seems sickened. "She was perfect, wasn't she?"

The *Herald* article lists some of Melissa's escorts. She got around, it says, was sincere in her ambition. Now it is over. A

couple of laughs, some small parts, a few good photographs.
Two are reprinted, one candid, taken at Cannes by J. Brizard,
the other a low-angle shot by Helmut Newton in a suite at the
Sherry-Netherland.

"I will definitely kill him," Billy says, as he wipes his
eyes. Peter feels Billy trembling, there is no doubt. This
morning in Ruben's Billy looks as if he would attack Toyer
with a dinner fork, anything. Telen will remember this morning as the beginning of his obsession with Toyer. Not a day
will pass from now on without Billy bringing the name up in
conversation.

He asks if they have been working, hoping they will say no.
They do. Billy smiles. The Uncastables have been reunited for
the moment.

TOYER

MAUDE KNEW he would not quit.
     A coyote trots from the gloom into the pool of
golden light from the streetlamp, back into the gloom, it trots
toward the front of Maude's house, checks out the tiny yard,
lifts its muzzle to the air. Waits.

Maude's disappointment is severe, she knows there is no
mental disorder like his. She has never read a book, she has
learned nothing, what she knows is false. She feels naked,
feels her bones pushing through her flesh.

Maude knew about Melissa Crewe first, twenty minutes before O'Land. Chleo telephoned her at home. There was nothing she could do. By the time she called Sara Smith who was
sitting in O'Land's office, they had already heard.

The coyote spots Jimmy G lying along the windowframe,
he stands breathlessly for an instant, staring.

Maude gets dressed, slips out of the house, drives over to the hospital to meet Melissa. Later, she drives down to O'-Land's office. Melissa Crewe hurts her deeply, taunts her, makes her efforts feel embarrassing.

"So as of this morning, Mr. O'Land, your beloved Toyer is taking credit for eleven women. He's back on a roll, what do you think, just getting up to speed again?"

"Don't blame me."

"God forbid, what if he slowed down? Or even stopped?"

Sara looks up, "Maude, don't, we all tried."

"But if he did, wouldn't the *Times* bury you?"

O'Land looks weary. "We all thought he quit. I even bet on it."

Sara says, "Jim found a Vegas bookie who sets odds on him."

"I'm glad you could show a profit. I won't worry."

"I lost." O'Land barely smiles. "Maude, I'm truly sorry for you, but I've got a hundred thousand words to get out."

"If I only read your paper, I'd never see any good in mankind."

"It's a big busy world out there, your Toyer's just one of many."

Sara looks at her. "Maude, you and I have got to keep trying to get to him ourselves, somehow. Maybe that's the best thing for your peace of mind."

"Maybe."

"I've got to go." Sara excuses herself. O'Land and Maude are alone.

"It can't go on like this."

"Well, he can't either, Maude, there's gotta be a break in it somewhere. You look terrible."

Maude starts to go.

"Would a drink help?"

"It certainly would."

While O'Land is bringing out the Paddy he says, "Can you wait an hour? I'll buy you dinner."

MAUDE

THAT NIGHT Maude's telephone rings, it is late, she has
fallen at last into fathomless sleep. She allows it to ring six
or eight times without knowing where she is, unable to reach
for it. When she does pick it up, she raises her head, propped
up on one arm, she knows where she is, who she is. She feels
the familiar late-night fear; it can only be the hospital. She listens without speaking.

"Maude?" It is an alert male voice, intimate, sonorous.

"Yes?" she says thickly.

"I'm sorry about Melissa, I really am" is what the voice
says before the phone clicks and the sound is a hum.

*All night long she hears his voice; I really am! I really am! I
really am!* It plays inside her head like rock music.

MEYERSON

AN 8x11 ENVELOPE on his desk, no return address. He
opens it. A photograph, the face of a pale woman asleep.
Melissa Crewe.

Written on the back of the picture:

July 26

Bob,

Here's a new face to hang in your office. I know we're all
getting used to it, but isn't she beautiful? I took this portrait
of Melissa yesterday.

She's number eleven by the way. But who's counting?

Maude

"Ciel, please get me Mrs. Kipness."

"She's already dismissed Doctor Garance from the Kipness."

"Can anyone stop this woman?"

"Legally, sir?"

TOYER

HE WRITES on a stolen word processor. It is the color of the dusky morning sky, the size of a science book, it snaps shut like a purse. Last year, on foot, taking a shortcut, he spotted it on the floor of an open convertible in the parking lot behind Le Dome. The attendant had turned the other way. In one motion, he reached in the car, walking in stride, swiped it up over the door, it was his. At home he erased its boring contents, columns of prices, and made it his own.

He hides it in a sixteen-inch space, slid between two wall studs inside the wall of his apartment. No one who visits him knows he owns a word processor.

Now, alone, stoked with word-generating espresso, he types. He puts his finished letter in a yellow envelope and for the first time, using his left hand, he addresses it to the *Herald* in large child's letters.

Two days after Sara's straight coverage, O'Land runs Toyer's unedited account of his encounter with Melissa Crewe, exactly as he wrote it to Sara. It has the mindlessness of a girlish diary, casual as coffee shop chat.

If that's what it takes. It is picked up by 1,958 syndicated outlets, the first money to be put aside for the Toyer Victims' Fund.

Toyer's Eleventh
Melissa Crewe
His Own Account

Special to the *Los Angeles Herald*. The following account is the complete text of a letter received by the *Herald* yesterday. It is written by the unapprehended felon known as Toyer. It is his account of the encounter with Melissa Crewe last Wednesday. Crewe was found in her Marina Del Rey condominium early Thursday morning, following telephone notification to the Los Angeles Police by Toyer. She is his eleventh victim and like the ten previous women, a victim of cervical cordotomy.

LOS ANGELES. July 26, 11:00 A.M.
I wake up this morning wearing socks and a shirt. I go to the mirror and check myself out. I can't figure out why I'm wearing socks and a shirt. I look at myself in the mirror. I can't for the life of me remember what I did last night. I smell my shirt. It smells sort of like lemon furniture polish only better. It's driving me crazy not knowing. I don't do drugs. Or do I? I can't remember so I take a shower. When I come out I feel better. But I'm still wondering. Then I see my pants, scrunched up under a chair. Dark spots all over them. Dry spots. The knees are covered. Pants are ruined. Suddenly I remember. Melissa Crewe. Then it all comes back.

The Marina, the high-class apartment, washing my fingers, the parking lot, driving back, the sunrise. I remember calling the police from her place right away. I throw up in her wastebasket. Is she going to live? I'm no murderer. I go out and buy a newspaper. She's going to be okay. She was different from the others. She's a big strong girl. When I first saw her she looked sort of like a big-eyed fairy, tall and thin. She's very beautiful sort of like a high jumper and I know she still is. The picture of her in your paper is the one I saw on her bedroom wall. I feel terrible this morning. Can't understand right now why I even did it in the first place. I remember my anger but not why I was angry. It's almost like I made the whole thing up but there it is in the paper. So I won't write any more about her until I have a chance to figure it all out.

It is signed *Toyer*.

"Maybe he'll slip one day and sign his last name," Jim says.

"And his unlisted number," Sara says.

Toyer's back. The *Herald*'s lost sheep return, they must buy the newspaper, they have no choice. There is no place to land a TV news helicopter. The *Herald* readers are over the moon.

MAUDE

SHE CANNOT SLEEP. She opens a can of tuna fish and divides it with Jimmy G.

The telephone rings.

She waits for her answering machine to speak. After the squee she hears the voice. "Hello, sweetie, I know you're there. Pick it up." It is Sara. "You'll never guess who just called." She picks up.

"Yes I can, he just called me. He sounded drunk."

"So you know."

"No, go ahead tell me."

"About the scalpel."

Scalpel. Maude feels her face pale, does not answer.

"Didn't you read about the scalpel they found at the beach last month, remember? The homeless man?"

"The scalpel—yes?"

"Well, he told me it was yours."

"Mine?" She breathes in and out, "Honey, I don't use a scalpel."

"I didn't think so, so why call me and say it's yours?"

"Who knows? He didn't mention it to me."

"What did you two talk about?"

"We were trying to decide on a movie, he's seen everything I want to see."

"Maude . . ."

"He called me to apologize."

"As usual."

"Well, he did it again. I hung up on him."

"*Why?*"

"Just an irrational response. I shouldn't have. That may be why he called you."

"I feel contaminated hearing his voice, it doesn't go away."

"I know."

"You okay?"

"Yeah."

"You want company?"

"No, thanks, I think I'll call it quits."

While she has been talking, she has been undressing, dropping clothes, when she hangs up she is naked, the telephone rings again, it is Dr. T.

"The line's been busy."

"Uh-huh."

"So late."

"Talking to Sara."

"I've got to see you."

"He just called me, too, Elias, I know what he told you."

"You do?"

"Yes, your scalpel."

"That's what he told me again, that it was my scalpel the

police found on the beach. My missing scalpel. Is that what he's saying?"

"Yup."

"Is he the one who called me before?"

"Yup."

"Why does he do it?"

"He's just doing what he does best."

TOYER

BY SOME OCCULT CONTRACT, *Time* and *Newsweek* run Toyer covers. It is the thing to do. He has made a comeback, he is for real, he has longevity, he is worth reading about.

Time's portrait is painted in the style of the late Francis Bacon; a torn man in tatters wearing a Punchinello mask. *Stylish dementia.*

Newsweek's cover shows an imagined photograph of him rendered in byte-square-shaped question marks. *Stylish cleverness.*

60 Minutes wins the right to film a docu-essay. Faceless. Cold, hard. *Stylish immediacy.*

In London, a thriller-to-be in the West End. *Stylish theater.*

A Hollywood studio's guarantee surpasses the ten-million-dollar mark. *Stylish commerce.*

In the East Village, a punk bar, Toyer's Toys. *Stylish punk.*

It is his openness, his mystery, his charity, his forthcoming book, his perfect danger. O'Land will call the *New York Times.* He is news that's fit to print.

MELISSA

BUT THERE HAS BEEN a problem with Melissa Crewe. Everything is all wrong about her, everything is different from the ten other victims. The coroner, who was brought in again by mistake, determined that she has fought like a bronc, and it is obvious. She was nearly equal to her adversary, District Attorney Yellen suggests.

There is no fist-heel print on the bedroom window. There is blood. For the first time. A pattern of arterial splattering on the wall above the bed; a subtle Jackson Pollock, more subdued. Expensive art. Not even the ceiling is left unmarked, residue blood has drifted in a fine mist onto the mirror. She is alive only because Toyer made an unprecedented call from Melissa's bedroom and spoke directly to the police operator.

The differences are so distinct that the police doubt it is the work of Toyer. There is real concern that some moron is imitating him.

Is this another copycat Toyer? He has always left his fist pommel mark high on a bedroom window to identify each victim as his. But here there is no mark. His ego demands an anonymous signature.

Listening to Melissa Crewe's answering machine, an alert detective has placed the times of the calls and realized that Melissa came home and made two drinks without hearing her messages. Would that suggest that she was with someone more important to her than her callers? Or someone she did not want to have hear her messages? Either way, her messages are still waiting for her.

Then, that afternoon, a sigh from the investigators, *all's well*. A detective dusts a partial fist mark on the elevator mirror, high, as if Toyer had rushed, been rattled, forgotten to leave it in Melissa's apartment, maybe in panic. It matches. It is Toyer, after all, the mark confirms that Melissa is his victim. But it answers only one question. It does not explain the bloody struggle.

On the fist print a trace of blood, not Melissa's. For the first time Toyer has been cut. Now the police have his blood group, AB, for whatever use they may find for it.

At the hospital just before dawn when she first sees her, Maude is overwhelmed by Melissa's beauty. The languid long-legged doll that lies draped in the hospital shift was part of the *beau monde* earlier in the evening. Maude parts Melissa's hair with her own pocket comb. She plays her *Songs from the Auvergne* until she can play Melissa's favorites.

In the morning, Sara's story in the family edition comes out bearing a headline heavy as car parts: *BLOODSTORM*. It is immediately transmitted via satellite to all news agencies, translated into dozens of languages. Into German: *Bludenkrieg!* The word *bloodstorm* will stick to Toyer, will now become part of the legend.

With Melissa's professional portfolio, the print media finally have la crème de la crème of super model photographs to choose from, better than all the first ten victims combined. The *Star Weekly* will bid against the *Enquirer* to publish a sensual but tasteful nude layout by a French photographer whom Melissa posed for three years earlier in *Oui*. It will make a handsome package.

O'LAND

ALL THE NEWS *that's fit to print?*
It is the focus of a hurried conference call between O'-Land and several editors in New York. O'Land has cornered the *New York Times* into a meeting by using its own definition

of news fit to print, it is a good question. Manfred Koch, the *Times*'s executive editor, who respects O'Land, answers: "If we run this Toyer stuff now, Jim, when's it going to stop, where's it going?"

O'Land says, "I dunno, no one does. Why not run it at the bottom of National News, page thirteen or so."

"Because people will read it there." Koch does not add, *Our newspapers are different.* "Bad taste, Jim, he's just not going to force us to fulfill his needs. It's dirty stuff. Not a question of whether his accounts of how he spends his evenings is news fit to print, but whether it's news at all. And it just ain't."

The meeting ends.

It is later that afternoon in New York, that William Speare, the *New York Times*'s publisher, calls Manfred Koch into his upstairs office. Speare has heard from Dunc Whiteside, his liability lawyer, who has told him that if there is to be compensation paid by the Toyer stories to the victims and if the *Times* does not agree to publish them, it may be held liable for withholding due livelihood compensation from them.

It is a windy season in New York and oddly enough, Senator Greenwald has also telephoned Speare. "It's a very real consideration, Bill, and one you would do well to acknowledge."

Speare speaks to Koch of the newspaper's duty.

"Rubbish," Koch says.

"Of course it's rubbish, Manny," Speare agrees.

"And legally, it's simply not so."

"Maybe. But don't be too sure, have you seen the current crop of attack lawyers?"

"What about all the other stories we don't publish that may cause suffering?"

"Unlike any other story." In overriding Koch's decision, Speare says that the Toyer story is unprecedented and so strange that no rules apply, that it is a huge pitfall. They have no choice but to cooperate with the *Herald* and print Toyer's future accounts.

Koch slams out. In an hour, after taking refreshment at Daly's Grill, he slams back in and is now seated at his desk putting out the early edition.

In Los Angeles, Jim O'Land, still in the dark about Speare's decision, dictates an editorial, *Is Toyer news fit to print?*

There will be no surprises. Tomorrow, readers will whack back their answers in immediate harmony, "More!"

Of course they want more.

BILLY

NO ONE SEES BILLY ANYMORE, he has gone underground again. He needs a tether, Telen says. Ten days, he has not come to the Group. The two Uncastables remember that the last time they saw their third member, he was too quiet, pale, he seemed drugged, needed a shave. He calls himself a freelance roofer like Peter but Peter has not seen him on the job. Now he has missed two sessions and Peter cannot reach him, his telephone is disconnected. When Peter knocks on his door, he can hear a television churning inside, Billy does not answer.

He lives in old Hollywood, 1920s stucco sliced up, there is no sun but a glare so powerful it makes Peter squint. A sullen man who slices smoked fish and meat at Horowitz's Discount Deli, David Horowitz, certifies Billy's mortality, assures Peter that the person he describes comes in for smokefish, lox, pastrami, scraps for his cat.

"But he doesn't have a cat, cats ignore him."

"Cats ignore everyone." David Horowitz shrugs. "So whaddaya want, he told me he was a stand-up comic with nowhere to stand up. Whaddaya having?"

Peter tells him he would like to order what Billy eats.

"Try the pastrami."

Peter orders a pastrami sandwich.

"What else?" David Horowitz asks.

"Mustard."

"What else?"

There's more? Peter leans over the counter. "What is gefilte fish?"

"*Gefilte.* If you have to ask, you shouldn't take it. Take the lox."

"Okay." He will bring it to Billy. Horowitz tells him Billy has stopped shaving.

"You want a pickle with the pastrami?"

"Okay."

"You want seltzer?"

"A what?"

"Seltzer," David Horowitz says, then he adds, "club soda."

"No, thanks." Peter feels blond.

Billy has given up trying to find an agent. He says that Hollywood acting is not a noble profession. He lives well on very little. He owns a black-and-white television set. There is the Grand Central Market downtown that sells day-old loaves of bread for a quarter. He has applied for his unemployment insurance, standing in a palm-shaded line, but now his check is delivered biweekly to his mailbox. It is easy to quit.

The shades are drawn. When Peter has gone, Billy will find the pastrami sandwich wrapped in aluminum foil outside his door.

Once at Ruben's he told them that his dream was to be interviewed by interviewers who regard him as sacred. Telen told him her dream, that she wanted to share her recipes in *Cosmopolitan,* reveal her beauty secrets in *Vogue,* read lies about her sex life in the *Star.* Her laugh was delicious, she was mocking him.

Billy does not bother to dress anymore. He lives like an Egyptian fellah, wearing secondhand pajamas from the Goodwill Store on Santa Monica Boulevard. He may curl up snug and die in the pink stucco studio on Lime Street just the way an earlier tenant did years before in the 1930s, an unknown actor who carved his initials in the bathroom door and needed to carve a star above them. The days are almost too bright to see pain. While his laundry tumbles next door, Billy tries to invent his next step.

TOYER

HE NEEDS to see Melissa. *What is it about her?*
The hospital is calm, it is after hours, lag tide, patients are being readied for the long night, calculations of their disillusion are being made.

He wears his slightly spattered white coat, enters Admissions, walks through the swirling corridors, carries a clipboard, pen, stethoscope, rides the elevator to the sixth floor. He is in the back of the elevator making space for an empty gurney when he realizes it might be Maude's back he is looking at. He reaches out and touches her hair so gently she does not know it. Abruptly he dislikes her, sees her for what she is, his mortal enemy. The woman who tried to slash his throat. The elevator stops on Three, she gets out, turns right, he continues to Six, turns left. Intuitively he finds Melissa's room.

He stands at the foot of her bed. She has gained weight. She is posed more elegantly than the others, propped up in bed beside a bouquet of dried wildflowers, the kind sometimes seen in graveyards.

They are alone. There is music playing in the room, pale sounds. He studies her beauty. Her eyes have vapid clarity. He touches her arm. It is like furniture, the arm of a chair. Then her cheek. No one comes to her room. They are alone. He feels a stirring in his groin, a sexual impulse. Minutes pass.

The music comes from a CD player on her bedtable close to her ear. Beguiling music, Arabic in style. He bends over the machine and removes the disk, reads the title, puts it back in. It is the score from the film *Justine*. She told him an audition had been arranged for her. The part of "Melissa." This was the last disk he heard in her apartment.

She makes her patients listen to music they know and love, something important to them, nonverbal.

He is aware that Maude Garance is liable to come by anytime, especially after visiting hours, even though she is on leave. He stays in Melissa's room, sits in the corner, watching her. He is strongly attracted to her. Suddenly he feels uncomfortable, in conflict between his desire for her and his inability to fulfill it.

It is 8:40. Maude enters, sits by the bed without acknowledging him. Both women have close-cropped hair, Maude's has grown an inch since the last time he was at the hospital. She takes Melissa's hand and whispers to her. Is Melissa aware of her?

Maude starts to pull the sheet down. She wants to examine her legs. She turns to ask the man sitting in the corner to leave, but he has already left.

O'LAND

WHEN SARA SMITH comes into Jim O'Land's office carrying the *New York Times* Syndicate and the Associated Press orders, drops them on his desk, she does her best to sound hurried, detached.

"Jim, when you get a minute, check these pickup orders from the *Times* and the AP."

O'Land halts his pencil in midair while he aims his bifocals onto the pages on his desk.

Under his breath he reads, "*. . . first refusal for any future communication the* Los Angeles Herald *receives from the alleged felon known as Toyer.* God, it's happened. We've won."

He slips from his chair to one knee, crosses himself, one hand on his desk. "I'm Irish Catholic, my hand still does this, I have no control."

"Get up, Jim."

Everything is in place. The *Herald* will copyright all future Toyer accounts and syndicate them to the world press through the *New York Times* Syndicate.

O'Land has made Toyer the darling of the morning, afternoon, and late-night talk show hosts. Jokes cued by tragedy.

With his eleven identically rendered victims now securely behind him, and with impeccable credentials, Toyer intends to rehumiliate the Los Angeles Police Department with his accounts of evenings spent with victims. It is as if he were a franchise, which he is.

It is a journalist's godsend, especially now, in the heat of a summer without news, a season without a silly trial or a handsome war to watch.

This is, of course, unprecedented, O'Land tells Sara again, everything about this is. No self-confessed felon extant has ever published ongoing accounts of his crimes. And the wide public, uninterested in any cause, only aware of result, applies constant pressure on Toyer to produce. It is a dry, distant summer, they need product product product.

TOYER

A SUDDEN NOTE to Sara Smith from Toyer is found without postage by the night watchman. It is definite. He will quit.

O'Land pencils in his headline several times, trying to get it right, to be sure, finally settling on one that Sara says she would expect in a Batman comic book, GOTHAM CRIME LORD RESIGNS. He chuckles. He says he wants it to sound trashy:

TOYER TO *HERALD*: I'VE HAD IT
I ABSOLUTELY QUIT FOREVER

Terminates Career in Crime

"The gravity of the event, Jim. It's a big deal. What's wrong with last month's headline?"

He runs it in 124-point boldface:

TOYER QUITS! CLAIMS HE'S CURED
CREDITS *HERALD* COUNSELING

States Kipness Doctor
Altered His Perceptions

Could Leave Area—Future Uncertain
Eleven Victims Remain Unconscious

It runs above Sara's story, which includes her telephone interview with Ray Yellen, the D.A., who tells her that everyone in his office is certainly delighted, but that he hopes this does not remove his chance at prosecuting him one day. To the *Herald*'s readers, Yellen comes away looking mean-spirited, self-serving. Toyer comes away looking clean, reasonable, sincere, caring. He has promised to quit.

Los Angeles. August 8. In a copyrighted story to the *Los Angeles Herald,* Toyer has stated unequivocally in a letter to Dr. Maude Garance, a correspondent of this newspaper, that he will no longer continue disabling women at random as he has been doing for the past year throughout Los Angeles County. There will be no more victims. The number will stand at eleven. A collective sigh of relief can be heard in all quarters of the city. . . .

Sara calls Maude to meet her for a celebratory drink, but Maude is not up to it, she will stay home.

"It's a beautiful letter," Sara says when she rereads it. "It's a great credit to you, Maude. I think he means it."

"I believe he believes he means it," Maude says, "which is not the same thing at all."

Four press runs sell out.

O'LAND

August 18

Dear Editor;

Should Toyer decide to surrender to the authorities our office would be delighted to pledge its services to his defense at no cost. I believe that this is what justice is about. My partnership with its collective experience will be at his disposal should he ever feel the need to elect us as his representatives.

> Buck Wassitch
> Wassitch, Lordell and Paine

Maude hurls the fluttering paper across the living room against the far wall. It lies on the floor like a shot bird. Jimmy G wakes, stares at it carefully, waiting for it to get up, to fly away.

It is the *counterlove* that comes from the people, there are thousands of them, in a mongering letter on the op-ed page, she has seen: *A posturing lawyer procures a client by offering sympathy to a diabolic killer.* She telephones Jim O'Land.

"Why on earth did you run that letter?"

O'Land says there has been nothing on Toyer for more than a week. And anyway, Buck Wassitch is a great believer in the majesty of our law.

"The majesty of the law is no match for the majesty's court jesters. Who are able to outwit their king at every turn." Wassitch is a Dallas lawyer who has somehow never lost a case, the author of *The Lawyer and the Lens*. The profile of a caring man who stoops to help another. It is that Wassitch probably would succeed in defending Toyer's rights that haunts Maude. *No one of any importance is ever punished in America.*

ELAINE

FROM THE ROOF he can see the ocean. Turning to the east he can see the gray bag that covers downtown Los Angeles where the zone of clustered glass buildings is hidden. Then, turning west, Hollywood, Beverly Hills, Westwood, Brentwood, Santa Monica and again, the bronze, high ocean, a dozen miles away. A wide, flat, unspirited view. His world.

The sun is just up, above the hills. Dew has drenched the roof, it coruscates. It is an easy pitch, maybe twenty degrees. He is enjoying his coffee. His roofer's trick is to get down off the roof by eleven, when the tiles get too hot to touch; that means getting started at first light.

For him, roofing has its benefits and this is one of them. He works for an unusual man, the father of an actor in the Group, a man who wants his roofs to last well into the next century. He is not so dedicated as his employer, sometimes skips a step if he feels it is unneeded, in order to get off the roof, tempting imaginary rainstorms.

Otherwise, he is good at it, he feels he can outwit water, he has excellent balance, he enjoys heights.

Now, it is nearly eleven. He is on his own. Ninety-five degrees on the roof. He has stapled the tarred felt paper down in straight rows and has worked the tarred tiles shiny from heat up to the peak on the east side of the roof. His work is nearly done. This is a small job. He watches the fleshy lady of the house come and go, uncombed, in a satin robe. Askew. Now she looks up to the roof, scanning it to see the roofer, her hand shielding her eyes, her mouth slightly open, her lower lip full. No one seems to be home except her. He can hear a television drama piping up the chimney. He can feel her breath. The woman makes this thing, her sex, uncomplicated.

But love is mysterious to him, the opposite of learning. He

is haunted by a love that does not have a brain in its head, has pretty animal eyes, does not add or subtract, that does not have a sex. How else can he explain his unbreakable bond to Elaine?

Two years ago he had decided to marry her and she had decided to marry him. She had been raised a Catholic and had begged him not to make love to her before they were married. *Impossible!* Yet he had done this unique thing: he had agreed, flustered and somewhat embarrassed, without telling a friend, had gone along with her request. The promise had been made and kept until their wedding day. She remained a virgin. It was not a long engagement. On their wedding night, three men got to her before him.

The story of her tragedy had been a briefly noticed case in the New York area, left unmentioned in the press west of the Hudson River.

Each detail of what these men did will stay in him daily, forever: Newlyweds. Summer honeymoon in New York. Visiting her relatives, car rental, a black Buick. Driving all the way down to New York City from Massachusetts just after the wedding. The temporary parking lot under the Highland Park Hotel late at night, construction equipment standing around to enlarge the parking lot, unpainted plywood walls, concrete dust.

A lone tattooed man seen putting on an eye mask. Bare arms. He is knocked down from behind, on his knees. Hands of a second man felt behind him. His mouth taped shut, arms and legs bound by insulated wire. Pain. Dark red whorls behind his eyes. Blank. Buzzing, unconscious, coming to, seeing her held from behind under the elbows by the first man, the man with tattoos. A third man. Three men in masks, fully clothed. Erections.

His head on cold concrete, eyes locked, watching, watching, watching his wife being held, bent, spread, inverted, divided, split, explored, spattered, kissed, fucked. Immortally naked. Nakedness to linger within him forever.

The unsmiling men labored over her, restless as hogs, sharing her equally among themselves on this special occasion. Someone's birthday? Ramming her in turn. Busying all of her muscles, keeping her bones working, her senses active, her brain alive; scouring her every nuance, pulling every moment out of her, prying into every soft crease, pocket, opening, hole on her body, every crevice, knoll, nook, slit, breath with dreadful thoroughness and expert knowing, careful not to kill her outright. As surgeons operating on a critical patient; experienced: they had performed this operation before, each doing his procedure in his turn.

The semen weeping down her thigh across the warm hood of the black car, coddled egg whites forced from her vagina. Her vivid, hurting eyes fixed overhead, yanked away from the hyenas devouring her. Then, near the conclusion, her eyes simply fixed, staring dead-eyed at him. Then, glazing over, they finally close, behind a vellum shade of night-deep trauma.

She never returned. She remained in catatonic dementia, in black, far away in another room.

They had never quarreled. Not even argued. They had always agreed. Tears had never flowed from them together. Until that night.

An immediate money settlement was made by the hotel. Generous and quiet. A frightened lawyer knows the price, does not haggle. The *New York Post* printed the story without photos, did not follow it up. As the months passed and no arrests were made, interest dried up. The file is open.

And their marriage stands forever on the threshold of its ceremony, waiting. It is still standing where it ended, on the ascent toward its zenith.

When they found him, he was in deep shock. He attacked two police officers in the parking lot. He did not recognize his wife. He was taken to Roosevelt Hospital. The next morning he recognized her but had to be taken away and kept in another room.

Following his first lucid interview with the police, he smashed the wall behind his bed and broke six small bones in his left hand. A week later, in the same hospital, he choked, with his good hand, a male nurse, who fainted either from lack of oxygen or from fear.

He was put under observation at Bellevue. He was prescribed Thorazine. After a week, he was released to go home and live with his wife. Her mother was already caring for her with the help of a nurse. There was nothing left to do.

Now, the pictures of the three men, masked, engulfing her are suspended in a safe vivarium behind his eyes where they collide forever without concussion. Now, a year later, he wakes each morning anxiously. He sees the images in gentle motion each day, each night. In them he understands what it means to be insane. Now, in his life he is content if nothing happens. He is constantly expecting tragedy. He is unsure of everybody, everything.

Now, he never feels calm except for a day at a time. Always feels close to a black void. Nothing impresses him. He is through learning. He cannot remember facts, dates, at times when he meets someone the name dissolves. At school he had been a three-letter athlete, basketball, gymnastics, track, now he walks like a racehorse gone lame.

Shouldn't he have rationalized his way into a divorce by now? Considered her lost, demoted her to an obligation or, at the most, a dependent? No. He needs the sorrow she provides him, or is she his raison d'être?

And so he loves. Pain and marriage are good neighbors, he thinks. And he gets along with her mother, in a painless son–mother-in-law love.

After the first months, he accepted some of the hotel settlement money for himself, not much, and bought a car. He found he had a taste for late-night cognac, then cognac with his first coffee early in the day. He watched morning television dramas, studying their neatly dressed misfortunes. He took a bottle of whiskey, gin, vodka, rum or wine to the movies every afternoon, sometimes buying a mix at the concession stand. He became an expert on programming sedatives. And each night slept soundly with a bottle by his pillow while what was left of Elaine lay awake or asleep, no one knew which, in the other room with her mother.

Still, the picture of her beauty in agony spread out on the hood of the rented car stood in front of his eyes, always, between him and the world, a dirty window he could not smash or pry open.

To him, suicide seemed like two weeks in Paris compared to living with what they had left him of his wife. Fresh ideas for suicide tended to cross and recross his mind throughout the days. Swimming, he was rescued a mile off the beach by a fishing boat. He kept running the car off the road late at night. He knew, though, that even a clean suicide would be abandonment.

So he began helping his mother-in-law, caring for her daughter, in small ways. He would wake up each morning fresh, in that first gleam when he still hoped his dream was not real and he would realize that it was. By midmorning he was drunk, whirling in deep depression. She was too busy with her patient to notice.

Finally, they drove west, the three of them, undecided where they would settle, what to try. The settlement money would take care of them and a part-time nurse. There was enough for a small house. They found Sondelius, a town to the north, a dry place with sun. His mother-in-law had always wanted to live where you had to pull the shades down in the afternoons to keep the sun out. She was sure her daughter would have wanted that, too. They were from Massachusetts where plain blue skies are a revelation.

They left behind them the silence of their wood-floored living room. The silver clock had struck the hour. Silence rushed in over the afternoons. The house that without her had once seemed so empty.

At the small house, she would prop her daughter up each

morning in the shiny wheelchair and strap her elbows to her sides then wheel her outside, if the weather was fine, and point her toward a eucalyptus tree she seemed to like. Her mother designed and laid out the flower garden she had always wanted. It was to be for Elaine.

His pain had ripened into a rich textured rage that woke with him every day. He watched his young wife. She looked less than alive in her wheelchair, regal.

It is impossible now for him to know the date this rage began. During the two weeks in Bellevue, he was a lizard suspended in a calm terrarium of trauma. No one examined the result of his shock, they just kept calming him down with pills. His wife was the endangered subject, the victim, not him. Gradually, his pain formed a texture so rich that it built a protective helmet around his head, while within it, his brain remained full of the leftover screams from Bellevue. No one noticed, they were watching for her recovery. No one was entirely sure then what progress she would make, if any, that was the concern.

He stayed at the small house in the sun for months. He helped turn the sandy soil for Elaine's garden. A green place for her to gaze. By the time it was fertilized and planted, there was nothing left for him to do there but blot her drool. He hitchhiked to Los Angeles, it took him two hours. He had not had a sexual thought in more than a year.

FELICITY PADEWICZ

HE DOES NOT FEEL that anger this morning on the roof. The heat of the day has leveled off. There is no breeze but it will not get any hotter. He feels calm. He had felt a whoosh of rage yesterday, always an alarming sign.

Elaine. He loves her, does not see why he should stop loving her. He thinks that she may still feel the same about him, if she can feel. When he is at the house up north, he talks to her mother, Ann; she has told him that love is a luxury given anyone, that to gauge love by need is another thing. He feels his love for her is based on what he believes is still alive inside her, he feels his love is supernatural because he has never wished her dead. Ann has seen him rage at her hopelessness. Of course she understands rage, she has survived her own tragedy-filled childhood in Brockton, Massachusetts, and knows all about hopelessness.

A final volley of commercials echos up the chimney. He looks at his watch; the television drama is over. He feels the familiar rush of tremors come up through the roof, through his feet and knees, pass through his gut, up his spine and stop, trapped in his ears, swirling.

He climbs down the ladder and wanders in the back door, undecided what he'll do, he may say he wants to use the phone or the toilet or ask for a glass of water or maybe a beer. Real workers prefer water if they intend to continue through the afternoon working in the sun, but beer if they are knocking off for the day. He will ask the fleshy lady with her hair and mouth awry for a beer.

She is still wearing her satin robe which keeps falling open revealing a low brassiere, an outpouring of breasts. Her lower lip is swollen, the size of a chicken giblet. She receives him without suspicion, lets him use her bathroom, where he washes his hands and genitals. He usually starts with the bathroom, where biographies are stored. When he comes out he sees the chilled can of beer standing on the kitchen table and that she has done something to her hair and lips. Are there traces of morning wine in her eyes?

Iris.

The kitchen smells of bananas and cantaloupe. She wants to feed him, guides him to a kitchen chair, makes him a sandwich with mayonnaise and thin meat. She insists. He sits gobbling it, he is her worker, elbows on kitchen table, cleared for their passion. Iris watches him, her robe open to the floor, she is watching *Lives and Loves* on the small kitchen television, a drama of lives more restrained than hers. *Iris*.

Lives and Loves takes place in Smallwood, a smallish urban setting without an outdoors where it is always Saturday. Its citizens have extra hair follicles, extra teeth, they have all been married to each other more than once.

Now the sun has passed over the roof-peak, drumming the tar on the unfinished side, turning the drab seams lustrous. His knee pads can still absorb the heat but his fingertips cannot. It is cool, sweet in the banana-and-cantaloupe kitchen. Without a word, she kisses his mouth and neck. Her craving awes him. Iris's muggy passion is sweet from surprise, her warmth far greater than his. She drops to the floor between his legs, tugs at his belt, plunges her hands into his open trousers. Iris trembles in fine small waves, the mere act of touching him causes her to convulse in tiny tremors. She cannot be this lonely. The beer is iced.

The front door opens and slams, someone is walking toward the kitchen through the living room. The sound of the front door key hidden by another television drama. Iris is on her feet standing by the sink closing her robe when a full-grown girl enters the kitchen, gapes at both of them, rumpled mother and rumpled worker. She sees his pants half-open, his shirt still out. Shocked, then angry. She is closely related to Iris.

"I thought you had practice," Iris says in a motherly tone. The girl ignores her.

"Would you *excuse* us?" she says to him. She leads her mother who has been a naughty girl out into the living room. He snaps open another chilled beer and listens to the girl berate her mother, *poor, fulfilled Iris*.

It goes: "The *roofer*, Mom? For God's sake, the *roofer*? Wow, Mom, way to go. Can't I even come home without finding you with the *roofer*?" Her mom has entertained earlier

craftsmen. "I *just* about came home with Dodie. I ought to put
a collar on you, with a bell." The implication that all service
people are subject to her lust. He likes the girl already.

When the two women reenter the kitchen, he has finished
his sandwich and his second beer. He has made a decision.
The girl glares at him hotly with crisp high school hatred. He
sets her age at sixteen, a more sharply focused version of Iris.
He likes the daughter for caring about her mother's well-
being, for her small, even teeth, for the curve of her legs dis-
appearing under her skirt. Iris excuses herself, maybe to get
dressed.

The daughter gets herself a Diet 7-Up from the refrigerator.
He has not heard her name yet. He stays seated, without guilt.
He faces her directly and tells her that loneliness is okay.
Risky.

She gapes at him. *Right.*

She clears the table of his dish, briskly washes it. He tells
the girl not to judge people by their status or by what car they
drive, that occasionally one does roofing because one enjoys
the view.

"What were you doing with my mother?"

He watches her mouth when she speaks. A neat fresh mouth
made to nip berries from bushes, a mouth that sucks the seeds
along with the juice. He wonders what it tastes like inside. He
wonders if she shares her mom's propensity for sudden sex. If
she is syrupy.

He never answers her question. The girl says nothing more,
continues to glare at him hotly. She takes his beer cans and
puts them in the trash bin. He feels her eyes on him when he
looks away, feels them on the tanned muscle lines running the
length of his arms. Long subtle lines. Not the cultured bulges
grown in mirrored rooms, but simple muscles earned hauling
shingles up to rooftops.

The kitchen episode constitutes an introduction to the girl,
he feels. He only needs to meet her alone to apologize for his
behavior, to begin their friendship, to activate the normal

vengeance any competitive daughter feels toward her mom, a natural force.

"What's your name?"

"Felicity. Yours?"

"Adam."

Tonight. He has made his decision. It does not seem dangerous, only thrilling.

When he stands to go back up to the roof, her eyes flick only once. His height surprises her, and his leanness.

He turns, catches her watching him, his lower back. She glares at him, her glare lingers over the limit. He returns it nicely, then turns away first. He feels her glare follow him out of the room.

She can't help thinking about what I was doing with her mom. She'll wonder about it tonight in bed, maybe dream about it. How can I possibly quit?

In an hour, when Felicity has left the house with black warnings to Iris, *poor sated cow,* he slips down from the roof and, without a sound, back into the house. He quickly finds the girl's room, locates from a mass of artifacts the salients of her brief life. Her name is Felicity Padewicz, that is all he needs to know. She is almost seventeen, a B-minus student, wears a C-cup. She has had one abortion, is taking birth-control pills, and is currently between boyfriends.

When he slips back out of the house he notices the kitchen door key hung on a string behind a jade plant, leaves it untouched, unlocks the laundry room window. He will come back after midnight when the house is dark.

He does not see any serious obstacles to a late-night visit to Felicity in a sleeping household; even if he fails, the risk will have been tantalizing.

VIRGINIA

VIRGINIA SAPEN. It all started accidentally, the horror, but he feels it came inevitably. His first week in Los Angeles. He had been fascinated by a girl at the beach without knowing why. She had been swimming, then reading a current fat novel, lying on one side, lying on the other, not reading, staring at the horizon.

Then he knew. Of course. Dark eyes and hair, slim arms and legs; Elaine. He sat near her, oiled, blond, his toes were tan. He had never known anyone named Virginia. He offered her a ride home, she accepted. It was her first time on a motorcycle. She locked her knees around his hips, there is no other way for a passenger to ride on a motorcycle. Delicately at first, afraid of her thighs. Later, while it was getting dark, they sat on her sofa playing a board game she had taught him, Snakes and Ladders. He turned on a shaded lamp. She did not want a real drink, something cold with ice, a diet soda.

He went to the kitchen. The phone rang, a girlfriend. She said she was playing Snakes and Ladders with someone. "No, you don't know him, someone I met" is all she said. She whispered a short sentence he could not hear, she listened for a few moments then giggled. He brought her a Coke. He asked her for a beer. She did not have one. He got himself a 7-Up. They continued playing Snakes and Ladders.

She said, *No, please wait,* when he reached his arm around her, pulled her toward him. He said okay, he understood. He did, too. He was gentle with her when he kissed her. He took her glass to the kitchen again. He opened the refrigerator. Something felt wrong, maybe the angle of the floor, an uncentered window. He turned, looked back at her sitting alone on the sofa, waiting for someone to marry her.

Virginia had said *no* to him, nicely. Too soon. Before he had

touched her. He wanted his wife. He had never made love to
her.

Now, standing in the kitchen, he felt a dizzying crash behind his eyes. Followed by a stabbing headache. He held on to
the tiled counter until it passed. He felt his rage stirring. His
eyes trembled rapidly. He dropped a triple dose of his own
nerve tranquilizers into Virginia's Coke and waited for the
fizzing to flatten out.

In less than fifteen minutes he watched her slip into a daze.
When she was nearly asleep, he pulled her shorts and panties
from her legs and tried to force his penis into her, calling her
by his wife's name again and again.

The phone rang. Virginia snapped out of it, saw what he
was doing, fought him off, hit him in the face with her fists,
screamed for the neighbors. Then she lost her strength,
slipped away, and he was able to resume making love to
Elaine. He was ecstatic.

Then it was over. She had hardly moved. He stood above
her cinching his belt, stunned. It had begun so suddenly, taken
so long. He went to the kitchen and found a pint of scotch left
behind by a date, poured himself a drink. He was ready to
leave. He had finally made love to his wife.

It was after nine when she stirred, moaned. He was still in
the kitchen, seated, holding a second glass of scotch in both
hands. *She knows my name, remembers what I look like.
There's evidence everywhere. She'll have me arrested. Jail. I'll
have to leave L.A.*

He stood in the doorway of the kitchen holding his glass,
staring at the half-naked girl whom he could see was not
Elaine. She was waking up. He wondered how much time he
had left to decide her fate. Maybe ten minutes before the
screaming began again. He poured himself another drink. *I
cannot kill her. I cannot kill.*

As he stood in the doorway abstractly watching Virginia
Sapen stirring, images of bottles appeared in his mind, rows of
aged bottles, wide corks in cured wax, slices of human brains

stood lightly suspended in formalin, a clear fluid. He had seen them the summer he had qualified for a job with false credentials as a diener in the department of neurosciences at the Cornell medical facility in Havers, New York. That summer he had assisted in the removal and preparation of brain specimens, he had seen a brain extricated from its skull, separated for inspection. An imposter, he felt the rush of a gate crasher at a costume ball. But it was the hand-blown bottles that had stood on their shelves since the last century that had captivated him, their crisp labels, amber glue stuck along the bottom of each bottle, written in sepia script describing their strange contents that had once wondered about the stars. *Medulla Oblongata, Thalamus, Corpus Callosum, Substantia Nigra,* beloved names from the surgeon's private world. He had stolen a bottle, taken it back to his room, poured the pale sweet-smelling fluid down the drain of his sink, slid the contents onto a plate where it lay firm as a slice of country pâté. Three pins of description remained stuck in it without a trace of rust.

The origin of evil is need. Often it is innocence. Virginia lay across the sofa, her face pressed against the armrest. He raised her head with both hands, tilted it forward, with his thumb he found a small lump, pressed it, trying to remember. The inion, the knob at the base of the skull. Now he remembered, *Below the inion there's a big hole that opens up into the brain. The foramen magnum.*

What he would do to Virginia would be a simple procedure. He had seen it done. In her kitchen, he chose the thinnest steak knife in the knife rack, boiled it in a pot of water. Charged with images of sliced brains, he began. As he remembered it.

What he did to Virginia was uncomplicated, bold, neat. He entered her brain upward through the hole at the base of her skull and with slight sweeping motions, imagining the fibers he was disrupting, he eliminated her consciousness, leaving her lower functions intact. *I cannot touch her breathing, her blood pressure, her heart.* An intuitive cingulectomy, an office procedure. She hardly bled at all into the bath towel draped around her neck. He watched her for a long time. She resembled his wife now more than ever. He wiped the blade and put it back in the kitchen drawer. Then he vomited in the kitchen sink.

No one knew he had been there. He called 911 on her telephone, wiped the receiver. He wanted Virginia to live, not to die. *Now she'll be all right.* He needed to tell a paramedic exactly what he had done, but instead, he told the police operator to send an officer to Virginia Sapen's address, he suggested she call an ambulance, not a coroner.

This is how it began.

That night he could not sleep. He felt a strong need to confess. To a stranger, to a lady on a bus, a drunk, a priest, anyone. Early the next morning he read a newspaper page by page. There was no article about the incident, the telephone call, the singular condition of the girl. Then, in the afternoon edition of the *Los Angeles Times,* there it was. He bought the paper and drove up to the house near Sondelius. He surprised Ann, his mother-in-law, brought them both flowers. When Ann had gone out grocery shopping and he was alone with his wife, he read the brief article aloud to her, told her the entire story of Virginia Sapen. What he had done to her. How much she had resembled her. How wonderful it was to have finally made love to her. He believed that Elaine was able to hear his story and approved of what he had done. He tacked the article on the wall in a place where she could see it.

The relief he felt calmed him, cleared him of any guilt, cleansed him of his rage. Nor did he go into a depression as he imagined he would. Nor did he feel his anger return for a long time.

Now, a year later, after telling Elaine about Virginia Sapen, Karen Beck and Gwyneth Freeman, Luisa Cooke, Lydia Lavin, Paula Straub, Nina Voelker, Melissa Crewe, he is still amazed at how light his cargo feels, the psychopathic horror that he is able to carry around with him with such ease, such freedom.

FELICITY

THAT NIGHT, Felicity wakes from a dream, she senses him sitting above her on the bed, his weight stirs the sheets, his heat. Confused between two realities, she forms a scream. He covers her mouth and smiles. *Shhhh.* She wriggles and writhes, her eyes watching him like a deer's, until she is convinced that he is not there to harm her.

She nods, she understands. He removes his hand. *He's cute, this is radical.* She is rebellious. They will get away with something, maybe the same thing. She does not want to wake Dad. *He's such a monster.* That whole Mom/Dad aggravation will start up again. They are pitted together against her monstrous dad. She is trembling, not from fear. He bends and kisses the lips he watched, tastes her mouth. His fingers touch the top hem of the sheet, raising it. The smell of soap. He is reaching out of the night like a man from the dark sea.

The choice is hers.

TOYER

NOT QUITE DAWN. The hills above Los Angeles. Houses are still dark, leaning toward the east, televisions sleep. Empty cars, waiting for their captains, point toward the day. The city below has been poured from a pitcher of costume jewelry onto a plate twenty miles wide.

He had not wanted to leave Felicity at three and has stayed on until almost morning. He rolls a borrowed motorcycle down the hill to a bright chorus of barks, the first bright fart from its exhaust always wakes at least one dog.

He stops at a telephone near a closed gas station. He dials the West L.A. police number and begins, speaking quietly. *This is Toyer. Tango Oscar Yankee Echo Romeo. There is a woman to be found. Born October 10, 1982, San Jose, California. Go to 1112 Alameda Drive in Encino. Felicity Padewicz.* He sets the telephone down.

He knows that Iris will never come forward. If news of their quick adventure, Iris on her knees, the roofer relaxing on her kitchen chair, her *quickie,* if it came out as Toyer's testimony at the trial, as it would, the public would lock arms against her. *What were you thinking?* And her husband, Dave, would leave his sinful wife.

Her choice of silence is governed by other rationales: *The roofer probably wasn't Toyer. Dave would beat me to a pulp the way he did the last time. Nothing will bring Felicity back. I want to put the whole thing behind me and get on with the rest of my life.*

MAUDE

AT 5:35 A.M. THE TELEPHONE RINGS. She is not asleep, lying in the dark. She lets it ring five times, she knows before she picks it up what she will hear. What the words are going to be. The words. Chleo. Chleo who never wants to call her but is the only person who knows how. First, she always apologizes, "Doctor, I'm sorry, but we've got a disabled girl in here. . . ." And then she says nothing. She waits for Maude to grasp what she has said and hold on to it, be able to ask her first question. "Is she steady?" Yes, Doctor, she has always answered.

Of course it is Chleo, calling for Doctor Tredescant: Felicity Padewicz has just been brought in. Number twelve.

Maude does not speak, does not ask if she is steady, does not say thank you, and as she hangs up, Chleo hears a choking sound, maybe a sob. It does not matter about her ego, her morality. What matters is that her methods have failed her, that he has let her exist for weeks under a perfect delusion; he made her feel that through her vast experience with psychotics, she was able to turn him away from his crimes, into a better person. She was not.

A psychopath, her patient, a practicing toyer, has outwitted her. She has been betrayed. There is no one she can talk to. Not Doctor T, not anyone. She would crawl on her knees to the shrine of Saint Bridget if she thought it would help.

She hears the voice now every night. She does not need to be asleep to hear it, sometimes there are several voices in a talking chorus. For a few moments it is quite beautiful but when she wants them to stop, they don't, they go on and on.

She makes a pot of tea, dresses for the drive to the hospital. She can hear his footsteps outside. He is standing there, a man on the sidewalk, about to attack her. But there is no sidewalk.

The telephone rings. Maude picks it up, listens, expects anything, holds it away from her ear, for several moments she can hear only faint smears of traffic. Then the sonorous voice.

"*Sor-ry.*" Two syllables. He hangs up.

There is something unhealthy about this kind of loathing, it is that the person being loathed does not mind. It leaves you with nothing.

She is able to drive to the Kipness as if her car knew the way.

O'LAND

SEVEN-FIFTEEN A.M. Sara Smith and Jim O'Land are eating breakfast at the Columbia Café twelve blocks from the Herald Building.

The telephone in his pocket chirps.

A woman has been found.

They both stop eating at once, lay their forks down carefully, as if in a fresco. Sara says, *Twelve.* O'Land calls the pressman downstairs below the newspaper offices, tries to delay the press run of the final. He must convince the pressman that the caller is really Jim O'Land, he tells him the combination for the key to stop the presses and manages to hold the run for an hour and a quarter, time for Sara to find out the details, check them, make sense out of them, type a box for the front page of the final. *It may not be Toyer after all, Toyer has quit.* That is the risk. They race their cars twelve blocks back to the *Herald* driving through all red lights.

Sara is on her car telephone all the way, calling for Felicity's last name, her address, listening to police calls on her CB radio. Nothing. She cannot get anything more than hints.

Upstairs at the *Herald,* she tries again. *If I could speak to someone who's been to the scene.* No one can yet be sure who is responsible. Of course every clue points to Toyer, and she might go with that as her story, *TOYER TWELFTH SUSPECTED.* But because he claims to have quit, this would be the perfect moment for a copycat to disguise his work. There is doubt now, Felicity is younger than the others, barely arrived. Sara intercepts a police report, she may be the youngest by five years. She was cordotomized while her parents slept in another part of the house. Nothing is familiar. *Why?*

Sara calls Maude at home. *Is there a pattern I don't see?* For the first time Maude sounds weak, beaten. She tells Sara that this is an ugly, dangerous change of pattern. *His range is widening.* Maude tells Sara that she hopes it is not Toyer, that this is a copycat at work. Sara agrees, it is barely possible; there has been the courtesy call, the small bloodless incision. She cannot write the story without proof, police corroboration. They will have nothing official for another hour.

Then Sara gets a signal from O'Land who has found Felicity's private telephone number in the Valley telephone book. The Padewicz home in Encino. She calls it and speaks directly to I. Perrino who is standing in Felicity's bedroom. "Can you please look for the mark?" It is called *the mark,* never *the handprint.* Outside of the police, O'Land, and Sara Smith, no one knows about *the mark,* no other reporter, not the mayor. "I'll hold on." Sara waits poised as Perrino dusts high up the window for a print. After several minutes he picks up the telephone.

"Don't quote me, but it seems to be him."

That is enough. When she sets the telephone down she calls O'Land back, "They found the mark on her bedroom window."

O'Land has been jotting anagram words that will make up his Toyer headline: Valley, 12th victim, youngest, Felicity Padewicz, sixteen, confirmed, Toyer.

SARA

O'LAND IS IN HIS OFFICE at 9:50 A.M., just before the morning news meeting. Sara Smith has driven out to the Kipness and has just returned to the paper. She has seen the victim, written a second story for tomorrow. The news has shocked her, no one wants to believe it, she trusted what Toyer had said.

Not so much of a shock for the readers who are just now getting comfortable for their morning coffee breaks at work, reading the opening sentences in a box on page one of the special final run of the *Herald*. Sara knows that without knowing it her readers share an unspoken sense of relief, a feeling of continuum:

TOYER BACK WITH YOUNGEST VICTIM

Los Angeles. August 22. Early Wednesday morning, Toyer shocked those who had believed he had quit when he left his twelfth victim for the Van Nuys police to find. In an unusual departure from his known style, he has disabled a victim in her parents' home. At 16, Felicity Padewicz is his youngest victim to date. Please turn to page three for Sara Smith's coverage.

It is a sickening jolt to those directly involved, those at the Kipness. Those looking for solutions, sources, causes, cures. The relatives. Those who know both sides, those who believed him when he promised, twice.

Maude has spent the rest of the night at the Kipness, sitting by Felicity's bed, holding her small intangible hand, speaking to her, playing her music. Twice, during the early morning hours, she has stirred, her eyes opened. The rustle of hope.

Finally, when it is light outside, Maude cannot stay any longer, she has been officially suspended. For the next few hours she cannot be alone. Doctor T is busy, washing up for surgery. She does not want to go home, she has nowhere to go. She follows Sara Smith back to the *Herald*, barely able to keep her car between lanes.

Maude is trembling badly when she walks into Jim O'-Land's office, it is like palsy. He half stands when she enters. They shake hands across his desk. It is a good handshake, as good as a hug. Better. She chooses the arm of the wizened leather sofa to sit on, refuses a cigarette, coffee. She is faint, pale with rage, helplessness. The tremble subsides.

Maude says, "It's not my ego, Jim, believe me."

Just before the morning news meeting in O'Land's office, Sara goes to the toilet to wash her face, comb her hair. O'Land and Maude are alone.

"God, I'm sorry for you, I'm sorry for the girl, too." He comes around from his desk, sinks into the sofa below her. "This is a bum rap for you. Your job, your reputation. He really put you on."

"Your basic toyer, Jim."

"Tell me what I can do. If I can do it."

She gives in a bit, lessens her rage. *Here he's got permanent crises, Israel, Africa, Bosnia, Iraq, Iran, Britain in Ireland to deal with and he looks whipped over what this psycho did to me.* She feels warmth toward him, surprised to find it. She could kiss him now. "Thanks, Jim, it means a lot to me. I'll let you know."

"Why do you think he switched, Maude?"

"Because he's a psychopath, Jim—that's what they do."

"You knew he would?"

"Yes." She realizes she was waiting.

"But you were still taken in." O'Land leans toward her, seems fascinated.

"I was hoping."

"Was it personal?"

"Yeah, he won a game." *I wonder what he calls it.*

"What's the next step?"

"Don't know."

"He's still dangerous, right?"

Maude nods.

Someone looks in, it is ten, the news meeting is waiting to form, Sara enters. Maude stands. "I know this, Jim, I'm through trying to help him. I'm going to try to take him down any way I can."

"Can I quote you?"

"Yes." Then she says, "No, don't. It's a threat and he would respond."

At one-thirty P.M., the late edition of the *Herald* carries a picture of Felicity wearing a white dress, floral, taken at her junior class prom. Her eyes are not quite open, caught in a blink, her arm cropped at the elbow, gripped by an unseen escort.

Maude's explanation of Toyer's reversal appears inside. *Because he's a psychopath.* Her piece is short, resigned, she knows she will hear from him soon. *He's very good at being a psychopath.*

She knows that the fox has retraced its steps, bided its time, and cleanly bitten the hunter.

DOCTOR T

WHAT MAKES A FACE IMPORTANT? Doctor T watches Maude pour coffee into their cups. *Curiosity marked by gentle intelligence.*

With her it is constant, she might ask me a question I've been needing to answer and in the same breath answer it. A thin face, never entirely simple, sometimes very beautiful, a face I might spend years watching.

"Your friend Meyerson called me and asked if by any chance I was missing a muscle scalpel. I asked why. He said last month one was found, he didn't say where. I told him I was busy today. It wouldn't be the sort of thing I'd notice anyway, that my nurses keep track of my instruments. The same question."

"You put him off."

"Yes. He brought up your name."

"My name? Why?"

"He wouldn't tell me why."

"He wants you to dismiss me for good." *Toyer called Meyerson.*

"Why would he want to do that?"

"He doesn't know why but he'd be right."

"He doesn't know why but he'd be right?"

Maude takes his hand, sits him down on the edge of the bed. He watches her go to the kitchen, fill a glass with ice and pour three ounces of scotch into it. She puts it in his hand, sits on the bed beside him. She longs to snip his nose hairs.

"Meyerson doesn't know it, Elias, I nearly killed that poor man in Venice."

"That man . . . that beach bum . . . you nearly killed him? But he was stabbed, his throat was cut by scalpel."

"It was your scalpel."

"What . . ."

She does not say anything. He watches her face, it is ringed with lines he has not seen before. She is trying not to cry.

"Maude, please talk to me now."

"Meyerson is guessing. He heard from Toyer that I tried to kill Toyer."

"Did you?"

"I did."

"My God," he says. Then, "My God." He is pale.

"It was me on the beach in Venice that night, Elias. Meyerson may know that he could have me arrested for attempted murder."

Doctor T is silent. He barely understands.

"You met Toyer?"

"I met someone else. It was horrible." Maude is crying. "I don't care what happens to me, Elias, I don't give a damn anymore, I just want him dead."

Doctor T has fallen dumb.

She slashed a man's throat with a scalpel. Maude. The woman I love . . . Incredible.

"Who else knows what you did?"

"The man at the beach. He didn't see my face."

"Beside him."

"Toyer."

"How?"

"He set up our rendezvous. He knew I was supposed to be at that certain spot in Venice at three A.M. Someone else just happened to be there. Toyer knows I did it. Then he read in the paper that they found the scalpel. Too big a coincidence. He called Meyerson and told him about the scalpel and me, that's the part Meyerson didn't tell you."

The intrigue, the chicanery. It is a nightmare, of course, it is all impossible.

He has always loved Maude, nothing will change that, now he feels more closely bound to her than ever. He feels the thrill of their conspiracy, he feels her dependency, her need of his power. A stirring in his genitals.

ELAINE

A HIGH-SKY BLUE SUMMER DAY. Cloudless. The day has no dimensions. There are tiny jet streams eons away.

He drives toward the squat two-bedroom house, up the incline, over stones the size of grapes. When Ann sees him through the window, she puts her shoes on. She is going out for a walk then market shopping. Elaine is sitting in the front room. Perched in her wheelchair like a stunned bird who will never fly. Sun ladders slowly cross the floor.

In the car, he has slipped a flat gold ring on his ring finger. He has brought wilting yellow roses for Elaine and a small potted jade plant for Ann. Ann has left.

He stands alone in the dark room in front of Elaine, she is strapped in her wheelchair. Their wedding rings match. He feels anger soar into his ears like cheap rum. He has set no ritual. He lays the yellow roses across Elaine's lap. He kisses her forehead. She does not nod. She smells faintly of soap and excrement. Ann has washed her. She might not know he's there. The ticking of the silver clock, a wedding present, on the dresser.

He touches Elaine's hand. Her fingers are strange as glass. He settles in the armchair opposite her. He reads aloud to her, Sara Smith's short piece on Felicity Padewicz.

Today he will tell her another story, the story of what became of Felicity. He will read her his account. He has written it on a yellow pad. Every last detail. He enjoyed writing his book.

He is the only visitor Ann and Elaine have. The others have long since drifted away. A few difficult visits, polite, honorable, then they disappeared. Elaine was too great a tragedy, Ann too strident, he was sullen. Not an easy house to visit. Caught in a heightened wracked boredom, visitors to the Sondelius house could not survive long surrounded by the three, without withering, feeling diminished, made terribly aware of themselves. The sight of Elaine showed them the hideous face that the world they fear wears. It was too close. They left the small house mourning themselves and never came back.

It was in March that Ann first noticed his visits connected with Toyer's morning headline. Whenever he showed up with flowers for Elaine, there was always that morning's newspaper under his arm. She has gradually come to wonder why. After so many months. The long conversations he has on that day alone in the room with Elaine, who cannot answer him. Ann tried once to listen at the door but he stopped talking and came out and politely asked her if she could get Elaine a cold drink. His visits are always religiously formal.

It is because of the morning newspaper and his appearance with it under his arm later that same day. Now she pretends that she has not seen the news. She cannot imagine that he might have sacrificed all those nice women for her daughter. Ann is awed by the possibility.

She wonders. Maybe he knows that she knows. She forms questions at night that she will never ask him during the bright afternoons when he comes to visit. She intends to but never can. If it is true, if he really is, what can she possibly do? His reprisals would be beyond her understanding, and yet in a dimly Catholic way, she realizes that even if he is, he is not killing anyone, the gravest sin of all. She cares for her garden, trims the grapevines she planted behind the house. She feeds her doves, symbols of the Holy Ghost. She has decided that even if he is Toyer, he would never harm her because he loves Elaine, who would die without Ann's care.

The silver clock ticks elaborately. He watches his lemonade fume. The room is airless. The window shade barely moves. The sweat he feels running down his chest is a benison. Today, a new story. He stares at Elaine, who stares at the floor. *She can hear me.*

He begins. He will tell his story as if it were a suspense novel. It will be a bestseller by Christmas.

An hour has gone by. The story is over. The lemonade is gone, its glass stands in a silver pond on the table. "The end," he says.

He looks up. The silver clock's hands show 5:35. He stares at Elaine across the room, she might have heard. And if she has heard, *Does she understand that I am fulfilling our marriage?*

The story is over. He is her storyteller. He stands up to leave. *Time to go home.* The sun ladder has touched the wall. Ann has returned, he hears her in the kitchen making supper. The silver clock ticks.

MAUDE

WITHOUT A CLOCK, Maude can now sleep through certain nights. But there are times when her inner voices reside in her bloodstream like tinnitus and tonight she has not been able to sleep at all. She understands the ability of the heart to shut down its own arteries to preserve itself. She understands that *not* destroying, for some, is a huge effort. She understands why a praying mantis will nibble off her mate's tiny head during sex, disconnecting the final lobe at her climactic moment. She understands that the route we choose each morning is of fatal importance.

Maude may never love again. She is a widow, in mourning, it has been two years since Mason died. She is fond of Doctor T. He spends the night at her house not more than twice a week, it is Maude who is holding the number down, not Doctor T. She is considering him.

Whenever she can, she sits alone in movie theaters, trying to distract herself. It amuses her to watch the enlarged, brightly colored movie stars who presume that she cares. The city surrounds her, its institutions. She believes in three people: Doctor T, Sara, Toyer. Four: Melissa.

MELISSA

MELISSA IS RESPONDING NICELY to Maude's clandestine tests, she is able to create sounds with the skill of a six-month-old baby. On her good days, while Maude is combing her hair, which is growing out beautifully, she is able to smile faintly. She opens and closes her eyes at will, holds a small rubber ball with tenacity. The Glasgow Coma Scale shows her to be on the gentle upward arc. But the light in her eyes appears and disappears with the sleight of fingerlings who dart among the shaded stones in the pond beside the Kipness courtyard.

Toyer keeps Maude up at night, but he is no longer responding to her. After a year, she is no closer to predicting his workings any more than she can predict the workings of the internal combustion engine that drives her to the Kipness each evening. Maude is afraid that unless she succeeds in Melissa's recovery, she will lose him forever. *He will never make another mistake and he will win.* Now she has shown herself. Doctor T knows, she is a felon: *attempted murder.* She expects everyone to see it in her. It is the guilt of the naive. She has never been more transparent. She is molded glass gone hazy.

SARA

SARA COMES INTO Jim O'Land's office, below them, the presses are running. It is a dreadful moment for her. Toyer has returned in full blossom. She has read the first chapter of his book, *No One Lives on the Moon?: Virginia Sapen.*

O'Land's liter bottle of Paddy is open, glowing on the table for all to see, sporting its huge Irish pub common man label, *PADDY,* as if all its drinkers were blind, which they sometimes are.

She brings it with her in a manila folder, drops it on the desk. Toyer's work is done. The *big book* is in the works, on its way, he promises her that chapter two will be finished in a week. There will be an even twelve chapters.

"He's done his research, God love him," O'Land says,

"now he's got to write it." The *Herald* will run interim articles, he supposes, but the finished book will be rushed to the printer's by fall.

As though they've just emerged from a great play, neither speaks. Finally Sara says, "It's good."

O'Land nods, "It really is. It kind of makes you want to read on."

"I'm afraid so." Sara has never hated him more.

In the morning she will cut it in half and edit what is left into two parts of 500 words each and run them over the next week. The *New York Times* Syndicate will pick them up as they are published and distribute them to twenty-two hundred markets. It is too soon to see the result. What has happened is that Toyer has caused deadline pressure to be put on him. *Imagine, he's on deadline.*

"I want to know how it ends," O'Land says.

Sara brings two paper cups from the water cooler.

"I cannot drink whiskey from Dixie cups, Sara Smith, it doesn't fit in the bottom." O'Land is talking like a Dubliner. "Smith's an English name so I'll make allowances for you."

From the toilet, he brings two tumblers, heavy as stone. The whiskey looks fine in them, its tint standing up golden roan from their thick bottoms. He raises his tumbler. "To your feckin' countrymen, may they get off our lovely green soil."

O'Land kisses Sara, she does not stop him, taken in surprise at his *beau geste*. She knows it is more out of celebration than it is for lust. Then his hands drift, gripping her to him by the small of her back, he kisses her again. She holds her breath. It is a good feeling, something she had not predicted or thought possible. His hands are firm, on her waist then down around her buttocks, one in each hand, pulling them up toward him, raising her slightly. She can feel his bones through her cotton dress. She cannot conceal her quickened breathing from him any longer, she gasps.

Without knowing how, she is deep in the sprung leather sofa; it is made for what they are doing; necking. His stubble scrapes, the whiskey is ripe on his breath. He kisses her well. Their mouths are wet, pressing, sluicing each other's. He has brought her leg over his knee, forcing her closer. It is a hot summer night in an old office. Its walls are primarily glass with varnished wood mullions, the night editor might wander by and look in. O'Land stops kissing Sara, stands. Straightens himself slightly, pours two fingers of whiskey into each glass. She shakes her head in protest. He offers her his hand as if to dance, they stand. She drinks half an ounce of whiskey, pours the remainder into his glass, sets her glass on the desk. She takes his hand in both of hers. She has been waiting, never more ready to make love to him than now.

"I want to come home with you, Jim."

"I want you to."

When they separate, O'Land leaves the opening chapter of *No One Lives on the Moon?* in the office safe for tomorrow's editing. He flicks the light off.

Sara's shoes have dropped off, up through the soles of her bare feet she feels the presses booming deep below her, the presses spinning in place as they have every night since 1911.

MELISSA

MELISSA CREWE YAWNS. She is lying on her back, as always, eyes closed. Chleo is in her room, she turns quickly, watches Melissa's face. *What did I see?* She cannot be sure. There is nothing to do. Wait. *Could she have yawned?* She tells no one, spends an extra hour in Melissa's room, sitting by her bed, from time to time yawning provocatively for her.

The next morning, Chleo comes into her room at seven,

opens the blinds, lets the early sun in. It will be a bright day. Melissa's head is facing the wall.

When she returns with her breakfast bottle to connect to the tube, Melissa's head is facing the window.

She calls Doctor Tredescant and asks him if she should notify Doctor Garance. He tells her *no*, he will.

On the telephone, Maude is cautious, she tells him that she will not come in, not yet. She asks him to see if he can verify what Chleo told him, and to tell her to take a reading with the Glasgow Coma Scale. If there is any change at all, it could mean nothing or it could mean the beginning of a very slow process.

When Maude hangs up the telephone, she is crying.

That night Doctor T brings her a dozen short-stemmed white roses, she smiles when he tells her that the white flower is invariably more fragrant than the flamboyant, brightly colored ones. He bears a plastic bag full of common wonders from a Chinese restaurant. There is eggplant in hot garlic sauce, mu shu chicken, prawns in black bean sauce, a couple of scallops for Jimmy G.

She has baked a cheesecake, which he adores. It is not a celebration. A celebration, of course, would be premature. He insists it is her birthday. It is not.

He asks what her plans are toward Toyer now that she has been humiliated by him again. She does not answer. He feels that in her confusion, maybe her helplessness, she will turn toward him.

She is emotional, weepy. While they are eating dinner from several bowls, she tells him how bad she has been and how much this small movement by Melissa has meant to her. She wants to tell him about her voices, he will understand her command hallucination.

At the kitchen sink just before bed, she leans into him, he holds her. She cries about Melissa's miracle. Imagine, she says, waiting all this time for someone to yawn. How small the miracle.

CHLEO CHUBB

IT IS MORNING, not yet light. Chleo wakes Maude. In the dark, reaching for the telephone, she smacks Jimmy G across his face. "She's trackin' me, Doctor, she's trackin' me." Maude snaps on the light.

"Chleo?"

"Yes, it's Chleo."

"What did you just say?"

"I say Melissa Crewe's trackin' me."

She knows. "Okay. Thank God, I thought this was one of your other calls. I'm awake, go ahead."

"Well, I walk in there checkin', you know, just using my penlight. I see her eyes open. So I go to close 'em and one of 'em moves." She is excited, tumbling her words.

"Slow down, slow down."

"One of 'em moves, follows my light. You hear?"

"I hear you." Maude imagines Chleo's wide lovely face radiant. They have been waiting.

"Honest, Doctor, I get goose bumps."

"Which eye?"

She pauses. "Right eye." *She's right handed.*

"Did you call Doctor Tredescant?"

"Naw, what for? I just thought you want to know."

"That's good. Now did you do anything else?"

"Naw. I shut 'em. I didn't want 'em to dry up." The eyes.

"Would you run a Glasgow Coma Scale for me, please?"

"Yup."

"Thanks, Chleo, I'm coming down." *Clever girl, Chleo.*

Maude releases a year-old sigh, puts the receiver in its cradle. She feels a high, deep flow penetrating her, a feeling that will last for days. In the light of the bedlamp Jimmy G has recovered from the blow to his nose. Should he retaliate?

"It's okay, Jimmy G, it's okay. It was unintentional."
Maude is glowing. But he studies her face, uncertain.

Elias lies facing away from the light, barely awake.

"Who was that?"

"Chleo."

"What?"

"Melissa."

He can tell by her voice.

MAUDE

WHEN MAUDE ARRIVES the room is dark. Chleo has
been waiting. The room has been carefully arranged,
Maude is able to cross it without a light. There is a bed on either side of the room, the other bed is occupied by Nina
Voelker who has never opened her eyes.

Maude stands in the doorway beside Chleo, letting the light
from the hall divide the room. She is tingling, it is an amazing
moment, in a year there has been nothing.

"Turn on the lamp beside her bed, please, Chleo."

Melissa is pallid yet beautiful, in full bloom, her wide-set
eyes and wide mouth running off the sides of her face. She lies
elegantly as a sloop at anchor on a still night, none of her riding lights lit, swinging slightly on the tide.

Maude leans forward, with a cotton swab wrapped on a tiny
stick she grazes Melissa's eyelashes. Her eyes flicker and
open. Maude takes Chleo's penlight and crosses her pupils
with its beam. Melissa blinks once, then again.

"Melissa, I want you to bite my finger as hard as you can."
Maude works her pointing finger between Melissa's front
teeth. "Now bite me." She waits. "Please try, bite me hard."

She waits. Nothing. She waits. Then she feels it, slight tug, less than a lover's bite.

She stands, Melissa's eyes stay open, Maude closes them. She takes her hand. "Melissa, squeeze my hand." She feels a flutter of life. "Squeeze." Maude waits. Then, alternating between tremors, Maude feels the bones closing innocently on hers. She nods to Chleo.

It has begun.

Maude carefully draws the sheet down her body.

"Chleo, let's take her tunic off."

She is nude. She is colorless, almost without contour, exasperatingly beautiful. Her feet are long, piscine.

"Is that your work, Chleo?" Someone has painted her toenails crimson.

"Yeah, I like to do that." Maude has told Doctor T that Chleo is priceless. "It passes the time."

Maude takes the foot gently in her hand, turns it slightly out and with the cotton swab, tickles its sole. Chleo is bent over Melissa's face watching for facial movement. There is none.

Maude lifts her foot, uses the silver tip of an automatic pencil. She pokes her bare sole.

Four things happen at once. Her toes curl, her foot withdraws, she squints, she utters a gasping sound.

Both know what is happening.

"My Jesus," Chleo says. It might be the prelude to a larger miracle.

"Let's dress her."

Melissa is aware, a tear runs down her cheek.

"What brand of whiskey do you drink, Chleo?"

"Why, if I take whiskey at all, Doctor, I am partial to the Irish whiskey." And she says it with a faint Irish brogue.

They laugh together instead of crying, breaking the emotional lock.

"I'll tell Doctor T later today, and you can be sure he'll know who discovered it, Chleo. But don't you tell anyone, not even the duty nurse. I don't want rumors. It's too soon for the cops to come down here with their picture books asking her questions, they could send her spinning backward into nowhere."

"To say nothin' of Toyer hisself."

DOCTOR T

IT IS A CELEBRATION. Maude will be reinstated at the Kipness, the Woman has agreed. It is the success of Melissa Crewe.

Doctor T removes his shoes whenever he enters Maude's house as if he were Hawaiian. It just feels right, he told her the first time. *Symbolically*, she had said, he is leaving the filth of the world outside. *Realistically*, he had answered. He did not add that he was beginning to undress for bed.

He has insisted on bringing along a good bottle of champagne. Expensive anyway.

"Do you have a can opener?"

Maude looks across at him. "For champagne?"

He waves a flat tin. "A can of sardines in water for your cat." Doctor T is too tall for the kitchen area.

Then he sees her. It has been a miraculous day. She is pale, gaunt as if she had been in solitary. She has lost too much weight. He does not mention it. It was he who called the Woman and insisted that Maude be reinstated so that she could continue to work with Melissa Crewe.

"Elias, here's to you." She raises her glass. "I mean it, you've put up with a lot from me."

He nods shyly, allows her to drink to him. He is an icon. He raises his glass to her, "Maude, now here's to you, for all the wonders that you've wrought."

Here's to you, my darling Maude, and the wonders of your

bed, I love sleeping with you, I want to live with your wonders from now on. How much of my own company do you think I can stand?

He has told her that he was dreadfully married to a dead woman for a long time and now he is not. Love always seemed to be a quaintness to him, a luxury, a purgative for sorrow.

He has taken his jacket off and laid it on the sofa. He sits well in the deep Timmons chair, it suits him. He is chief-of-service at a leading neurological center where she is on staff and he feels like her bashful admirer. He is wearing a startling cologne. He came through his adolescence pardoning himself to girls.

Lying in bed, when the champagne bottle is empty, by the light coming through the door from the living room, he looks at her, "What are Melissa's chances?"

"Good."

He waits.

"She's different, Elias, she's willful. I found that she may not be like the others, I don't believe her cordotomy procedure was completed."

Doctor T nods. He feels her excitement. "Do you think it's possible?"

"I've put eggs back in their shells before. But still, she's a broken yolk."

"What do you think, really, wouldn't it take a miracle to reassemble a broken yolk?"

"Well no one's ever stood behind God and seen his back, either, but I wouldn't give up looking for His ass."

In the morning, early, after Doctor T leaves, instead of going back to sleep, Maude, revived, sits at the dining table and begins writing her weekly letter to Toyer.

By the end of the month Melissa will be able to give the police his description. Maude believes it. Five people know. She has made them all swear, Melissa's progress is to be kept secret, no one else must know about it, especially Sara Smith.

MELISSA

MELISSA CREWE'S EYES are now moving consensually, it is very exciting, both pupils widen when Maude brings her finger close to one of them, both pupils shrink when she fills one of them with light, both eyes follow her across the room when she enters it or leaves. *She wants to know me.*

Melissa is turned over every four hours rather than every six, her lungs must not congeal. Maude wants her to be kept alert, she has raised the head of her bed six inches.

When Maude touches her uvula with a tongue depressor, she gags. She has made her first sound, a long *ghaaaaaaaaah*, raspy as a baby camel.

It has been three days since Doctor T agreed to withhold details of her progress from I. Perrino, now he is adamant, he will not wait a full week.

Assistant District Attorney Meyerson's office calls the Kipness every other day. Doctor T asks Maude *when?* He tells her that what she is doing is wrong, maybe it is time for Perrino to show Melissa photographs of males. She might indicate his age group, ethnic type, skin color, hair color, eye color, height, weight, by squeezing Maude's hand. Doctor T tells her that keeping her progress secret is dangerous, that withholding evidence is a felony. Maude worries about Melissa's stability. With the police hovering, she will suddenly become valuable, maybe threatened. The media will find out, there will be leaks.

She tells him to wait one more week, it might be safe then. Doctor T barely agrees. There is no suspect.

THE GOOD LIFE

BUT MAUDE cannot stop herself from wanting to tell Sara, she knows how much it will mean to her. She telephones her.

"What is it?"

"I can't tell you on the phone." She asks to meet her for lunch tomorrow as Chez Bostwick, an outdoor café on Sunset Boulevard near La Cienega Boulevard.

"What time?"

It has become too exciting, she will tell her, she will trust her silence.

At lunch they sit facing each other across the littered table close as Smith roommates who have not seen each other since graduation, neither understands the other's profession.

"Melissa may be waking up gradually." *Maybe, maybe.* She describes the signs.

Sara understands immediately that a positive description of Toyer might be coming from Melissa. It might be only a matter of weeks before she will be able to identify police sketches of him.

"When?"

"Maybe never, but maybe soon. You can see how dangerous it would be. Hold on to it. Don't do anything 'til I tell you."

Maude swears Sara to silence about Melissa. It will be Sara's story. *My story.* If word leaks out now, Maude does not know what Toyer would do about it. She would require a twenty-four-hour guard sitting outside her room. The district attorney, Yellen, would need to be photographed visiting her. So would Meyerson. TV news cameras waiting in the wings would enter in the third act. A night nurse might grab a snapshot of Melissa, her gaunt face stunning, surrounded by her growing hair, and sell it to the *Enquirer.* Tension at the hospital. It could affect her recovery. And the threat of identification; Toyer cannot disappear, not now.

A man has been watching them from a table close by, trying not to be seen listening. He has recognized Sara Smith, *But who is she with?* His index finger has closed one ear, he has raised his menu discreetly to cup the sound of their conversation. He hears the name Melissa. Sara says, "Do you want a cappuccino, Maude?" *Maude Garance.* It is all he needs. They order cappuccini, stand up, walk toward the ladies' room. *Why can women go to the toilet together and men cannot?*

When they sit down again their coffees are there, waiting. A photocopy of Toyer's latest note is on the table, unfolded.

The man comes over, stands above them. Robin Tessander.

"Sara Smith, it's you. Have you had the crab penne? I recommend it, celestial." He leans forward, his small hands on a chair back. Robin Tessander is positive that he has charm. He can work a room.

To Maude: "How do you do, Doctor? For some reason, Sara's not introducing us, I am Robin Tessander of the other newspaper. Have you been talking about . . . ?" He pauses, eyes widened.

Sara folds the letter.

"Who?"

"I think you know who I mean, Sara Smith. Our favorite chatty felon."

Silence grips the women. He has small perfect ears pinned to his head.

"Yes, as a matter of fact we were, Robin," Sara says.

"Have you heard from him today? Doesn't he stay in touch?" He makes an abrupt hysterical laugh. "Don't you find schizophrenics are the only worthwhile people? God, I do." Another abrupt laugh covers everything. "Isn't it like being with a small family?" He has seen her fold the note. "I'd love to look at one, may I?"

"Robin."

"I'm damned good with handwriting."

"He uses a word processor, Robin, you know that."

"That's right. Like me. No. Really, I do understand him, I b'lieve."

"And he understands you." They laugh without looking at each other.

"I b'lieve I could talk some sense into him. Read me what he says, anything. Off the record. Look, chills." He reveals a pale spotty arm out from under his seersucker.

Sara opens the page, quotes, "My mortality is not the question, my immortality is."

"Lord," Robin says, "the audacity!"

"Yeah, he's getting grander." Sara folds the letter.

"*Such* a c.u.n.t." He spells the word.

Sara mentions Maude's notion that Toyer has the anxieties of a movie star.

When Tessander has gone, Maude says, "What was that?"

"The society editor of the *Times,* writes a people column called 'The Good Life.' " Then she tells her again how dreadful she looks.

Maude only says that she has been dreaming of Melissa, the same dream she dreamed of Nina Voelker and Lydia Snow Lavin before her, elegantly spread on a bed, their petals opened wide. But this time she is speaking to her and Melissa is answering her. She sees her standing, walking nude into her bedroom. She cannot tell Sara anything more, that she hears whispering whenever she is alone, that she cut a man's throat. She orders a second bottle of white wine, this time a Vouvray.

Robin is back, like a red ball, at their table.

"I know who you are, Doctor Garance, excuse me, I admire what you're doing." His card is out, in his hand. "D'you mind if I call you for a chat?"

"I'm sorry, I'm too involved." She speaks to his bow tie, not his face.

"Too-too for a chat?"

"I'm sorry."

And he is gone. His card is on the table. The next day:

THE GOOD LIFE

By Robin Tessander

. . . spotted at Bostwick's on Sunset. Wasn't that noted medic Dr. Maude Garance sharing a chilly bottle of Vouvray with Toyer's favorite Boswell, Sara Smith? What's cookin', gals? Stay tuned . . .

There is never a check at Bostwick's for Robin Tessander.

TELEN

THE CLOUDS over the ocean make a map of France. There is Brest and Le Havre and Marseille. The sun, a robin's egg yolk, stands just below France, ten minutes from setting.

"Ever been there?" Telen says.

"Where?" He glances up and sees the cloud formation, "Oh, France."

"Have you?"

"Yeah, but I was too young to remember." He could be lying.

She feels Peter's mystery, his strangeness, his strength. She wants them to be hers the way someone wants to own a treasured amphora. She decided yesterday.

He is the same age as she is, almost handsome, straight. He is not like anyone else. She has decided that she wants him to move into her apartment, sleep with her each night, have their mornings together. She turns her face close to his, makes sure he inhales her breath.

"Peter, let's live together."

"Us?" Then he touches her cheek. "Us?" As if it were a far-fetched idea, like taming hawks. He kisses her again, this time deeply but without promise. *He kisses beautifully, with me in mind.* He lets her settle away from him.

"Us get involved?"

"Yes, you and me." She laughs but of course she is serious.

She looks away, he stares at her while she looks out across the dull-waved, silver ocean. *What makes her ears so pretty?*

"Your ears aren't pierced."

"I've always known that, I'm glad you noticed."

"Did you start a trend in high school?"

They are not alone. There is a man standing a long way above them on the bluff looking at the same things they are looking at from a higher angle. The three form a tall narrow triangle.

"I can imagine watching us from up there." He points up the bluff behind them. That he can be where that man is and hear them talking from the bluff while he is still down here with her. She says she is not able to do that.

She puts her hand around his. "I don't mind if you have a problem."

A problem. He stands, his bare feet in the sand, walks away, picks up a shell or something worn.

They have been dating. They neck, they go to movies, Telen cooks dinner. Sometimes he stays over, he sleeps without touching her.

She is waiting for him. She knows it is important. She trusts love at first sight, at second sight, love is a lasting first impression, a confirmation of it. For a while she has felt the beginning love between them. Waiting for him has made her keenly sensitive to his accidental touch, stimulated by an off-hand kiss.

"Yes, why not us?"

"No."

Telen's mind is blank. She pushes a sigh through her closed lips. Her only answer.

"I need my place, Telen, I need to do things."

She thought he might say yes. "Keep your place, stay with me sometimes. I'll give you a key."

He waits another moment.

"Don't you want to know why I can't?"

"I don't need to know."

The dog they have been watching on the beach looks at them and yawns luxuriously. Telen smiles. Her long upper lip flattens against her teeth. She has perfectly straight teeth. Child's teeth. He removes strands of her hair from her mouth. *He's full of romantic gestures.*

The map of France has vitiated into the Russian and Chinese land mass. At the moment the sun goes down, a cool breeze touches their arms. Precisely. They have reached the glass-edged limit of their conversation.

Telen looks downward, saddened by rejection. She is exhausted from wanting him. He takes her hand and puts her palm flat on his thigh. She begins to knead his thigh firmly, like pasta dough. The long corded muscle surprises her. She eases her hand higher, continuing. Her breath is uneven. After a while she says, "Let me, please. I want to."

"No, Telen."

She whispers, "Don't worry, it doesn't matter about us."

"Yes it does matter."

Later, at her apartment, they finish a bottle he finds in her freezer of very cold white wine, a Chablis, and he opens another.

He knows everything; how, when it will end. He feels the hidden power of her sex; still, he needs to lie beside her again without a word in her silent room. In her own silence. He imagines her asleep. He knows how her body will shape itself to his like an animal seeking to conserve its heat. He wants to watch her face heal. She is innocent. He wonders if he will ever be able to feel himself surge into her as if her innocence were all that was needed to solve his problem.

It is evening, the room is almost dark. When it is time to know, when they are completely undressed, lying on the bed, her back to him, she feels his heat, hears him whisper the name *Elaine, Elaine, Elaine.*

But he cannot do what she wants him to do to her, what he wants to do to her. He cannot. For a long time in the dark he sweats onto her. Then she feels him roll away off the bed. She hears the empty wine bottle smash against the wall, shards fly onto rugs and cushions, crumbs of emeralds on the sheets. Her framed photograph of La Madeleine is shattered. The fragments of the other bottle in the bathtub.

The act of a lunatic. He cleans up the glass. She sees that he has been crying. He is dangerous, he remains fascinating to her. *His impotence is absurd, a minor problem. I can change that. I can make him want me.*

In the morning, in the stale air, he says, "I wonder if I could ever love you."

Telen catches her breath.

"Maybe if you get over Elaine."

"What?" His face is open.

"Elaine, you called me Elaine when you were trying to make love to me."

"I did?"

"Yes, it's me not her." She is serious. She has left her bed for the bathroom. The door is nearly closed.

"I want to tell you something, Telen, the most important thing in my life."

"You're married."

"Yes. I'm married." Without a pause. "Just between us, okay? I don't want Billy or anyone to know."

Telen closes her eyes, she realizes how simple it would have been to love him.

"Do you love her?"

"Yes."

"Well, how serious is it?"

"It's very serious."

She covers her mouth, sighs. She wants to die spontaneously.

"Peter." She comes into the bedroom, her hair is pinned back, she is wearing sweatpants, a white bra. "God. Why couldn't you have told me? You had plenty of chances. Why couldn't you have had the honesty?"

"My wife is an invalid." He explains about Elaine. The unfulfilled marriage. The honeymoon rape in New York. How the police never found the rapists. How the three of them came out here. About his visits to Sondelius. His mother-in-law. By the time he is finished, Telen has made them coffee, cut squares of cantaloupe and put them into bowls.

"How awful for you, Peter." She is delighted. "You've been secretly carrying this huge weight, that's why you're so detached."

"Fucked-up is the word, Telen."

"Are you still angry?"

"Still angry." He takes her hand dramatically. "Never got over it."

"But you never show it."

"Yes, I do."

"I never see it."

"Do you believe me?"

It has not occurred to her to doubt him.

"Do you want to meet her?"

She does.

ROBIN TESSANDER

IN THE *LOS ANGELES TIMES*, a blind item:

THE GOOD LIFE

By Robin Tessander

Word has come to "The Good Life" via cognoscente in place close to the source that one of Toyer's last victims is recovering nicely. Natch, I can't reveal which one but she may be well enough to finger the real Mr. T as early as next month. We're just dyin' to find out who-o-o he may be. Robin to Toyer: Enuff awready. You've destroyed twelve excellent, lovely women. You've baffled the judicial system by telling them you don't kill. You've outwitted science, conquered the LAPD. Okay, okay. You're a legend in your own eyes. Now just go 'way, will ya? Give L.A. a break.

It is his profession.

MEYERSON

MEYERSON CALLS Doctor T at the Kipness. The paragraph in the *Times* by Robin Tessander.

"My secretary read that piece in the gossip column. Any truth to it?"

"I don't know, Mr. Meyerson, I haven't seen it."

"It says one of your victims is a whole lot better. I want her to talk to Perrino, look at photographs, give him a sketch, anything."

In the afternoon Doctor T calls him back. "I spoke to Doctor Garance, unfortunately it's not true. Much too soon, maybe in two weeks."

ELAINE

SONDELIUS. A hot white sky. Not a cat is visible. Birds are dark in the shade.

Peter twists the flat gold band on the sweat of his finger. Telen waits in the car, hidden. She sees Ann leave the house, walk to her six-year-old Buick, drive away.

After another minute, Peter comes to the front door, signals to Telen, brings her inside, through the dark living room to meet Elaine. There are abrupt flares of sunlight on the sills beneath the closed shades. She will meet his wife.

It is the first complete silence Telen has heard since she came to Los Angeles. She stands stupefied in front of Elaine six feet away. The silver clock is silent.

She can see beauty in Elaine's face. "How old is she?" is all she can think of to say. Telen never sees them, they are in shadow on the wall behind her: a row of newspaper clippings.

After a moment Peter says, "Almost twenty." Then, "Wait for me in the car."

When she has left the house, Peter speaks to Elaine.

"Elaine. Do you want me to be with her?" He waits. He says it again. Elaine gives him no sign.

PETER MATSON

LATER, downtown Los Angeles, after drinking too much iced black tea in Chinatown and eating dim sum with cheap chopsticks, they walk through the Mexican streets. Telen clings to Peter's hand. Elaine is unforgettable.

They try to eat *albondigas* soup at Las Mananitas, the Mexican restaurant next door, the sweet heat of the soup makes them sweat. Their elbows stick to the patterned oilcloth table covering. Peter says that twenty million people live in Mexico City and all they can come up with are tacos and burritos and soup with hamburger balls in it.

At Telen's apartment they lie together. "I'm so sorry for your burden," she says.

With her fingertips, she tours his penis gently as moths. She wants him now. It is obvious, when he touches her clitoris it is exquisite, more tender than anything. They massage each other until she comes, when she releases his penis it is unchanged. Defeated, he falls asleep. Telen feels Elaine lying between them all night, her wheelchair standing above them by the bed.

In the morning, waking up he finds a note saying that she has gone out to read the classified ads, she is looking for a job. *I still loved last night, Peter.*

Still. It is written on paper that looks like little girl's underwear, pink with white lacy borders.

A coffee grinder, some coffee beans in a jar and a teaspoon in a cup mark the note. The counter is stained. Without looking, he finds a small teak cross with the silver body of Christ, nearly naked, glued to it. There is lipstick on a cup. Her panties, bras, T-shirts, are piled in a corner of the closet waiting to be laundered, strands of her hair have gathered in the sink. She is all around him.

On the way home to Silverlake, he realizes he has only one choice, he must either make love to Telen or give her to Elaine.

MAUDE

IN THE MORNING, he is startled to read what Maude has written to him in her column on the op-ed page, she is brusque, intuitive:

Toyer,
I know who you are. You are neat, repetitive, precise, compulsive. You have charisma, you are attractive. You have a rich fantasy life. You believe that your inhumanity is mixed with humanity. You feel rage rising in you and you transfer it to an innocent woman and destroy her. I don't believe you want to do what you're doing. You can't convince me of that. If we could sit down, I'd do my best to free you. When the source of your pain is eliminated, you will free yourself. You will feel your anger abate and you will have no reason to continue. You will disappear into the crowd. You might one day be well enough to feel remorse for what you've done to us all. I'm going to suggest that you do the most difficult thing I have ever asked a patient of mine to do. Instead of destroying another woman, destroy the thing that causes you to destroy. You know what that is. You will need to destroy it only once and then you will be free. Kill it. It might even be something you feel you love, but kill it. For us it would be an answered prayer, what about you?

It is signed *Doctor Maude Garance*.

Am I reading you right? He reads the letter again. *Kill the thing that drives me to be Toyer. If not, I will continue ad infinitum? Kill the thing I love as if it were a roach? We've got to talk, Doctor Maude. You want me to kill her? My totally innocent wife?*

TOYER

NOON. He is standing in Maude's living room looking into the bedroom. A few minutes ago from across the road he watched her drive away. Entering her house was easy, he has kept the back door key.

In the bedroom, the bed lies gaping, sheets spilled onto the floor, books askew, two open on the bed. The turned-wood bedposts catch his eye. They are low, he grips one, solid. He picks up a beige brassiere maybe the one he has already seen. It is barely visible, it could not fill an espresso cup. The photograph of "Mason" in the silver frame is gone.

He feels a presence in the room. Something moves by the window. He flinches, half turns. A sleepy cat. Jimmy G wakes, glares at him for the necessary moment, turns away, grooms himself, prepares to sleep. He does not remember seeing a cat the other night. *She doesn't live alone.*

The dresser is cluttered, glass beads, pearl cuff links, plain earrings, several small bottles of spray cologne, he puffs from each on his neck and arms. *Why not? She'll never sense me here in her bedroom.*

There are messages on the answering machine. One from a man who says: "Darling, I read it today and I think you're being reckless. Freeing him is not the same as making him well, is it . . . ?" A message from Sara Smith, "Brilliant, Maude, you're playing his game, he's got to respond to that."

I may. I may just respond. Maybe tonight, in the dark. I need to speak to you. We'll do it with my magician's bag.

Hours later, after dark, in the thick air, he stands outside the living room window. There is a large man reading on the sofa holding a glass. The woman in the bedroom is undressing, exercising, watched by a cat.

She has told him: "You must kill the thing that causes your rage. When the source of your pain is eliminated you will have no reason to continue doing what you've been doing. You may even feel lighthearted."

Must I kill Elaine? Is that what you mean by kill the thing I love? Yes, Telen or Elaine. Which? I can't have either, not while the other is alive.

ELAINE

NEAR SONDELIUS the next afternoon, Elaine finishes her dying. On a blue day with unlimited visibility. Her period of ambiguity is over.

Driving up in Billy's bronze El Dorado, Peter has never seen such a glorious day. Baking sand, scrub sage, Joshua trees, the desert blooms, shimmering heat rising forms limpid mirages, the car drives toward pools just above the road ahead. The magic desert suddenly alive in spite of food stands and gas stations.

When he knocks on the door Ann peers out, the permanent look of stress on her face. He has not been expected today, she feels fear. There has been no victim reported in the news. The house is a mess. Elaine is being fed but has not been washed.

"I was in the neighborhood." She nods. Something is wrong, there is no newspaper under his arm. "It's not important," he tells her. Ann knows for certain that he is Toyer. She drives away to the market.

Peter pays Elaine homage, standing in front of her wheelchair with the tribute of cut flowers, always roses. They are too red, their perfume too rich. The wedding band is on his finger, the silver clock ticks bluntly against the wall.

"Elaine. Thank you. For being my wife. Thank you." He lays the flowers across her lap. Today she smells of urine. Roses.

He waits for a signal.

Her years have been one long dumbstruck night, lasting from New York City to this instant. The destruction of her mind, her soul, her eyes, her person. It has been nothing. The executed roses lie on her hands.

He waits.

He is facing a garden of silk flowers where nothing ever dies; of past alien wills, forced penises.

A single rose slips and falls from her lap to the floor. He does not pick it up. He reaches forward, with his thumb, he squeezes to a stop the measured drip of her fluids. He drops to his knees, puts his head in her lap. As always, he grieves the questions he cannot ask her, too late, she has been dead too long. A wife with whom in life he could never share, talk, live, make love. Tears run down his cheeks.

She remains in the wheelchair with her head to one side, drool seeping from her mouth. He waits, watching the clock trying to tick its way out of the room.

The moment her hand falls, her head drops forward, her shoulder pulls against the strap. Peter walks away to the window. Without knowing it, Elaine would have lived long enough to witness the third millennium from the vantage point of her wheelchair.

The moment Ann comes home from the market, she knows. The air has changed in the small house. She walks into Elaine's room, sees Peter on his knees, his head in her lap, praying. It is all over for Ann, too, her expression does not change. She is free.

Later, driving home, Peter feels expansive, in a rush, tingling like a winter-dead tree whose branches suddenly feel the possibility of leaves.

PETER

IT IS OVER. He drives to his Silverlake apartment via the café, his mind reeling from espresso. It is still light.

There is a telephone message waiting. No definite word from his Velveeta cheese audition, the agency says. He will never succeed as an actor. Should he call Telen?

She has been worrying about him, she says, where was he? He tells her where he has been not what has happened. He needs to see her, he says.

Late, they meet at the café across the street from his Silverlake apartment. It has no name, simply, *Café*. It is closing.

In his rooming house, climbing to the top floor, Telen ahead of him, step by step, upstairs to the third floor. A long-term tenant from the second floor examines her gradually, a soiled man in his fifties who sleeps in ashtrays, smiles as they pass, but it is not a smile to be returned. On the final staircase to the lone attic apartment, Peter watches her shining calves spinning ahead of him, he touches the backs of her thighs whirling up her skirt. The staircase is narrow, lined with fingernail marks.

At the top step Telen turns the key, opens the door, he grips her ankle, yanks it back, lowers her to the floor, twisting her legs, pries her apart. He enters her against the open door, blocking it so it cannot close. She gasps, surprised, shocked by his power. She comes immediately.

Anyone standing in the hallway below can hear them, might even watch them if they wanted to look up. They do not care. It is sudden, quick and mean. She has been ambushed by his want, frightened by his passion, excited by the source of her own.

She falls back breathless, suspended. They slide into the apartment, half crawling along the uneven floor, the dust. Her own tremors continue flickering across her loins. He kicks the door shut. Sweat, saliva, semen, her own oils, the grime of the wood stairs baste her face and arms and buttocks. He drops his head against her breast so she can only see his neck. With her fingertips she rubs his sweat into his hair. She feels soft jolts pass through him. Peter is crying. His ear is just below her breasts, he can hear her quick heartbeat through her brassiere, *lub-dub, lub-dub, lub-dub, lub-dub.*

I can forgive him anything.

Inside his apartment, he switches on his floor fans, they snarl like terriers. He falls back on the sheets of the bed, she pulls off his pants. With his knees up, he can smell the scent of her thighs, she remains on him.

"My God, Peter," she is breathless, surprised, "What happened to you?"

"I feel free. Scream, yell, cry, I want everyone to know." His first true sexual feeling in more than a year. Soon, he will need her again.

Amazed by each other, they make love by twin candlelight, he rubs every muscle in her body with his thumbs before he penetrates her. Afterward, silence, lying apart, barely touching toes, staring overhead at the old ceiling rooflines in the dirty light.

In the gray morning, reflected in the bathroom mirror Peter sees himself, a man in his twenties, this morning his eyes more green than brown. Everything is new. *It's over. They'll be discussing me for years. Wondering. I'll be elsewhere.* He is exuberant. In the mirror he sees himself, he sees his ancestors who walked to Kentucky. He feels American. They will travel across the country by car.

When he comes out of the bathroom, he stands in front of the bed, he is grave, he tells Telen that Elaine has died, that he did not want to say anything about it last night.

"I'm so sorry, Peter." She is ecstatic, he is hers.

"Well, she was dying for a long time."

Telen knows it will be a good thing for them. She does not say more, then she says that Elaine has been spared, that it is a blessing, she is free at last from her wheelchair. *And so are we.* They can both feel it in the thrilling morning, it is clear, as if the vapor had risen between them. Love. They are Priapus and Napaea. There has not been another man, she has been celibate. So has he.

She knows. Peter has become everything she has ever wanted in a man, bright, funny, sexual, not handsome in that dangerous way that is a constant worry. He is kind and she cannot ever imagine him harming her. Some women on the verge of formidable love stop and say their name with their lover's name attached: *Telen Matson.*

For Peter, it is the first time he has felt anything truly good stir in him since the honeymoon in New York. Once again, the stars wheel in harmony, making sense. It is love. His body feels its coils.

MAUDE

NO ONE KNOWS ABOUT THEM at the Kipness, maybe Chleo.

Doctor T seems cleaner, more closely shaved, he is shiny from soaping. His hair is parted, he wears men's perfume. His shoes are smaller. Maude's hair is now nearly long enough to style, sometimes she wears a dress, low heels. The couple whisper vivaciously in offices, kiss in elevators, touch each other in front of her patients. When they pass in the running hallway they smile at each other secretly, appearing to be only colleagues, as always, as before.

They are in bed when Chleo calls.

"Doctor Garance, did I wake you?"

"Yes, Chleo, you did." She says it nicely, it does not matter. Doctor T is waking slowly, his arm across her hips.

"Well, you said to do it if it was important."

"I know I did and it's fine, it's okay."

Chleo takes a moment.

"Melissa's edema went way down around five-thirty this morning, I think you oughta know that."

"I ought to, thanks, great news, any change in the Glasgow Coma score?"

"I believe she's up to twelve."

Whoosh. Out of a possible fifteen. Maude is awake. "How do you break it down, Chleo?"

"Well, Doctor Garance, 'cause she was already a nine, right? *Verbal* is still at two. *Eye* is definitely up to four. *Motor* is up to four maybe five, so that's giving her twelve." *Eleven.*

"That's eleven. Eleven tops, Chleo."

"Yeah, somethin' like that."

"What about motor?"

"She's pushin' real hard."

She's thinking. "What about verbal?"

"She's pushin', you know. She's got somethin' she wants to say."

She'll be talking soon. "What time you got, Chleo?"

"Seven."

"Maybe I can persuade Doctor Tredescant to perform a craniotomy on her later today." She kisses the top of his spine. He is impervious, thoroughly feigning sleep.

"If he does, I'd like to assist," Chleo says.

"You go home pretty soon, don't you?"

"Supposed to go at six but I'll stay here. I'm gonna lie down in the sixth-floor nurses' room, you just wake me when you come in, Doctor."

"I will, Chleo, don't worry. I'll get in touch with Doctor T now. Thanks again, Chleo."

She sets the telephone down gently as if the ringing had not woken him. She puts her face against his wide warm back.

"Elias, are you awake?" He sighs, rolls on his back, eyes closed. "Did you hear that?"

"If she's ready, I'm ready."

"Elias, Elias, Elias." *What a beautiful sound.*

MELISSA

THERE IS THE RISK OF DEATH or death itself, either one, nothing else. Maude watches Doctor T open a flap in Melissa Crewe's skull with a Gigli's saw. He is irresistible, his hands are jeweler's hands, large, finely turned, he is sure. She watches him through a glass pane, he is astonishing under the lights, his finesse is overwhelming, the opened patient becomes small under him. His power enters her through the open door he has carved in her skull. The glimpse of mortality, Maude's, is always left lying on the operating table whenever she watches him perform an operation.

They will know soon. Afterward, they talk outside in the hallway. Melissa's brain has been decompressed. He has drilled through three layers of skull, three layers of brain, connected his hopes, and has succeeded in reducing the swelling caused by the water level inside her brain tissues. The craniotomy is a success. Melissa's head has been shaved, she looks starved, the eyes of a Holocaust survivor. Later in bed, bandaged, she appears elegant, even fashionable.

Maude is emotional when she leaves Melissa, she finds

Doctor T in the waxed hallway on Six. She kisses him on the mouth in front of Chleo, who makes her unique crowlike sound.

ELAINE

SHE IS DEAD. There will be a funeral this afternoon at three at the Heavenly Rest Cemetery between Sondelius and Ojai. Peter has already told Ann to go ahead and get a stone cut, using the hotel money, of course.

The view from Telen's apartment. No matter how many times he looks out the windows, it will never be worth looking at.

"Want to come to the funeral?"

"Sure." Telen has no choice. *Our first real date. Mass, breakfast, funeral, dinner, fucking.*

Peter is lying in bed, Telen is in the bathroom. Under the sheet is a nomad's tent of their smells combined, scents of their essential substances drying out. Nothing familiar that Peter has smelled anywhere else, unlike beached seaweed, oak leaf mold, sweet candle wax. A unique smell, theirs, a lovely trick of nature.

Telen stands on tiptoes at the open closet reaching high, she is naked. She reaches her summer hat with a ribbon, puts it on, it defines her nakedness. She has a pure girlish look, slim-hipped, mild-breasted, but she can be overtly female, convey adamant feminine sexuality. He feels himself harden. It is a new feeling. He cannot have enough of her, he will want her all the time now. He asks her where she got her eyes, from which parent. He constantly engages her in conversation. No one knew she would be so light-eyed, she says, her eyes as a baby were navy blue.

"What'll I wear?"

"Beside the hat? Shoes."

She sits, folds one leg over the other, slips on a pair of high-heeled sandals with many thin straps.

"What'll I wear?"

"Beside the shoes and the hat? Wear the red dress."

The red dress. Men in restaurants who do not want to be seen gaping at her give her severe looks over their menus when she wears her red dress.

"Red isn't for mourning." *It's for celebrating.*

"Your shoes are black."

"I can't, Peter, not red."

"Yes you can, Telen, she's gone to a better place."

Into the red dress then, line by line, he watches her disappear. He is watching an amazing person dress, she is prettier and smarter than he is. He loves her, he did not know this would happen. He wants her to know about him. He wants to find a way.

"Shall I wear panties?"

"Yes."

"What color?"

"Your call."

She slips on a sheer pair of black panties.

My grief.

MAUDE

MIDDAY. Maude sits in her murky office. She dials the assistant district attorney. "I'd like to speak to Bob Meyerson."

The chirpy woman asks who it is, hears Maude's name, clicks her on hold without a word. Rudeness to people of her choice is part of her day. When she clicks back to Maude, she is no longer chirpy, she sounds delighted with her news. "I'm sorry, *Doctor*, Mr. Meyerson is in a meeting all afternoon."

"Would you please take a message?"

The no longer chirpy woman sighs clearly, so clearly that Maude makes the effort not to hang up on her.

"What's the message?"

"Tell Mr. Meyerson that Melissa Crewe will see him now."

PETER

PETER SEEN FROM ABOVE, alone in an empty church, praying. A wooden Greek Orthodox church on Third Street. Bright morning seen through an open door, simple colored windows. An old Greek woman sweeps with a straw broom raising dust in the beams of sunlight.

The church doors were open so they came in, they had not intended to, but it is a church after all, and a good one. Telen climbed the stairs to explore the choir loft and is looking down at Peter. His shoulders are bent in prayer, his kneecaps touch the floor. She can hear a piano being played, someone rehearsing in the basement, below the wood floor, repeating a single elegiac phrase.

It is what she has written to him, Maude. She has brought him to this place, given him his ecstasy and his sorrow. How could she have known all along that it was Elaine who drove him, that she was his spectral queen, the ruler of his life, his incapacity. Elaine. That he woke up to her every day, saw her at all hours.

Peter's first image as a Catholic. He was six when he saw the nailed corpse hung from a wall above gold objects on a counter, he felt sick then frightened. A pale bluish corpse no bigger than his, jogger's legs, not long dead but dead as a fish on ice. It resembled his father. He stared at it, hoping its eyes would open. They did not and he fell asleep but he came back to look the next Sunday, fascinated, worried, excited.

Telen has slipped downstairs from the choir loft. The old woman sweeping regards her, the red dress. *That is a child's dress. She's not one of us, look at her, dressed like a Paphian.*

From the pew behind him, Telen can hear him crying gently, hears him whisper, "Thou shalt not kill." She touches him on the shoulder. He turns back to her, waiting. It is in his face.

In an instant she knows. In the next instant, it is all right. Telen loves him, his heat. She feels a cool surge rise between her buttocks up her spine. *I accept it.*

She comes around and sits beside him. "We can divide it between us, Peter," she whispers.

And what about the others? Shall we divide them between us too?

Telen's compliance excites him. He reaches down and removes her cocktail sandals, kisses them. The old woman is watching. *What is the cretin doing to her shoes?*

They kneel in prayer against the pew in front of them. Peter slips his hand up between her legs, his fingers inside her mourning panties, with his other hand he takes hers and puts it inside his open trousers. Using their fingers as sculptors' fingers, silently, it is the house of God, their eyes closed, they shape each other's clay until Telen's soft moaning ends and Peter cries out too loudly. The old woman flees in search of authority.

ELAINE

TWO O'CLOCK. They are waiting for the priest. The three of them. Watching them, a small Mexican man with a new shovel sits in the shade. There are few trees, the gravestones are modest, it is farm country, there are patches of tough grass and here and there a tiny flag, Mexican or American, pots of dried flowers.

It was once an ideal place for a cemetery, on a slight rise, but the neighborhood has come to it, there are children watching them from a window, the comforting murmur of a freeway.

There are three of them, not counting Elaine who lies in a shiny black box on canvas straps above a deep hole.

Ann is wearing a simple gray bag. *She has no idea what she looks like anymore.* While they are waiting for the priest, she walks over to the Mexican man sitting in the shade. He stands when he sees her approaching him. His name is Manuel, when he removes his straw bullrider, she sees he wears his hair pulled back in a ponytail. She asks Manuel if grass will grow on the new grave. He says, *Jou never know, it's pretty dry here.* She thanks him, maybe she will bring seeds and water, it depends. He touches his hat and sits. She does not know about tipping gravediggers if only for good luck.

"I feel really out of place," Telen says.

"One is meant to in a graveyard."

"I mean, it's that I'm your lover and this is your wife's funeral."

"Elaine would get it. You look fabulous." She does. Her legs emerge from the red dress at just the right place, her slingback sandals are no match for the dusty green, the sun clips her bare shoulders hard.

The priest arrives on a motorcycle, he is named Father Josh

and he is nondenominational. He reads from Dylan Thomas and Stephen Spender, two of his favorites. It is quite beautiful. Ann cries openly, clinging to Peter's arm. Throughout the brief ceremony, Manuel cannot remove his eyes from Telen, her sandaled feet, her thin dancer's legs, the suggestion of her loins, her unblemished face, her tidy hair, the hint of her pudenda, she is the gravedigger's dream.

When Manuel lowers the coffin in jolts, they drop sods. Peter manages to slip Manuel a ten-dollar bill. As they walk away, Manuel is shoveling the dirt back into his hole, one of the children watching from a window calls out at Telen, *"Puta, puta, mamame la pinga."*

"What is a *puta?"*

"It's a compliment, especially coming from those kids."

Afterward Peter invites them to breakfast at Mister Smith's Waffle House on the road home to Sondelius, a huge orange and blue chalet where every price ends in .95. They order buttered waffles and syrup. Peter is ravenous, the waffles are perfect, he eats Ann's.

Ann tells them that she plans to stay on at the Sondelius house for a bit longer, until the lease runs out around New Year's. She is thinking of moving to Canada, there is very little to move.

"Why Canada?" Peter says.

"I don't know why. I've always wanted to go there."

While Peter has been eating, he has been rubbing Telen's thighs between her knees under the table, but now that Ann is talking to them, she has clamped her knees together, blocking his assault. They are still at that stage when she can lock her knees.

Telen says to Ann, "I hope you didn't mind my coming along today."

"No, no. Peter said you knew Elaine."

As though they were friends.

When Peter goes to pay the bill, Ann reaches across the

table, catching Telen's hand, she is a small woman with a strong grip.

"You love him, don't you, Helen?" Telen does not bother to correct her.

"Yes, I do."

Ann's face is wild. There are tears budding.

"He is still very upset."

"I know."

"No. I don't believe you do. He is upset over everything."

"What happened in New York."

"Yes, *and ever since*. Is it going to stop now?"

"You mean his being upset?"

"That and *the other thing*. It's wrong . . . Helen."

"I don't understand."

"Make him stop. You can do it."

Now she can see terror in the woman's face, it is truly there, the tears are nothing.

"If he loves you, he'll listen to you."

"I'm sorry, Ann, I don't know what you mean."

"He doesn't know I know. Don't ever tell him what I said to you. Promise."

She nods, *Yes*. Peter is coming toward the table.

"Now Ann, tell me all about Canada."

TELEN

THAT NIGHT. He lies, after love, his head below Telen's breasts, listening to her heartbeat. She is smiling at the ceiling eyes closed. So is he. He cannot have enough of her. He has torn her open and has danced a flamenco inside her. He has chafed the lips of her cunt.

It is a confessional. He has just told her that he knows he loves her.

Before she met him, she says, she has been in love four times. Not really once.

He says that they are both virgins. That you are a virgin until you fall in love for the final time.

They lie face to face in the dimness, matching heartbeats, watching each other's hair grow.

And hours later, sometime between the widening predawn light and the gray morning, Telen lies awake, remembering Ann's vivid teary face, her fingers gripping her hand, wondering what she meant when she said, *Make him stop.*

RAY YELLEN

THE SUNDAY MORNING'S *Herald* is spread across District Attorney Ray Yellen's desk:

TOYER QUITS!

"Quits my ass."

Assistant D.A. Bob Meyerson is sitting in the district attorney's office. Detective I. Perrino and a tall female aide are standing. The front page glares up at them.

"He keeps doing this to us."

"Yeah, yeah, yeah." Yellen is taking it badly. He has called a special meeting.

"I guess we're supposed to rejoice."

"Yeah, let's have an office party."

"You got that doctor to thank, Ray."

"What doctor?"

"Doctor Wacko." Meyerson takes it personally. "I don't want him in therapy, I want to prosecute him."

"First trial, then rehab. Not the other way around."

"First arrest, then trial. We need an arrest."

"What's stopping us?"

"Invisibility. If he's quit, he can go underground for good."

"Maybe he's already out of state."

"You got that right."

"We've got what, zip, his blood type? A couple of fist prints? A shoe size, a hair sample?"

"We've got no net that fine."

Meyerson repeats himself. "I want him nailed, not cured."

"I know, Bob, if we don't nail him they'll hang every one of us."

"The press."

"You think this is over? Just 'cause he quits? We've got his fucking book to look forward to, excuse me, ladies."

"His book?"

"They're publishing a goddamn book with pictures."

"When?"

"Christmas."

"It's going to be a long winter."

"You got that right. Pictures of all twelve girls. Before, after. Pictures of their apartments, our station houses. Maps, charts. The complete enchilada. We got all that ahead of us."

PETER

MORNING. The first eerie smell of day. The agitated floor fans whir on, yanking themselves back and forth in quarter arcs. Telen is dozing, wide, lying in child-bearing position, Peter is curled like the child she has borne, awake, afraid of the day.

It is two days since the funeral, he is anxious to buy this morning's *Herald*, read his letter of farewell to Maude Garance.

In the street, the *Herald* has already been sold out. *Stardom. I'm quitting on the ascent.* He will wait for the late edition. Against his will, he buys the Sunday *Los Angeles Times*, hauls it back down the street to his café, shedding its leaflets.

He sits alone outside under an awning across the street from his apartment, orders an espresso, signaling through the window to the man behind the copper bar. Finally, at ten, the *Herald* truck rolls to a stop at the corner, drops a cube of newspapers to the pavement.

There it is. Four thin bars bordering it. His letter is called *news*, not a personal account. Today's headline is the lead story, at the upper left-hand side of the front page:

TOYER QUITS!

CAN WE BELIEVE HIM THIS TIME?
TOYER FINALLY BIDS FAREWELL
CLAIMS RELIGIOUS PRIORITIES
By Sara Smith
Special to the *Los Angeles Herald*

Peter had wanted it there, today, forced O'Land to print it Sunday by dropping it off Saturday morning.

Los Angeles. August 26—Yesterday Toyer delivered what he claims to be his final communication to this newspaper. Following a unique procedure we have come to expect from him, the letter below was received in our editorial office by mail. We have no reason to question its authenticity.

Dear Dr. Garance, I read in these pages last week that if I destroyed whatever drove me, I would no longer do what I was doing to women. I have destroyed that thing. It was harder to do than you'll ever know, but I did it. It's gone now. Of course I can't tell you what it was, but I am through being Toyer. A lot of people can thank Dr. Maude Garance for that. Of course, my women and their families won't call this a happy ending, but they'll agree it's a happier ending than what might have been.

The Chicano waiter sets the cup beside Peter.

"I never killed until last week," Peter says to him, "I swear to God."

The waiter nods, smiles. *Not a clue.* Stormy moustache, large extra teeth. Peter absorbs the black slap of espresso, continues reading. Toyer has quit to be close to someone . . .

. . . who loves me and understands me. I can now begin to lead a normal life with this woman I love. I intend to put the past behind me forever and get on with my life. . . .

His own words. He has signed the letter, as always, *Toyer.* It is over.

Now he can glimpse Telen, this woman he loves, through his window across the street, his own bedroom window, toweling herself, slippery from her shower. And she sees him, reading the newspaper to himself, moving his lips. He wipes his eyes with a paper napkin. Telen watches him.

For two and a half days, since Ann gripped her hand at the waffle house, Telen has wondered what she meant. *Make him stop.* Why did she seem frightened of Peter? Without wanting to, she has been looking for clues.

She cannot ask Peter, of course, she has sworn to Ann. She is the only person who can tell her.

The window is open, Telen is humming around the apartment, touching its oldness, dressing, making the bed, then in the bathroom again, smelling his shaving cream, blowing hot air on her hair.

Out the window, she watches him read, it is his chin, his nape. What is he doing wiping his eyes? *Is he crying? Something in the newspaper makes him cry. Is it something about Elaine?* He puts the section he was reading on the chair beside him, picks up another.

She snaps on her skirt, ties her hair in a loose wad, clumps downstairs in flat low heels no socks or stockings, crosses the street to the café.

She sits touching his knee, then above his thigh, through the fabric she can feel his excitement, barely twenty minutes without her. It is a clear promise, they will make love long before the sun sets. "I love you, Telen." He says it with finality, an announcement. He touches her hand. He is completely happy.

"I love you, too."

They belong to the café, they are weightless. He continues reading the paper, she picks up the section he dropped on the chair. There is nothing on the top half of the front page that could bring him to tears. An article about a bomb in the Middle East. Articles about Congress, baseball. Another that says Toyer has found the woman he loves. Nothing remotely possible. She folds the *Herald*.

His eyes are moist.

"Is it Elaine?"

"Yes."

So that was all it was, the tears. But it is an opening. "Peter, I feel so sorry for her. Ann, I'd really like to talk to her again."

"She doesn't have a phone."

"Why don't we drive up there Saturday?"

He makes a mild groan, does not look up.

"I can make lunch. I love the drive it's so pretty."

He puts the paper down as if it might shatter. "I'd really like to put all that behind me, Telen."

"I understand. Why don't I go alone?"

"No." He is reading, disguised.

"Oh, Peter, why not?"

The silence is too long. *I wouldn't ever go there behind his back.* The waiter comes, he never answers her.

"But why are you so against it, Peter?"

"Why are you so for it, darling?"

"Is it a problem?"

"Yes it is."

"Not for me. She's just a sad little woman with thick ankles living up there all by herself." *I don't even know her last name.*

"It's a very bad memory."

"I know, Peter, but it's not mine."

"Yes but." He stops, suddenly her face is between his palms, he is staring into her. "Leave it alone, Telen."

"What is it, Peter?" *There is nothing he can't tell me, nothing, nothing that will ever change my mind about loving him.*

"I'll tell you. Not now."

She does not know why, she reaches for the newspaper on the chair again. She feels a small surge of apprehension but does it anyway. *There must be a clue.*

The front page. She shakes her head. "So depressing."

"Yup, that's why we like it."

"I suppose. One more bombing. Oh, Toyer's gone, good riddance."

"Looks like he's walking away for good." Peter says it is probably the last time she will ever read anything written by him. Then he adds, "Might not be such a good thing after all."

"What makes you say that?"

"Well, how would you feel if you were Felicity Padewicz's folks?"

"And him in Miami working as a fashion consultant or something."

"Yeah, but he's a bigger star than I could ever be, that's for sure." Peter does not blink. His eyes are lighter than the sky.

"Star?"

"Yeah, another kind of star. It's not what he is it's what we say he is."

He waits, carefully. *This is a beautiful letter no matter who wrote it. Somewhere deep in the belly of your lovely mind you must see that, Telen.*

"You don't respect him by any chance, do you?"

Peter does not answer.

"You do. Oh, my God." She is smiling. Then she laughs.

"I respect what he is trying to do right now."

"He ought to kill himself."

"He can't kill, Telen. Nobody's picked up on that, he's probably Catholic."

"He's probably schizophrenic."

He folds the newspaper, signals the waiter.

"Doesn't the waiter remind you of Zapata?" She does not know of Zapata. Peter orders a second espresso then changes it to a machiatto. Telen shakes her head.

"I'm sure you're right, Telen, schizophrenics can watch themselves do something that's absolutely crazy and they know it, but they watch themselves do it anyway like any by-stander, they can't stop themselves, it's the damnedest thing." His eyes have been roving while he talks, moving quickly from her face to the windows of his attic apartment across the street. "It's as if you could be over there at my window and watch yourself sitting here with you at the same time." *It's what he told me at the beach.* "You're *that* detached."

Telen feels a sparkling wave wash over her, leaving sweat on her neck. It is a wave of uneasiness. She wants him to make love to her to make it go away.

MAUDE

JILTED. There it is. In Sunday morning's *Herald*. *The write-off. He's quit once and for all to be with someone who loves and understands him. Free, young, happy. He'll never trouble me or anyone again. It was just a phase he was passing through.* Jesus God.

Sara calls. "Such a pleasant little note of farewell. Just think, he's beginning a new life. Just like the Duke of Windsor when he abdicated the throne of England for the woman he loved."

"I love the 'put the past behind me,' part," Maude says, "and the 'get on with my life.' They all say that. Politicians, businessmen, criminals, they all say 'get on with my life.'"

But the letter is what Maude needs; it is a way in.

"Answer him, Maude, sit right down now and answer him immediately. You've got to get it downtown by three 'cause it's Sunday and Jim'll tell them to get it in tomorrow morning."

Maude knows that she cannot cure Toyer, no one can, that it is a lie. She wants him found, she does not want him to withdraw to roam free and happy, she wants him incarcerated for the rest of his life. And if he is, his scalpel story will never be believed.

It does not take long to write, by eleven it is finished. Maude calls Doctor T, they meet for Sunday brunch at Sam & Sam's Deli in Beverly Hills.

Scottish smoked salmon, lemon, cream cheese, capers, sopping beefsteak tomatoes, fine sliced Maui onions, toasted bagels plain. The *Six-Day War*, Doctor T calls it. He frowns while she reads her response to Toyer. He knows it is all she can do, her final volley. They will meet for dinner at Bouffe le Dindon and afterward, the night.

By two-thirty she has delivered the letter to the Sunday news editor, her twenty-year-old admirer with erupted skin has saved space on the op-ed page in the early Monday morning edition. *It might just work.*

PETER

NIGHT. They are at opposite ends of Peter's living room. The light from two candles wavers on the shadowed attic beams. Both have a floor fan blowing air directly at them. He is on the floor, lying naked on pillows, staring at the ceiling, taut. Telen is relaxed, she leans back on a wood chair, her willow legs stretched out, wearing a black half-slip, her brassiere unstrapped, a pair of panties dangles across a string in the bathroom, drying.

It is Peter's move. An invisible chessboard floats somewhere in the dimness between them, suspended near the canted ceiling. Incredibly, Telen has introduced him to mental chess. The game is mysterious. For the first time, Peter can feel his brain within his skull, moving like a trapped squirrel, as if it had tiny fingers, as if it were part of his body, active, not locked away in a safe. He is using his brain gymnastically. Telen has done this. When she was nine, she met Bobby Fischer.

He is holding their first five moves in his mind, imagining the board hanging between the beams above him. "You're scouring my brain pan, you know that, don't you?" He can feel friction from grains of sand in the fluid between it and his brain pan. "I need to lubricate it."

"Your move. We'll lubricate it afterward."

He is smiling. He can no longer concentrate. He enjoys losing to her, watching her win. After a moment he says, "King bishop to five."

"No."

"Why not?"

"Your pawn's on queen knight four."

He imagines her hands flying across the board. *Chess is finite but boundless,* she says. *Compared to love, the choices are overwhelming, the number of possible games you can play.*

She wins easily with the black pieces, casting a spell on the game early by obviously sacrificing a rook for a pawn, preventing a central counterattack when Peter's strong pieces become stuck in a backwater.

"I resign," he says.

"Remember, you're supposed to say, 'Thank you.' "

"Thank you. I was pretty good, wasn't I?"

"You were. If you'd stop trying to throw me off." Telen moves her heels apart, separates her legs. "Now what was that you said about needing to be lubricated?" *There is always something better to do, something we wish we were doing. When will he tell me?*

Maybe she should not know. She has found her man, she has made her nest. And when the summer heat has left the nights, she wants to sleep in his white cotton shirts.

MAUDE

TELEN NEVER BUYS newspapers but this morning she does. It is as though she were meant to read Maude Garance's letter.

The *Los Angeles Herald,* August 27. The op-ed page:

DR. GARANCE'S RESPONSE TO TOYER

Toyer,

If your promise to quit forever again is to be believed, it will be a miracle equal to none.

You say you have found a woman to share your life. You have convinced her that you can offer her "normal love." People change. I understand that. But you have not been cured. Love may feel good, but it is not a cure-all.

You say you are "normal." How would you know? You have a normal side to you, all schizophrenics do, the side that gets you in the door. But you are the same psychotic you have always been and always will be.

The furious, torn feelings that shaped your psychosis into the persona we know as Toyer are still alive in you.

You promise this woman you love a "normal" life. You may even act "normally" toward her, but you are not normal. You are capable at any time of reverting. It will take only one adverse act on her part.

Have you told this woman that while you are dancing with her, your twelve victims are rotting in special rooms in care centers, in wards, in their parents' homes? Or do you skip that subject?

If she truly loves you, she will understand your recent career. So if you truly love her, you must tell her.

                    Dr. Maude Garance

Telen assimilates the letter, turns the page.

TELEN

SHE IS RIGHT. There is no romance in Hollywood, she tells Peter, immigrants find that out for themselves. It is all too easy, there is nothing but time in Hollywood. It is too close to Mexico, by comparison a truly romantic country.

Long nights of chess and sex, losing, winning, he stimulates her with his Rubenstein Variation, penetrating her Nimbo-Indian Defense again and again.

"Did you know that chessmen are afraid of the dark?"

"No, I didn't." She surprises him.

"Yes. When you put them back in the box they hold each other. The queen picks one of the pawns and takes him into the castle and lets him make love to her. It's her right as queen."

"What about the king?"

"Nothing about the king. Sometimes he goes off with a bishop."

Tonight, she beats him so quickly that it takes him an hour to want to make love to her. He is dazzled and intimidated, he likes the feeling. She overwhelms him variously with her needs.

She has changed since they have been close, she looks at people and wonders who they are, not whether they like her or not. She walks differently, without lolling her head, straight in good strides, she does not dress for strangers, shop for new shades of pigment, she does not care. That was all Hollywood was good for, it was never meant to be more. Now she can leave.

They both have changed. Peter wants their affair to be like a marriage, less provocative.

She would be too smart for Hollywood, her mother warned her, she had taste, background, a good mind. Telen told her she wanted to try it, she was still young enough to waste a year or two. She refused to be deterred. It would be a *goof*. All she ever wanted was to be allowed to enter Hollywood and play in an improvised world where everything was temporary, in motion, where anyone could feel important, could invent his days. She longed to be scrutinized. Her mother said that within the year, she would either marry an actor or be killed by one. It was an interesting choice. But when she arrived, there was nothing. She has been in town a year and has not even been mugged.

She feels ill. *Maybe I'll ask him tomorrow.* She feels vomit rising below her throat. She goes into the bathroom, closes the door.

PETER

THE NEXT MORNING when Peter returns to his apartment in Silverlake, he opens the windows and sets his two small fans whizzing on the floor.

He has found a pigeon in the alley near the garbage cans, behind the house. The pigeon has a bad leg, a swollen pink stump. It is now in the living room in a flat box under the window, pecking at wet bread. Occasionally it stops eating, looks at him and wurbles. As if asking for permission to die.

He switches on his word processor and begins to write. It soothes him. After minutes his eyes droop, he yawns, cuts off the switch. He is constantly in danger. Stands, strips, lies spread out on clean sheets, ties a silk handkerchief over his eyes to darken the room. He sees Maude bending over Melissa. It is a beautiful scene.

But he cannot get Telen out of his mind. Anyone can describe beauty, he cannot explain it. He holds his penis. Afterward, he sleeps. He thinks about what he has done, it is beginning to terrify him.

MELISSA

THIS EVENING Melissa Crewe seems to understand what Detective I. Perrino is trying to do. The telephone message he has been playing for her begins: *"Tango, Oscar, Yankee, Echo, Romeo."* Maybe she will remember the voice. Once again, Perrino holds a small tape deck close to her right ear and plays her a tape recording of Toyer's telephone call, made from Melissa's apartment to the Santa Monica Police Precinct. The recorded voice is intimate, clear. It begins, *"There is a woman at this address to be found. Her name is Melissa Crewe. . . ."*

When she hears Toyer saying her name, she knows, blinks twice, releases tears. Very slightly, she turns her head away.

This is the fifth day there have been sessions with Melissa, they are brief, no longer than five minutes. With Detective Perrino tonight is another man, a police artist, an internist, and Chleo. Melissa has been tired. Chleo holds the watch, when she tells them that their time is up, Perrino and the police artist withdraw to the cafeteria, wait an hour until Melissa has rested, then they will begin again. It is coming together tonight. Perrino will call Assistant D.A. Bob Meyerson the moment they have a sketch.

There have been contradictions. Sometimes Melissa is able to blink twice when she sees an image she recognizes, sometimes she slips back into her tide pool.

Piece by piece Toyer is being assembled. He is male, white, his hair is light colored, slicked back as it was on the only night she knew him. He has strong, well-scrubbed hands. He is six feet tall, lean, tan, light-eyed, maybe blue-eyed, wears black. There are no tattoos, he is heterosexual, he does not smoke, he is clean. When Melissa is shown a composite sketch by the police artist, she blinks twice.

I. Perrino calls Meyerson at home, tells him that he has enough to go on, he is ready to roll. Tomorrow he will order a guard to be stationed outside Melissa's door. Meyerson calls his boss, Ray Yellen, also at home, tells him that they are ready, they have the sketch, he suggests that this is the moment to call a press conference early tomorrow, in time to catch the morning talk shows, the first editions of the *Herald* and the local *Times*. Ray Yellen will stand onstage in front of the Great Seal of California, the usual flags, facing the glare, Bob Meyerson on his right. He will release to the world the first known image of Toyer, his exact description. Of course, there have been helpful aides, but it is his office that has delivered Toyer to them. There will be reverence paid him in the room, the press can do that.

Meyerson calls back. He wants to see a fax of the police sketch. Perrino asks Chleo where the fax machine is. Chleo says she will show him.

SARA

DOWN THE HALLWAY on Six, Sara Smith, wearing white, is standing at the public telephone, speaking to O'Land. She holds a photocopy of the police sketch, which Chleo has made for her. It is of someone she could not possibly have known. He has no redemption, she would never allow him in her house. A map of a man's head. Almond-eyed, doorknob-faced, without distinction. The face is not Hispanic, is not black. It is white, light-eyed, slicked-down hair, a longish nose. Nothing more than a man's rumor. A lawyer might say, *It does not rule out any suspect.* No one you know. Police sketches never look like anyone you know, living or dead. Diagrams of inhuman faces, all of them guilty.

She dictates her story to O'Land over the telephone. Under her byline, he will give her copy a four-inch box with the sketch above the fold on the front page of the bulldog edition. Another Sara Smith scoop:

> Finally, "the long-awaited" police sketch of Toyer as recalled by Melissa Crewe from her hospital bed. It has been drawn by a police artist. Melissa conveyed the details of her attacker's face by blinking her eyes in response to his questions.

In a few moments, she will fax him the picture, scooping the universe. She no longer trembles at the thought. O'Land asks her what she is doing, Sara Smith, for the rest of her life.

When she hangs up she calls Maude.

AMALIA MALDONADO

THE WAITER at the café gave her the business card. *Readings, Sra Maldonado*, the address around the corner.

This is crazy.

Why did he hand me this card? Why didn't I throw it away? She feels a draw. It is more than curiosity. On her way to Peter's apartment she passes the neon sign hung in the first-floor window on Cadogan Street below Sunset Boulevard two blocks away. The crimson neon outline of a hand hung in the window, she has never seen it unlit. The word *READINGS*. Written with red crayon in a cursive style on white paper, taped just below the neon hand: *La Señora Amalia Maldonado.*

"I am Señora Amalia Maldonado." A rich scornful voice, the certainty of the Spanish royalty. Telen's eyes are not yet used to the darkness of the small foyer. Maldonado is a grand tub of a woman. *Why am I here?*

She offers her hand, a soft dry hand, leads Telen into the close living room, backing into it as if she were rolling on casters concealed beneath her full-length dress. It is a huge dress, ornate, quilted. *She's wearing her bedding.*

"I really can't stay, señora, thank you, I'm running late. I'm sorry."

"No-no-no, stay, pay me nothing if you want." Maldonado is used to the hesitation of beginners, sometimes the fear. She puffs her lips into a smile, raises her chin, she knows who needs her.

"May I please use your phone?"

"Here there is no phone." Maldonado shrugs. *We are way beyond telephones.*

Telen stands, she is wearing a pale blue buttoned dress that Peter likes. It is awkward, Maldonado fills the doorway to the foyer.

"I don't need no phone, miss, what's it for?"

Telen cannot go forward, cannot sit. There is sandalwood incense, three lamps lit, still not enough light. It is a salon cluttered with dead life, monthless magazines, a stuffed animal with an unfriendly face in a bell jar, walking sticks, a pelt rug that had at one time hunted critters. A German helmet. Ornate silk rags, a seashell, thin white bones.

"Please." Maldonado holds her palm over a reddish velvet chair, the client's chair. She is a disheveled woman with small groupings of facial hairs. "The color is Goya red, do you know of Goya, miss?"

"Yes, of course."

"He is my ancestor." Señora Maldonado is from Spain, not Mexico; to clear up any confusion before it arises, she tells Telen that she is from Saragossa.

"Why are you here to see me, miss?"

"I really shouldn't be."

"I don't know why not, you have many troubles."

Telen sits.

"You need to know about a man."

"Yes."

Señora Maldonado looks at Telen without haste, nodding. Before she speaks again, Telen opens her purse. She has heard that fortune tellers require money on the table in order to foresee. Amalia waves it closed. There are many rings.

"Pay me what you want." As if money disgusted her, as if she has given up on it and exists in the still room at the pleasure of her guests. "Pay me more if he is dead." There is a scent of incense in the gloom, a sweet gloom of it laid over a darker scent Telen can smell rising from the carpet. A dog is absent, she doesn't ask where.

"He is alive?"

"Yes, he is."

Maldonado sighs. "The living can be so troublesome." Carefully, she lifts out of a leather satchel a crystal ball the size of a baseball, polishes it with her scarf, watching Telen, sets it on a scrap of velvet with black tassels. Telen watches her position the crystal ball, she tries several times for the ideal aspect, turning it again and again until it is right. There are tiny black hairs growing between her fingers in the crotches above her rings.

"You are very 'fraid."

"Yes." For the first time Telen hears her own words. *I am afraid of the man I am in love with.*

The woman continues to stare into the ball, she does not need Telen's assent. She raises her eyes, watches Telen carefully. "What is it you fear?"

"I thought you might tell me."

The woman shifts, nearly closes her eyes, continues to stare into the crystal ball. "What crime has this man done?" There are local felonies.

Telen says quietly, "It is a new crime to your neighborhood, señora."

"You are not the first girl to come crying to Amalia Maldonado over a wanted felon. *Asi es la vida.*"

It is time to go. The woman cannot help her. Telen half rises, covertly opens her purse again, slips three five-dollar bills onto the table. *More than enough for being wrong twice.*

Maldonado puts her hand over Telen's, stares down into her crystal ball, shielding her face, her dark eyes brilliant, her expression benign. A minute passes. Telen can smell flowers. She can feel a dog watching her but she cannot see it. Amalia Maldonado shifts her weight grandly. She seems to have stopped breathing. Abruptly her body jolts, as if her train had come to a sudden stop. When she speaks, her voice is light, inquiring, "There are dead?" She asks it simply, as if she wanted to know the time. It comes from nowhere.

"Dead?" *Why would she say that?*

Maldonado says it again, definitely, as if in discovery. "There are many dead." She makes it seem not quite possible.

Telen does not answer, her fingers are damp, she feels the grip of the room on her. Pale, her face resembles milk glass.

"There are dead, miss."

It is an edict. Immediacy and certainty. The woman covers the crystal ball with the suede bag as if to protect it from Telen. She looks up at Telen, her benign expression is gone, her black eyes are sure. Telen sees ferocity, the great eyebrows have joined. The woman rises, large.

"Please kindly get out." Señora Maldonado touches the back of Telen's hand.

The massive dog who has always been there stands in the gloom beside Señora Amalia Maldonado, ears high, alert.

"Please return my card. Say to no one you were here, I did not see you."

Obediently, Telen hands the woman back her card, passes through the foyer, opens the front door, feels the thick gush of heat, totters outside, barn blind into the stunning brightness of the early evening sun. As she turns to close the door the woman is there, she reaches out and touches Telen's arm. She says, "Run, child, I see many dead."

Telen is stunned. *She knows.*

Señora Maldonado balls Telen's bills and tosses them into the air after her, causing Telen to stoop to the sidewalk to pick them up, the door slams.

TELEN

THE DRIVE to Sondelius is exhilarating. *Leaving Los Angeles is.* Without Ann's address, she will find her house. She knows she will remember a house or a street but once there, she cannot, nothing is familiar, it is a small town but there is no center, too many roads.

At the gas station she asks directions to Heavenly Rest. She will start there, find her way back, remembering the route they took after the funeral.

The plan works. Ann is not at home. Telen opens the screen door, the back door is unlocked. "Ann? Ann?" She pushes her way through the stale kitchen. She expects anything, a body, there is nothing to steal. A toaster. The house is in shaded light. At each door she says, "Ann?"

The living room, its lamps at attention, the unclean sofa. The bedroom, a small bed neatly made, frayed veneer. The bathroom, its false tiles. Rust sparks behind the sink.

Elaine's room. It is as it was, cleared of carpet, the bare wood floor. The wheelchair shining from the corner, folded. Clean. The smell of dried shingles, the shades half drawn, outside light bounces on the ceiling, the walls bare except the one behind the door.

There they are, the row of narrow clippings. From left to right, each one a pretty name, Virginia Sapen on through to

Nina Voelker. They might be titles of books being reviewed. Names of smart women brought to rest.

Why? Who put these women on her wall? Was it Ann? No. Ann was terrified. Is this the other thing?

Dry-mouthed, Telen feels weak, she will collapse if she does not sit, she pulls open Elaine's wheelchair by the window, falls into it, leans forward. But it is no better, she may vomit. The feeling that she may or may not, it is her choice. Out the window the brittle oaks shimmer black pools of shade, a land without water, Telen imagines sheep, cows. She does vomit, suddenly, too soon, before she can rise. Up and out it goes, her chartreuse breakfast, she sits staring stupidly at the vomitus on her ankles and pretty shoes.

With knots in her stomach, her imaginings uncontrolled, she washes her feet one at a time in the kitchen sink, cleans the room, the sickness hugs her. By the time she is done cleaning it is three. She cannot wait any longer for Ann. It has taken too long. He will wonder. What will she tell him if he asks, will she lie? She has gone behind his back.

What she dreads and what she believes have come together in her mind yet she cannot hold them there for more than a moment. Driving home, she can barely keep her car between the white lines on the freeway.

Immediately Peter sees a change in her, walking in. He looks at her too carefully. He picks her up and drops her on the dining table. She submits. He shatters her, it is as close to rape as possible, her panties are torn off to one side. She is not ready for him. He fills her. Gradually during the long screaming moments she is made well.

In the afternoon wide as her bed, they make love again, this time nude, damp from the shower and on clean sheets folded back, but it will not go away. When it is over she feels ill. She feels a rock lodged inside her chest just below her breasts.

After dark when he is asleep, Telen lies on one side and then the other, repeatedly dreaming the same dream, a busy din in her brain. She has heard the din before when she has had too much wine or coffee, but tonight she has not drunk either. Finally she begins to fade.

She wakes with a jolt. A fathomless sleep, a brutal waking. It is late. Her wristwatch is elsewhere. It must be three or four. The purple light made from streetlamps and headlights muscles its way between the shades into her apartment, it lavishes Javanese shadow puppets on the ceiling.

She does not know the exact moment it comes to her, because it has come to her in her sleep. Impressions have been fitting into a shape that is so dreadful she cannot imagine it.

She feels Peter's eyes click in the dark. He is awake.

"Telen."

"Yes?"

"What is it?"

"I'm so frightened."

"I can tell." He says it lightly. He is staring at the ceiling, waiting.

Telen is trembling. She starts to sob from her belly.

"I don't care anymore, Peter, it just doesn't matter what you do to me. This is the first time I've ever been happy with a man and I feel like I want to die. . . ." She condenses herself, sobs, her eyes are closed, her fingers are in her mouth. Her crying excites him, the threat of hopelessness. Abruptly he enters her. It is as if his cock were the answer.

She does not stop sobbing. She cries now with all her body while he punches into her from behind. When he withdraws, she finds his sperm with her fingertips and smears it on her breasts. With one finger she paints it into the tears on her face, under her eyes.

After a while, he says, "Be calm and think very carefully about this. We're free now, Telen."

"Are we free?"

"I'm through with my life here, we can leave L.A. anytime."

"Can you tell me everything?"

"No."

"Please?"

"Whatever it is you're worried about, is it in the past?"

"I suppose."

"We all have pasts. Some more unforgettable than others."

Unforgettable?

"But it's over. What about the future? Why do we always worry about the past? Can't we talk about the future?"

She begins to sob again, overcome with the horror of loving him. She cries, her screams muffled into the pillow.

"Don't tell me don't tell me."

"Telen. There is nothing left to tell." Peter holds her, whispers, "Everything is behind me. I'm starting all over again. I want to do it all with you." He waits. "Telen. There is nothing *to* know anymore."

She whispers, "Does *anyone* know?"

"Go to sleep, Telen." His fingers close her eyes in the dark.

After his wife's ordeal he lost his mind. Okay. He killed her. But how can I wake up every morning, wondering about the others? How can I if I know there may be replicas of women he left behind. If it is true, if it is him? Can I try? Go to sleep.

The walls of her bedroom dissolve into a mist of clouds. She cannot answer. *Sleep.* She wonders over and over, *Is it possible?* She believes, she knows. When she first came here, LOVE was a songwriter's word, she believed in the lyric. *Can't li-ive, if livin' is without you. Sleep, Telen.*

Lookin' for Love in All the Wrong Places.

Leave Los Angeles? Why not. Easy to give up my silly strange ambition. No one will ever know. Writing for movies? I met producers. I tried. Movie scripts are pencil sketches of orgasms. Sleep. We could settle in a town up north with seasons and greenery, dusty afternoons and aged wood, where old people say good morning to you without even thinking about it, where streets are named after species of trees and birds. Where grocery stores smell of food. Sleep. Where there is no ambition to be anything but what you already are. Can he be a better person for all the horror he's created? Sleep. Can I be able to sur-

vive it? *Can my love for him turn this gangrene stink into fragrance? Is that my definition of love? Genetic survival? The strongest force? In our best interest? Sleep, Telen.*

But she cannot, of course. Something is leading her away from her bedroom. She dresses and walks a block to an all-night market. There is a shatteringly bright café attached.

The pay telephone is broken, so Telen taps in Billy's number on the counter telephone. She is glad to hear his taped voice rather than his own.

"I'm out, right?" The hunter out hunting. "Hi, Billy, Telen. I called to say goodbye. I'm going away." She says it gayly, then adds after a pause, "I love you." She interrupts her pause by hanging up.

Back in her apartment, she undresses just inside the front door, lies down naked trying not to wake Peter. She is as close to dying as she has ever been, that is, feeling the perfect relief that only death might provide.

PETER

PETER WAKES TOO EARLY. It is still dark. He has heard a sound, a sharp sound, something has fallen, he does not know what. He feels for Telen with his foot then with his hand. He is alone. He calls out quietly, "Telen, Telen." Silence. He knows that she is nearby somewhere in her apartment.

He assembles himself, gets his feet on the floor, ears screaming, feels himself pushing through the room knee-deep in marsh-water.

Telen is curled in the bathtub like a child. Her blood has made a simple line to the drain. It is a dark, masculine flow.

It is written too neatly, in beautiful script. On the porcelain wall of the bathtub, in black felt marker:

11 Nembutal, 5 Seconal. It could be a baseball score.

A ritual suicide. Without realizing it, Peter has shut Telen in a perfect chamber, sealed, without windows.

TELEN

I T IS A DAY as ordinary as yesterday. In her hospital bed, Telen is dove gray but well enough to go home. Billy sits beside her, his wildflowers nearby in a plastic vase. Peter stands in busy silence at the window.

The tranquilizers have been sucked out of her, the wrist cut is sewn and bandaged. She had cut one wrist, not deeply, with a fruit knife, avoiding the artery. The police have come and gone. Attempted suicide is not a crime, anyhow, it is not clear to them that was what it was.

Billy is whispering. He has a new life. He has spent a week in San Diego, through Peter, he has met a Hollywood agent, a dry salvage named Buck who has gotten him a job as master of ceremonies and sometime stand-up comic at the Laugh Lounge, a noisy room on Melrose with tiny tables. He is making payments on a new car. He is on top of the world.

"It's legit, I'm legit."

He never asks Telen why.

When he leaves and Peter is alone with Telen, she says to him, "You know what I thought, don't you." It is not a question.

"Do you still?"

"I'm almost past all that." *Kill me for knowing. Kill me for not knowing.*

PETER

LATER IN THE CAR, something happens to Peter. He is driving Telen home, east on Sunset Boulevard, barely moving, inching past sharp sealed office buildings. All the car's windows are open. The sun is too hot. Telen is sedated, mildly aware that they should be moving forward and are not.

The radio is playing, its aerial is a straightened coat hanger. It can only be heard when they pass between buildings. As they emerge from a sound shadow, a woman's voice emanates from the radio. A woman's voice, midsong, unaccompanied, singing without words. Lifelong breaths. Peter catches a hint of the melody, needs to hear it all.

The street is cramped with cars. They are anchored dead center between the four corners of buildings at an intersection when the light changes. When there is an opening, he rolls ahead, the voice fades into static hissing. He stops, backs up, the voice returns. The horn behind him shrieks. He eases forward, the voice fades. He backs up. He cannot lose her, who is she, what is she singing?

In the voice he hears a woman, its female largess. The voice swells. A woman's voice. The rich guttural, then the clean high notes, swooping upward. It reminds him of longing, he does not know for what, something within him, a need he does not know he has.

Stuck to a standstill, horns shriek. He creeps forward, the pathetic antenna fails, they enter another sound shadow, the voice fades again. He stops, leans forward his head touching the crazed vinyl of the steering wheel. *What is that?* The searing full notes changing without blemish. *The blood of woman, how can it be this beautiful?* Telen watches him without speaking. He cannot drive. It is too strange.

"Peter, drive."

He cannot move. He does not raise his head. He is trying to catch every note. The melody journeys toward substance, a certain end. The sun overhead does not matter, the horns, the breathless street. The presence of the singer, it is everything. He listens. "Listen, Telen, please listen, this is the answer. Listen to her." Without knowing what it is, Telen absorbs it. She is moved by the music.

A man has been yelling from a perfect car behind them, a woman is driving. Telen reaches out the window, waves for them to pass, but the wedge has tightened. No one can move. Horns blast on three sides of them, clarions from Detroit, shrieks from the Autobahn, trills from Japan. An urban omelette.

Peter rolls the car forward again, her voice fades. He eases back a few feet until her voice is clear, full. He kills the motor. He pulls the handbrake up. He must know the name of the singer, the composer. It is important, it has something to do with him, something depends on it, something he has never been aware of but he knows is there.

The man behind them has gotten out of his perfect car, slammed the door. His wife is shouting at him.

Peter is deeply concentrated. In the rich contralto he hears the depth of a woman, the depth of her sorrow, her longing, her supreme joy, the woman's great beauty, all in her voice and in one melody from sex to childbirth, early death, rebirth. The woman emerges, reaching out of the dashboard, beguiles his soul. Everything, the high heels, the rampant delicacy, the wondrous lab. He has never heard a sound like it. In this voice he hears weather, salvation, lives of centuries. The history of women to men, men to women, the ancient debt. A miracle.

The man is at the window, a well-turned-out man, combed, clean as a baby. Cool from his air conditioning, late for lunch. He is trying to slap Peter. Peter rolls his window up, catching the man's arm, then his hand. The clean man yanks his hand away through the crack between the glass and the frame. He hits the window with his ring shouting basic school words. Telen is frightened.

Peter, head down, concentrates, eyes shut, he listens, sweat running down his face. He cannot imagine how anyone could compose music so simple and so full, so endless. Elaine's misery is there, too. He must know what it is. He sees his life as a dream, in it, he is alone. He feels his mind rise from his body, above the steering wheel, pass through the roof of the car and look down at the three of them. Telen wonders if he is crying.

The clean man is screaming through the window, raving, pounding the hood, bending the windshield wiper back and forth until it comes off in his hand. He cuts his hand. There is blood on the windshield. The man thrashes the hood with the wiper then holds it stupidly and hurls it at the car. He could die right there, over the hood, under the sun. His wife is standing by their perfect car, waving him back. The clean man is for the moment insane, the man inside the car is insane.

Peter cannot raise his head. He listens, leaning forward, close to the steering wheel, the music binding him, more important than Telen's fear, more important than the man outside his car, more important than his life.

Another man has abandoned his car, a pickup truck, and is walking toward them holding an iron bar, a steaming man in a hurry.

In one sustained note the ending comes too soon. A fragment, it has been three minutes.

"I have to hear what it is, I have to know the name of the singer."

From the radio, a man's calm voice says, "You have been listening to the *Vocalise* composed by Sergei Rachmaninoff, from an old recording sung by Anna Moffo in 1964." That Anna and Sergei could touch them here, now, today, their souls. Without words. Words that would reduce the solo melody to thoughts.

The lane opens, Peter drives. After a silence, Telen says, "He died in Hollywood, Rachmaninoff."

He does not answer.

"He did, really. He died during the Second World War right here."

"Can you blame him? Look at this toilet."

They feel the presence of Rachmaninoff.

"I know he lived nearby," she says. "One of these streets, maybe over there." They look up Larabee Street at one of the four-unit apartment buildings that is not meant to be looked at for any longer than it takes to read its number. It is where Sergei Rachmaninoff died.

When they stop at a light, Peter holds Telen fiercely against him, he knows that if she can survive this they will live forever. Telen is the one. He marvels at her. He begins to cry. It makes her cry to see him cry. Unable to drive, they park, sit, crying. She does not want the responsibility of knowing for certain, of forgiving him.

At her apartment that night they lie side by side and stare at the enigmas on the ceiling. It comes to him that his life is not a dream. That the soft area just outside his vision is his to go to. It is his invention, he created it, he owns it. That he can find something else, create something better. That he can change. That if he wants to, he can destroy Toyer himself. Anytime. He believes Maude has been trying to help him. He understands that. Her words told him clearly what to do. Her words joined the *Vocalise*, they came together at a perfect time. It is his first entirely lucid moment since the New York City night.

Telen holds him, he does not hold her, she does not know if she wants him inside her, she cannot make herself touch him there. She whispers, "Do you seriously think we can live? And do ordinary things?"

"Elaine is dead. I keep telling you we're free."

Peter slides his hand under her buttocks and turns her away from him and penetrates her. She does not want him inside her, it is too soon, she has not decided. She is drained and resists, exciting him. She shudders. As always, his cock is the answer to everything.

His face is wet, drops run into his eyes. The sheet is moist with his sweat. Her buttocks slippery against his stomach, his loins. Her neck shines in the streetlight, hair stuck to it. He combs it aside, with his fingers he numbers her cervicals without realizing that he is doing it. He stops. He circles her ear with his lips, drenching it with his tongue. She grips the mattress with one hand, the bed table with the other and lasts until it is over.

SARA

EARLY EVENING. Sara is meeting Melissa Crewe for the first time. Maude has asked her to write the first article to be written about her recovery.

She is stopped from entering Melissa's room by a police guard, a black woman. "I'm sorry, you'll have to wait here for clearance." She reads Sara's name tag, calls downstairs on her intercom: "Miz Smith from the *Herald.*"

Through the glass panel, Sara sees: Melissa, her head raised on a pillow, wide eyes open staring at Maude who sits beside her holding her hand. Doctor T has looked in on them both. He stands behind Maude looking down, his operation has been a success.

"Okay. You can go in."

Sara stops in the doorway. Music emanates from the corner of the room, it is the film score from *Doctor Zhivago,* another one of Melissa's favorites. What Sara beholds is quite moving to her. *Perfect. A vivid tableau.* None of the three has seen her. In a moment Maude turns to her, comes over. Whispers. "Hi, Sara, come on in." She is radiant.

Doctor T turns. "Doctor, this is my friend Sara Smith, Doctor Tredescant." *So formal.*

"We met briefly, remember? When I picked Maude up for Telen's play?"

"Yes, of course I do. Have you been well?"

"Lovely, thanks. Maude's been telling me about your work." *And your nights.*

"And she has been telling me about yours." Doctor T is not a fan. He is leaving.

"I mean it, Doctor, congratulations. Your patient looks wonderful. I was standing in the doorway just now before you saw me. You three looked like the Currier and Ives print called 'The Healers.' "

"Cut it in half, Sara."

"Would you please let me take you both to dinner tonight?" Sara catches him in the doorway.

"I cannot." Doctor T half bows. "Unfortunately. But I can certainly come by after nine for a cognac if the restaurant is not too far away from West Los Angeles."

"We'll pick a spot and let you know," Maude says.

He is gone.

"He can't forget how I corrupted you."

"Oh, he'll be fine." Maude sits and takes Melissa's hand. "All we need are results and he'll get over it."

"That's the other reason I'm here, Maude. I've had a great idea." Sara waits for Maude's attention.

"Well? Want to tell me now or over dinner?"

"No, now. Instead of writing to him, why don't you write one last letter to her?"

"Who?"

"The woman he loves."

"Brilliant."

PETER

TELEN BELIEVES it may all be possible. At six the next evening, Peter and Billy ambush her coming out of the hospital where she has gone to have her dressing changed. They will take her to dinner in an orderly mall named Robertson Village.

They choose The Source, where the food is either brown or green, they order spinach and bean salads, a bottle of cold Chardonnay. The three friends toast to the Uncastables. Telen's left wrist cannot be seen. When they are finished eating, Peter reveals his plan.

"Plan Nine," he calls it. He has seen an ad in an Oregon newspaper. Unbelievably, he says, he and Telen can rent a house in Portland for a third of what they would pay in Los Angeles and still have a room for Billy when he visits. Then, later, if they become bored by urban life, they can find a house in a nearby town where Telen's old people will smile good morning to them from their porch swings as they walk by. Peter can do part-time roofing, Telen can work at computers or at anything she wants, even apply to the University of Oregon and study art. There will always be a guest room waiting for Billy. As an alternative lifestyle, Peter announces, he will propose marriage. They laugh together. They toast themselves again. Sun shines through their glasses. It is their life after all. They are standing firmly in the present tense. When they have eaten, they walk, cling together, as if it all might break. It is the final meeting of the Uncastables.

From a distance, Billy watches the three of them drifting through the mall. He knows that Telen belongs with him, not with Peter. Didn't she tell him she loved him just before she tried to kill herself?

Nothing is broken in Robertson Village. Nothing leaks or

rusts here. Unlike anywhere else, everything at the village works, a nineteenth-century village, cobbled alleys lined with corporate outlets, national franchises disguised as Cornwall shoppes. School Street, Telegraph Street. Its blueprints are new. The sky is glass, the night is viewed overhead, sealed out, framed by ficus trees. It is a world unlike any other. There is no horse manure, no smell of wet straw, no poor children, no one is deformed, there is no influenza.

They walk around the perfect village, hand in hand, as browsing citizens, chatting. *Why can't we live here?* Telen is enchanted by Peter's idea of life in a small town in Oregon.

"When do you want to leave?" she says. *I want it to come true.*

"What about next Friday?"

"Let's break our leases and head north." *I can make this work.*

I can make it work, Peter thinks.

"Which car do you want to take?"

"We can drive up in mine and Billy can bring yours up later."

"I need the whole weekend to pack."

"Monday. Monday night. We'll get there Tuesday morning and have the whole day."

Her mind is swirling. It is decided, they will leave L.A. Monday night. She believes in them. She knows that tomorrow she will wonder what she is doing today.

Nothing is impossible at Robertson Village. But at 10:00 P.M., a guard asks the three friends to leave his village and return to their own. His village must be sealed for the night against intruders.

MAUDE

M ONDAY MORNING.

A MIRACLE TOO BRIEF
TOYER STILL A TERROR

By Dr. Maude Garance, M.D.

I want to thank the editors for giving me one last opportunity to express my views. I had not planned to write on this page again. This letter is addressed to one woman whom I believe to be living in the Los Angeles area. She is the woman described by Toyer as his reason for "walking away," as he puts it, "for a woman who loves me and understands me. I can now begin to lead a normal life with this woman I love." It is my hope that this letter might alert her to the truth. I believe this reckless woman has no idea who the man is whom she loves.

Dear Reckless,

Yes, he has indeed changed, and for the moment he seems normal. He is toying with you the way he has toyed with all of us. That is why he's called Toyer. I know who you are, dear Reckless, you are a nice-looking girl, in your twenties. You are probably religious, you are romantic, capable, trusting, and, oddly enough, intelligent. I try to see you and I almost can. He has only chosen the best women and you are one of them.

As I have said to him I'll say to you: He promises you a "normal" life. He may even act "normally" toward you, but he is not normal. He is in remission. He is capable at any time of reverting. It will take only one adverse act on your part.

You have chosen to love a human being who is a sinister deviate. You have a perilous future ahead of you, young woman, and please, don't let me make that sound glamorous.

He is someone who has enjoyed watching the light fade from his victims' eyes. To quote a colleague, Toyer is "what is scraped from colons during autopsies."

If you suspect him, do not share your doubts with him— the moment you do, your life will be over. You could easily suffer a diabolic fate. You will most certainly be his next victim. Your duty, as you read this letter, is twofold. First, you must think of yourself, save your own life, run. Second, once you are safe from him, your duty is to come forward. Contact the police at 911. You must do it for all of us. Please understand this.

Please, dear woman, whatever your name is, for the sake of his next victim, yourself, come forward. He is extremely dangerous. My heart goes out to you. Do the right thing for all our sakes, and especially for yours.

I am also giving you a telephone number at this newspaper. Your call to me will be confidential. You have my word. Please call me, your life depends on it.

                                        Maude Garance, M.D.

PETER

PETER has picked up a check at his friend's roofing company and on his way home drops his car off at the brake shop down the street from his apartment. He buys a copy of the *Herald*, takes it upstairs to read in the bathtub full of cool water. It is early evening.

On the last page of A Section, Maude's letter to Telen glares at him. He had no idea. He is jarred, bewildered, he thought she was through with him, through writing for the *Herald*. *She's swallowed a scorpion.* He feels her rage flattened out against him, overwhelming him, he has been too casual, too open. *Too fucking stupid.* He is shivering, the water is too cold.

He calls Telen, no answer. She is out shopping for the trip.

Maude Garance is telling her to run from him as fast as she can, to identify him to the police. *Has Telen seen it?* He reads the letter over and over, flings the newspaper out the bathroom window, it flutters to the alley below. He cannot lose Telen.

He calls her again, no answer.

She's trying to break us up. She told me to kill Elaine. I did. Not enough. She wants to take us down.

Peter is out of the tub toweling himself. It is after six. Telen is bringing her bags over at seven. *No, she won't have read it. We can still get the hell out of town without her seeing it. It'll be in the wastebasket tomorrow.*

He is packed, waiting. Carefully he cleans the tar out of each fingernail with mineral spirits. At seven he calls her apartment, no answer.

Why should she read the paper? She never does. Someone's going to tell her to read it? I don't think so. By seven-thirty we'll be driving north.

By seven-forty she has not shown up. He calls her again, then the brake shop. Half an hour more. He writes her a note, telling her to wait for him inside, sticks it on the door. He borrows a neighbor's motorcycle, rides to her apartment, stone deaf.

He turns the key, opens her front door. His eyes are like a falcon's. Her place is silent, reeks of abandonment, he can see haste. He goes into the bedroom, turns on the ceiling light. Her dresses are missing, her blouses, her red dress, yanked from their hangers, her hats are gone, her heels, her underwear, the book she was reading is gone, her chess set. Both of her wristwatches, rings, hairbrush, hair dryer, toothpaste. She has packed, not for Oregon.

He goes into the kitchen, there it is on the stove:

Dear Peter
    Please please please don't look for me! You won't find me I promise you. Don't try. If you do, I will call the police. I promise I will.

                                                            Me

She believes every word that woman wrote her. She did it. I want that woman.

It is over. Telen could be anywhere. Driving. Peter feels his headache scrape, his eyes ball up with pain. He stands in the dark kitchen, swaying. He has a key to Maude Garance's house.

THE END

THE END

MAUDE

THE HEAT is withdrawing from the nights, it is September. Maude nearly did not play tennis tonight. When she left Melissa's room, she sat with Felicity during her feeding, then with Nina until she could no longer look at her. She left the Kipness in the early evening. In Nina's room, she heard a television weather personality predict that this would be a sultry night. She skipped dinner.

She kept her tennis date with Rex Voss, a new doctor in pediatrics, at the public courts on Cheviot Hills Park, it was 8:20 when they got on the court. She has beaten him before. Their games have been slow and vocal.

The courts are busy, brilliantly lit. Now it is a quarter to ten. The floodlights blink once, warning the players, *ten o'clock blackout*. Curfew and dismissal. Some players have already quit, others are quitting, winding down, toweling, walking by off the courts. Two courts are still in use.

Maude, leading five to one, serves an ace. Point. Each time she serves an ace, she makes a small cry. She is finishing Rex off. Point. She puts old anger into her serve, leftover anger from her long day at the Kipness. Point. No talk. Sweat.

She wears a white tennis skirt, a loose white top with wide shoulder straps. Traditional. Rex has been eliminated from the competition but keeps going, like a white mouse on a wheel. He is no longer smiling, occasionally calls out jokey threats that he really means. He would not mind quitting. He is slow picking up the loose balls, towels himself each time. He is younger. He is attracted to her, he came to play tennis not to argue with her across a net. Maude is intent on annihilating him. They will probably never play tennis with each other after tonight.

Cheviot Hills Park, dark as a myth, surrounds the bright players. Full Tacoma bushes, black and deep, crowd the chain-link fence running the lengths of the courts. Peter stands among the Tacoma bushes, hidden in shadow, watching Maude chase down every shot, try for every return, make nasty, unreturnable serves, curt calls. There is one game left in the final set.

Peter studies her, the force of her will. He has been watching her thighs, they are in fluid motion, they jolt to a stop then surge again. The long cords of her *vastus lateris* muscles leading to her pubis are rigid, strong. Her body, a perfect ectomorph. Her femoral muscles, churning, enticing, arms taut. *Stroke, stroke.* Point. *Stroke.* Thighs. Point. *Stroke, stroke,* pubis. *Stroke.* Buttocks. Point. *Stroke.* Her skirt swings away from the rise of her pudendum. Her hips in motion, slugging away, backhand, forehand, backhand. Point. Game, set, match. Maude's cool *yip* of victory, uniquely sexual, Rex's groan of exaggerated agony, relief.

Watching her play tennis for blood has not tempered Peter's rage against Maude, it has honed it, disciplined it. But he is surprised by her athletic beauty, her meanness on the court, her fierce sexuality. He has watched her the way a matador watches a Muira cow tested for bravery at a *tienda*.

Suddenly it is ten. The floodlights go black. Cries of despair from the two other players, laughter because it is dark. Amber lamps remain lit, the park is dim, not black.

Maude and Rex do not leave arm in arm, nor do they speak, no awkward diplomacy. Peter feels a bolt of excitement. He skirts the courts outside the chain-link fencing, walks the long circuit around them, sees her white car parked nearly alone in the parking lot. He straddles his borrowed motorcycle, black on black, between the bushes at the far end, just off the lot. By the time he gets to the lot, he sees Maude toss her racquet onto the front seat, get in, turn on the ignition. The motor will not start. Other motors are being started. Rex drives by behind her, honks curtly, *beep-beep*.

Peter watches Maude sit back, coolly towel her hair, then try the starter again. Grinding noise. He has been here an hour. Another car drives by, its lights flashing as it passes. Then another, the last one. Silence in the parking lot. Maude is alone.

Inside her car it is stifling. She turns the key in the ignition, pumps the gas. Grinding noise. She says, *Fuck*. Not one of Elias's favorite words. She senses a headlight in the lot behind her, looks around. A single headlight at the far end. She reaches her racquet out the window and waves. A man on a motorcycle wearing a helmet slows to an idle beside the car door.

"Trouble?" She can barely see his face.

"Yeah," Maude says.

"Yeah," he says. He doesn't dismount. Bike idling. Biker pose continues.

"Yeah," she repeats. *Let's say yeah at each other for a while.*

Peter levels his bike, appears ready to gun it. Maude is suddenly exhausted. *Not good Samaritan material.* She opens the door, puts a foot on the pavement.

"I think I'll call Triple A."

"They don't fix cars."

God, what's wrong with him?

"Look, I'll pay you. I'm in a rush."

"What happens when you turn the key?"

"I get a grinding noise." She demonstrates.

"That's right."

"You know what's wrong?"

"It's your throttle linkage."

"Oh, yeah."

"You knew about it?" *Is he being rude or does he think I'm funny?*

"Not really."

"Something to know about."

"I guess it is." Maude has half-a-dozen diplomas depicting years of learning. She cannot tell coolant from windshield fluid.

"Do you have any wire?" His voice is surprisingly gentle.

"No." *Except for the piece under my bra.*

"What about in your hair?"

Maude's hands fly to her hair, it has grown to a certain length. She removes a hairpin she wears for tennis, holds it out. *He* does *think I'm funny.* He reaches out from his motorcycle, takes the hairpin from her, puts it between his teeth.

"Pop your hood?"

She does. Gradually he dismounts and raises his visor. He is surprisingly fair-complexioned, nearly blond. He removes his gloves and releases the hood catch, lifts the hood, the hairpin still between his teeth as if he were sewing. *A feminine gesture.*

"Hold that, will you?" he says, handing her a small halogen light, already lit, its stiff white beam scours the pavement. He bends under the hood and removes a piece of steel, small, bent and oily. He hands it to Maude who takes it as if it were part of a cockroach. She holds the light for him while he fashions her hairpin to imitate a throttle pin. After another minute he stands, slams the hood. He is sweating.

"That gizmo *may* get you home. Tomorrow take it to a garage and you tell them, don't ask them, exactly what is wrong with it. They'll give you a little respect. You're probably afraid to pick up your own hood."

Maude fishes around in her tennis bag and comes up with a loose twenty-dollar bill.

"Thanks. Would you accept this as payment?" She reaches the bill out to him, as if it were a cigarette in need of a match.

He ignores it for a moment then takes it, slips it into his side pocket unfolded. "Throttle linkage, remember." He mounts his bike, lowers his visor.

"I will, thanks."

"Which direction do you live?"

"Randall Canyon, why?"

"I don't know if that hairpin'll hold. I can ride behind you."

"I'm sure it'll be fine." *But the garages are closed and the Automobile Club doesn't do repairs.*

So superior, so prissy. Even so, she has always admired passersby who simply stop and help, they remain a rare blessing in Los Angeles. She turns the key slowly, as if the motor might burst. It starts quietly, a pretty sound. She looks at her watch: 10:12. From prognosis to cure it has taken six minutes.

"Okay. Please follow me."

He hops once on his starter and drives a distance away down the parking lot, waits for her to pass him and lead the way home.

TELEN

SHE KNOWS everything and nothing. She sits in her car, her overnight bag on the passenger seat, her dresses and blouses spread across the backseat, her books, pictures, dishes, pretty shoes in the trunk. She has been parked on Melrose Boulevard for more than two hours. It has gotten dark. The air inside the car is soiled white, there are cigarettes everywhere, short butts, long butts, crumpled packs. She has started smoking again.

It is him, the letter was very clear.

Traffic passes, wheezing buses sparkle, sneeze. Stores have closed around her, across the street, an optician's window glitters like Christmas.

First, it was Billy, she wanted to call him, "Can I come right over?" *He'd love to have me sleeping at his place. No. God knows what he might do about Peter. Would he call the police? Peter could walk in anytime looking for me.*

Sara. She's very clever. She'd get everything out of me. Sara is not a friend, it was just that one evening with Peter and Billy and they did not talk. She has no one.

Telen turns the engine on then off, she cannot drive, she has nowhere to drive to except Wisconsin.

It was nothing. When she met Peter Matson he was with Billy. As if the three of them were passengers who had met on a train heading for the same city. They sat and talked and looked out the window. She did not want anything more than friendship, not sex. The year before in Chicago was as if she had lived through a failed science project with her as the lab animal. Men were not wonderful or necessary. She was not looking for romance. She could not imagine romance in Hollywood; a practical, maybe elegant form of body exchange. The boys were fun, Peter and Billy, and acting class was a goof, but she wanted more than they did. Memorizing words, pretending to be other people, was not a grownup life. There was more, wasn't there? No, not here. She could write, she had always been good at it in school, she still wanted to write stories. Writing scripts for movies? She met producers. Tell me your idea in one sentence. Not too many words, please, scripts are charts for directors, conceptions. There was nothing for her here.

She has been ready to leave Los Angeles for months, she has only been waiting for the music, she has read the words: *THE END.*

MAUDE

WHEN MAUDE SLOWS THE CAR in front of her house, before she stops, she catches the single headlight of the motorcycle in her rearview mirror, it snaps off and on, *Goodnight*, turns in a U and vanishes. The Samaritan is gone.

She enters her house, tosses her towel and racquet on the sofa. No phone messages. Jimmy G stands, blinks at her, waiting to be addressed, focuses on her face by nodding his, arches his back in a high arc. His wide face is calm. He watches her stoop to empty a small can of food into his bowl on the floor by the sink. When she stands, after an appropriate pause, he crosses the room.

Maude's inner voice comes back to her wave by wave. She hums, tries not to grasp the words. She makes herself an icy gin and tonic, walks through the living room to the bathroom, turns on the bathtub faucets. Her tennis skirt is moist just above her buttocks.

Her inner voice follows her like the sea, whispering. She takes an ice cube from her drink, opens the CD player, slips in a disk, sits deep in the leather Timmons chair, legs wide, like a jock, head back, moves the ice cube under her ears, inside her thighs. The disk begins, she inhales, anticipates the reliable opening notes of *The Pearl Fishers*. She can no longer hear the voice taunting her.

She allows the full, longing voices to sweep over her dropping solace like pale rain. Eyes closed, sips her drink. Jimmy G dines on Gourmet's Choice. *The Pearl Fishers* rages, rising toward certain climax; the two fishermen, brothers, who have fallen in love with the same girl, are deciding again the correct thing to do next. Maude slides the melting ice cube back and forth on her neck and shoulders, on her thighs. She is wet from melted ice, her sweat, her own estrogen. In the far background, far below the music, the dribble of the bathtub, filling.

Knock-knock-knock.

Maude twitches. A dry triple-knock on the front door. Maybe an envelope being delivered from the hospital. *No, not tonight. Not Elias.*

She straightens, tries to project her voice through the door without lowering *The Pearl Fishers*.

"Yes?"

A voice paler than the singers', "Me, again."

"Who is it again, please?"

"The person in the parking lot. You know, outside the tennis courts. I started your car?"

Oh, him, of course. She stands, holding her dripping ice cube, dims the music. *What's his name?*

"What can I do for you?" It is different now, she is at home.

"Nothing much, just wondering if I could get my light back."

"I don't have your light." Maude is at the door, facing it, a foot away.

"My little light, you know."

"No. I don't have it." *Maybe he can't hear me.* "You mean the little light I used, don't you?"

"Yes. It's a good one. I'm hoping it's in your bag."

"*If* I have it, which I don't think I do." She feels unprotected. "Hold on. I'll look." There it is, nesting in her tennis sweater. Small, heavy, shiny. *How could I have taken it?*

"Found it," she calls out.

She opens the front door to the four-inch limit of the steel chain and passes it through. "I'm terribly sorry." She catches a glimpse of his hand. Clean. She is surprised, he has just fixed her car. "Thanks again. You certainly saved my life. Goodnight." She is being rude, of course, she knows it. *He was, after all, a good Samaritan.*

She goes back to the CD player, restarts the disk.

Knock-knock-knock. Brisk. *Is this why Samaria was destroyed thousands of years ago?*

She opens the door again to its limit, through the chained split, sees half his face clearly, a water-blue eye. A face nearly without expression, blank, a tabula rasa.

"Can you make one quick call for me, please?" Maude's eyebrow muscles contract. "I've got to call my roommate."

"What number, please?" *It's too late for all this.*

"If he isn't home yet, he's probably at Outrageous."

She's seen Outrageous in West Hollywood, never known for sure what it was. Is it an art gallery, a boutique, a café? "What's that number there?"

"Uhm, four six four . . . seven two . . . eight." He sounds edgy.

"That's six numbers. I can't call six numbers." Then, with a sigh, "Shall I call Information?"

"That'd be great."

"It's past eleven."

"That's okay, they serve 'til two."

"Why don't you just go home and wait for him?"

"I have the wheels."

"What is Outrageous?"

"It's, well, you know, it's a gay bar."

He explains about his roommate. "If he's at Outrageous, see, he's way over *there* . . ." He points east. ". . . where I was headed when I met you. *If* he's at home, he's way over there in Santa Monica." He points west. "I can't guess, frankly. So here I am in the middle. I've got to go one way or the other and I don't know where to go."

"Why don't you just go home?" She is inconvenienced, bored.

"What if he needs a ride home?" There's a female whine in his voice.

"I'll call." She hears the rudeness in her words, changes her mind. "No, wait a sec." She closes the door gently in his face, slides the small chain, lets it drop, opens the door.

TELEN

THE CAR IS AN ASHTRAY. Almost three hours parked on Melrose. Diaphanous fumes, they have joined the upholstery, her hair, the car reeks of death. Her mouth feels spray painted. Aside from going home to her mother, she has found she has five choices: call Billy, call the police, call Sara, call Peter, drive drive drive away. She feels as though she has given too much blood.

The radio: *Love, love, lo-ove.* KLUV, the love station. Hours of music that depends entirely on love, it enters her body like breath. The traffic has thinned.

The word *no* keeps coming up. Maude Garance's letter was sharply frightening, but was it written to her? *I wouldn't be here if it wasn't for the letter. It could be to anyone. What if it isn't him? The word NO. His thrilling smile his shattering eyes. I never looked for love, I didn't look for sex but sex is what I got, the incessant primary fucking of a man who has abstained for years, a young friar set free from a monastery, fucking that will go on for forever.*

The box of chess pieces on the seat reminds her of Peter. She can feel her body being drawn to him. She feels the black cave-tide of his needs. He has made her part of them. She wanted to share the worst of them with him, now she does not know. To her horror, she aches for him. He is the only lover to have shown her the way.

But what if it is him? Concentrate. Say, He's the one. He won't continue doing what he did, he has no reason to. He won't harm me. Say, I do love him enough to stay with him. It's all behind him, he said it and I believe him. He snapped. He did it all for his wife. Then he came to me, I gave him a reason to live normally. I can understand that, I read about women who marry death row inmates. It's a moral judgment, isn't it? Those are for outsiders to make, I'm an insider. If I love enough and I do. What he's been through makes him what he is right now, this incredible man. He engulfs me, he's never even slept with his wife, the virgin man. If love were enough. It is. I know he's changed, his cock is my proof, his cock is my release.

We'll travel across America like he's always wanted to do, he says. Cross the borders, the deserts, the Rockies, the Great Plains, eat huge unhealthy breakfasts at cowboy cafés, sleep late in one-story motels, dance in empty roadhouses, camp out under the stars. Nature's its own reward, nature will cleanse us both, it will make us well. We'll make love across America, he won't always be evasive. We may marry one day.

But there is no way he is Toyer and even if he was, he isn't anymore.

She feels wrong about everything, she has made a terrible mistake. Before she can stop herself, she has gotten out of the car and telephoned Peter from a sidewalk telephone shell, left him a quiet message on his answering machine, "Where are you?" She calls him darling, he likes that, she says she will be going to his Silverlake apartment, she will wait for him there. She leaves him a second message on her own machine at her apartment, he may go there looking for her.

It will be an occasion. She will find him. *I'll go to Hell with him, I'll go anywhere. I Will Follow Yo-ou.* Take her chances. *And with you, I'll always be-e.* She looks back at herself in the rearview mirror. Her thighs actually tingle. She starts the motor, looks behind her at the sparse traffic and in a careful arc makes a U-turn, and drives toward Peter's Silverlake apartment.

PETER

LORD, THIS IS *FUN*.

The decor. He stands in the doorway, his jacket is open, helmet in his hand, he regards the living room, the coolness of the place, the inventions of glass, stone, and chrome. *She's a lot calmer at home.*

Maude is aware of his thinness, his tallness, the tumbled coif certain gay men affect. "Please close the door, the entire bug world wants my flesh tonight."

Courtesy laugh.

"There's the phone." Maude is tired, she stands to one side, letting him pass, closes the door. *She has real beauty.*

The living room is lit by one lamp, a pyramid lamp on a strictly angled glass table. There are three rocks grouped like cats on the low gleaming sharp-edged table. The effect is sensuous, *if river-washed rocks can be sensuous.*

"Great lamp," he says gayly. *He's sweet.*

The ceiling fan spins so slowly Peter can see a dark rim of dust on the edge of the white blades. *An immense delicious challenge tonight, a dessert tray.* He picks up the telephone and dots out the three numbers for Information. The tub is dribbling in the next room. He is crowded with ideas.

He feels rigid, standing across the room from her. He knows her better than she knows him, the encounter seems unbalanced. She seems so ordinary at home, so innocent, he feels a touch of guilt. Tonight, he will make her stand at the edge, leaning out, looking all the way down. She may slip and fall. He shivers, a brief tremor runs through him.

To Maude, he seems slightly embarrassed, out of place, ready to fly. She does not know his name, of course, does not realize how much hatred she has squandered on him, how many nights dreaming, how many orgasms, how well she knows him.

He speaks into the telephone, "I want the number for a café-bar called Outrageous in West Hollywood, please. Thank you," he hangs up, writes the number on a white pad. "I'm always thanking taped voices." He laughs. "She might not even be alive anymore."

There is a tin-faced wall clock with a mean-looking roué in top hat smoking a Gauloise. "Is that the right time?" *11:12.*

"I would assume."

"I'm so very late." Peter taps out the numbers again and waits. "You'd love Outrageous. I see women alone in there all the time." *Gay women.* He sets the telephone down, "Busy."

He slips easily out of his leather jacket, drops it on a chair. Maude can see his litheness in the manner gymnasts are lithe rather than weight pushers. She stands in the kitchen area, never too close to him.

"I'd like to give them one more minute if it's okay. If he's not there . . ."

"You'll go home."

"That's right. And if he's there . . ."

"You'll go and pick him up."

"Yeah."

Uncomplicated, refreshing, he's too shy to look at me. He stands shifting his weight, hip to hip, seems awkward in her small house, anxious to go. He quickly presses the numbers again, shifting his hips. She drops two teabags into a teapot, puts the kettle of water on the stove, it is electric, she can never be sure when anything is going to be ready.

"What was that music?" he asks. *We are going to spend the evening together.*

"Opera." She has turned it way down.

He mouths an *oh.* "How come you don't know anything about cars?"

"I'm a doctor."

Another courtesy laugh. "I knew you were *something.*" *I feel chatty.*

Maude feels herself aging. "Is it ringing?"

His head is down. "Three," he waits, "four." He looks at her. "Different me having a roommate than you, isn't it?"

"I suppose." *Meaning that it's easier to imagine women in each other's arms than men in each other's arms.* "Still ringing?"

"Six," he waits, "seven."

"Maybe you dialed wrong."

"Maybe so." Carefully, he taps the numbers out, waits, head down. "Busy."

I don't want this. I want my bath, my tea, my music and I want them all by myself. And I need to pee.

The kettle screams. Peter jerks around. Maude grabs it. Its scream whimpers and dies. He watches her pour the water into the pot. *We are nearly touching. We're big fans of one another Maude; we want each other dead.*

Maude is conscious of her damp tennis outfit clearly showing the nibs of her breasts, the rise of her mons. "Please make your call." She scoots into the bathroom. Alone, Peter sets down the receiver, slides open the top drawer under the telephone, scans the contents. The silver-framed photograph of Maude and the dark-haired man, Mason, has been put away. *Thine, Mason.* He deftly opens and closes the bottom drawer, sees a small revolver, its bullets lying on a sweater. The toilet flushes. He closes the drawer, hangs up the receiver in a single gesture.

Maude reappears wearing a wrap-around skirt and a loose silk blouse darker than deep sea. He is pouring tea into her cup.

"Oh, don't do that, please."

"You take milk?"

She sighs. "All right."

"No sugar."

"No."

He smiles awkwardly. *Is he trying to make me feel rude?*

He leaves the cup on the counter and goes to the telephone, taps the numbers. Waits. "Talk, talk, talk." He puts the telephone down gently. He stands motionless. Outside, he senses a black river flowing by the front door, he can feel its currents.

Jimmy G passes through the living room on his way to the bedroom, Maude opens the door for him, he enters, tail high. He will wait for her there.

Peter stands, one finger on the telephone. "So you're a doctor. I'm Peter."

She does not answer. Together they listen to the bathwater dribbling.

"Horrible water pressure," he says. After a moment, he says again, "I'm Peter."

"Maude."

"I love that name, *Maude.*" He picks up the telephone. "So, you're a doctor." *She's not going to tell me she's a shrink.*

"And you're a mechanic."

"No way. I make my living as a palmist." *Why not?*

"A what?" She is caught off-guard.

"I read palms, professionally. I do Outrageous. It's fun, I'm like a psychic, I go over to their tables, sit, they ask me whatever, they pay me what they want, parties I get a hundred a night."

Like a hooker. She doesn't say anything.

"You think it's tacky, right?"

Yes, indeed. "I don't believe that the lines in someone's palm have anything to do with their future."

"Well, I hold someone's hand and simply tell them what I *believe* they ought to do with their future."

"I'm exhausted. I'll have to ask you to leave when you've made your call."

He indicates her hand. "Show me." *I'm inside a melody I don't want to get out of, I can't stop now.*

She keeps both palms closed. "No."

"Please?" Peter begs, putting the telephone down.

Maude, across the room, transfers her teacup and holds up her right hand, palm forward as if she were asking a question in class.

He squints across the room at her palm. "You've just come out of a depression."

"Who hasn't?"

"I haven't." Peter says, "You have misgivings about something at work."

"Who doesn't?"

We're both clairvoyant and I'm whiling away a sweaty summer evening with a gay palmist.

"Your little finger's *much* too short, you have a stubborn thumb. And look at that! Where it joins your first finger, it's called a lascivia." *He's kittenish.*

"A what?"

"I won't tell you." *That's it. Out.*

"Time to go, Peter."

Peter lifts his jacket from the chair with his middle finger, turns to the front door. "Does anyone live back there? Up the hill behind your house?"

"Why'd you ask?"

"Not important." He pauses. "I saw something moving in the trees out there. Maybe it was a deer."

"Out where?"

Peter is at the front door. He points past the living room window out to the back of the house.

"Was he wearing one of those jogging outfits?"

"Should I call the police?"

"No."

"This Toyer thing's got everyone paranoid."

"I am not paranoid, Peter. Paranoia's an advanced mental disorder."

She's good. "You're saying Toyer jogs?"

"He is not Toyer, he's only a voyeur."

"I'll call the police." Barely shifting his body, he is able to tap 911 on the telephone.

"Don't bother, it's all right. They came last month. They don't do anything."

He holds the telephone to his ear, waits for someone to pick it up. "Detective Rosen, could you send a car up here, please, we have a voyeur hanging around." He listens. "Randall Canyon, Tigertail Road." He looks at an envelope on the bureau, "Eight two oh one." He listens. "Maude . . ." He looks to Maude to finish her name.

She says, "Maude Garance." *I've made her tell me her name.*

He repeats the name into the telephone and hangs up. "Nice lady." *He's such a girl.* Maude is almost enjoying herself.

"They're sending a woman?"

"You've got something against women?"

Touché. She holds her cup lightly, touching it with ten fingertips.

"I want to see your voyeur." *Then I want to flick my tongue between your fingers.* "What does he do?"

"Apparently, he stands on my nasturtiums, watches me, and . . ." *She will not say masturbate.* Peter laughs.

"That's drinking deep from the cup of life."

"I don't think it's funny what he does."

"I don't either."

"I sympathize."

"I know. I do, too."

"It's not that uncommon."

"What if I got myself a drink?"

"No."

"Okay. I'll take a look myself."

"No, don't . . ."

"Why wait for the cops?" Before Maude can stop him, Peter has opened the front door and vanished. She sits at the kitchen counter cooling her tea. The dribbling water from the bathroom reaches a higher note. The tub is filling. She considers locking the door. His leather jacket slung over the back of the chair.

TELEN

AFTER DRIVING for five minutes she turns east onto
Sunset Boulevard. Stopped at a traffic light, she dumps
the smoldering refuse of her ashtray out the window, a man on
the sidewalk yells at her, a lengthy curse that ends in *Butthead*.
The traffic light is changing, she squirts away east down Sunset.

STOP. Blinking lights. There is a DETOUR sign. Rushing
water from broken water mains that have burst under Sunset
Boulevard causes traffic to be detoured.

She notices that the water from the broken main running by
her tires like a brook has improved the look of the street, has
turned the patchy architecture into riverfront property. She
turns south to Santa Monica Boulevard, east again, barely realizing she is driving toward Silverlake, slowly, letting the
lights blur, letting the car drive her blocks past her turn. Telen
allows herself to be driven too far east by her car. There is an
air of inevitability that frightens her. She is at Sunset Boulevard and Hollywood Boulevard, where the two rivers join,
more than halfway to Silverlake. She can easily turn the car
around, go back home, call Billy, watch his favorite television
shows with him, sleep alone, hide from Peter, maybe without
explaining herself. He does not mind if she smokes.

She slows, changes lanes, does not stop. She can still go to
Billy's. The car continues carrying her east. She turns on the
radio, hoping for instructions. Peter's door key is on the key
ring that dangles from the ignition.

PETER

THE NIGHT FALLS on Peter's head as he closes the front door, he is outdoors, the swell of the night. Past the butter-yellow porch light. Up behind the house the sky is clean, jammed with stars close to his face. In the Valley, the warm air is rising, cooling the sweat on the arms of people already asleep.

He takes a moment, sees what he is doing. *This is fabulous.* He feels his way, touching the wooden surface of the house with his fingertips as he pushes through nasturtiums and bushes. He steps on a rake, picks it up, balances it on the top of a windowsill and a low limb. The slightest impulse will make it fall, clatter against the house.

There she is. He sees her between the shade and the win-dowframe. A small fragment of Maude seen through a slit, her pale skin. She is standing still now in the middle of the room, listening. He taps the window. Maude turns quickly toward him. *The rush of the voyeur.*

She does not lock the front door. When he reenters the house she is sitting again, flushed. "That was unnecessary," she says. "Please go."

"I'm leaving, but I think someone definitely is out there up the hill."

"Go. Really, I have to get up early."

"Fine." Peter shrugs. "Let me call my roommate real quick."

Peter taps out the number written on the pad. "It's ringing! Happy ending." He waits another ring. "Hello, Carl? This is Peter, is Peter Too there?"

After a few moments listening to the bartender tell him that Peter Too left with another man, he chooses outrage. "That cunt. Fine, thanks, Carl, fuck him. That's it. Thanks for telling me." He bangs down the telephone, turns away from Maude, gripping his own elbows.

"I'm sorry, Peter."

"I'll live."

Maude is curious, ready to listen. *Just waiting for the tub to fill.*

"His name is Peter, too?"

"*Was.*" *Why couldn't I do Adam again?* "Can I make myself a quickie for the road?"

"You may turn the kettle on again for tea."

"I don't *need* tea."

Maude sighs. *A lover's pain. Why not? I'd like one, too.* "There's tequila, gin, there's even coffee liqueur." The Kahlúa is from Doctor T.

Peter goes into the kitchen area. "Why don't I just mix them all together and name it after me?"

"Right behind you. Glasses above. Ice in freezer."

Peter pours tequila over ice using both hands, quick as a bartender. "Nothing for you?"

"An ounce of gin, there's tonic water in the fridge." *He is fun to watch.*

Peter knows that she is beginning to find him diverting.

Los Angeles yawns, turns down its sheets. It is past twelve. Metal-faced celebrities stand outside restaurants that serve flaming desserts from trolleys. They are waiting to see their cars again, driven toward them. Soon the nights will be cool.

TELEN

A LIGHT IS ON in Peter's apartment on the top floor, the rest of the house is asleep. Telen parks and sits. A minute passes. The house is large, old, private, from a time of servants and vast families, in a grand neighborhood gone poor.

Upstairs, at the narrow head of the stairs to the attic, on the top step where they made love last week, Peter driving her backward on her buttocks, pushing his front door open with her back, she knocks, using her fingertips. He does not answer. He could show up anytime.

She waits outside the door in the hallway amid boiled odors risen from rooms below, trapped all evening in the stairwell. She waits, her dress will smell of sauces. The hallway creaks like a schooner at anchor. She waits another minute in the silence of the sleeping house.

She puts her key in the lock, but cannot turn it. Her hand is trembling.

MAUDE

"NOBODY'S OUT THERE," she says. "I don't believe it."

"I do."

"I don't. He'd be long gone by now."

"Not your jogger."

"Someone else?"

"Toyer."

Maude laughs.

"I'm serious."

"Come on. He doesn't work that way."

"So how does he work, Maude?"

She feels a distinct chill. *It could be.* It is a very real possibility. *He knows the way.* "Why are you fixated on him."

"Why couldn't Toyer be a voyeur?" *This is good.* "He could be anything. Just because he doesn't kill?"

"He kills."

So do you, sweet lips.

"Well, they're not dead, Maude."

"*Everybody* knows they're not dead, you—" She does not say *bimbo.* "That's his point, that's *why* he's called Toyer, get it?" *She almost called me an idiot. I love this.* "Put yourself in a wheelchair, pushed into your Outrageous, can't move your arm, can't speak, you're watered like a fern."

"Like a living toy?" He holds his glass out at arm's length. He swells from the tequila. *Let her think I'm high.*

Maude is flushed, angry. *Where the hell's the police?* She sits, crosses her bare legs, legs still taut from tennis, warm legs. *I really could use a massage and another drink.*

Peter is thrilled by her anger, excited by her excitement. To be standing a few feet from her. They have known each other a long time, after all, not as friends, but known each other. They have talked, they have corresponded, she has tried to cut his throat. He feels close to her.

TELEN

WITH THE FINGERS of both hands, she is able to turn the door key. The lock unsticks, the door swings open. A pinched squeal. Now she smells the chocolate smell of ninety-year-old shingles, varnished timbers. She turns on a lamp. The large gabled room. It had once been divided into three servants' rooms, rooflines are everywhere, part of the room's plot.

She closes the door behind her. The air is aged, dry. She turns on the lamp by the bed, two oscillating fans.

The bed is made. *What a man, neater than me.* She turns on his answering machine. One message, hers. *I sound very young, strange.* She erases it.

There is a scrap of torn newspaper in the wastebasket. Maude's letter to "Reckless." Her.

She has come back here full of hope, expecting to tell Peter it is all right again, ready to submit. She has brought him a present. It is the *Vocalise,* sung by Anna Moffo. She managed to find it at the Robertson Village and has been saving it for the right moment. This is the right moment.

Frightened and excited for a future with the man she loves. She imagines Peter. Makes herself smile. There is nothing more to know.

She finds Peter's pigeon dead in its box, the lame pigeon he had rescued from the sidewalk, she had once given it a name, now it is garbage. She lifts it out of its box, startled by its lightness, there is nothing there. Feathers. She wants to bury it, wraps it in a paper towel. There is movement behind its eyes, tiny worms. She drops it out the window into the dark.

It is too strange to imagine. Waiting, she begins to tremble. *Can love cope with this?*

Yes.

PETER

SILENCE. All night long, the city below cleanses itself like the ocean floor. In parked cars east of Cahuenga Boulevard, jolting whores in cavalry boots ride away on their steeds, earning their wake-up money.

Peter has poured Maude another gin and tonic and, without mentioning it, a tequila for himself. He hands it to her, she accepts it. She sips, sets her glass down on the glass table. *Alcohol looks wonderful through cut glass and ice.*

"I've always wondered if Toyer . . . you know," he hesitates, "you being a doctor . . ."

"Does he fuck them?" Maude leans back, stretches.

She's definitely loosening up. "Yeah. Okay."

"Maybe he does maybe he doesn't. Do you care?"

He feels a warm gush shoot up his spinal canal through his upper cervicals into his brain. He feels the familiar flooding behind his eyes. Hears the familiar hollowness in his ears. He lifts his chin high to shorten the back of his neck, to ease the weight of his head. It always begins this way. The small darkness behind his eyes. His prelude. He trusts his hatred, it is calming, it is not a burden. He can continue playing this game, *A different sort of tennis*. The game being played is for her, she is the silver cup, her mind, her spirit, her integrity, her taste, her will. Her body, her skin, her eyes, her hair. Each part of her. Every part of her.

Maude's mind seems to be elsewhere, far out of the room.

"Are you still here?"

He accepts the penalty.

"Okay, okay, maybe I'd better go.

"Goodnight," she says without looking up.

Outside, at that moment, a breeze rises, a branch moves, the rake falls, as if on cue. *Perfect.* Maude turns. *What was that?*

"Your admirer is back."

She listens, her head tilted toward the window. She stares blankly at the shade. *Could he be right about the hillside?* Peter goes to the window pulls the shade aside, stares out.

"An admirer is not someone who stands outside windows watching women undress."

Peter shrugs. "What do I know?"

Apparently nothing.

"The last time my admirer admired me, he stood right there." She points to the window. "The curtain moved, he said my name, again and again."

"Nice."

"The window was open of course, he could have ripped the screen and stepped right in. Then he said it again . . ."

"What was that?"

"I love you."

"The police came?"

"Oh, they came all right. They found one clue and asked me if it was mine."

Maude holds out her hand, palm curved. "I'd never seen it before."

Peter sucks in his breath. *My serve. Let the game begin.*

"A pocket mirror."

She looks directly at him for the first time.

He's right.

"How did you know that?"

Oh, Maude, I want to kiss your neck barely touching it, Maude, feel you quiver, Maude, make you want me to give it all to you, Maude.

TELEN

TELEN SITS tentatively on the arm of the armchair legs dangling, slides down into the cushioned seat holding Maude's letter cut from the newspaper. The chair smells of old people.

She puts the disk of Rachmaninoff's *Vocalise* on the player. It is an extended female sigh, squeezed up from between boulders in epochs before her time, a woman's plea from women who were greater than she. Peter loves the *Vocalise*, he once told her it was his turning point. *He loves women in the best sense, he loves their womanliness.*

When he comes home, she will not ask him any questions. She is waiting for him seductively and she will seduce him. She is wearing the cotton panties that he bought her at the drugstore across the street the morning after the first time she stayed over at his apartment. The night before, he had torn her fine panties to pieces while she was wearing them. A set of two panties size *small* came in a clear plastic envelope. *His favorites*. She will say, *I love you*. She has washed and dried her hair, it no longer smells of reduced nicotine.

Sharply, out the window, the burst of a motorcycle slowing. *Wake up everyone!* She knows the harsh sound of shredding sheet metal of the rebuilt Harley Davidson. It passes in a ripping flourish. She has been waiting too long. The surprise is dissolving. She is dun-eyed, dry; nervous. Estranged from the world. Midnight. She watches the street below through the window. Lifeless.

She telephones her own message tape, presses the two-digit code. One message, Billy. He wants to make sure he knows her plans, is she still leaving *tomorrow? Call me.* She balls the newspaper clipping up, tosses it out through the small eaves window.

She wakes Billy up, he sounds relieved. "God, I'm glad you called, I didn't want you running away without talking to me." She feels awkward about asking, but has he seen Peter? No. Or heard from him? Not tonight. He does not ask why. He is stoic. She promises she will write him, she will give him their telephone number when they get one. He can accept Telen being with Peter, he has admitted to her that they look well together. It is like that with Billy.

"By the way, Telen, I do love you, I want you to know that." *In case my romance with Peter doesn't work out.* Last week, when she told him she loved him, he knew what she meant. She was in the basement of her self-esteem and her words did not count. He knows about her doubts, nothing about her fears.

She sits leaning her head out the window, smokes a cigarette down to its filter, flicks the butt out to the street. Peter will not know. She rinses her mouth, brushes her teeth vigorously. It is well after midnight, 12:25. For the first time she realizes he may not be coming home tonight.

She stands. She has never been here without him. It is all so very neat. All of his things are put away. *So unusual. Eerie, as though he expects to be judged.* She opens and closes each bureau drawer. No rings or chains, accessories. No secrets. T-shirts, undershorts, socks folded. Everything in order. A bottle of citrus cologne. She splashes a few drops in her palm, cools her neck and arms. She goes to the stove to see if there is coffee. Everything is washed and put away. There is a red metal tool box full of his roofing tools. *What an unusual hammer.*

There is nothing unusual here and yet there is. There are scraps of paper, lists he has typed, numbers, hours he has worked, requests for overtime pay. They are crumpled in the wastebasket, all made by a computer printer but there is no computer or printer in the apartment. On a high kitchen shelf there is an unopened ream of computer paper. *For a computer that isn't here.*

Anxiety prods her, she feels intuitively curious. She snoops, down on all fours, between the refrigerator and the wall, in the back of the closet. She snoops. Nothing is hidden.

Twelve-forty-five A.M. Her anxiety has turned into suspicion. It surprises her, not because it is there but because it is so intense. It has grown from casual snooping into clear physical images of him making love to another woman with the same torrid force that he made love to her yesterday. She has been betrayed. His unfaithfulness was never a possibility, now she realizes he may be capable of it. Disbelief. She is shocked.

All I want is loyalty. I came back to him tonight, I committed myself to him against all my doubts, and all my better instincts. Who the hell is he with right now?

She needs an answer, a quick reason to continue believing in him, or a reason to dismiss him. Either way. Immediately. There must be a name somewhere in the apartment, a telephone number.

She scans the steep, shadowed room where once a cook, a driver, and two housemaids celebrated the Armistice in 1918. Only in places this old can there be true hiding places. Building conditions have changed since then. She searches the living room first, its elaborate shape, nooks and gables, the desk area with his few books. Then the partitioned bedroom, its closets, the bathroom. Areas sectioned according to the cross rooflines. *Damn. It's here in this room and I can't see it.*

MAUDE

HOW'D YOU KNOW about the pocket mirror?" She is not making too much of it. But something dry clicks in, she is startled by the breeze in her ears, she stares at Peter, waiting for an answer. "Absolutely no one knew about it."

He smiles warmly. "Do you still have it?"

Somewhere. In the bathroom. She stops herself. "How'd you guess? I'm just curious."

"I told you, I'm a palmist."

She forces a laugh. "I need a rational answer."

"Okay, then, I dropped it."

Maude feels a draft chill her sweat. *So this is what he looks like, my peeping jogger. He's younger than I imagined.*

"Don't upset yourself."

"Not at all." *I can handle this, keep it simple.* "You're a voyeur, it's your mirror. Now, it's suddenly very late and I think I've been very patient with you, Peter. Thank you for fixing my car. I bought you a drink, you made your call. Let's call it even."

She thinks that'll work?

"You happen to be a voyeur. Fine. We live in a voyeuristic society, mirrors and cameras everywhere. It's called scopophilia by the way."

She's irresistible. She's dazzling me with psychobabble.

"There's a new word for you, Peter, *scopophiliac*, a guy who likes to watch females in various stages of undress without being seen."

"What about watching males?" *Keep the gay guy alive.*

"Absolutely." *Control him.*

"So. I'm just an ordinary guy."

"A very ordinary guy." *Don't belittle him.* "It's not a crime if you do it at home. Helgen says a scopophiliac is a person who simply refuses to be seen obtaining his sexual gratification. Peter, it's just a unique way of saying 'Hey, I'm shy.' "

"That's me all right. A cheap date. How can you spend money on a date who doesn't even know you're with her?" He laughs.

Her laugh scrapes. "And you seem to be able to relate to it with humor. So, why don't we call it a night?"

"Yeah, maybe we should."

So far, so good. "But don't let the police catch you. If they don't get it, they tend to shoot."

"But *you* get it."

"I do indeed. I'm a psychiatrist."

"I thought you were a doctor."

"Among other things. Call me sometime at the Kipness. Doctor Garance, I'm attending in psychiatry, physiatry."

"Thank you, Doctor Garance."

"Now get the hell out of here before those idiot cops come banging in here."

"They're not coming."

"Oh?" She smiles.

"No."

"You called them."

"No." He says it gently.

Silence rings in her ears. *He's only a voyeur.*

Peter has formed an equilateral triangle between himself, Maude, and the front door, which is unlocked. He is casual, he knows her capabilities.

Maude indicates the closed bedroom door. "Okay, Peter, I hate to say this but Karen's in there asleep. Maybe she's been listening to all this. Let me warn you: go, now."

"There's no Karen in there."

"Oh, no?" *What the hell is he doing?*

"No. Karen's not in there." He pushes the bedroom door open with his toe and asks the dark room quietly, "Are you in there, Karen?"

Silence.

"I didn't know she'd gone out."

"She's out, all right."

"I think you'd better go."

"Maybe I should."

"In any event, my fiancé's coming over here tonight very soon."

There's no end to her guest list. "Mason?"

Maude nods dumbly.

"Mason's not coming over here." Peter speaks sympathetically. "I'm sorry."

Maude opens her mouth to answer him, stops.

"Would you go now? I will even say please. Leave. Okay?" She is maintaining control, supported by her years of professional experience. "Look, I'm getting pissed off at you. Go."

"I don't think I can."

"Why the hell can't you?"

"I wish it was that simple."

"Then let's have another drink and discuss it."

"Sorry."

"Stand over there, Peter."

"I'd rather not."

She refuses to believe that this situation is in any way beyond her expertise. "I'm not afraid of you, Peter. You're maybe a nice person but this is going to get you in a hell of a lot of trouble tomorrow. And you know it."

"I know it might."

"So, may I ask what the hell you think you're doing?"

"I've been watching you."

"I realize that. Why?"

"I love you."

"Peter, you don't love me. You're fond of me. And I'm fond

of you." There is comfort in her voice. "I know you're shy and I know you might have a special aversion to women, but you should have made yourself come over to me at the tennis courts when you first saw me."

"We would have gone out to dinner, right?"

"I'm ten years older than you are, Peter. But you should have expressed your feelings, anyway." *Careful.* "I understand about obsessive people, I've worked with them. There's something uncomplicated about obsessives, something sweet . . ."

"You think I'm sweet?"

"Well, no. Yes, certainly. Not sweet in the conventional way, in a new way. And I can see you're a very deep person. Anyway, I wish you'd spoken to me first."

"That's not exactly the way I do things." He pauses. "Why did you smile at me in the parking lot?"

"I don't know, Peter, did I?"

I smiled directly at him when he fixed the car.

"I remember your smile."

"All right, Peter, you're a voyeur which is okay, and as such you don't need to touch women."

"Yeah."

"You simply like to watch women undress, don't you?"

He nods, shyly.

Her mind is racing. "And because you're fond of me, you wouldn't want to force me to do anything I wouldn't want to do. That's right, isn't it?"

"Yeah." *Where the hell is she going with this?*

TELEN

FIFTEEN MINUTES, *1:00 A.M.* There is nothing hidden in the apartment. She makes a small pot of tea, pours it into a

mug, sits again. She listens for the snarl of his motorcycle.
She has casually searched the two rooms, found nothing, now
she begins again as if it really mattered. She feels her way
around the back wall of his closet, tapping it gently for hidden
panels, smelling Peter in shirts. There is no light, the little silver flashlight that stands on his bed table is gone. *Why did he
take his flashlight?*

She knows his clothes, she can imagine what he is wearing
by not finding it. His black leather jacket. Black jeans. Black
on black. She cannot find his helmet. Usually he rides without
his jacket, especially on these hot nights, but he has taken his
jacket with him.

The oval mirror above the bureau is from an earlier time.
The gilding around the glass is too bright, as if it were meant
to be seen only by gaslight. She feels the wall behind it, she
lifts the mirror down. The mirror is gravid, decaying, the glass
is bleary, as though it has been a mirror too long, worn out by
its reflections. She examines it. Uneven wood slats behind the
black glass. There is nothing there, nothing hidden, no papers.
Listening to the street, she is about to hang the mirror again.

Now, in the wall behind the mirror, she catches sight of
something concealed. A bright nail head. There is a slat above
it, the slat can be turned. The plank is loose. Inside, tall and
narrow, dark, it is four inches deep. Something is wedged between wide timbers, something new between the old hairy
wood. It is a beige case. She lifts it out. A small computer.

She sets it on the bureau, it sits like a puppet, waiting to be
awakened, waiting to be told to speak. Her throat closes. She
has found something. Maybe it is what she was looking for
and did not want to find. Telen stares at it. The computer is as
small as her purse. She feels its invisible power, she knows
that its bland look is a lie, that it is all in front of her. Something worth her life that she does not want to find.

The night is too hot. The jigging fans are worthless tonight.
She plugs the computer into the wall plug. She takes her shoes
off, steps out of her skirt, pulls her T-shirt over her head,

loosens her hair, sits in her underwear, knees apart, toes way back, straddling the chair like a jockey. She sits facing the tiny computer.

If she hears his motorcycle in the alley, she will have to snap it off, dump it in the wall, hang the mirror, jump on the bed, pretend to be asleep. She will have a full minute. She does not want him to catch her snooping, not tonight. When he comes in he will be shocked to see her, then delighted. They will forgive each other. In spite of everything, she will tell him that she loves him. It is the truth. She gets up, pulls back the sheets on the bed. He will make love to her.

The *Vocalise* is over, she has played it three times. She sits again, snaps open the computer, *click*, like a compact, slides the On switch sideways. It springs to life making tiny frog noises along with its first demand. She understands computers, it takes her only a few seconds to enter, to find her way in to the directory of files. The flashing green markers beckon to her like harbor lights.

MAUDE

MAUDE IS FILLED with a sudden gust of controlling energy she has not felt since she first began treating patients: from her inventions, psychodramas, dark experiments. Maude has not felt this euphoria for years. The rush of danger dizzies her. She will stay in charge. He is only a voyeur, after all.

"Let's make a deal, Peter."

"I'm in." *And fascinated, I might add.*

She faces him openly, unprotected, as if she were speaking to a psychotic patient, which she is. Peter is not sure about this part, it can go several ways.

"This bra is killing me. I'm wearing a silk blouse. My breasts would feel much better against my silk blouse. So why don't I simply unbutton my blouse and take it off? Then take my bra off? And after that I'll put my blouse back on without my bra and button it up again. I'll feel much better, I'll be cool, my breasts will be free. Would you mind if I did that?"

"Now?" *This is incredible.*

"Yes."

"I don't know. . . ." *Am I caught off guard, or what?*

"Well, if I must change clothes, you probably wouldn't want me to do it in the other room where you couldn't watch me, so I suppose I'll be forced to do it right here, in front of you. If that's okay?"

She stares at him until he nods.

"Yeah, okay." *I couldn't have written the scene better.*

She continues speaking so softly he can barely hear her. Slightly hesitant. "But it's not really polite of a total stranger to watch a woman he doesn't know take off her blouse and her bra and look at her breasts, is it? Shouldn't you lower your eyes?"

This is the part where she attacks me with the scissors.

"But if by any chance you did catch a glimpse of me undressing, changing my clothes, then afterward, would you leave?"

She's talking to me like a voyeur, which I am. Very sexy.

"It'll have to be *yes*, Peter." Maude stands behind the sofa, head tilted, staring at Peter eye-to-eye. Peter hesitates.

Jimmy G enters from the open bedroom without noticing them, laps water from a bowl near the refrigerator. Starts back to the bedroom. It is then that he stops as if he has been told to stop, he turns and regards Peter. Only Maude notices his ears. They have flattened as if for attack. It is so strange a thing for him to do that for a moment it distracts Maude.

"It'll have to be *yes*, Peter."

"Yes." *Incredible.*

Maude centers herself, unbuttons the top button. She lets him see her neck. *Brains equals guts.* He stands facing her across the room, watching her directly. She can see he is embarrassed.

"No. Wait. Stop. Stand over there." Peter points toward the bathroom door. *I'm the voyeur, I give the orders here.* He opens the bathroom door wide and sets it at an angle. *This is how they watch.*

"Okay," he says. "Face the mirror."

Obediently, she faces the mirror. "If you insist on watching me undress, maybe *I'd* better be the one to close *my* eyes."

She does. She bends forward, her fingers touch the second button of her silk blouse, she unbuttons it. She is aware of him standing behind her, several paces back. She closes her eyes, unbuttons the last buttons of her blouse, lets it drop from her shoulders, letting it slide down her back to the floor behind her. She pauses, then, still keeping her eyes shut, uncouples her brassiere and leans forward, letting it slip down her arms to the floor at her feet. She straightens for a moment, cooling her breasts, letting her nipples expand.

"There. That feels better." *She's as brave as a matador.*

Maude has submitted meekly. She has kept her eyes closed throughout her experiment. She opens them, stands for a moment inspecting herself in the mirror. She seems fascinated by her ability to control Peter. She feels her breasts, lightly holding them from below, watching her nipples lengthen slightly.

Peter watches her impassively, without expression, voyeuristic detachment. *Jesus, is this a great moment or what. I can feel these nipples growing in my mouth.*

Peter decides to ask nothing more. To end it.

"Thank you," he says, indicating dismissal.

Maude swoops to the floor, snags her blouse, slips it on and buttons a few buttons. "See how easy that was?"

Peter watches her breasts disappear within the rippling green silk blouse. She ignores the brassiere lying empty at her feet. Her ordeal, degrading, risky, brilliant, is over, her contract fulfilled. They nod at one another. He lifts his jacket on one finger, stands at the door.

"Thanks, Maude."

"Goodnight, Peter." *I've won.*

Peter's hand rests on the door knob without turning it. He does not move, he looks away. "I wish I could leave."

She reaches a hand to the telephone. "If you break your word to me, I'll call the police."

"You really don't know, do you?"

TELEN

OUT OF ITS LONG PAST the attic room comes into the present tense, she navigates inward toward the computer program's center, legs wide around it. Her fine child's fingernails flick the keys *cluck-cluck-cluck-cluck*. The files align themselves. There are very few names under *LETTERS*, little correspondence, he does not write to anyone. Mailing addresses of newspapers, magazines in various cities. The *Herald*. There are telephone numbers, not hers. There is the local telephone number of the *Herald*, Sara Smith. These are the categories. Notes. A file near the bottom of the directory.

She chooses a file named *QUAKE*.

She presses the ENTER key. Instantly the message flashes across the screen bright as neon:

KEY CODE DOES NOT EXIST.

Telen types WORD:\QUAKE.DOC., presses the ENTER key. After a couple of bee-buzzes, the computer spreads the green message:

NOT A VALID FILENAME.

She must begin again. There is a second program inside. She needs the password to enter it. The computer is locked.

MAUDE

WATCHING HIM, eye-to-eye, she presses 911 without looking down at the telephone.

"Are you going to stop me?"

"I don't need to, Maude, the phone's dead."

She listens. There is no dial tone. *Jesus, it is dead.*

"I promise you, I'm going to scream." She feels a hush thicken the air.

Peter shrugs. "You should definitely scream if you want to scream." He says it as if screaming would be in her best interest, therapeutic, a needed catharsis. He takes two steps toward her. "Try not to sound like your teakettle."

Maude hears herself screaming, a high, bright scream. He watches her appraisingly. Jimmy G wakes wide-eyed, sums it up, he is used to opera, closes his eyes again.

"All better?"

"Get out." *Stay calm.*

"You really *don't* know what's happening, do you?" He seems surprised.

Peter is no longer at the front door but has drifted toward the sofa, deftly narrowed the triangle.

"I don't jog, Maude, I can't even look at joggers."

I really should introduce myself.

"Guess who I am."

The familiar name, the unspoken, the invisible screams to be heard. Maude, in the deep chair, uncrosses her legs.

"This is what's happening, Maude, in case you don't already know: I'm not your jogging voyeur. I do not have an aversion to touching women." *And, by the way, I would like to smell the inside of your thighs and you will let me do so.*

Peter makes a small tour of the living room, eyes never off Maude. He knows everything. "Handgun in bureau, small caliber. Sort of a club behind that door. Letters under your lingerie, you favor white. Neat medicine cabinet. A man's shaving brush and razor."

Peter moves to one side, a dance step, maintaining the triangle: Maude, himself, the front door. He turns to the stereo, watching Maude, switches it to jazz-rock, the volume low.

Now.

Launching herself from the deep chair, Maude hurls herself through the open door into the bathroom, slams it shut, locks it. Perfect timing. She has beaten him. The other bathroom door opens to her bedroom, she locks it. She slides open the bathroom window, she will slip through it and run.

That was quick. Peter is at the bathroom door. With his toe, he pushes open the bedroom door. The bedroom is dark. He sees the second bathroom door, a line of light under it. He pauses in front of it, turns the knob. Locked. If he tries to break it in, she will be out the other door, gone. She is an athlete. The chase exhilarates him.

"That was nice."

He listens, standing ready, on the balls of his feet. *The window.* He hears Maude sliding it open.

By the time it takes her to climb up and crawl through it and drop to the ground outside, he is waiting to assist her. He clips her arm behind her, with his other hand closed on her neck in a delicate but painful thumb-and-index-finger grip, he marches her back into the house.

Inside, he chains the door, drops her on the sofa. Maude stares at his throat, her mouth is half open. She has aged.

This is Toyer.

TELEN

THE PERSISTENT HAMMERING of steel on metal. *One-fifteen A.M. Bizarre neighborhood.* Someone is using a ball-peen hammer, maybe fixing a fender. Telen knows the sound. She grew up in a small town. Older men working on trucks in the garage turned and studied her as she walked by, studied her limbs and extremities, her lines, and at night wondered what it would be like with her.

It is madness. She cannot get into Peter's secret files.

She types WORD:\QUAKE.DOC. again, presses the ENTER key, the message: *NOT A VALID FILENAME.*

She knows there must be files underneath the files she is looking at. *Something is in here being hidden and protected.* It is a maze from a dream where what she fears most could be to her right and what she loves most could be to her left. She taps in various drive letters, software names, file names, she tries again and again but there are limits. The invisible barrier standing between Telen and the files has turned her casual curiosity to desperation. Then by a chance meeting of macros, a second directory appears. *September 3* is the most recent entry, yesterday. It was made at 18:41.

Last night?

PETER

"**C**ONFUSED?"

Maude is on the sofa, her mouth is askew. He stands in front of her, looking down. He is polite, restrained.

"Maude, I couldn't call the police because I cut your phone line."

She looks at the line going into the wall, it seems intact.

He nods to the window. "Out there. That was before I went down to the courts and disconnected your throttle linkage." He pauses. "Okay? A full hour before you waved to me in the parking lot behind the tennis courts. I thought you'd figured all that out."

Maude puts her hand over her mouth. *He's way ahead of me.*

"And you've also been wondering what he looks like. Well, this is what he looks like, Maude. Sort of above-average profile, nice cheekbones. Honest face, future Republican congressman. Golf. Lunch?"

The walls surrounding her mist and melt. *He seems just as smart as me, just as quick, but stronger. Keep dancing.*

"You don't know me at all, Peter, there's more to me you haven't seen. We might become friends. We might be good friends."

"I hate to degrade you like this."

"You're not degrading me." *Just bribing my executioner.*

"You're so optimistic, it's beautiful. You think I'm not going to . . . touch you. That you'll be fine tomorrow."

He never takes his eyes away from me.

"I'll be fine."

"See? Optimism. As for myself, I'm always a little gloomier about tomorrow."

"I really think you're very sensitive, Peter, very strong."

"And that I'm going to say, *Night-night* and go away."

"I will not take any drugs."

"You took them a quarter of an hour ago."

In my drink. Her fingers distance themselves from her arms. She stands.

"Sit down." She feels the first signs of her strength beginning to decompose. He waits. She does.

"In your own words, can you tell me what your problem is."

He shrugs. "No problem. I meet a girl. I cordotomize her. What problem?"

"Only women."

"I adore women."

"But you're a homosexual."

"But you're a psychiatrist. You know, helpful to people like me."

"There are no people like you."

"You mean I'm fiction?"

"There are no others."

"No, probably not. But I'm just standing off to one side, watching the pageant."

She has counted the steps it will take her to cross the room and crash out the front door. Five.

"Insanity works, Maude. I was one nasty little boy, I borrowed these goldfish and dropped them in a bathtub filled with lemon Jell-O and watched them swim slower and slower until they, well, just stopped. Then I went to the movies."

One, two, three, four to the door, yank it open and run some more. Right, left, right, left. I can do it, I can do it.

"I'm always touched by someone I can completely control. And you've got enough muscle-relaxant in you to drop a rhino. Do you feel like you're swimming in Jell-O, Maude?"

Maude makes a lunge, yanks the door open, the chain snaps out of the wall, she is outdoors, on the dark porch, down the steps, she faces the night for an instant before Peter brings her down, catches her neck cleanly from behind in the same paralyzing finger hold he used before. He raises her with only his fingers on her wrist pressure point, brings her back inside. "Please stop doing that, Maude. I'm quick. God, I'm quick."

He slips the bolt closed on the front door. He shows her to the deep chair, closer to the floor, as if he were a host seating a guest. Maude obeys, head down, disoriented, stunned. *And he's silent and calm and strong and unruffled; marks of a superb athlete.*

"It's what happened with Melissa Crewe, a chase. Does

bloodstorm ring a bell? Let's try not to have another *bloodstorm*."

Now she feels truly afraid, close to drowning, she thinks, *I'm going to be one of them.* But she must have spoken it aloud because he answers her.

"You sure are. Sort of, well, you know."

Peter brings her to her feet, lifting her weight by the same three fingers now clamped on one wrist not on her neck, it is a paralyzing hold, he leads her across the room to the shelf with the stereo.

"Play us an opera. I don't care which, something different."

Maude finds a disk, puts it on. It is too loud.

"Turn it down."

He leads her back to the deep chair and seats her again, standing behind her where he cannot be seen. The opera rises like the tide of discovered love.

"Are they singing about love?"

She nods.

The two great lovers now merge in duet rising to hurricane level in mouth-to-mouth ear-ringing harmony, proclaiming, through each other's headbone canals, their eternal love for one another.

Sara said she'd call me tonight. Who knows? She could be standing outside right now, listening.

TELEN

TEN MINUTES. She cannot get into *QUAKE*. Her impulse is to lift the tiny computer and throw it out the window into the street. To see it shatter into pieces. *No one needs to know. Why not?* It is only a memory bank like her own and she is willing to destroy hers. *God knows, the sword is mightier than the laptop computer.*

She is waiting.

She snaps it off and on. Back come its odd manners. Maybe that is where she should start, with the formal inquiry.

It is so simple. It comes to her that the files she is looking for are not kept inside the computer. Maybe there is a disk.

The date is on the E drive, not on the main drive. She goes to the wall and lifts the mirror to the floor. She reaches down into the panel. She feels loose supports and pulls one up. It is a mailing tube sealed at both ends. She cuts the tape at one end with a kitchen knife.

Rolled into the tube are magazine articles. Out drops the *Time* magazine cover, the *Newsweek* cover. The big articles. The announcements to publish a book, the article where Toyer announces he will give benefits to victims. *Our memory book. A scrapbook for our grandchildren.* Even scanning the *Newsweek* words, they resound. She tells herself she has come to terms with his past but she cannot control herself, it is truly terrifying.

She needs a disk. She reaches down in the wall, there are two more tubes, then, feeling her way up, above where the computer was, along a narrow shelf, her fingers touch a single disk. She dislodges and brings it out. It is an unmarked 3.5-inch disk.

Telen slides the disk into the computer, chooses the E drive, types E:\WORD\QUAKE.DOC., presses the ENTER key. Instantly the message flashes across the screen bright as neon:

INVALID PASSWORD
This file is password protected.
Enter the password you used when saving the file.

Password protected? The file *QUAKE* has been programmed to be opened by a secret password known to one person. The way files are protected at the Data Bank where many people use the same computer and no one can alter someone else's work file. Maybe Peter changes it frequently. She notices the date, September 3, again.

ENTER NEW PASSWORD

Blocked, she releases the file. But instead of returning to the directory, a lone sentence appears along the bottom frame of the window, unblinking green on black:

_____ are also able to predict earthquakes,
but how can they notify us?

Then:

To continue, enter name of species.
Answer one question: What species can predict
earthquakes that isn't able to notify us?

_____ are also able to predict earthquakes,
but how can they notify us?

It is a puzzle.

PETER

ACT ONE IS ENDING. There is unrequited love, unequal pain, death. The male voice is threatening, dangerous, the female's is angry, defiant.

"You opera lovers die so much better than we do. You've had so much more practice." He says it charmingly. He is hard to hear above the voices. She doesn't react, watches his lips. *He could be making a joke.*

Peter snaps it off, severing the aria as its crescendo peaks before it descends into grief. He doesn't seem to notice. It is an ugly moment. He stands in front of her, she sits in the deep chair. "You know what you did to me, don't you?"

She doesn't speak.

"Fucking me up with that letter?"

She nods. She is staring straight ahead.

"You did it to fuck up my life, didn't you?"

She nods.

"Guess what? It worked."

She nods. She feels no triumph.

"So here I am."

She is truly afraid. She is trembling like aspens. By seating her deep in the Timmons chair he has forced her to give up any chance of escape. "I thought you needed help, Peter."

"Is that why you wrote me, I was what they scraped off colons during autopsies? Did you believe that would help me?"

"I was quoting someone, remember?" Her mind is white. "But yes, I did." Her courage makes him smile.

"You also called me a rapist of minds not bodies. That wasn't a quote." He says it without anger, without raising his voice, even sweetly. "When we make love tonight, Maude, remember, it will be as beautiful as it's ever been for you, and we will make love only because you want to make love to me."

"I would never make love to you."

"Well, okay, then, let's just say *no* to any further mention of sex." He smiles pleasantly. He no longer seems upset.

"Murderer." She says it quietly, to the floor, not a thought in her head.

"No, Maude. Not murderer at all. Personally, I abhor violence and I fear death. You know I don't kill. And you'll be going someplace far more fascinating than the afterlife. You'll always have your opera, Maude, dead people don't have opera. That's the big difference."

These are his words, he believes them.

"So just try to remember, you're safe with me. You'll be known as my thirteenth and final chapter, 'The Woman Who Got to Me.' I will *mortalize* you. You'll be sympathized with by everyone."

He rambles, Maude barely listens. *This is his mind. This is his pleasure.* She cannot move.

"I've always assumed that should something happen, should I ever go to trial, the event will be covered in the best taste. I've already discussed this with a lawyer, a nice man."

He is the most coherent psychotic I have ever met.

He is casual, loose, he travels in a foxtrot, his toes never leave the floor, he never loses control of the room.

"But enough about me. What were we saying? You were planning your day tomorrow. You were going to visit our patients? Lunch with your doctor friend? I hope not that poor idiot you beat at tennis? Doesn't it bother you you're not going to do any of those things tomorrow?"

Out the window just above the trees a police helicopter fingers the dark houses. Routine night security without suspicion. Cords of light swish past Maude's curtains. She looks up to the ceiling. The helicopter thunders by, seen through the leaves, carving its way through the sky, a stiff bird with a rod of light that pokes people from a fresh angle scanning their last possession.

TELEN

TELEN STARES.

Species of animal? Typical Peter. Well, how bad can it be? Animal? She types *cats.*

The computer ruminates, makes a small *peep,* then announces:

INVALID PASSWORD

_____ are also able to predict earthquakes, but how can they notify us?

She types in another word. *Dogs.* Immediately the computer peeps and responds:

INVALID PASSWORD
This file is password protected.
Enter the password you used when saving the file.
ENTER NEW PASSWORD

She types *birds.* Waits. *Horses.* Waits. *Pigs.* Waits.

Then: *Chickens. Hens. Apes.* All followed by the same brisk reprimand accompanied by a peep.

She types *sheep, cows, snakes, lions, goats, raccoons, mice, roaches, foxes, rats, otters, squirrels, hamsters, deer, birds, bears, monkeys, apes, gorillas, worms.* Each time with finality:
INVALID PASSWORD

She quits. It is 1:35 A.M.

She remembers the afternoon she was caught swimming nude when she was twelve, with two older boys in the pond at La Madeleine.

MAUDE

GET YOUR GUN. *Dead Mason's. He said shoot for the legs. Only to stop not to kill.*

Maude throws herself to her left, jerks the bottom bureau drawer open, spilling its contents, grabs the gun in a flurry of silk scarves, squats on one knee, holds the barrel aimed at Peter's face. It has taken her two seconds to get from the sofa to the bureau to the gun. She is able to stand, hold it at arm's length.

Peter looks appropriately impressed, betrayed.

I've got him. It's over.

She is wobbly, she steadies the gun with one hand under the other. Her voice is shaky, her command is strong, her index finger is precisely in the right place.

"I'll shoot you if you so much as twitch."

"Twitch?"

"Just stand there."

"Are you positive you don't want me to twitch?" He is half smiling.

"You think it's funny?" Maude feels comfortable holding the gun aimed at his eyes. She is trembling.

He seems deliberately calm. "Aren't you supposed to make me do something now? I'm trying to be helpful."

"I'll shoot your right eye out. Does that sound okay?" *What do I want him to do?*

"Look, why don't I just lie down here with my hands behind me? They do that a lot."

"Do it. Over there." *What next?*

"Okay, okay." *Peter gets to his knees. This has elements of comedy.* "But isn't the theory behind it to—"

"Shut up."

"Right."

"Flat on your face. *There*." He lies on his stomach.

Jimmy G, who has been roused, watches them with Chinese eyes. He stretches, walks between them, jumps to his place on the windowsill. *Much too late for all this action.*

Maude stands, aiming down at Peter. It is a revolver, too shiny, made in Spain, she has never used it. Her mind is clear, she knows she is in charge. *What comes next?*

"Hadn't you better tie me up with something?"

Yes, of course, but with what?

"Why not use one of those scarves?"

"You're having a little too much fun." Maude points the gun at his head. Mason told her always to keep three bullets in the chamber, no less. She pulls out a sheaf of scarves from the drawer. She tosses one to him.

"Tie your ankles. Together. Stop smiling."

"I really like it when you talk rough."

Peter sits, wraps a scarf around his ankles then stops. *He still thinks it's funny.* "I'm just hopeless at knots, Maude, always was, even in Scouts."

"This is not a joke, Peter." She aims the gun at his nose. "Tie your ankles together or I'll kill you." Her voice has gotten steady, resonant.

He ties his ankles together with a bow, a gift knot. "Okay, how does that look?" *Why isn't he taking this seriously?*

He gets up on his knees, then stands, swaying, lightly hobbled, almost without moving, facing her across the room.

"I love you, Maude. Really do." He seems deeply touched by her.

"Back on the floor." *No phone. How am I going to get the cops?*

"I love psychiatry, don't you? So full of nuances, somewhere there's a cure for all of us."

"Shut up."

"Look, Maude, you've had a dose, you're probably dizzy. Why don't we sit down again, let's finish what we were saying."

Maude aims carefully at his right leg. *Shatter the tibia.* She will disable him with the first shot, fire again into the other leg if she needs to.

"I'm counting to . . . three."

"For what?"

"For you to get back down on the floor."

"Come on."

He does not move.

"One . . . two . . ." *He ought to know I'm capable of shooting him.*

They both know it. She has the gun, the position, the experience, the motive. "I'll do it. I don't care. I'll tell the police . . . you came looking for me and I shot you. Everyone will understand."

"You'll be a hero." He says it mildly.

"Move!"

He does not move.

She aims at his kneecap. *I will.* Slowly she pulls the trigger. *Click.*

"Oh, dear." He says, "Not empty?"

She holds the gun aimed at his legs and pulls, *click,* aims and pulls, *click, click click, click.*

He reaches out and lifts the revolver out of her limp hand. *She might want to throw it at me.* He unties the bow on his ankles, the scarf falls open with a flick.

The bureau drawer that she's opened. "There they are, the little rascals." The bullets are among her scarves, on her cashmere cardigan. "They can stain silk, you know."

He pushes her backward into the deep chair, traps her below him, his arms on its arms. She is off her legs, beaten.

"If I didn't know you better, I'd think you were just trying to kill me again. Now, where were we? Oh, yes, tomorrow. It's going to be different for you tomorrow, isn't it. You'll be this pretty pale flower, wheeled around, fed, loved."

She releases intestinal gas. *How embarrassing. I'm facing*

Toyer and I fart. But if that embarrasses me it means I haven't given up.

He's rambling. "Ever thought about Saturn's moons? Nothing deader than a moon, right? But it goes on revolving, rising and setting. What about trees? Who buries a tree when it dies? No one. It stands there elegant, clean, strong. You're a sexy, good-looking woman, Maude, with a headstrong beauty, brilliant mind. Why would I ever want to see you buried. Eyeless?

"Did you do that?" The gas. "Perfectly normal, Maude, don't give it another thought. I know you don't feel much like talking now, but this is you we're discussing, not somebody else, don't you care? Is this actual denial? Can't you show me a couple of tears?"

I've been expecting it.

The words surface, ". . . expecting it . . ."

"Strange, isn't it, that fear of predestiny? We all have it, in one way or another."

Maude hugs her legs and bends forward, her head between her knees.

Here he is. Here I am. All these months, dreaming about him, fucking him, trying to kill him, trying to outwit him, writing to him. Here he is. Here I am. I'm losing it all to him. He's beaten me.

She feels tears slipping down her nose dropping onto one bare knee. *He wins.*

TELEN

THE METAL HAMMERING has long since stopped.

It is one way the mind can work. Telen has caught a glimpse locked in a corner of her memory's eye, a small vision: At the Sondelius house at a time when she was not noticing because she had been staring straight ahead in horror at Elaine drooped gaga in her wheelchair, she remembers something on the wall behind her. She now realizes what it might have been. A line of newspaper articles, tacked side-by-side, neatly cut to their length. A *display*. But it did not matter then, she was not looking. Now she remembers. Were they Sara Smith's articles? The names of the towering victims. She cranes her memory but there is nothing more to see. It is nearly two-thirty.

I can solve this. Who can she call about earthquakes? The libraries are closed. The newspapers? She calls the *Herald*, the night editor does not know, he always thought it was dogs. She calls the *Times*. The man at the news desk tells her that his wife can predict earthquakes. Her name is Dale. Look for one in November.

She sees a four-year-old telephone book under the bed, supporting a leg. She finds *Earthquake Center* at Cal Tech. An 800 emergency number. She pushes the numbers and waits. No recording. Good. She continues to wait. Finally, after twelve rings, an ancient being answers. The voice seems hesitant, "Cal State Center for Earthquake Research," as though his telephone has never rung before. He seems to be sleeping, unsteady, maybe surprised to be alive.

Telen explains that she needs the names of animals that are known to predict earthquakes. The man, still in his dreams, follows her down her list, discrediting each entry. He believes that she is telephoning him in search of a decent animal she can purchase tonight that will protect her from an imminent earthquake. He might be humoring her, it is late.

"So we've pretty much covered all our domestic animals."

"Yes."

"And our domestic birds?"

"Yes."

"Have you tried fish?"

She feels a twinge of excitement. The idea of fish.

"No."

"Well, as a matter of fact, there is a species of fish that reacts strongly before an earthquake. It's the damnedest thing. It goes into an alarm pattern of swimming, you'd think it'd gone nuts . . ."

"What fish?"

". . . you really got to see it to believe it. Truthfully." His voice trailing off, chuckling.

"Which fish? Please."

"Any number of fish in the order of Ostariophysi."

She is let down. *I need eight letters or less for a file name.* "I've never heard of Ostriophysi . . ."

"Os*tari*ophysi. Ever heard of a catfish?"

"Yes."

"It's your catfish."

Telen feels a cool rush, blesses him and hangs up.

Seven letters. She types in the word, *catfish.* No peep. INVALID PASSWORD does not appear.

Her fingers are shaking badly. She taps in the file name. There it is:

NO ONE LIVES ON THE MOON?

The introduction. Twelve chapters, one for each victim. A nonfiction book. A page-turner that the public requires. Then, she is looking at it. The lone word:

TOYER

spreads across the screen like a horror movie marquee.

It is all here.

She scans. This is exact, there is no more doubt. These chapters are fuller than the newspaper articles, more detailed, rambling, personal.

She is paralyzed, scanning calmly, logically, hurt, pretending she's known it all along. She has, she supposes, and has not realized it. She scans the file from beginning to end, noticing familiar chapter names as they fly past.

She scans:

*What Doctor Garance said was 100 percent true.
She said all I needed to do was destroy
the thing that made me Toyer. Well, I
have. Elaine died just as she lived,
without knowing it. I can't feel bad
about it because
I have been given the chance to lead a
normal life with a woman I love. And I
intend to, nothing will stop me. We will
disappear. It is a big country.*

August 27

She hears his voice saying it. A week ago, the date was August 27.

She skips, skips, skips reading words as they stick between impulses. All the way to the bottom, scanning. Familiar names, the now famous names, news legends, tick by one after the other, each one a chapter heading: Virginia Sapen. Gwyneth Freeman. Luisa Cooke. Karen Beck. Lydia Snow Lavin. Nina Voelker. Melissa Crewe. The prettiest names their parents could think of at the time of their birth, compliments paid their daughters at their highest moment of hope and life.

Queasy, Telen stops after page 321. Chapter 12, *Felicity Padewicz.* The last chapter. After that the screen is blank. The end of the book. No more surprises. Then a letter:

James O'Land
Officer, Publishers' Consortium
The Los Angeles Herald
1 Herald Square
Los Angeles, California 90019

Dear Mr. O'Land,

Today is Wednesday. NEXT Wednesday I'll be sending you the complete book. There's a Chapter 13. I have not written it yet because I have not actually met my subject. By next Wednesday, hopefully, this book will be on its way to the Publishers' Consortium.

I realize that we do not have a contract. We have at best a verbal agreement. My representative is Mr. Buck Wassitch of Wassitch, Lordell and Paine. I have explained my needs to him over the telephone. He understands that the Consortium is to take no more than its expenses and that the remainder of the profits will go to the *twelve* families of the women. Not the *thirteenth*. Nothing will be paid to her family or guardian.

I am proud to do that. These twelve women constitute the best of the American world as I know it. I don't think of them as victims. They are my beneficiaries. Their share from this book not only here but in Paris, Moscow, Sydney, Singapore, Mexico City, Buenos Aires, Toronto, will make them and their relatives rich.

The letter is signed *Toyer,* dated August 29.

The gnarled force of the words hits her full-face, numbing the nerve endings in her cheeks. Her mind goes blank. When it refocuses, she knows. He is not finished. *He took his flashlight, he wore his leather jacket. He's doing it again, he's out there now.* She feels like an imbecile. It is not another woman, he isn't being unfaithful to her. *It's not a date, it's a victim, for the love of God.*

Telen sits in her underwear, pale from fear. It is the fear of being so very close to a man she loves who can still end a life. *The answer is in front of me. It is up to me.* She has begun trembling visibly. *It will be my fault.* He is out there somewhere.

She presses the *Page Down* button once, twice, the words

climb the screen: *Chapter 13*. The chapter is blank, it has not been written. He will know what to write by morning.

Telen's mouth opens, she feels her head tipping over, toppling forward, tries to steady herself, faints into the screen, catches the corner of the desk with her cheekbone on her way to the floor. She lies still maybe half a minute, crawls to the bathroom, lays her neck over the edge of the tub but cannot throw up. Eventually she raises herself to the sink. Her cheek is bleeding, a welt is darkening under her right eye. She runs cold water on her hands and rinses her face, wipes her eyes and cheeks with a towel that smells sweet, doglike, unlike her.

Should she call the police? Maybe Sara. Somebody. Billy?

PETER

"**D**RINK, DARLING?" It is a scene from a Noël Coward comedy. Maude doesn't answer. Peter drinks, continues gushing as if tequila were truth serum.

"You know, Maude, when a pack of wild dogs catches a zebra, one dog grips the zebra's nose in its teeth and one grips its tail, while the other dogs begin to eat out its stomach. It's a routine. The zebra's standing on his hooves, and these dogs are eating him. You'd think he'd fight, wouldn't you?" He takes another sip of his melting drink.

"Well, he's through fighting. He's been expecting this. It's been happening to him for twenty million years and he doesn't even feel the dogs eating out his stomach. He's already gone away. Have you . . . gone away?"

She lolls back in the deep chair, he is directly in front of her, his hands loose at his sides. He touches the crown of her head. Maude jumps, grips the pillow more firmly.

"This is your life we're talking about, Maude, not one of your patient's. Where's your rage? I want to see tears."

"Fuck off, mind fucker."

"Good start."

"Fuck. Off."

"More doctor talk?"

"Who the hell are you to make people live or die?"

"Oooh, I love it when you flare. Have I disappointed you in some way?"

Maude is breathing too quickly. *It's gone. Everything. Over. My work. My career. Elias. All I wanted. He's done it to me. I can't believe it. It's over.* She cracks. She bends further forward, sobs in muscular spasms, helplessly. She longs to hear a car, Sara's, Elias's, Mason's, to hear people talking in the road outside the house, a dog's bark, to smell flowers, cigar smoke.

TELEN

B Y THE TIME you see buzzards circling over your head, they have been watching you a long time.

She knows immediately: *Sara.* She will wake her of course. But she does not, her telephone rings until it is picked up by her message machine. Telen leaves her number, says it is urgent. Waits. Ten minutes. No good.

She calls her at the *Herald,* hoping that she is working late.

"News Desk," an easy voice says. The presses are rolling, tomorrow's edition has been put to bed.

"Sara Smith, please?"

"Not here. Call back after nine A.M."

"It's urgent."

"Okay. Tell me why."

Telen must answer him, she hesitates, mentions Toyer.

"I'll have her get back to you, miss."

"No. It has to be right now, tonight."

He hears the true tone of urgent tension in her voice.

"What's your name?"

"Telen, she knows me."

"What's your number?"

"Five five five one two two nine."

He is intrigued just enough.

"What else can you tell me, Helen?"

She says she cannot say any more.

"I'll give her a try."

She sets a kettle on the electric stove, sits down to wait for the water to boil, wait for Sara Smith to call. Whichever comes first.

The telephone rings. She picks it up on the first ring, does not speak, waits.

"Hello, Telen?" A pleasant voice, calm, alert considering the hour.

"Sara?"

"Yes, it is." Sara is lying in bed in the dark, the telephone is glowing. "You called me at the paper so I guess it's pretty important. You mentioned—"

Telen cuts her off. "Yes, I did." She does not want to hear the word again.

"What have you got?"

Telen cannot go on. She presses the receiver with her index finger until she hears the dial tone.

SARA

TELEN'S VOICE sounded harsh, broken. Sara knows she will not be able to get back to sleep unless she speaks to her again, hears why she called so late. Sara is not at home, the night editor knows to call her here in emergencies. She lies for a few more moments in the dark, barely touching the back of the man, Jim O'Land, lying beside her. *The phone call probably woke him.*

"Jim?" she whispers. "Sorry about this."

He moans several words she cannot understand, she brushes his hair with her fingers, grooming him. She has not turned the light on.

"Go back to sleep, Jim, this may be nothing."

But she knows. She is a reporter. It is real. There is a pad and pen by the telephone. Telen woke her for a reason. Sara waits another thirty seconds, presses the REDIAL button on the lit face of the telephone. She must be gentle. Telen picks the receiver up during the first ring.

"You okay, *ma petite cousine?*"

"Yes, I am."

"I don't think you are, Telen. You wouldn't have called me at three something."

"I'm really sorry I woke you."

"Not the point, dear, the point is what's going on?" She says it sweetly.

Silence. Telen cannot speak.

O'Land shifts his position, so as to be half-aware of the conversation.

"Is anyone there with you? Telen?"

"No."

"Now, tell me."

"It's nothing really, nothing concrete. I have my suspicions but it's nothing more than that."

"Look, I get Toyer calls all day long but never this late and never at home. I called you back in good faith because one summer long ago my father slept with your mother's sister. And because you told the night editor it was about Toyer. So let's go, Telen, I want to stand up or lie down."

"I have a real conflict, Sara."

"I would tend to agree. Now tell Aunt Sara one single fact, one piece of hard evidence."

"I have one, I think."

The pause is too long for Sara. "Okay."

"I'm trying to get into his computer files now."

"Whose?"

"You know." She still cannot say the word to her.

"Toyer's?"

"That's right. I'm close to something."

Sara feels a thrilling flush. There is nothing like it.

"Where are you?"

"No."

"Tell me what you're looking for."

"I'm not really sure, not yet."

"Can you give me a name?"

"No."

"Can't or won't, Telen?"

"Both. Please give me some time." Telen is trying not to cry.

"No, Telen."

"Yes."

"How long?"

"Until morning?"

"What time in the morning?"

"*Sara.*"

"Okay. You're having problems with this, I can wait until nine. Call me at the paper at nine. But tell me one thing now, one detail in good faith. Give me something specific so I can get back to sleep."

"Okay."

Sara pauses a moment, thinking. "What makes you think it's him?"

"I think he kept every one of your articles tacked up on a wall. He killed his wife because Maude Garance told him to."

Silence.

"She told him in a letter to kill the thing that drove him.

Well, that was his wife." *I wonder how many other wives died because of her note.* "I can't think straight right now, Sara."

"I know. But there's just one more thing. Can you describe him to me?"

Finally, Telen begins to cry.

"This is hard for you, what does he look like? Please try to tell me." Sara waits, she listens to the silence of the telephone line. Maybe she will turn the light on. She hears Telen suck in a breath.

She speaks slowly, Sara can barely hear her. "He's good-looking, light-haired, almost blond, he has a good chin, dark blue eyes, long straight nose, he's lean, athletic, smart. He's six one-and-a-half inches tall, he weighs about one sixty-five."

The man Telen is describing brings Sara to an upright position in bed, then to her feet. She is stunned. She stands barefoot by the bed in the dark, listening, thrilled to the soles of her feet. It is true to Melissa's description, there are no contradictions. Sara is breathless, she keeps her voice steady. "Okay." Sara has moved into the bathroom, she is getting dressed in the dark. "Tell me his name."

"Peter."

"What's his last name?"

Telen cannot say his last name.

"Do you know him?" She turns the light on over the sink. "Yes."

"I'm guessing wildly, Telen, forgive me. You don't mean it's *your* Peter?"

Telen hesitates.

"It was."

Unbelievable. Stay calm. "You two broke up?"

"How'd you know?"

"You used the past tense."

"I broke up because of what Maude told me to do."

"So you think you're the woman she wrote that letter to?"

"Yes, I do."

"I can see the conflict."

"He's out there, Sara, I think he's . . . he's doing something."

"Do you have any idea where?"

"He might be in Sondelius."

"That little town on the way to Ojai? Why would he go there?"

"It's a house owned by his wife's mother."

"His wife?"

"She just died, I told you."

"Maybe her mother knows where he is."

"She might."

"What's the phone up there?"

"She has no phone, you have to go up. It's less than an hour this time of night."

"Does she know about him?"

"Well, she told me she suspects him, but he doesn't know she does."

"So she's probably safe from him, I mean she's not the only living witness."

"He's not going to kill her, if that's what you mean."

"Yes. Okay, what's her name and how do you get there?"

Telen gives her the street address, tells her how to find Ann's house. "Speak to her, I know she'll want to talk to you, she knows everything."

"Okay."

Telen adds, "Her name is Ann. Ask her to show you Elaine's room, that's her daughter. That's where I think your articles are. It's like a shrine to her. You've got to see it for yourself."

"Okay, Telen, thanks. I'll bet I can probably drive up there in thirty or forty minutes, I have a paid-up press card. Now what's this number I called you at?"

"You called me at his place."

"What if he walks in?"

"It's okay. Sara, he loves me."

Tough love.

"Will you still be there around four-thirty? I'd like to call back."

"Yeah, probably."

"Better give me the address now."

She does. She tells her to close the front door very quietly and tiptoe to the top floor, the attic apartment.

She remembers. "Okay, Telen, thanks, be careful. I'll call you from Sondelius after I speak to Ann. Before four-thirty."

Telen hangs up the telephone. It is three-twenty-five. The house rocks with silence.

PETER

PETER LINGERS on behind Maude where she cannot see him, puts down his drink in its own puddle on the glass-top table. He watches her for some moments with a cognoscente's pleasure. She is so obviously beaten.

He leans forward from behind, barely touches her shoulders. A tremor. He speaks.

"Okay, Maude, okay. That's enough. Maude. Can you hear me?"

She does not answer, she seems catatonic.

"Hello. Maude, can you hear me? Listen to me, I've got some good news."

Maude holds in her breath between sobs but cannot look up at him.

"I've done something pretty dreadful. See if you can forgive me. Maude, you're going to do all those fun things you said you were going to do tomorrow. Understand? Lunch with your friend, visit your patients, et cetera, beat the crap out of that poor doctor again. Whatever. It's all back on for tomorrow." He is elated, touches her shoulder. "You're going to stay just the way you are."

Maude remains head down, does not react. *What?*

"Maude. I've got a present for you. I live at eight-two-eight-oh. Down the hill? Practically your neighbor, see you drive by every morning. You win."

Maude looks up at him, red-eyed. *I win what?*

"I didn't mean for it to go so far. I was playing this acting game with you and it just kept getting worse and worse. I really feel badly, I'm so very sorry."

"What?" *Is this happening?*

Peter is smiling, relieved. "Maude. I'm sorry. None of it's true."

"What isn't?"

"Everything, nothing, I'm an actor."

Maude repeats the word dully. "An actor."

"I'm a professional actor. Peter Matson. The actor. You came to the Actors Group, I was the old man lying in the bed shouting in Telen Gacey's play. I never got out of bed. I was in a wig. That was me, remember?"

Yes.

"Anyway, don't hate me, I was trying something, an improvisation. Did Sara Smith tell you about our improvisations? The stuttering one?"

Yes. One of Sara's friends.

"I didn't mean for it to go so far but it was going so well, it was . . ." He stops before he uses the word *fun.* "I just got carried away, but believe me, I made it up, I made it all up." He is euphoric.

"I hate actors."

"Of course you do." Then, impulsively: "Can I say something?"

"Get out."

"Can I say something? Please? Can I say something?" *Think fast.* "Anna, Anna Blouse, and you remember this very good actor, Billy Waterland, they both told me to create a character; complex, believable, one that breathes, taken from real life, okay? Become that character and test him out on a stranger. I wanted to do Toyer."

That's what Sara said.

Maude looks up, watching him, dazed. Peter is volleying around the room like a suburban host.

She stares up at him with sea-washed eyes, forms the word, "Why?"

"All week long Toyer's been in my brain. How he stands, how he walks, talks, what pisses him off, why he does what he does. I even used one of your letters to him. Finally I believed him. Now all I had to do was to make you believe him. You of all people. Doctor Maude Garance. And you did. When I met you in the parking lot, I said *now*. Big decision. I had to make you believe it. The ultimate test of my performance. If you didn't—" He snaps his fingers. "— no scene. And we had a scene." He has gotten high at his own party.

Thickly, Maude answers. "Yes we did . . . have a scene."

"Right?"

"Right."

"What can I tell you? You let me, understand? You're so tied up in this Toyer business, you were willing to take my word for it. You've been expecting it! I just fed you cues."

She speaks dully. "You didn't break my car?"

"No, no, no, not at all."

"How could you know all those things about me?"

"You're a doctor, you're not going to have a messy medicine cabinet." Contentedly, "Fortune cookie material."

"What about Mason?"

"His picture's facedown in the bureau. What can I think?"

"The gun?"

"I snooped."

"I'm trying to imagine what you could possibly get out of what you just did to me."

"I told you, acting. Sara Smith told you about the Group,

she's writing an article about us." Maude, still slightly in shock, abruptly realizes she is going to be all right.

Peter, unguarded, turns his back to Maude for the first time, relaxed, flushed, comes down from his greatest Hollywood performance, greater than the stuttering scene.

"Acting per se has been kind of a marvelous thing for my persona. I've definitely grown. I've defined my priorities. I know who I am. I like me. I believe in me."

"Yes, you do." *I'm witnessing the flowering of an actor's ego from bud to bloom.* "What about me? Did you believe in me?"

"Sure." He says delightedly, "But you believed more in me, that I was this Toyer who'd killed, excuse me, disabled, all those girls."

"Have you lost your mind?"

"I don't think so, no," he says judiciously.

"I think so. You're insane, I can tell by listening to you."

"Fine, if that's *insane,* then I'm *insane.*" Peter is piqued. "Aren't you supposed to use the word *psychopath?*"

He goes to the kitchen area. "I'm getting another, okay?"

"Oh, sure, have a drink. Send out for Chinese food. Better still, why don't you just get the fuck out of here?"

"I am definitely leaving, Maude, but first I need one little drink."

"There's a faucet just above the sink."

Peter opens the refrigerator, squats out of sight, takes a handful of ice. "What'll you have, gin and tonic?" He spots half a bottle of gin in the freezer, takes it out, flaps around the kitchen like a sea gull, waving the bottle. "What about one for the road?"

It's over. She smiles, realizing. *It's over. Yeah, why not? One for the road.*

"Gin and tonic."

"Gin and tonic. Yeah. If that's crazy, then I'm crazy. There'll always be people who don't understand you."

"How true," Maude is able to say. "You've always got to be on the lookout for us."

It is the epicenter of the night, the turning point from where all directions emanate toward morning.

SARA

THE BATHROOM LIGHT is lit, the door is closed. Sara is dressing, pulling on jeans.

Poor Telen. I can't imagine what she's going through. She loves him, he's a monster, she's got to turn him in. That's the real story. Christ, it doesn't get any rougher than that.

She regards her face hurriedly in the mirror. *Such an unkind mirror.* Her fine shoulders, her breasts. She raises her chin. She is tingling, ecstatic, she feels the morning will lead her to Toyer. *There is only one moment,* she whispers to her own image. *I thought it came yesterday.* She can see excitement in her eyes looking back at her.

She writes Jim a note, turns off the lights. She acts matter-of-fact, without excitement. Jim would appreciate that. She leaves him the address she's driving to in Sondelius, the name Ann. Her license plate number in case there's an accident. Telen's telephone number in case he doesn't hear from her by 8:00 A.M. Even the number at Peter's apartment.

What about Maude? She should know. At three-thirty? Why not, she'll be so excited.

But Maude's telephone line is out of order.

TELEN

WHEN TELEN HANGS UP the telephone, she passes out again. She does not know for how long, maybe only for a few moments. When she comes to, the full horror slams her again. What has happened to her life comes back to her in a whoosh, her dreams have turned to bile. She goes into the bathroom, kneels, waits for the vomit to rise. Afterward, she rinses her mouth with water, wipes her eyes with a towel, then her tongue.

Chapter 13? What he told her was over, is not. She cannot stay in his apartment a minute longer. She knows too much, far more than she wants to know. Except the title of Chapter 13. What is the name below the number?

There is a quiet knock at the door without a sound from the hallway, as though someone has been standing outside the door for a while, listening. Telen stands motionless as a forest deer.

Of course it is not Peter. He is not coming back for her, it is an irrational fear. Still, her heartbeats pound in her chest and arms, she cannot feel her fingers, her legs are gone, she has never been more frightened in her life.

Another quiet knock. She tiptoes to the door.

"Yes?"

"Is everything okay?" It is an old voice that cannot sleep, hoping something is wrong.

"Yes, of course, why?"

"I'm Mr. Fuotto. I live downstairs."

That dreadful man who sleeps in ashtrays and tries to look up my dress whenever I go upstairs.

"Well, I'm sorry, Peter isn't here, Mr. Fuotto."

"I know." It is too intimate. *He knows.*

"Well, thanks for checking, Mr. Fuotto, everything's okay."

He knows I am alone in the apartment. He probably saw me making love to Peter in the hallway the other afternoon.

There is no sound of shuffling movement outside the door.

"By the way, Mr. Fuotto, do you know what time Peter went out?"

"He went out a little before six."

"Thanks very much, Mr. Fuotto."

After half a minute, she hears shuffling sounds, he is going downstairs.

PETER

THEIR GLASSES are empty, the ice cubes have melted into ovoids. Peter takes Maude's glass to the kitchen.

"You were beautiful," he says. "I'm sorry, but you were." He looks at her admiringly. He is still preening. She no longer cares.

In her glass Peter brings her an ounce of iced gin and a splash of water. She drinks it. Gulp. Sets the glass down. He snares it, saunters back to the kitchen, fills it, moving in bartender's choreography. *She's getting high.*

"I know you weren't acting, but your behavior choices were valid."

"Go." She feels too weak to push. "Just go."

"You still feel pretty bad?"

"What do you think? God damn you."

Peter hands her the glass. He sits on the sofa beside her, not close. "Well, of course you've got to come down. So do I."

The idea of coming down. "Doesn't anything embarrass you?" Suddenly she laughs, surprising even herself, this has been a game, nothing more. "Just go, I'll be all right." She can barely assert herself other than to laugh.

He nods and abruptly sits forward, elbows on knees, looking away from her. "Wait, wait, wait, I want to say something. Okay? You'd make a hell of an actress, Maude. Don't hit me. Hey, I could care less, but you would. You might like it as a hobby. You and Sara come to the Group next Saturday morning, see for yourself. We could do a scene. You'd love it, we could do *this* scene. This exact scene. I could even type it up." He raises his right hand in solemn oath. "I swear it wouldn't be embarrassing."

"This? Again?"

"You've got presence, depth. Plus, you really believe."

"I wonder why."

"Okay. Just come and watch. Don't go near the stage."

This is actor-babble. "No. Get out, I'm feeling nauseated."

"Will you think about acting?"

"Yes-yes-yes. Now get out, whatever the hell you are."

"You don't remember me?"

Maude doesn't remember him.

"No?" He pauses. "Maybe I'd better stay."

"Why?"

"Just to show you that it's all innocent." He shrugs nicely. "That I live down the street and that I'm a friend of Sara Smith's, that's all."

"No! Just shut up. Look, I don't care. What to believe, who you are, anything."

Peter goes to the front door, unchains it, opens it slightly.

"I got all my ID on my bike, okay? Be right back, that might help."

He is gone. Maude stares at the door, nodding slightly from the gin. In an instant he pushes the door open again, leans in, smiles.

"Remember I said I cut your phone line? Try it. See if it works. That ought to help."

He disappears. Again, he leaves the door ajar. Maude, alone, turns to stare at the telephone on the bureau. She feels embarrassed by her doubts. After a long moment, she gets up and goes over to it. She picks it up and listens. She bends her head, covers her ear, tries to hear the dial tone. She pushes the disconnect button. She listens again. There is no dial tone. The telephone is dead. Dead telephone. Her throat solidifies.

She feels him behind her, turns. He is standing in the open doorway. He has never left. He smiles sweetly, shrugs.

"I love you," he says.

TELEN

IN THE JOHN, peeing again, her hands shake so badly she grips the towel rack as she rides the toilet like a toboggan. No one in the world knows where she is tonight. Only Sara Smith, Mr. Fuotto. If Peter walks in now, she has no chance, she may as well jump out the window. She knows what he will do to her.

She closes down the computer, leaving the files unchanged, as she found them, snaps it shut, leaves it in plain sight on the bed.

I've got to talk to Billy first.

After four rings, she hears his taped message, the night hunter, stalking prey. "I'm out right? But your message is important to me. . . ."

"Billy it's three-forty-five, if you come home in the next couple of minutes, call me, I'm at Peter's but I'm leaving. Please please, it's very urgent."

I have to show Billy something physical, I can't just tell him, he won't believe me, I need a copy of a chapter. The printer has to be here.

And it is, a small one, she finds it in the closet, less skillfully hidden than the computer, it is in his duffel bag. He has made no effort to conceal it, there is nothing incriminating about owning a printer.

She opens the computer, sets it on the desk, connects the printer, prints two pages of the Felicity Padewicz chapter. She dresses quickly while it is printing, folds the pages and slides them down into the seat of her panties.

She writes Sara a note.

Sara,
   Sorry, I couldn't stay. The computer on the desk is open to the book files. In case you lose it, the secret word is CAT-FISH. Call you later.

Telen

She will drive to Billy's place, wait for him there. She turns the fans off, makes the bed look as it did when she came in. She leaves the apartment unlocked.

She takes her shoes off, afraid of alerting Mr. Fuotto, her admirer on the second floor, tiptoes barefoot down the wood stairs, through the dry wary house.

She runs to her car as if she were being chased by demons, locks herself in, drives half a block, parks.

He's killed us both is all she can think again and again. *I love him and he's killed us both.* She cannot stop crying, sobbing hard. Across the sidewalk ten feet away, the crimson neon outline of a hand hung in the window, the word *READINGS*, written in red crayon below it. It frightens her that Señora Maldonado knew.

MAUDE

MAUDE GRIPS the dead telephone.
   She sets it down in slow motion, dazed, not in the cra-

dle, it does not matter. She is drained sober, her eyelids flicker. Peter closes the door, slips the chain in the groove, takes a step toward her. He speaks gently, as if to illuminate. "I love you, Maude." He takes another step, another. Halfway across the room he stops.

"I do love you." He stands poised, his hands out, palms toward her. The annunciation, he is Gabriel.

Maude feels ill, leans a stiff arm on the kitchen counter for support. She stretches her other hand to the wall by the alcove. Leaning on her arm, she reaches under the counter and snaps off the switches for the room lights.

The house is black.

Peter stands a moment then backs toward the front door, eyes wide, alert, feels the wall for a switch, switches it. The yellow porch light goes off. He finds another switch. Nothing happens. Old house circuits. Dead.

"Just kidding around, Maude," he says, sounding cheerful. "Game's over."

Maude, crouched in the darkness, reaches up to the knife-rack on the wall, slips out a jib-shaped Sabatier dicing knife. *I will.*

"Turn on the light, Maude." Peter stands at the front door, talking continuously, listening, feeling for a light switch. "Maude, I was just kidding, I swear, I'm an actor, a lousy actor, for God's sake, it's a stupid actor's game. Let me explain."

Maude crouches small under the counter, still as a rabbit.

"Hey, I lose." Peter takes a single step forward and another. "Come on in. You win. You're home free."

He listens, takes a step toward the kitchen area. He listens, not a sound. Maude throws her address book to the wall behind Peter. He turns.

"Maude. Actors' games."

Don't breathe. Wait for him to come to me. She waits.

There is no moon. Outside the black house, on the hillside,

the midnight-blue sky spreads out above the pinchbeck villages below.

Peter touches his jacket, pulls his small halogen light from the pocket, shines its thin beam around the room. "Maude, please, listen to me. It's over." The light flashes quickly past her.

She has slipped out from behind the counter and is now crouched in the bedroom, waiting.

"Maude, for Christ's sake, you must know I was only joking."

He scans the bedroom with his light, she is behind the door, he doesn't quite enter. "You're a bright girl, Maude, come on give me a break."

She stands, the knife is out in front of her. She is trying to breathe silently, her mouth wide as a grouper's, *He knows I can kill him.*

"Maude? Come home, all is forgiven. It's just a game, promise." Peter turns back into the kitchen, turns his light off. The rooms are black. *He knows he's the one in danger, not me.*

She cannot see him. She slips from the bedroom through the bathroom and out into the living room again. She gets to the front door. She is open-mouthed, dissipating the sound of her breathing.

He touches the light switches under the counter. Light floods the kitchen, the living room. Maude is caught standing at the front door, the wide knife is at her side. She faces him.

He reaches his arms out, holding his flashlight, palms toward her, straight to her, fingers wide. "Friends?" He comes toward her, smiling, a slight spring to his step. He hasn't seen the knife. He is a dark target.

Now. Without a thought, blank as her need, she takes three steps, quick, directly into him, led by the wide blade out in front of her, the knife held low, aimed at his genitals. She is too quick.

He is caught, completely surprised. Trapped. Overwhelmed. He can only dodge aside, half turning away, off balance. It will be very close.

Up Maude's knife flashes, arcing toward the ceiling. Peter is caught by the blade, the leather sleeve gives way for the flesh of his arm. He screams, staggers backward, stumbles, falling onto the sofa. The small light flies out of his hand, high toward the ceiling, then down loud on the glass table.

Maude stands over him, panting, sweating, the kitchen knife ready for more, its point on his stomach. Peter lies stretched on the sofa, prepared to die. She has slashed him through the leather sleeve, and he lies holding his left arm tightly. There is blood.

"Not a breath."

Peter looks ill. *She'd do it. Get yourself out of this one, asshole.*

Maude keeps the tip of the knife to his throat, dimpling his larynx. Maybe a minute passes, her eyes glaze. Peter is fixed, motionless, breathy. He is out of ideas. He is pinned.

Maude has not moved. She has already tried to kill him at the beach. She feels the same momentum that led her there. She is dazed, unable to push the blade into him or to take it away.

Peter tries to swallow, he turns his head away. The knife tears his skin slightly.

In an instant he is raving. "Call a doctor! For Christ's sake, call a doctor! On the phone. Plug it in." He nods toward the telephone jack on the wall behind the bureau. She looks at it for an instant. It is unplugged. She stares at him blankly. He is close to hysterics. She has seen hysteria before. He ignores Maude, concerned about his wound.

"Call a doctor, you work at the Kipness, you must know a doctor."

"I *am* a doctor." She has not moved, nor has the knife, it is always there, pressed into some part of him.

"A real doctor, you're a psychiatrist. I can sue you."

"Don't push it." Maude is coming around, well armed.

"I'm serious. We had a drink, we had an argument, you tried to kill me."

"I should cut your tongue out." She moves the knife up his chest, once again it touches his throat. "I may do that, Peter, you know I can." He knows. "I cut a man's throat once."

"I didn't touch you, remember? I'm not your fucking Toyer. I may be, on the other hand, an asshole for getting myself into this."

He's probably right, psychopathic personalities usually don't harm anyone but themselves.

"Could you please move that knife?"

She doesn't. She hovers over him, watching him carefully.

"I am so sorry, Maude. Okay? Now do me a favor and call a goddamned doctor, on that phone, now, before I bleed to death on your sofa."

"Is it that bad, Peter?"

He tries to look at it, tries to roll up his sleeve. "That bad? It's bad, very bad, it's terrible."

"It's a scratch."

"It's red and it's deep and it's long and you did it. You're afraid to call a real doctor because you stabbed me. I won't say you stabbed me, don't worry, I'll tell them we were having a party, whatever, the champagne blew up."

"I can do scratches, Peter, nine years' training, six years' practice."

"You *had* to stab me, right? You couldn't grasp that this was a game. Okay, okay, so maybe I was fucking with your head. But I wasn't using a kitchen knife, was I? I was using my brain. I thought you were using yours. People like you are supposed to be smart, obviously I was wrong about you, stabbing me was dumb." He begins to sob.

"Shut up and take your shirt off."

"Why don't you just slash it off me?"

He wriggles out of his leather jacket, lets it drop, then his shirt. "God I hate blood. Especially mine."

"It's not a vascular area, the outside arm. It's a muscle cut, that's why it's bleeding. But there's no artery there."

Peter is bare-chested. Maude can see that he is lithe, spring-strong. A good-looking adult male specimen. The sun has sketched an undershirt on his chest and shoulders.

She holds the knife ready in her right hand. She runs the fingers of her left hand up his arm, turning them red with blood. She cannot leave the beach. Blood in her hair, on her breasts. She leads him to the sink and rinses her hands. She is horrified, watching it swirl away. "Would you run water over it?"

"No, I could not run water over it."

"Do it."

He quickly bends over the sink, throws up, runs water to wash his mouth, turns on the garbage disposal. She waits, runs water directly on the cut. He squirms. For an instant they seem to be at the sorry end of a children's game that's gone too far and one child has gotten hurt.

"How many stitches? Goddamn you."

"No stitches, Peter. I'm getting sick of you." *I don't consider him dangerous: narcissism, castration complex, feminine weaknesses.* "Wait there." She goes into the bathroom.

Alone, Peter berates himself. "What the fuck am I doing here?"

Maude returns with a bottle of peroxide and a bandage. Sets them down on the counter. "Impersonating Toyer?"

"Is a very sick thing to be doing."

"Not just sick, reprehensible. I wish I'd been a split second quicker."

"You're absolutely right."

"Don't agree with everything I say."

"Do I do that?"

She ignores the question, blots peroxide on his cut.

I want to make you want me, submit entirely, submit willingly, feel you in my mouth, feel you spread out under me, open.

TELEN

TELEN DRIVES to get away from Peter's house, drives one block to Sunset Boulevard, turns and parks, unable to see. Her eyes clench from squeezing out the tears, her throat aches from gulping sobs. She sits and waits for the waves to calm down, too sick to drive.

She still loves Peter. Whatever hope she had for life with him has just been killed by the tiny green lights darting across the computer screen. She sits. For the first time in her life she wants to be someone else, older, living someplace, not Los Angeles, in a new house like all the others in the neighborhood, with children, a messy husband. She wishes she had a brother. She wonders if her piano is still in storage. She wants to be famous. She wants to go to bed.

Telen Gacey has no resources. She is a girl who came from a small town where men whispered about her. When she was six her mother told her that she had a pretty voice. In high school, in her sophomore, junior, and senior years, she sang the national anthem at the Thanksgiving Day game. No one in the school's history has ever equaled that, before or since.

She sees the dim light of a half-lit telephone shell down the block.

MAUDE

ENTIRE NEIGHBORHOODS are asleep, their televisions cool, resting for the long day ahead. A coyote passes close to the house, raccoons, possums, owls, mice. This is their time. The deer drowse. Sometime earlier, Peter has turned the stereo low. Barely heard music seasons the night.

His arm is bandaged. Maude has not put the knife down. She gestures with it. She is deeply upset, relieved. She has not killed him but she knows how close she came. Again. "I cure people, I try never to murder them."

"Actors, we're disposable." His laugh is weak, more of a whimper.

"I'm really sorry."

"Don't. You're apologizing for saving your life."

"I tried to knife you with a wound they can rarely fix in Emergency. I've seen knifing victims wheeled in on gurneys. It's all gone, stomach, kidney, intestine, sometimes lung. No hope. That's terminal hemorrhage, when you shoot someone it's simple shock."

"Well, if it's any consolation, you also tried to shoot me." He reaches out his hand to her, "C'mon, Maude, anyone can kill."

She ignores his hand. She continues to visualize what almost happened and did not.

"Drinky?" He makes a monkey face, rattles the ice in his glass.

She pauses, she gives him a sudden, stunning smile. "Why not?" She picks up her glass and starts to the kitchen. "Why the hell not?"

Peter jumps up. "No, no, no, let me do it."

He is ashen and wobbly, but he takes her glass and his to the kitchen counter. With one hand he pours two gins over ice and brings them out, hands her one. "Friends." He toasts her.

Maude doesn't toast.

"At least stop waving that knife at me, okay?"

She drinks, sets her glass down and stretches her arms back, knife in hand, out over her head. "I'll be fine."

"Me, too." Peter cradles his hurt arm. "You must feel relieved."

"*You* must feel relieved. You almost were my *corpus delicti* over there by the fridge."

"Yes, indeed I was." *I need to enter you, bend you around me, penetrate your brilliance unhinge your mind and slam it shut forever.*

She stiffens into cat stretches. "I feel somehow fatigued."

"But sky-high."

It's true. She is on the verge of smiling. They catch the other's eye in a flick. He winks at her. This is the arrangement. One is not a killer, one is not a corpse.

Beyond the sighing house, a screech owl screeches and is answered by a distant screech owl. *What an incredibly beautiful sound.*

The lavender loom of the expired city dissolves in whispers. Maude loosens the fingers that grip the Sabatier dicing knife. She sets it down on the glass table beside the three river-washed rocks. Together they form a calm arrangement, the rocks, the glass, the ten-inch blade.

Whatever he is, he's an amazing man.

BILLY

BUT THERE IS NO RECEIVER on the pay telephone. Telen has been scanning the closed sidewalks for one that works, all the receivers have been torn off of them. Finally, at a gas station, she calls Billy again.

"Please pick up, please."

He does after four rings, the same moment his answering machine picks up.

Billy is asleep, the telephone feels warm against his neck and the pillow.

"Please Billy it's Telen please Billy wake up Billy please."
She does not care if he is with a girl. He is not.

"Telen?" He forms the words, "Tomorrow I'll definitely be
there . . . swear to God."

"No, Billy, now, wake up. I'm coming over. Let me come
over." Billy dreams of interludes with Telen.

"Why?"

"Because it can't wait, Billy."

"You crying?"

"Yeah. You will be, too."

Billy wakes. "Peter?"

"Yes."

"What?"

"I have to meet you."

"Come on."

"No, not on the phone."

They will meet at Ruben's in twenty minutes. *Billy Billy
Billy.* Telen stays parked a few minutes longer by the telephone shell at the gas station on Sunset Boulevard wondering
if she should call the police. She has recovered well enough to
drive. She starts the engine.

It is four-twenty-five, the long night is ending. The wide
town has this one splendid moment. When the boulevards exhausted by the sun lie deserted and, still drained of life, point
toward day.

MAUDE

THEY FINISH their drinks. Peter collects their glasses,
takes them to the kitchen, pours another round, brings it
out.

"Will it leave a scar?"

"I wouldn't think so."

"I'd like it to leave a scar. My turning point." He raises his glass. "I'm through playing with the big girls now."

"If you ever played with them at all." Maude looks directly at him, raises her glass. "What an amazing feeling."

Peter affects an actor's French accent. "Yir f'rst creem de passione, ma'mselle?" He laughs.

"Funny, I've been told I lack passion."

"Oh yeah? Well, you got it. They're pretty close, hate and passion, they lie side-by-side in the brain."

"Don't start." She laughs back at him. "There isn't a lot I don't know about love-hate and you're a real stack of *Time* magazine clichés. I knew exactly what I was doing every second. How do you think that feels?"

"For a rational person who solves problems logically? Educational."

"Yeah, always nice to grow."

She holds out her glass, he goes to the kitchen for another gin-on-ice. "Why, Peter?"

"I enjoy it. She enjoys it. Everyone goes home happy."

"It's a sport, right? And you get to play what position? Let me guess: God." Maude drinks. She feels a drunk euphoria.

He stands, watches her from the kitchen. *She's right.* "A sport," he says aloud to her. *But a euphoria that never happens in sports.*

"Women. We're all so fucking scared, aren't we? Mention the word *rape* and if we can't escape we become pliant."

Pliant, I like pliant. Peter hands her a drink. *Get pliant soon, Maude.*

Maude, red-eyed, looks up at him. "Why do you do it?"

"The truth?"

"Oh, why not?"

Tell her. "It's a visceral thing."

"Sexual? I was supposed to be turned on by it?"

"Women love it, what can I tell you?" *Full disclosure.* "It's a total reversal."

"The closeness of death. An aphrodisiac?"

"You let me take you in, show you around, bring you out the other side. I mean you were *there*."

He means it. "My, my, your absolute power over me acts as a drug. The closeness to death gives me a rush that leads us into my bed?"

"Something like that."

"Is that all this is about? Fucking?" She notices the proportions of his body. "You're only a rapist?"

"Well, in slow motion."

"It actually works?"

Of course it works. "Maude, I hate to say it, but you wanted us to love each other any way we could."

"You ought to be put away."

"Maybe." A rueful smile.

"Bastard."

"Bitch." A radiant smile.

"What the hell are you?"

"I'm an actor, Maude, I can be anything you want me to be."

"Hasn't anyone ever tried to kill you?"

"One must be on the lookout for that."

"But you consider it part of the sport?"

"Very much so. I do love the brink."

"You know what I hate you for? For making me think I was about to die just so I'd say all those . . . things."

"Yeah. That's death for you, really wakes up your alternatives, doesn't it?"

"It's a truly degrading experience. I would have done anything for you."

She's coming around, she's starting to play. "Like?"

"Too late." Maude laughs suddenly. "So take that dumb look off your face. But you name it, I would have done it." She adds, without smiling, "With pleasure, just so I could see tomorrow."

"Adequate reason."

"So what happens now?"

"Whatever."

"Whatever?"

"Happens, happens."

Far from Maude's doubts, the city barely breathes. In all-night cafés, puffy men eat their soup. A small woman with exciting shoes has just been killed by a man she scarcely knew, behind a parked car in an alley where people urinate.

TELEN

SUNSET BOULEVARD is the longest city street in the world. Its final address is in the twenty thousands, at Malibu, across the street from the Pacific Ocean. Telen is in a dream, maybe she will drive its length. On its way to the sea, she passes the burrito stands of Silverlake, then the stagnant swimming pools of Los Feliz where dead movie stars swim to gramophone records of Enrico Caruso. She does not need to be anywhere. She has always loved the way Sunset Boulevard rises through Hollywood, celebrating its demise in a thicket of billboards, then the sheer dream of Beverly Hills where theme mansions cling to their properties like clichés, then through Brentwood's landless estates, Bel Air, built against seasons that will never come, on toward the Pacific Palisades that are made of dirt and down to die at the edge of the vast modest sea.

There is a *thump*, a pleasing sound. Telen has hit something soft. A person is lying on the pavement in front of her car, over the hood to the right she can see the remnants of an overcoat. It is a man, maybe dead. A fellow human being. She sits in the stopped car, holding the steering wheel, her head pressed into it, eyes closed.

The struck man has raised himself on one elbow. He had

drifted out from the curb in front of her right fender. Telen had slowed for a red light, but had kept rolling, barely moving without looking. The struck man is now crawling to safety toward the curb, glancing back at Telen over his shoulder. He moves sideways like a beggar, someone close to the ground. Telen is afraid of beggars, she does not like the feel of their eyes on her. She wants to wave to him and drive on, but she parks. He sits on the curb. *He's not hurt, please.* Earlier tonight Telen had a solid dream of death, now she hopes a beggar will not die. He is sitting up straight on the curb. He looks well there, at home.

People are watching. She stands beside him on the pavement in her little dress, bending down. He has beautiful, oily skin, radiant from the sun and rain. He has the finest head of hair she has ever seen, it glows in waves. He has the teeth of a movie star. He has peed in his pants earlier in the week, she can smell his recent history on his clothes, urine, alcohol, vomit, smoke. His breath rises from his being, made up of vodka-rotted intestines. He is drunk.

Several Hispanics study Telen, *¿Que tal señorita?*, keeping their distance, afraid she may jump in her car and crush them too under her wheels.

The beggar has a rich, guttural voice. "What's your name?" She tells him.

"You hit me with a car, Helen." It is not an accusation, it is pure wonder at the event. *Hit by a car. Think of that. Cute broad. Wow. Here I am. Alive. Jesus Christ, is this a good life, or what the fuck.*

"That's okay, it was only my coconut." The pleasing thump Telen heard was made by his head striking her hood as if it were a kettledrum.

"I'm so sorry," she says.

"Hey, I'm sorry too, I did not see you coming."

"Are you all right, sir?"

"Yeah I'm good, but you oughta give me something."

"What do you want?" *I'll give you anything.*

"Whatta you got?"

"Well, I've got some money. How would that be?" *Give him some nice money.*

"In that purse?"

"Yes." She has been holding it like a fullback.

"Well, look, gimme what you got but I don't want 'em to see it." He nods his damaged head toward the hyena-eyed Mexicans standing in front of the closed spaghetti house.

Telen nods, goes to her car, and empties her purse. There might be a hundred dollars. *Good.* She wads it into a handkerchief, comes back to him, uses it to wipe his forehead, then puts it in his hand. *He gets it.* His beautiful skin feels like a horse's hide.

"Thanks. Now get lost, I don't want to see a cop tonight."

"Goodnight. God, I'm sorry."

"Have a good one." And, in afterthought, he squints at the ball of money. "Come back and hit me anytime, lady."

She drives away, waving. She sees herself making love to Peter on the top step in the hot afternoon with their clothes scattered around them, loving each other's pure skin. She remembers every moment with him. Where is she driving? She remembers that she is waiting to die.

MAUDE

THE NIGHT, gray as elephants, shuffles down the hills.

Jimmy G, pale orange, showing a whitish belly, shifts in his sleep on the window seat, his paws are crossed as though he has dozed off while reading. It is late, late.

Peter collects their glasses from the glass tabletop, takes them to the counter. The clatter wakes Jimmy G, who yawns lavishly and watches the scene. Not seeing anything worth staying up for, he closes his eyes. Maude has thrown one leg up on the sofa. Casual neglect.

"Of course, I'm meant to respond to you now in a *new* way, calmly grateful for your gift of life."

"You're free to respond the way you feel." Peter is in the kitchen inspecting the contents of the freezer.

"Under the circumstances, I'll pass." She wants to laugh at him.

Think about it, Maude, I need to taste you enter you bend you around me penetrate your brilliance unhinge your mind slam it shut forever.

"Why tell me you're gay?"

"I despise that chipper little adjective, don't you?"

"But why?"

"I never said I was, Maude." He sips the gin.

She pauses, nods. "So I'd open the door."

Peter smiles. "So you'd open the door."

The kitchen light is off. The bedroom is dark.

"By the way, what was all that garbage you were telling me about zebras or gazebos? Was that your creation?"

"Just for you."

He offers her two glasses. "You get the last of the gin or the first of the tequila."

"Gin." She points.

He empties the bottle in a glass, tosses the bottle into the wicker basket. "The end of the gin." *Clank.* He hands her the clear glass, keeps the one with two ounces of gold tequila among clear icebergs. "The tequila refused to mix with coffee liqueur. It lay in the bottom and sang 'Maria.' "

"I sure opened the door, didn't I?"

Yes, you sure did.

Jimmy G can't seem to sleep, he comes over to watch, it is too late to see people. He sits. This is a very strange night for a cat.

"Why me?"

"You're an extraordinary woman, Maude, that's why."

She detaches herself easily from the compliment. "Oh, yeah?"

"Tell me something," Peter says. "Why did you chop your hair off?"

That was last year. Now it is two inches longer, still boyish, the color whiskey turns milk when you add a taste of it to a glass.

My hair. "I used to wear it long as a palomino's. It was so thick I could go swimming and it'd still be dry at the roots when I came out." A week after she faced Virginia Sapen she had it shorn, she called it her prison camp cut. "I cut it because of Toyer. Syndrome called empathy."

Only the pyramid lamp is on, sending specters to the ceiling. Somehow, there has been music the whole time, now a quiet, meandering jazz quartet. Both hold melting drinks. Maude on the sofa, her head whirls pleasingly, just behind her eyes. She feels relief, in her release from death. *My entire diastrophism.* She is free, stronger than anyone.

Peter stands over her, holds his hand out to her, open, slightly curved. Michelangelo's Man reaching a hand to God, beautiful, she lets it hang in the air, admiring it. *I see you, your hips, your waist.* Maude studies Peter, the long evening and night in her face. Her eyes are direct, vulnerable, plain. She looks from his eyes to his hand to her own, to the clear fluid in her glass. She sets the gin down too hard, glass on glass, bright as an altar bell.

She feels a hand raising itself, reaching out to his. Hers to his, hers to his. It can only mean one thing, it is done. He pulls her up, perfect tension, close to him but not touching him. She feels his strength. For moments a jagged line of light stays between them, then she comes against him. There is a nice wetness where they touch. The room is dim, it spins nicely for her.

A relief of sentences form without her knowing it, from a vault of words she has not spoken in years, passes her lips into his ear, "I can feel it all falling away from me, Peter. I'm spinning down through the floor into the sky. Can't you feel me spinning? I'm not sure how long we've known each other. Has it been long?"

"Yes." Peter is settling himself nicely between her legs.

Spinning, spinning.

"How long has it been, Peter?"

"A long time."

"I left my keys somewhere else, left them in some drawer. No one's called and I'm not busy tonight, or any night, and no one knows I'm alive except you. And I want you to see me. . . ."

Spinning, spinning.

Peter passes his hands over her, she passes her hands over him lightly. They kiss beautifully, dancing, like a famous photograph.

". . . drop my layers . . . cloth, silk . . . show you me. Find out what it is, if I'm all right for you. If that's what I'm for."

The music moves over the dancers, she is drunk as the ceiling in the stars. "Whatever the hell this is between us, this thing, please, *please* don't ever let it deteriorate into friendship."

Spinning, spinning. He is an actor, Sara told me about her actor. She can do it, I can do it, I can take an actor to bed for one night.

They dance. He unbuttons her blouse with his left hand. She does not notice. Minutes pass like planets.

"Peter, you were beyond belief."

Once again Maude's blouse falls billowing. Her wraparound skirt drops easily. The room turns, they are barely dancing, moving. Everything is theirs, this is all she wants. She undoes Peter's belt, opens his pants. He holds her hips with both hands, moves her backward, down on the sofa, separates her knees. He kneels on the floor in front of her, between her legs, after the long expectancy, and distends her, entering her with too-full strength; the full soft rage an act of love can assail upon the woman receiving it, her entire body open, as if the creation of lovemaking had been based on this moment.

Elsewhere in the wide town, men in unfamiliar rooms dress in the dark, standing on one leg. Using tissues, women dry their vaginas, roll on their sides.

SARA

SONDELIUS. 4:50 A.M. It is a town without street lights. There is a moon, the shadows of the trees are stronger than the trees. Sara doesn't need her flashlight to read mailbox numbers.

There it is, *471*.

After a moment, Ann is standing in the open doorway, she expects nothing. She is no longer frightened, her face is passive. She is wearing a robe over her pajamas.

"Yes, miss?"

"I am Sara Smith, a friend of Peter."

"Oh! Is something wrong?"

"No, nothing's wrong, I only came because a mutual friend of ours, Telen Gacey, asked me to, I'm sorry it's so late but she told me something . . ." Sara says she would have telephoned. Ann has no telephone, no friends. She smiles. She can only sleep in the morning light with the television set on, after the sun has come up. Ann knows everything.

"Are you Elaine's mother?"

They sit in the kitchen like mourners. Ann has nothing to live for. She has no plans. They talk about gardening. There is less than an hour left until daylight, soon enough Sara will know what there is to know. She is fresh, subdued with excitement.

Now they go into Elaine's room. Ann goes in first, turns on

a lamp. The wheelchair has been pushed into a corner, folded. It is an amazing room, cheap veneer walls. The tomb where a dead person lived every day for a year and a half. There is a glass vase with a bouquet of dead roses in blackened water. There is the broken silver clock that Telen mentioned. Ann will tell her.

On the bureau, a photograph of Peter smiling shyly, he is wearing loose trousers, a cotton jumper knotted around his neck, he is leaning against a sailboat, not his, on a beach. Because of his atrocities, this image of a relaxed young man, hair tousled by wind, multiplies the horror.

There they are. All of her articles, tacked side-by-side along the wall. There are so many. Sara scans the breathless headlines. No effort has been made to preserve them, they are there, tanned, curling, in no order, pressed into the plywood veneer with red thumbtacks, fifty to a card.

Ann will tell her why.

"He loved my daughter so very much."

"He must have" is all she can say. Sara is discreetly writing her observations in a slim notebook with a ball-point pen.

Afterward they are sitting in the kitchen again.

"Tell me about him, Ann."

"He brought her roses every time he came, he brought me plants for my garden. One day he brought me two white doves, they are symbols of the Holy Ghost, you know? I call them Titi and Coco. He was a wonderful boy."

Ann keeps busy in the kitchen while they are talking, afraid to stop, she is dissolving powdered coffee into a pot of hot water from the sink, she has set out half of a cherry pie from a supermarket. Sara has accepted both.

"What about the newspaper articles on the wall?"

"He brought them for her."

"But she couldn't read."

"I think he read them aloud to her."

"When would he bring them?"

"Always the day they came out in the newspaper."

"Did you ever ask him why?"

"No."

"Didn't you ever wonder?"

"Only at first I wondered. Then I thought he must have been showing her that there were others as bad off as she was."

"Do you think that's the real reason?"

After a moment, Ann says, "It's a good reason."

The cherry pie is not new, the magenta jelly has stiffened from the cold of the refrigerator, it has oozed onto the aluminum plate and hardened. Ann does not want Sara to leave, it is as though she understands, that she is a friend.

"Tell me about Elaine."

"She was his wife."

Ann tells Sara the story, what happened in the parking lot the night of Elaine's wedding to Peter.

"What happened to him?"

"When the police came in the morning they found her sitting in her own blood. They thought Peter was dead, he was unconscious. When he came to, he didn't know where he was, he attacked the police. He'd gone crazy. They had to tie him to a stretcher. He didn't know who Elaine was either. He was put under observation at Bellevue for six months and he never fully recovered. You see, Miss Smith, Peter and Elaine never touched each other before their wedding, they were very religious, they were a very rare couple who decided to wait until their wedding night."

"So unusual."

"He became even more unusual, that's why I didn't ask him any questions."

"You were afraid of him."

"Well, I still loved him but I never saw him again the way he was before."

"Did they ever catch the rapists?"

"Oh, no. No, such a big city."

"So you moved out here?"

"Yes, nearly two years ago, isn't it? Maybe less. The hotel gives us money."

That's when it all started. Sara begins to see. *Maybe my articles on the wall form some sort of restitution, a continuous homage to her. Is each woman sacrificed for her? Evidence of his love for her?*

Sara cannot sit any longer, she must telephone O'Land, she will need to meet a photographer here later today. The deadline is not until evening but the story of Sondelius, Elaine and Ann, will be useless until someone is arrested.

"What is Peter's last name?"

"You don't know? I thought you said you knew him."

"I do know him, I just never knew his last name."

Ann is suddenly alarmed. Sara has been unethical, she has not told her that she is a reporter.

"I don't think you know him."

"I do." *We danced together once.* "I'm here because Telen Gacey was looking for him."

"That's the girl Peter brought to the funeral."

"She's been quite worried about Peter."

"Well why didn't she come with you?"

"She's looking for him in Los Angeles."

"I don't believe you." Ann is a small woman, in the dim, amber light she has come to life. "I like Helen."

"Why don't we call her?"

"I don't have a phone."

"I do, it's in my car, I can bring it in."

"I think you're a reporter with the newspaper." *This interview is over.* "Isn't that what you are?"

"Yes, Ann, I was the one who wrote those articles on the wall."

Silence. Ann is stunned, afraid. She pushes herself up from the table, crosses the kitchen to the back door. "What are you doing here?"

"I have to write about Peter."

"Is it true?" Ann's eyes fill with tears, tiny diamonds. "It's true, isn't it?"

"I think it is."

"Leave us alone."

She pushes the screen door open, holds it open until Sara walks through it. She is finished talking to her. She closes the door.

"I'm sorry, Ann," Sara says through the screen.

She will call Telen from her car.

MAUDE

MAUDE IS NAKED, asleep on the sofa, seen by the dim light of stereo dials. The unending phrases of music circle and circle.

Peter lies buckled on the rug at her feet, his pants around his knees. He wakes, pulls them up, gradually gets to his feet. He watches her. He lays her blouse over her thighs, carries her still asleep from sofa to bedroom. He cradles her into the bed under a sheet. Jimmy G does not wake.

"What time is it?" She is murmuring up at him, smiling, her face wreathed in slumber.

"I don't know. Night."

He goes back into the living room, sits, drops his shoes, pulls his pants down over his ankles, lays them on the sofa. Taped to the inside of his calf is a gleaming trocar. He untapes it, raises it at arm's length above his head, lays it quietly along the top of the doorframe leading to the bedroom. He takes a sip from Maude's glass of summer night gin with melted ice water, winces. Maude calls thickly from the bedroom.

"Where the hell are you?"

"I'll be right in."

She is swaying in the bedroom doorway. Leaning on both sides. The trocar is balanced on the doorframe a foot above her head. Peter is lighting a candle.

"Lie down." She does.

In the bedroom, Peter, barely dressed, looks at Maude curled on her side of the bed in his candlelight. He sets the candle on the floor, kneels on the bed beside her, turns her toward him, spreads her thighs under him. Through the wall, bygone jazz made by ghost musicians continues to be played, low. Maude moans.

SARA

SARA CALLS O'LAND from her car a mile down the road from the Sondelius house. "Wake up, Jim, I've got it."

O'Land is wide awake. "I'm up, hell, I've been waiting. This'll be good, won't it?"

"We've almost got Toyer, Jim, I'm not kidding."

"Where have we almost got him?"

"That's a bit of a problem."

"Who is he and where is he?"

"I'm calling from Sondelius. I've been at his mother-in-law's house. He matches Melissa's description. His name is Peter, he works as a roofer and he's a part-time actor."

"You have art?"

"Yup." Sara slipped the snapshot of Peter into her purse.

"Okay, that's who, what, when."

"Where is the problem."

She is turning onto the deserted freeway heading south.

"Okay. What about calling the cops?"

"Not yet. I can cope. I need one more hour."

"He's dangerous, Sara." He stops there. He did not say,

Please take care of yourself, Sara Smith, if anything happened to you I'd be destroyed. He has just realized that she has become more important to him than the story.

"I'm calling his girlfriend when I get off the phone, she's at his apartment in Silverlake. He's gone out somewhere, I'm heading over there now to meet her, she found his computer hidden in the wall with the entire *No One Lives on the Moon?* file in it. I want that disk."

"Sounds like evidence."

"It does, doesn't it?"

"Call the cops. We have enough for the story without it."

"I will, I will, Jim. Let me do this." She knows. "I just need to copy that disk. If I don't do it now, we'll never see it again, the D.A.'ll tie it up for years."

"If this Peter is apprehended."

"He will be, Jim, tonight or tomorrow, I know it. He and his mother-in-law own a house up there in Sondelius. I've just spent half an hour with her, I've got everything. I think I get it. He was probably doing it all for his wife. It's a very sad story."

"And a great one."

"Yeah, and a great one. Okay, I've got to get off and call her. I think we've almost got him."

"Want me to meet you?"

"Next question."

"Let me have everything you've got."

"In case I get lost. Her name is Telen Gacey, she has an apartment in Hollywood at 1311 Larabee. I know her." She gives him Peter's address.

But when she hangs up she calls Telen at Peter's apartment. Telen does not answer. Sara is driving at 80 m.p.h. on the freeway, she will be at Peter's apartment in twenty minutes.

BILLY

BILLY IS WAITING in the Uncastables' booth. Telen is late. The instant he sees her, he knows it has something to do with Peter, that he has done something to her, something dreadful. Billy's instinct from the beginning has been to protect her, he sees her as frail, maybe too good for Peter, maybe for himself. The small cut on her cheekbone. He leans forward, touches her arm above the elbow. "What'd he do to you?"

She does not speak. She lights a cigarette thin as a chopstick. The waitress is there. Telen looks ravaged, pale. He has always wanted her to cook him a huge breakfast after a night of lovemaking, to pick out his shirts for him.

"How'd you get cut? Tell me."

"I fell."

"Okay, don't tell me." He is nervous, angry. "Is that why you woke me up? Not to tell me?"

"I did fall, Billy, I sort of fainted. It's all part of the same thing."

"Which is what you couldn't tell me on the phone."

When the waitress has set two cups on the table, filled them with coffee from a glass globe and left, Telen leans forward and whispers, moving her lips so distinctly they can be read from the street.

"Peter is Toyer."

Billy recoils. "Right!" He leaps up out of the booth, pirouettes, does a comic half-turn. "Get. Outta. Town." He poses, he slumps, he regards her with exaggerated disgust. "Don't do this shit. Don't get me outta bed at four to do this shit to me, Telen."

"It's true."

She is whispering. "Listen, Billy, believe me, what I'm telling you is true. *Understand what I'm saying.*"

"This is like my brother you're fucking me with." He lies down in the booth, arms binding his head. He feels skinned.

Through the plate-glass window, Telen sees the night ocean, purple-black and changeless, surrounding them. It is a Van Gogh background painted just before his death. She cannot believe who they are anymore, what has happened to them, the three of them, the Uncastables. She tells Billy about the computer, *catfish*, the file named *Toyer*, the book with thirteen chapters.

Billy has grown numb around the cheeks. "Wait a minute, wait a minute, I don't believe you. This is not Peter, okay? This is not even evidence. This is something else, a few details."

"You don't want to believe me."

"I wonder why."

He is on his feet, her face is close enough to kiss. She puts her hand on his neck, pulls him down, kisses him on the mouth. Her tongue is strong, sharp. *It's crazy.*

"Do you love me, Billy?"

"Yes, I love you, I'm here for you."

"I'm glad."

"Always." Is all he can say. He sits, takes a breath. He is being broken in two. "Jesus. This is Peter."

"If you love me, Billy, can you try to believe me?"

He can no longer escape. "Okay."

"He's married, he didn't tell us that."

Billy shakes his head, repeats the words, *Peter is married.* "Where is his wife?" He is gaunt.

There are voices everywhere. Two drunks sobering up on coffee discussing a baseball game they bet on and lost, the cook in a white cap telling a joke to the cashier.

Telen takes Billy's hand across the table, whispers in short breaths. "Her name is Elaine, she was paralyzed on their wedding night. They never made love. They were in New York, he watched her get raped by three men. She was in a coma. She lived up north with her mom. She was a vegetable. He loved her. He visited her all the time. He never recovered."

Billy watches her, his face has no shape, it is a pale smear. He is weeping, tears form and drop without his knowing. Billy cries a lot, as much as a woman. "Where is she?"

"She died last week."

"How long since the rape?"

"Two years."

"Toyer started only last year."

"He was in Bellevue for a while after that."

"What's that?"

"Mental hospital in New York, under observation."

They are holding hands across the table, she is trembling. She tells him how different Peter acted toward her the day after Elaine died, how free he was. She does not mention his sudden ability to make love to her, his renascent force, she only tells him that a burden had been lifted off him and that he asked her to marry him the day she died.

She lights a cigarette, waves the smoke, dashes the air. *God, she smokes beautifully.*

"My own brother." It is a line Marlon Brando says to Rod Steiger in *On the Waterfront.* Billy relies on filmed moments. His voice has changed, it is softer, there is nothing behind it.

"I don't know him anymore, Billy."

"You don't still love him, do you?" *Come home and live with me until this is over. Watch television. Walk through our living room naked. You can smoke in bed.* "Do you?"

"No." This morning she could never have imagined saying it. "Billy, how could I still love him?"

Now Billy starts to cry, he is sobbing. Telen is crying, too, weeping. They are both frightened, weeping. They sit there, facing each other, blubbering. People stop talking, watch them shyly, wonder who died. Billy slides over beside her. He wipes his eyes, then hers, jacks his head up on all his fingers.

"I never stopped loving you."

She puts her arm around him. "Look, Billy, we really don't

have time for this. Peter's a . . . you see that don't you? I got scared, I ran."

It is after five now. Outside Ruben's, the night ocean is no longer wine, it is verdigris, the first gloaming of day. Two late-night blacks fresh from dancing, hipping and sliding by the booth, check out Telen.

Then the pale waitress is back, smiling a sweet crooked smile, holding the globe of coffee in her skeletal arm. "Refills, anyone?" She seems too young to be out, working this late. She fills their cups, leans forward, whispers, "You really *know* Toyer?" It is as if he were the president. She has heard the word *Toyer*, it is enough. The name.

Billy stares up at her. She is there, ready to believe anything. She has moved to Los Angeles from Ontario. Her teeth will always need to be fixed. She whispers the name again, as if Billy did not hear her. It is a famous name. Does Billy really know Toyer?

"I didn't say Toyer, I said lawyer."

She is supposed to get autographs. "Do you know *anybody?*"

"Sorry, no."

She leaves with her black globe of coffee.

Billy moans. It seems impossible, after all this time, knowing Peter, the most impossible of the impossibles.

"I can't believe we're having this conversation."

He holds his breath, trying to die, staring at the tiny coffee lakes on the tabletop. It was Peter who paid his bail, Peter who wrote him his comic monologue, forced him to perform it. Peter who got him his agent. Peter who gave him confidence, turned his life around, found him his niche: talk shows, comedy shops. The bare table glows between them like a desert under the moon.

"You were never going to tell me any of this, right? You were just going to leave town."

She nods. "Probably I'd have just said goodbye to you."

"So, what changed your mind?"

"Did you read Maude Garance yesterday?"

"Sure."

"She wrote it to me. She told me he'd never change, no matter what, and one day he'd do the same to me."

"Jesus, Telen. You."

"Yeah. That was my letter." She lights her third Ruben's cigarette, crumples the pack.

"I'm still not convinced," he says abruptly, hoping it will go away.

"I've been living with it."

"How long?"

"I loved him." *Past tense.*

"How long did you know about him?"

"Don't accuse me. It wasn't true for a long time then I was afraid but I never knew, then tonight I knew."

"How could you be with him?"

"*I didn't know,* Billy."

"Don't holler."

"I told you, I loved him, don't you understand?"

She uses the word *love* as if it were a virus.

"I'm telling you, we went to church. He wanted me to know but he couldn't tell me."

Billy is not listening.

"He betrayed me," Billy says. "Like he was a spy only worse."

"Even if it was true, I was telling myself he could change."

"How could you believe anyone could change from doing something like this?"

"I could." She is crying. The words harden. "We were going to get married." Cement.

"How? Was there some way?"

"By promising each other we were going to get out of here, forever. Remember that talk about living near Portland? I can forgive the past."

"But he was already married, no?" Billy sounds desperate.

"No, she died the day before."

"I know him. Peter? It's not possible. I'm thinking about it. It's not possible. How is a thing like this possible?"

Billy is dried toast. He realizes what they must do now. "You know what we gotta do, Telen."

There are actors who do not belong in the tragedy but are in it anyway, who are hired to read lines and to follow directions written in the script. Accidental players who have not read the play and do not want to know the ending, the consequences of their actions.

She touches his arm, nods toward a booth. Two hatless police officers are ordering coffee from the waitress. They are fresh, ready for the day. They have just come on watch.

Billy walks over to their booth, gets their attention. "May we talk to you gentlemen?" After all, *To Protect and Serve* is written on the door of their car.

Both police officers look up at him politely. He could be anyone. Billy cannot speak the words.

"I just think you guys are doing a fabulous job. I'm serious, I just wanted to tell you that."

They do not know what to think.

"Thanks," one of them says. The other nods, resumes talking.

"Nice try," Telen kisses Billy's cheek. "What are we going to do?"

"I gotta see proof before I commit."

She reaches up under her dress and down the seat of her panties. She pulls out the curved pages, flattens them on the tabletop. Two wrinkled pages. Felicity Padewicz in her parents' house. He glances at them. They immobilize him.

"This is out of his computer? How could he have a computer? I don't own one you don't own one, where does he get off with a computer?"

"It's a little one. He kept it hidden in the wall behind the mirror."

"Did you put it back?"

"No, I left it out."

"So he'll know you were there and come after you."

"It doesn't matter anymore."

"No?" She can barely hear him, his head is in his hands.

"We really ought to go over and tell them, Billy."

It is for him to say, not her, but it does not matter who says it, he is ready.

They stand. There is a pyre of smoldering butts in the ashtray between them. Billy drops a too-large bill, a five, on the table.

"I didn't know you smoked."

"I know, it'll kill me."

They turn around, the police officers have left.

MAUDE

THEY ARE ASLEEP. Before she slipped away, he made love to her as if he had come home from sea after too many months dreaming of it, afraid of losing her again.

She knows. He is not Toyer. He cannot be. Toyer never makes love to his victims.

When he fell away from her, when she thought it had ended, he began again, he could not stop. She was astonished by his hunger. It seemed that making love was the most crucial thing he could do, he made it matter more to her than to him. He pored over her body again and again as if he might neglect some aspect of it, so thoroughly that she felt she were lying on an autopsy table, until finally during her final orgasms her body became so highly sensitized to his touch that she writhed to get away from his fingers his tongue his penis, but she could not and when she pushed him away and he slipped off the bed, he slammed her face into the pillows nearly drowning her, pinned her with his legs as if he were a boa constrictor.

There was cruelty in it, even hatred, her moans turned to smothered screams. He whispered that cruelty during sex never leaves proof.

When she passed out in her cavernous sleep, she fell between planets. Now, rising toward the world again she dreams. And in her dream she is standing again in the stained hallway of the tenement, the narrow walk-up inhabited by women who never speak. He is standing close beside her, he whispers in her ear. What is he saying? She will live there as a tenant, one of his women. The calm women in white. They are upstairs looking down the slim staircase, her hand on the newel post, but it is not the newel post. She feels herself being raised by his arms, she is naked, her dress has vanished. Against the railing of the narrow stairs, he fucks her. She sees his face, it is Peter.

O'LAND

DAMN. He stands at the bathroom mirror, lathering his face, killing time, his only recourse. It is twenty-five minutes after five. He loves the chase. There is only Sara Smith out there, alone, miles ahead of everyone. *Story of the year, and it's mine, all mine.* He is talking to himself. He lives alone. It is a natural part of his day and he does it well, sometimes the conversation is good, sometimes not. *Fine woman,* he adds.

As always, he will make up the front page at eleven but there is nothing more for him to do about Sara's story now. He has assigned a photographer to go to the Sondelius house but he cannot go without her, not until she calls him, there is nothing for him to set up. He can only reserve space. She will tell him when she knows.

You've got until six-thirty, my darling Sara Smith, then I come looking for you. It all depends on you. He is facing himself in the mirror, a man alone, shaving slowly, talking. *Lord, I admit to eccentricity, the alpha wolf, but you know, Sara, a man's nature shows itself in small ways, generosity, silence, humor, his fiber, quick solid decisions, a battling nature.* He smiles at himself through the foam, suddenly laughs in his own face. *Who the fuck am I kidding?* He cleans his razor, splashes water on his face. *My darling Sara Smith.*

No one knows this, but Jim O'Land has a fear of women, their inborn power, their magic, their blood. It is his secret.

Now, Sara, your average woman's afraid of spiders, snakes, but nothing personal disgusts her, an entire fertilizing lab is inside all of 'em, and she's smarter than we are.

Sara Smith's on the biggest story of the year, chasing it down, figuring it out, gathering, leading the ogre to the gallows. It's a moment like this that separates us from the workers selling crap people don't want, morticians, bankers, stockbrokers. Swapped lifetimes, front to back, chasing the buck no proof you're alive. Only pass this way once, pal, not even once some of 'em, slipping through life stillborn. Journalism. Bringing in the developing story, the waiting, the discovering, the outwitting, the look of the page, the wastebasket.

Damn. Bring it in, Sara Smith. Bring. It. In.

SARA

THERE ARE NO CARS on the freeway. The dashboard is dark. On all sides, the mute impossibility of the stars. She is driving fast in the slow lane, driving south past Northridge at eighty-five miles per hour, sometimes the speedometer touches ninety, she will turn off in downtown Los Angeles in less than ten minutes. She dots out Peter's number on the telephone. Still no answer. Telen said she would wait for her call. Sara turns on the light, finds Telen's home telephone number, calls her there. No answer. For the moment, she has become lost on the freeway at high speed. She would like to talk to Telen but it may not be necessary tonight. She guesses her next step but what about his next step? Did Peter show up? Should I get the cops? He is very angry.

She sees the sign, takes her foot off the accelerator, glides toward the East Hollywood turnoff, flaps down.

TELEN

FROM THE STREET TELEPHONE in front of Ruben's, Telen calls 911. Billy is hovering. She is patched through to the West Hollywood station. A woman answers.

"I'm calling about Toyer." She says it suddenly, no longer thinking.

The unexcited voice says, "Hold on, please, miss, I'm gonna getchou a detective." It is twenty minutes to six.

After a quick series of clicks, a man answers, a more alive, tenor voice; "Detective Nathan Smith."

"I know who Toyer is."

"Yes, ma'am. What is your name?"

"Telen with a T, Gacey, G-A-C-E-Y. I live at 1311 Larabee."

Pause.

"Your telephone number is 555-3236?"

"That was quick."

"Now what did you say about Toyer?"

"I know who he is, his identity."

"You do, do you? What makes you think he's Toyer?"

"I'm looking at a computer printout he made about Felicity Padewicz."

"Give me his name." Detective Smith does not sound convinced.

"His name is Peter Matson."

"Last name Madison?"

"Matson, M-A-T-S-O-N."

"What number are you calling from?"

"I can't tell you that." *As if he didn't know, he's already sent a car.*

"Would you like to come in, Miz Gacey, and talk to us?"

Telen hangs up the telephone.

"I can't, Billy."

"See?" He smiles for the first time. "Not so easy, right?"

"Let's get out of here, they know it's this phone booth."

"We'll go in my car." Billy is making payments on a white oval Japanese car that belongs in a soap dish. His first new-car smell.

"No smoking in the car." *It's allowed at my place.*

Telen stubs out her cigarette on the sidewalk. In spite of losing Peter, Billy is beginning to believe that it is possible, that Telen has come to him, that she can return his love. He imagines their house, he imagines childbirth.

PETER

WITHOUT TOUCHING MAUDE, he lifts and pulls down the sheet, away from her, he sees her entire being, naked, the instrument that has destroyed his life. There is less than an hour before dawn, it will be light enough to bring her breakfast in bed. He watches her dream, he would like to crush her head like an egg.

He is restless, he can feel hatred massing. Last night was good, today will be better. Last night was challenging, erotic, dangerous, there were moments when he could have easily lost patience and given in to baser methods, God knows he felt like it. But today is coming, nearly here.

BILLY

THEY DO NOT KNOW what to do, so they will do this.

They are driving slowly west in the direction of the West Hollywood Police Station. The streets have not cooled, he has sealed the car, the air conditioner blows dry icy air. Billy's ears are ringing, he can hardly hear Telen whispering.

"Billy, I'm so scared." She came to the city. She came alone.

"Be sad, Telen, do not be scared."

"Not for me. Someone else, something's happening right now, he's with someone. He's on that horrible motorcycle."

"Where?"

"I don't know. Anywhere. I know exactly what he's wearing."

They are stopped at a light. He takes her hand, driving, his eyes are running freely. It was Peter who got him off the roof, who brought an agent to see his act, bailed him out, constantly challenged him, saved him from himself. Peter has given him everything, without him, he would not have the new car he is driving.

Telen brings Billy's boneless hand up to her mouth, kisses it. "I do love you, you know."

Now he has given him Telen.

MAUDE

VAPORS RISE, smokelike from the roof. Morning dusk outlines the hills. Clothes everywhere. Stereo dial lit, digital numbers, station, volume, time. Furniture seen as shapes, black and gray, colorless before sunrise. Bedroom askew. Maude has fallen asleep again, she lies partly under a sheet. Consciousness. She stirs. Slight leg movement, fingers twitch. She cannot stop dreaming. She is looking at Mason. Alive, no longer lying in the dead box. She is standing on a railroad station platform in a country where she has never been. Italy? The train with many compartments is leaving, the platform is crowded. There he is walking a distance away. His hair is cut, combed. He is wearing a suit she has never seen, a tweed suit, carrying a pair of English suitcases. He is boarding the train, Maude is walking quickly, trying to catch up to him but the crowd jolts her, slowing her. The train starts to move slowly. Mason leans out a window, spots her, waves to her. She begins to run, pushing through the crowd. A conductor stops her, holds her arm, asks to see her ticket, she opens her purse to find it. The contents of her purse empty onto the platform, people are walking on her passport, lipstick, her comb is kicked by someone's shoe, the train is pulling away, moving faster, Mason is waving goodbye, she swears to the conductor she bought a ticket, she tells him the price, she begs him, he tells her to keep looking for it, Maude pushes him, ducks under his arm, runs after the train, but the last car has already left the platform, she watches it slide down the track toward the sunlight. A new dream, a new day.

"Hello again, don't touch that dial, child, it's only moi, your papa, Mister Morning. . . ."

From the living room stereo low-volume music has faded

into the too-intimate male radio voice, personally bringing Maude the summer dawn with mindless drivel.

Jimmy G wakes, stretches on the window seat, pads to his cat box in the bathroom under the sink.

Maude's eyes have opened slightly, sleepy, they stare at the ceiling, the vanishing night. *Jesus, what a night.* The room glints, she feels scoured, renewed, incomparable, angry. She remembers, harvesting details from the strange hours behind her, as if she were putting together the plot of a film that she had seen last night. The events in random order, the games played, the fear, the elation, wrapping herself around Peter in a noose, the intense sex, the relief. But there was blood, too.

"*. . . so I'm here to tell you it's going to be another run-of-the-mill sunshiny fabulous Monday all day long and if that ain't e-nuff not to worry about the temp, looks go-o-od from here like a big ol' break in the heat wave you been waitin' for, all the way down to the mid-eighties, my good friends . . .*" The heat has passed.

"You are not *my* good friend, Mister Morning," Peter says, face down, into the pillow. "Go away. I'm begging you, Mister Morning, shut the fuck up."

It is Peter's voice. She had not noticed it last night, the metallic contempt, the featheredge. This voice that could make her do anything, her memory of the night darkens. The strangeness of it overwhelms her, embarrassment creeps over her. At some time . . . when? . . . being abruptly aroused, her face held pressed into her own fingertips while he forced his way in between her buttocks, where she said she never would be penetrated, pain, disgust, crying into the pillow, powerless spasms, oblivion.

How could I? Some of the night's fragments fit, to her horror she feels the strength of the truth, that he outwitted her again and again, dominated her, the good Samaritan who fixed her car, the gay guy who admired her taste, the voyeur who caused her to strip, *to actually strip*, in front of him, the voice that said "I love you" not once but three times and she remembers each one of them, standing in the doorway, "I love you, Maude." He absolutely convinced her he was Toyer in all his dreadful charisma, then took it away and absolutely convinced her that he was not, that he was an actor improvising a part without costume or props, then suddenly he was Toyer again, then he was not.

There was blood. Then he was a vomiting infant she held in her arms. Later he became a lover and an extraordinary lover, more lover than she has ever known.

The knife. She opens her eyes, raises her head to confirm the scar on Peter's arm. *Yes.* A maroon tint on the sheet. Skid marks here and there.

The dreadful radio voice. "*. . . Okay, so where's my mama? Gracious, she just walked in lookin' like so much kitty litter . . .*"

Outside, the mist is rising from the hills, the cool sun, a whitish gray.

And now?

I don't want him in my house a second longer than it takes him to shower and leave.

SARA

EVERY CITY is beautiful just before sunrise. It will be hot again today, there is haze. Peter's house stands like any other house in Silverlake that still has pitched roofs, cornices, finials, corbels, gables, eaves, dormers, porches. It has survived nearly a century without preservation from an era when houses were built as vivariums for sprawling families.

It is getting light when she climbs the wide steps to the portico. The front door swings open easily, weighted by etched glass. The house is not awake. The used air is cool from the night. A stained-glass trefoil glares redly down from the first-floor landing. Up the stairs the smell of time-dried lumber. On the third floor she hears sounds of talk, smells coffee, aromas of morning.

The narrow staircase to Peter's attic apartment. She expects anything, cocked in her left hand, she holds the small canister of Mace she has never had a chance to use. In her right hand she carries the doorstop she picked up by the front door, a brick covered with shantung. *A better cudgel than my shoe.*

A stamped metal number 8, painted over, is nailed on the muntin of the door to Peter's apartment. She has been here before. She hesitates.

Driving down, she has imagined what she will find. She will knock. Peter will answer the door. She will say, "Remember me?," spray Mace in his eyes, causing him to stagger backward blindly. She will knock him unconscious. Telen will come out of the bedroom. Sara will call 911, the police will arrive in ten minutes to find Toyer trussed up like a turkey and Telen in a talkative mood. Her article for the *Herald,* written in the first person, will be brief, breathless, modest.

Sara knocks gently, waits, knocks again. She holds the Mace canister in front of her. The door is unlocked, the doorknob turns, the door opens, the apartment is as Telen left it an hour ago. Her note to Sara is on the bed. The computer is on the table glowing green.

It is fully light in Silverlake. Peter's windows are bright, the fans are whizzing, their bearings on fire. There are blue jays yabbering in the tree just outside the open window.

The telephone is in the kitchen. "Jim, I'm here." She speaks into the telephone. She gives him Peter's address and telephone number. "No one's here. I see the computer. Laptop. I can see my disk. I see the printer. I haven't touched anything yet." She is talking low. "No matter what happens, it's all here. I'm not going to stay long, not a second longer than I need to, I'm a little antsy, you understand. You've got the number here."

"What do you need?"

"A couple of minutes, I've got to look around. I'll test the disk then get the hell out of here. If I can't read it, I'll take the computer and run it on its battery."

"That's evidence, Sara."

"Yes and I'll be driving that evidence over to the West Hollywood station to turn it in after one quick stop at my apartment to make a printout."

"I hate to say it, Sara, that's obstruction."

"I know it, Jim, I feel sick about it."

"Call the police, Sara, it's time."

"No, not quite yet, by the time they get the disk it'll all be over, anyway they'd screw it up. Jim, let's do it my way. His girlfriend knows he's out there somewhere, she doesn't know who he's with of course. The disk is priceless right now, tomorrow I don't know if it'll be worth anything."

"I'll be right over."

"I'll be long gone, Jim."

"Okay. Get busy then get the hell out of there."

"Don't worry."

O'Land holds the dead telephone. *I'm proud of you, Sara Smith. Will you look at us? We've traded places.*

Sara sits on the bed, pulls the computer to her so that she faces the front door in case Peter pushes it open. She scans the directory, there are dozens of files, chapters, topics, each separated by its own title.

A document file marked *BOOK*. She punches it in: *NO ONE LIVES ON THE MOON?* A document file called *DoctorMG* catches her eye, she punches it in, waits for the little computer to pull itself together, bleep. Then in a sudden flash:

WORD:\BOOK\NO-ONE\DOCTOR.DOC

CHAPTER 13
DOCTOR MAUDE GARANCE

MaudeGaranceMaudeGaranceMaudeGaranceMaudeGarance
MaudeGaranceMaudeGaranceMaudeGaranceMaudeGarance

MaudeGaranceMaudeGaranceMaudeGaranceMaudeGarance
  MaudeGaranceMaudeGaranceMaudeGaranceMaudeGarance
MaudeGaranceMaudeGaranceMaudeGaranceMaudeGarance
  MaudeGaranceMaudeGaranceMaudeGaranceMaudeGarance
MaudeGaranceMaudeGaranceMaudeGaranceMaudeGarance
  MaudeGaranceMaudeGaranceMaudeGaranceMaudeGarance
MaudeGaranceMaudeGaranceMaudeGaranceMaudeGarance
  MaudeGaranceMaudeGaranceMaudeGaranceMaudeGarance
MaudeGaranceMaudeGaranceMaudeGaranceMaudeGarance
  MaudeGaranceMaudeGaranceMaudeGaranceMaudeGarance
MaudeGaranceMaudeGaranceMaudeGaranceMaudeGarance
  MaudeGaranceMaudeGaranceMaudeGaranceMaudeGarance
MaudeGaranceMaudeGaranceMaudeGaranceMaudeGarance
  MaudeGaranceMaudeGaranceMaudeGaranceMaudeGarance
MaudeGaranceMaudeGaranceMaudeGaranceMaudeGarance
  MaudeGaranceMaudeGaranceMaudeGaranceMaudeGarance
MaudeGaranceMaudeGaranceMaudeGaranceMaudeGarance
  MaudeGaranceMaudeGaranceMaudeGaranceMaudeGarance
MaudeGaranceMaudeGaranceMaudeGaranceMaudeGarance
  MaudeGaranceMaudeGaranceMaudeGaranceMaudeGarance
MaudeGaranceMaudeGaranceMaudeGaranceMaudeGarance
  MaudeGaranceMaudeGaranceMaudeGaranceMaudeGarance
MaudeGaranceMaudeGaranceMaudeGaranceMaudeGarance

an instantaneous green blaze, parading downward, top to bottom, full screen, unending, unending, out of sight, maybe hundreds of pages down into the black bank of the computer's memory. *He must have typed her name, hit the* INSERT *key and held it down, printing it thousands of times. I don't need a degree in psych to spot obsessive disorder.*

CHAPTER 13. MAUDE.

He's with Maude. Hardly realizing what her right hand is doing, she taps in 911. She is immediately transferred to the

West Hollywood station. She gets patched through to Detective Nathan Smith who takes the call seriously.

"Detective, this is Sara Smith of the *Los Angeles Herald*. I have a location on Toyer. I believe he is at eight two oh one Tigertail Road. That's the house owned by Doctor Maude Garance. He's there right now."

He says, "Got it."

She hangs up. She punches Maude's number into her telephone. Busy. She tries again, hoping she has made a mistake. *Who would she be talking to at six A.M.?*

Busy. She punches 0, waits, "Operator, this is Sara Smith with the *Los Angeles Herald*, this is an absolute emergency, please help me. I must know immediately if this phone is busy or out of order or off the hook. It's a matter of life or death."

Faced with this load the operator demurs, transfers her. Sara tells the supervisor as few details as possible, learns that Maude's telephone is indeed out of order, their computer check runs only as far as the telephone box outside the house and stops there. The telephone is not off the hook, the trouble is outside the house. *Their impulse does not even reach the box.* Does she want a repairman? They can schedule an appointment for the following day. She hangs up. She has lost five minutes. She runs down the wooden stairs, waking the house. The disk is in her purse.

TELEN

A T THE DESIGNER West Hollywood Police Precinct there is a frenzy of excitement. A lifeboat drill on a small ocean liner. Detective Nathan Smith holds a telephone.

"Ed, get Perrino down here *now*. We've got a make on

Tango Oscar Yankee Echo Romeo, and an eyewitness. I believe her."

He listens.

"I don't care, get him down here now."

A computerized All Points Bulletin has been dispatched to all stations and precincts and cars with Peter's description, what he is wearing. The black motorcycle.

SARA

DRIVING TOO FAST to Maude's, she runs a red light on Sunset Boulevard, then another, hoping to attract a police car, an escort. She clips a parked car, keeps driving. When she regains control, she calls O'Land, she is sobbing.

"Jim, listen, crisis. It's Maude. He's at Maude's. He's at Maude's right now. Understand? Toyer is at Maude's. You hear me?"

"He's at Maude's. I understand. Did you call the police?"

"Yeah, but call them again when I hang up and tell them who you are just to double it. West Hollywood station. Ask for Nathan Smith. Dispatch them to *eight two oh one* Tigertail Road. No working phone number." She repeats the address.

"Jesus, Maude Garance. I thought he liked her."

"Up to a point. I'm such an imbecile. Telen told me—that's Toyer's girlfriend—that she broke up with him because of Maude's letter in the *Herald*. Remember what she said? She told Telen to run for her life and she did. *She* was the woman Toyer loved. Maude brought him out of retirement." She hangs up.

Sara sits in her car stuck twenty minutes from Maude's, Santa Monica Boulevard is solid with stopped cars, she is waiting to get past Highland Boulevard. The police will beat her there.

MAUDE

PETER LIES without a sheet over him, face buried, chimp palms open to the ceiling.

The too-intimate radio voice persists. *"... an' here's your early-ayem shock 'n' rock ta ease yer pain, have a good one Los Anjeleeze."* The voice fades, blending with elemental crispy-rhythm-walkin'-down-the-road melody, music nearly harmless enough to let play. Mister Morning has gotten inside her house, her bedroom, close as her cat.

"Maude. Kill him."

She stirs, reaches one foot to the floor then the other foot, slips out of bed naked, works her way up the wall to a standing position. "I'll put some real music on."

"No opera, please."

On her way to the stereo, she passes through the bathroom. Pees. At the other bathroom door, she leans against the doorframe as if the house were in forward motion. *The most implausible night of my life.* Robed, she enters the living room, scans the sofa for bloodstains, sees none, cuts off the morning-friendly voice just as it is reentering their lives, slips in a cabaret disk, a *soigné* young man singing songs of Cole Porter, Park Avenue people who wear white tie and tails exclusively, the high-stepping society slumming in 1935 Harlem when class wars were unheard of. The music is as strange as the sunrise dazzling the room, as strange as her life last night and now this morning. As strange as Jimmy G.

Far off beyond these dancing lords and ladies, the privileged women at the Kipness, Felicity, Lydia, and Nina are also being roused, their night tubes are being unclipped, exchanged for their breakfast tubes. Maude sees each of their faces moving in her drapes, waiting to speak.

Jimmy G has been watching Maude from the doorway, waiting for her to bring him something from the refrigerator, his favorite room. Anything.

She goes into the kitchen, still adream, split by doubt, sets the kettle on the stove. Jimmy G is walking on point, finely stretching his tendons, tail high, looking up at Maude's eyes, flat-faced. She gives him a scrap of chicken, a lesser being. She finds orange juice, a banana, sets them out. Abruptly she remembers her inner voice. *Where is it?* It hasn't spoken to her all night long, not since Peter has been in the house.

"Time to get up," she calls out, trying to sound cheery. She hears him groan, goes back into the bedroom and stands above him. "Come on, Peter. Up up up."

He yanks her down onto the bed, she drops hard, bouncing, the luxury of a child. She tries not to touch him, then does. Peter's eyes remain stuck. The night will not be over until he is gone.

"You've really got to go now, Peter, so do I."

"It's still night."

"If you'd open your eyes you'd see it's day."

He leans over, flips her on her stomach, throws her robe up around her waist, kisses her lower spine just above her buttocks. She wavers. He moves calmly, eyes still closed, reaches around and touches her face blindly, kisses her neck.

No.

"I want you to get up and go, Peter."

His eyes remain shut.

He rolls on his back, pulls her over him, tightens his grip around her. He is ready for her.

"Think of me as a stallion you are about to mount to gallop away through the morning."

What the hell am I doing?

It is not the improbable night or the night's shame that makes her feel uneasy, it is his presence in her house.

"I said no, Peter, I'm not kidding."

She frees herself, goes into the bathroom. Peter rolls out of bed with an elaborate sigh and shrug, puts on his undershorts. After a moment, he can hear shower water smacking the walls. He is groggy, his new scar is inflamed, it resembles thin lips. He goes into the kitchen area, assembles whatever he finds: banana, orange juice, honey, celery, raw egg, puts them together into the blender, switches it on. He samples his mixture, seasons it with a dash of finely ground cayenne pepper. He unscrews the small halogen flashlight, drops the batteries into his palm. There is a plastic capsule. He cuts the tip and drips clear fluid into the blender.

Maude has stepped out of the shower, left the shower water running, has gone into the bedroom looking for shampoo. Between doors, she catches sight of Peter, he is doing something that takes his concentration. *What?* She cannot see what it is, he is standing too still, his back is to her. Without looking, he deftly replaces the batteries, screws the flashlight shut. She watches, chilled, a shiver, suddenly alert. *Something's gone very wrong.*

A minute later, she emerges from the bathroom, her body slim within her robe, towel wrapped around her hair in Queen Nefertiti's style. The hot water has made her skin glow.

"Aha," Peter's voice, "try this." He brings her the sunny glass, a bib of foam above its rim. "Jump-start you without cables."

Water glistens on her skin, her nipples are taut. She reaches out, fingers wet from the shower, her body cool.

"I think I'll call this Peter's Surprise." He is grinning.

Maude, back among the living, raises her glass to Peter. She sips, barely kissing the foam, licks her lips, swallows. *There it is.* The taste of mint.

She covers her shock. *This is it.* Smiles approvingly. "Minty."

"Minty? No mint in there."

But there is. Mint means Xylazene.

The kettle screams.

Peter smiles, "Remind you of someone?" He leaps behind the kitchen counter and snaps the gas off. He raises his thickening drink to her, toasts her, glass high. "Screaming always sounds better at breakfast."

"Always."

This is him. But how can it be? He fucked me. Toyer never fucks his victims.

THE WEST HOLLYWOOD STATION

DAWN. The West Hollywood Police Station.

Billy and Telen are sitting near Detective I. Perrino's desk, numbed celebrities, waiting for the D.A.'s car to arrive.

A captain, a sergeant, two detectives from the West Los Angeles Special Task Force, who have been aware of the Toyer case since it began, are on their way in. They will meet Telen and Billy and send a computer expert to the Silverlake apartment. They have been promised protection from Peter.

There is a Peter Matson in the Los Angeles County telephone books, a high school wrestling coach who will always remember being yanked from sleep just before dawn by a bullhorn mispronouncing his name and the battering of his front door by a Special Weapons and Tactics police force. Telen's Peter Matson, the actor and roofer, is not listed in the telephone directory.

Billy whispers to her, "Was he laughing at us the whole time?"

PETER

JESUS. *It's him.* Maude sips again, tastes a hint of Xylazene. Her mind races. She is fixed to the spot. *He's always been here. All night long, watching me, fucking me, now he wants the rest of me.*

She closes her throat, tries not to swallow. Smiles radiantly. Slips into the bathroom, smothers her choke, gags secretly. She empties the contents of her mouth into the sink, then the glass.

She holds her breath a full minute. She grips the sink on both sides, leans her head forward until it touches the mirror. She holds her breath again, maybe longer this time. Too dizzy to stand, she sits on the toilet seat, head down on her knees. Her hand touches the faucet. Runs water. *Make noise, sound busy.* A hairbrush clatters on the tiles.

Numbly she watches her reflection. In the mirror, her eyes burn back at her, her cheekbones protrude, her mouth is too low. She sees the outline of her skull, her mummified cadaver. The bathroom will be her tomb. *Sara's friend, the one who put a sack over her head and didn't rape her.*

He is standing just outside the bathroom door, waiting for her. She watches herself; pallid, weary, breathless. She has the face of a doll, pale ceramic whose eyes are too precise. *I can crawl through the window, call the police from a house down the hill. I'm wearing a robe. I'm still wet from the shower.*

Her toes chill on the tiles. She looks down, they resemble the white paws of a rodent. Her hands are trembling. She holds on to the sink for support.

Get out. The window. Run the shower, make noise. He won't hear me open the window. He doesn't know I know. Advantage. I'll have a good head start. He'll knock on the bathroom door. He'll break it down. I'll be gone. He won't know where.

Stay. It is her command hallucination. *Stay*.

She frees her hands, runs her fingers into her hair. She stares back into the mirror, into her own eyes. Eye-to-eye. She watches her eyes blur with tears as she tugs the roots of her hair.

Her inner voice shrieks, a terrible whisper, *Kill him kill him kill him . . .*

"No!"

Kill him kill him kill him . . .

"No!" She puts her hands over her ears. She focuses on her own image. "No. No."

"Maude?"

"Be right out."

Do it do it do it do it . . .

"Shut up shut shut shut up."

"What?" He calls through the door.

He knows I've got five minutes until I'm supposed to go down. Those five minutes are mine. I can run, if I run he'll escape, he'll go free. He's too smart for them.

She stares at herself. It is the opposite of life.

I'm not running.

She leans forward and touches the mirror glass with her forehead. "Me." She kisses herself on the mouth. She says the words "I love you." *Five minutes.*

She reaches down, finds her medical bag below the sink, pauses for control, counts five meperidine pills, pills no bigger than spots, coated with the red dangerous reptiles use to warn, she drops them into her palm, pockets them in her robe, flushes the toilet, reappears in the living room wiping her mouth, glass empty, smiling vivaciously.

"Exquisite." She sets her glass on the kitchen counter beside Peter's. "More." He is smiling at her.

"What were you rambling about in there?"

"Morning prayers."

She starts straightening up the living room, picking up last night's detritus, glasses, scarves, turning cushions on the sofa where he made love to her. She busies herself, head down, whisking clothes and fluffing pillows, busy until she can regulate her voice well enough to speak normally.

"Take a shower, Peter, wash." She smiles. "You smell. Of me."

"Yes. That's exactly why I'm never washing it again."

"Do it for the neighborhood. Coyote bitches in heat running around out there."

He laughs fluidly.

Four minutes.

"I'm making coffee," she says. "You do drink coffee, don't you?"

Peter goes into the bathroom, closes the door, the extraordinary thrill of Maude's innocence rushing through him. Moments away. His heart is racing. Her intelligence. Her helplessness. Under the shower, he stands in the cool spray, limp, his cut arm hung over his head, letting the water smite his armpits, his groin, never more naked, feeling his nerves drain away, slowing his heartbeat.

Three minutes.

Maude is pouring boiling water into the coffee filter directly into his cup. She adds one, two, three, four, five meperidine tablets. Tiny, dreadfully red. Watches them foam and disappear. She is careful not to overdose him.

She calls out, "How do you like it?"

Peter's voice above the shower, "Never forget it as long as I live." He turns the hot water on.

"Your coffee, Peter, not me."

"Oh. Cream, if you have it. Milk."

Two minutes.

Peter rubs sweet soap into his hair. The thrilling moments just ahead. Dismantling Doctor Maude Garance, physically, sexually, mentally. He is calm, his anger lies elsewhere. He turns the hot water off, chilling himself.

She brings his mug of coffee into the bathroom. Gives him a light-of-love smile. He stands in front of her, baby naked. Takes the cup. "Sniff me. See? Smell all gone."

"You're dripping everywhere."

"I apologize for last night."

"Don't apologize, I loved it, really. I've always secretly wanted to kill an actor." Maude laughs radiantly, goes into the living room and sits on the sofa. Sips her coffee. "I don't mean to sound cliché, but I grew up last night."

"You did?" Peter follows her out, rubbing himself with his towel.

"To know for sure if I would enjoy killing someone? Now I know. I wanted to kill you, it felt good. Thanks."

"I hope you don't still feel that way."

"Drink your coffee."

"It's excellent."

"Yes, it is, isn't it?"

One minute.

SARA

O'LAND REACHES SARA on her cellular telephone.

"They dispatched two West Hollywood police cars, they're on their way to Maude's. What's next, Sara Smith?"

"Okay, Jim. Call Doctor Tredescant at the Kipness, she's very serious about him. I don't have his home number but they'll give it to you. Be very careful when you tell him the facts; God knows what to expect, he's in love with her."

There is traffic, men alone in cars.

"I'm still ten minutes away from her place. Cannot get there any quicker."

"Don't run over anyone, see you later, take care, good job."

THE WEST HOLLYWOOD STATION

THE DAY IS AGING BADLY. Two cars have been dispatched for Maude's house, sirens to clear traffic. *Woop. Woop.* Only flashing lights, no sirens, for the last two miles. They could be there in ten minutes.

Telen is still seated at Detective I. Perrino's desk, Billy is holding her. They are profoundly depressed. Outside, the lifeless morning, the burnt ends of trees against the sky, if there is a sun it has no body.

Now there are eleven of them in the room, mostly standing, eight men and three women, officers, detectives, a lieutenant. The early heat of the day. Some already wiping sweat from their faces. There is an air about them, they feel it is going to be over this morning. Nina Voelker's killer. That's what it is, Meyerson says, killing. They all see it as murder. Toyer has invaded the morale of this station, brought down one of them. To a cop, there is nothing more fulfilling than avenging a cop killer.

Telen feels their attention sucking at her, feels their professional exhilaration, their glow of relief. She has done well, she has brought Toyer to them.

Telen has given them Peter's address, she has whispered the password, *catfish,* as if it were still a deadly omen. The word has been respectfully telephoned to a police car waiting outside the apartment at Silverlake, an officer has relayed *catfish* to a computer technician who will search the apartment but will not be able to find the disk.

A mile from the police station, a circuit judge in his

bathrobe signs a search warrant on his kitchen table for Peter's apartment.

Inspectors are already at Peter's, waiting to enter, to search drawers, pockets, unscrew jars, lay underwear out on the bed, open envelopes.

She has given the police her only photograph of Peter, a badly welted three-by-five glossy photograph, his description, the Harley-Davidson's description, what he is wearing. They are common knowledge now. But the information is useless, it is only a matter of minutes until the first car reaches Maude's house.

"He's really very vulnerable," she said to the wrong officer, earlier. He did not answer her. "He has a good side," she had said. Billy told their small audience that Peter helped him get work.

"He's gone through so many changes," she told them. They watched her lips.

Billy said, "His wife died last week."

"Did he kill her?" the booking officer asked.

Billy sits there, unused, except as corroborator to a point that Telen is making. "He isn't that good an actor" is all he says. *But of course he is.*

PETER

NO MINUTES.
     Maude understands Xylazene, its quick crawling symptoms, she knows precisely how to react, to show its effect on her. She will wait a few more seconds, then, when she tries to stand up from the sofa, she will pretend to fall backward. In that time, the dose of meperidine will have begun to paralyze Peter's muscles. He will hardly realize it.

Now, with Peter watching, she rises. She takes a small step to steady herself. She grasps the air for support, balance. Her arms fail her. Wordlessly she slips back down struggling to the sofa. Peter looks away, opens the refrigerator. "Do you have any bread for toast?"

Maude starts to answer, stops.

Peter, still half nude, goes to her, looms, toweling his face. *Finally.*

"You okay?" With sympathy.

She stares at him a long time, innocently puzzled. She speaks with effort. "My head feels like a board meeting."

Her helplessness excites him, he becomes chatty. "Is your face prickling?" He is drying his ears with the towel.

Maude touches her face, thick-fingered. "Why should my face be prickling?"

"Just wondering."

Clumsily, she reaches for her empty glass. "And my arms don't function right." She slurs her speech slightly.

"Maybe it's your throttle linkage."

"What do you mean my . . . throttle linkage?"

Silence. In performance, Maude suddenly realizes who Peter is. She looks up, "Jesus Christ."

"Ain't no Jesus around heah dis moanin', Miz Mowde." Accented deep South. He smiles widely.

"But if he was . . . he'd kick you in de balls."

He laughs delightfully. *I'm having fun.* "And don't think my feelings are hurt because you don't remember me from the hospital."

Maude doesn't speak.

"I was in Melissa Crewe's room, sitting behind you."

I never saw his face.

"Do you know why I'm here?"

Maude doesn't answer.

"You want to know why I'm here? You invited me. You wrote that fucking letter to her. I was through with this shit, I wasn't going to do this again, I was going to finish writing my stupid book and drop out of sight with her in Oregon. But you brought me back, Maude, you pushed me into Chapter Thirteen. You hear me? I'm here because of you, it's not random like the others, you sent me that invitation, and it feels just right. That's why I'm here. You ruined my life. You're a cruel bitch."

Maude stares stupidly up at his eyes, watching for signs of the meperidine, waiting for it to kick in.

Maude sounds drowsy. "I always knew . . . you were a . . . psychopath."

"We-ell, one really isn't supposed to know these things about oneself. Isn't that for others like you to decide? If I'm sane enough to know I'm insane, how can I be insane?"

"You're not, don't worry . . . you're borderline, just like me." *He's got to go down right now.*

"But if I'm ever picked up, of course I'll be a model patient. All my inhuman—what would you call them?—inventions. Wouldn't it be weird if I wasn't insane?"

What's holding him up?

"They won't punish me, they'll make a study of me. I've been extra bad, so they'll be extra good."

Peter is standing over her again, a towel around him. He has found a black china marker. Politely, he tilts Maude's head forward, on the nape of her neck counts four cervicals, draws a tiny vertical rectangle surrounding the fourth at the top of Maude's spine, the base of her skull. He is outlining his incision. He raises her head, stands away from her.

"You know, I had an exciting thought last night when we were dancing. Do you realize that your name on my book will boost sales even more? And that extra money will go right to your patients? Now beg."

"What."

"Indulge me; beg." Peter points at the floor. "On your knees, beg for your life."

Maude is forming the words *fuck you.*

He picks up Maude's arm, estimates her pulse rate, drops it. "Your system is fighting pretty hard now."

He tours the room impatiently, waiting for her to drop. He makes a fist, stands on the window seat and presses his heel-fist print high up on the window. The bench mark. "My sense of continuum. Fair play, I guess."

Like cricket, Maude whispers. Peter does not hear her, he is restless, waiting for Maude.

"I've touched seven things in this room, glasses, bottle, phone, gun, doorknobs, this, this. What else? You." He rinses glasses, bottles, fills a pan with water and sets it on the stove.

He opens the lining in his jacket, unwraps a small scalpel and a hypodermic syringe. She watches him reach up along the top of the doorframe of the bedroom door, for the trocar. She has not seen a trocar since the first morning after the long night with Virginia Sapen when she discovered how it was being used. Simple as an ice pick, the triangular blade catches the light. He sets it in the pan.

Her robe has come open. Maude rolls to one side trying to close it.

"I'm not crazy about your ability to fight off high-potency drug doses."

Or yours. Maybe Peter's Surprise slowed down the meperidine. Some psychotics have superhuman tolerance.

Maude watches him heavy-eyed, slumped to one side, robe open. She can show no effort to cover herself. He runs the hot water faucet, locates a roll of paper towels, washes his hands and arms, prepares for minor surgery.

Why didn't I overdose him?

He comes back to her. He pulls her robe away down onto the floor, slips his arms under her thighs and back, picks her up and carries her into the bedroom and stretches her out on the bed, spreads her knees.

"You wrote me, how could any woman want to touch me? Let's find out."

You're going to fuck me again, one last time, you necrophilic bastard.

"Was it good for you last night, Maude?" He pulls her by the ankles to the edge of the bed. Her toes just touch the floor. She feels like dead prey.

"Were you faking those orgasms?"

You shouldn't even be able to talk, much less fuck me.

"Are you ready for me, Maude?"

I am so ready for you. I'm so ready.

She sees his excitement over her apparent stupor. He drops his towel, kneels in front of her. She feels his erection graze her thigh.

Fall, damn you, fall.

He falters, clambers backward to his feet, sways back against the wall. Stares dumbly down at Maude, bewildered.

"What. Is. This." He catches each word. *Where are my legs?* He grips the drapes, recovers his balance against the wall. Feels a tremendous rush of dizziness, overcomes it. He cannot move. He feels his head zoom. His head is gone.

TELEN

SHE HOLDS a Styrofoam cup clipped in her teeth, it hangs down under her mouth on her chin. She has been trying to be helpful. She has not been told that Maude's house is the scene. They have not told her what they are doing. She is only a witness.

It's a crude process, not as smooth as it is on television, they really are cold and determined, nervous, cool, simple, efficient, thankful.

They have staked out the Silverlake apartment from the rooftop across the back alley, an undercover officer watches the building from across the street. When the warrant arrives, a detective will search the apartment. He will find the computer, not the disk.

Telen is trying to behave normally, she is struggling not to break down, the fingers of one hand are pressed between her thighs. She has not asked what will happen to Peter, where he is, where the police are, how it will end. If they will shoot him.

She decides. Today she will visit her mother in Lake Stern. Madeleine Gacey writes that her condominium is painted rose, it is three miles from the lake. There are many boats with happy names.

DOCTOR T

DOCTOR T has called the West Hollywood police station. Detective I. Perrino takes his call.

"Can you tell me what's going on, please?"

"We have everything under control, sir."

"What are you talking about, 'under control'? What's going on?"

"Are you a relative?"

"I am her husband." *Not exactly, maybe, one day.*

"Where are you calling from, sir?"

"From the Kipness, where she works."

"That's North Malibu."

"It is." The Phone-scan confirms this. *He's far enough away from the scene.* "Sir, we have reason to believe your wife may be held hostage at this moment. We've dispatched tactical force, they're on their way to the scene now."

"What scene?"

"Her house."

"Held by who?"

"We think it might be Toyer, sir."

Doctor T feels the numb helplessness bystanders feel witnessing a street killing.

"What are you doing about it?"

"A special team should be arriving in minutes, sir, don't worry. We can handle it."

Doctor T hangs up, tells Chleo to get on the telephone and postpone all his surgery today, trots toward the elevator, dropping his white coat on the polished floor behind him.

MAUDE

PETER HAS SLIPPED onto the wooden chair in the bedroom, its back against the wall, he stares at Maude, a stunned bull with a neck full of *banderillas*. He tries to give her a deadly stare but it melts down his face.

My head is flying through the ceiling. His legs go bad again. He rises, sits down hard on the chair, awkwardly. With a muscular lunge he tries to rise again, fails. *Christ, what's going on?*

Maude comes around easily, arches her back, stretches like Jimmy G, who joins her, landing softly on the bed, strutting over stiff-tailed, he puts his paws on her lap.

She is on her feet in a single bounce, taking Jimmy G with her, she opens the bottom drawer of the bureau and yanks out a few bright silk scarves.

"What are you doing, Maude?" He is unable to move.

With the scarves, she ties his wrists to the arms of the wooden chair, ties his ankles together. She ties the last scarf across his chest, under his arms and around the back of the chair. They are both nearly naked.

She bends over him and neatly rolls an eyelid back using a

swab. Peter squirms without muscle. "Tell me what you think you're doing to me."

Maude smiles, "One thousand milligrams of meperidine," she says, then adds cheerily, "I hope you don't die."

"In . . . me?"

"You're swimming in it, lover."

"When—?"

She goes to the kitchen area, warms the pot of coffee on the stove, brings her small medical bag from the bathroom, drapes a towel around Peter's neck as if it were a bib.

"Tell me something, Peter, are you sorry you wrote that letter?"

"What . . . ?"

"That first letter about Marla."

"I had to send it."

"I know you did, you were worried what people thought, but are you sorry now, looking back?"

"You mean . . . the chain of events, like I wouldn't be here if I didn't send it?"

"Would you be here?"

He knows that the first letter he wrote led to his killing of Elaine, his love affair with Telen, Maude's purge of her. He feels defeated rage. He can barely speak, he melts a grade lower into his chair.

"Are you reminiscing?"

"I suppose you could say that."

She just saves the coffee from boiling, preserves it, pours herself a perfect cup, it shoots through her extremities, a healing serum, she feels her spirits sail away. She could not be happier. Jimmy G butts her leg with his head, enjoying the action. She sits, picks him up, sets him on her lap, feels the rattling purr through his chest and stomach.

"One thing leads to another, Peter, the here and now."

She leaves Jimmy G, pours an ounce of milk into his bowl. She slides a Giacomo Puccini disk into the player.

"What . . . are you . . . doing?"

"I am going to listen to *Madama Butterfly*." She smiles, smiles, smiles.

TELEN

THERE HAS BEEN A LEAK. Channel Five News arrives at the West Hollywood station, there are moles everywhere.

Telen and Billy are holding hands now, rocking slightly. She will call her mother as soon as she can, she will explain. She will ask Billy if he would like to come home with her, she does not want to be alone now. It will just be for a few days. He will say yes. Her mother will rent a car for them, they will drive up to Lake Stern together. They will help each other get over Peter. Telen's ears are still unpierced.

Another news channel van arrives. They can see the new activity in the parking lot. Now, four television networks have parked their vans outside the West Hollywood station. They have been told that a Toyer suspect may be arrested and brought into custody this morning. The police lieutenant cannot give further details until 8:00 A.M. Outside the station in the parking lot, a newslady with a wire clipped to her head is waiting to speak to a camera in front of a small bank of lights. Nearby a newsman has already started speaking to a camera and another pair of lights at last. It is a *breaking story*, the best kind of television story there is. Breakfast shows are being interrupted.

Billy told Telen earlier this morning that the trick to finding Mister Right is knowing that at first he looks like Mister Wrong.

No one notices when Telen and Billy slip away from the police station, still holding hands. They get into his car and drive south toward the airport. They can buy their tickets for Madison this morning and eat breakfast together at thirty-five thousand feet where the temperature is sixty degrees below zero. Telen will take Billy to Wisconsin for a few days. There, they will become lovers. It is the best season, it is almost fall.

MAUDE

BUTTERFLY singing *"Un Bel Di"* fills the small house.
Peter is becoming aware of what Maude may do to him. He is terrified, stares at her wild-eyed, suspended in the Jell-O of the drug.

Maude's command hallucination guides her, whispers to her, *Do it. You can. Do it. You can. Do it. You can. Do it. Do it do it do it.*

"You really ought to call the police, Maude, I'd never tell them we slept together . . . I swear . . . not a word about the scalpel. Don't be afraid. Please. I swear."

"No." She is pathologically alert. "I'm doing this because you told me we turn the page and I don't want to turn the page. Remember? The real crime is not the crime, the real crime is that we know about it and turn the page?"

"Oh, God."

She finds a maroon textbook with a broken back on the bottom of the bookshelf, paper clips mark past references. She sets it on the glass coffee table propped up by the river rocks, held along the bottom by the Sabatier dicing knife. She thumbs past illustrated procedures, finds *Lobotomy*, reads aloud to Peter. "Lobotomy, Spinal, Lobotomy, Cervical. Loss of all motor and sensory functions, phrenic nerves." She turns to Peter, "That's your specialty, spinal cordotomy."

Peter is trying to speak.

"How did you ever come up with it? I'm curious."

My Cornell summer.

Maude studies the procedure, barely noticing him. "This ought to be a simple office procedure."

She continues talking to herself, reading aloud.

"Or shall we try this? Lobotomy, prefrontal. Prefrontal lobotomy? Such an archaic operation. It says 1936 here. It's historically obsolete but it'll maintain your motor and sensory functions with only the loss of your personality and reasoning power. Doesn't sound too damaging. Leaves you aware of what's happening around you but unable to do anything about it." She reads. "Yes, that's the one. Okay? Let's definitely do that one. If anyone asks me why, I'll just tell them the procedure was based on my considered prognosis; it seemed like a good idea at the time."

Peter is trying to writhe, wrestling for stability, to speak. He cannot. He is through speaking.

Stop, stop, I beg you.

She puts her thumbs on top of his eye sockets, thoroughly feeling each bone. "These bones are very, very thin."

Still wearing his pen marks on her own neck, she locates her entry point, marks his forehead with the felt-tip marker, making a bold tic-tac-toe pattern just above his nose and brow, between his eyes.

"There. No finesse, but it'll do. In it goes here and up across the cerebrum, snip a few fibers and out. Right? Do you know what all that means, Peter? Those are medical words. I always imagined you were self-taught, is that true?"

He tries to shake his head. *Jesus, she's really crazy. Stop her, someone stop her.*

"I hope you approve, Peter, I may be a little rusty, I haven't had the practice you've had. I want to make you proud of me, even though it's still absolutely wrong."

His pan of water is boiling away on the stove, she turns it off, picks up his trocar with a pair of tongs, passes it close to his face.

"May I use this?" She goes to the kitchen area, holds it under the cold water faucet, cooling it. "I hate to borrow instruments, but I left mine somewhere."

Peter watches Maude, barely conscious, terrified, clinging. He tries to speak. "Maude . . . I love . . . you."

"It's just not the kind of love I'm looking for, Peter." She smiles.

He glares at her, fish-eyed, up from the depth of his aquarium. *Please, Maude, please, please, please.*

She touches areas of his brow, refreshing her memory, referring to the open book. "This procedure's simply not done anymore, Peter." She bends down and whispers in his ear like a lover. "Except by me."

The first true bolt of fear. Tears are streaming down his cheeks. He wants to speak. He feels warmth between his thighs, soaking the towel under him. *I'm pissing.*

The smell of orange vinegar. She sees his urine dripping, wetting the wooden legs of the chair, her cream woolen rug. She kicks him on the shin. "God damn you."

Now, she hears the solemn whisper, prodding her gently. *Do it do it do it do it . . .* She returns the scalpel to the boiling water for an instant, stirs it in the pan. She feels excitement rush through her fingertips.

She takes a small packet from her medical bag, breaks the seal on a pair of clear latex gloves, snaps them over her fingers. She takes a breath. Waits a moment. She picks up the scalpel with the tongs and cools it, dries it with a paper towel, wipes the blade, holds it up in her fingers like a pencil. Stands in front of him and presses the scalpel to his brow for the initial penetration of his skull. A fine rivulet of blood runs along his nose, over his top lip, into his mouth.

Maude stops. She stands back, wipes the scalpel with a surgeon's tissue, goes to the stove, drops it back into the pan, drops the trocar loudly on the table. Peter watches, barely able to follow Maude with his eyes. She turns to the window. Her inner voice shrieks in a whisper, *Don't stop! Go on go on. Don't stop!*

"Shut up!" She yanks her head around. "Will you shut the fuck up?" Her palms are over her ears.

Peter has been watching her, *Who's she talking to?*

She strips off a glove. "I don't have any words left in me to describe you. So I'll just call you Peter. I think I may not do this after all, Peter."

Thank God. Oh thank God.

Her voice shrieks, *No! You can't stop! Don't, not now. You can't stop. Nina, Virginia. Melissa, Felicity, Lydia, Gwyneth, Paula, Luise, Karen, Carol . . .*

"Stop! I'm not listening to you." She leans on the bureau, her head tilted to one side, she waits for the command hallucination to fade. It takes a minute.

"I can't, Peter, I wanted you lobotomized, I didn't want you cared for by professional healers. I never wanted you set free. I was positive I could do this, but I can't."

Peter can dimly hear her voice. *She's not crazy. She's not crazy after all.*

"I'm not what you are." She picks up the gloves and tosses them into the wastebasket. She stares at Peter tied, crumpled forward in the chair.

"I'm calling the police, quick, before I change my mind. Tell them that their treasured Toyer is up here in my living room. Let them give you the stardom you so richly deserve, the best care money can buy. But I'm still on the edge, Peter, so while I'm deciding . . . be very careful."

He sits, dimly watching her movements.

She goes into the living room, picks up the telephone, listens. The telephone is still dead, of course. With her eyes, she follows the cord to the plug near the floor. It is unplugged. She crawls under the table and plugs it in. She lifts the receiver without emotion. The telephone is dead.

Now, she follows the telephone line from the wall plug, along the floor to the hole where it disappears into the wall. She opens the window, looks out along the wall, sees where the line emerges from the wall. It runs into a gray plastic circuit box. On the other side of the box, it stands out, the black line in the shape of a U. A clean cut, a diagonal, has been sliced through it, showing the glint of copper, tiny spots of colors. Silence, the morning is still. The cawing of her inner voice rolls on distantly in her ears like tinnitus. The pepper tree leaves are motionless, damp from the night. There is a hummingbird, a tiny bishop standing in the air, dressed for Easter. An ant is walking too quickly across the windowsill, late. Jimmy G sleeps on. Silence.

She feels a puff of leftover night air blow through the open window from far down the hill behind the house. Inside, it will remain cool for another hour, until the true heat of the day comes. The hummingbird vanishes. She closes the window. A new day.

She sits beside Jimmy G on the edge of the window seat. He does not wake. She listens to the drone of her bloodstream flowing through her veins, then to a helicopter throbbing comfortably in the distance.

She hears her voice, realizes that she is speaking aloud. "I knew a girl named Felicity Padewicz for a short time, but I didn't know her well . . ." She is suddenly in tears. "I didn't know any of them very well."

She goes into the bedroom, Peter's eyes are open, his head is a cantaloupe. Maude binds him with two more scarves, it is unnecessary, he will be immobilized for four more hours, aware of everything around him.

"I'm going out for a while so don't get into trouble." At the closet, she brings out cotton blouses on hangers and lays them on the bed.

"What does one wear to surrender Toyer at a police station before lunch? Pearls? A simple denim ensemble? Slacks and blouse?" She shows him two blouses, one blue. "Which? Perhaps not the blue?" Her robe slips to the floor, she stands naked, facing him. "I think the cream, don't you? For credibility." She is past excitement. She sits then lies back on the bed, nude.

"Wanna hear a story, Peter?" She knows he can hear her, waits for no answer. "Oh, why not tell you a story, as long as you're sitting there. I was eleven years old and this little girl I hated didn't turn up at our after-school movie party. Nicole Klein. We'd dropped her off to get masking tape and she didn't come back. When she didn't show up, we knew right away, but we didn't know *what*. No one just *didn't come back*. Anyway, it turned out that some freak had used her up and tossed her body out in the woods that first evening. The police didn't find her for a year. When they did, the little animals had divvied her up, her bones were found hundreds of yards apart because what they can't eat they take to their burrows. The head is the hardest part and so a fox will drag that a long way off but they never found Nicole Klein's head. This was before I had my first period, it was a little hard to follow. So we couldn't do certain things after that. Without knowing why. Then they found the freak and put him in a hospital but we weren't allowed to know anything. We heard he didn't get punished. So when older guys started looking up our skirts at bus stops we'd play a game, Spot-the-Freak, and we'd giggle when we spotted one. Freaks like you. I've just spotted one in my house." Maude giggles.

She gets up from the bed, naked, opens a drawer, takes out a white brassiere, puts it on then lets it drop onto the bed. She stands a moment, thinking.

"I'm a little confused at the moment, I have to think. Maybe I won't go to the police at all. Maybe I'll give them a call tomorrow instead." She has stopped dressing. "Don't think this has anything to do with Nicole Klein, she was a ratty kid and she was teacher's pet in sixth grade."

Peter watches her, he is drooling.

"See, I'm very much like one of those little forest animals, a possum or a marmot that sits there all its life eating a berry then one day jumps sixteen feet in the air. No one knew it could do that, but it can. Me, too. Thanks for showing me how versatile I am, Peter."

There is a freak in my bedroom. He is going to be institutionalized. He will be rehabilitated and made well and integrated back into society. Maude stares at Peter, the morning is still ahead of her. She takes a brush from the dresser and brushes her hair quickly, a dozen strokes.

"I wish I knew what to do. Maybe I should just drive down the hill real quick to the market and call 911, before I think about it any more. Not from a neighbor's house, I don't want to start talk." She suspends her brassiere from one finger. "So which is it going to be, Peter? Do I call or do I cut? Give me a signal."

Peter blinks twice.

"Guess that means I call."

There is no tension. The man in the chair does not stir. The woman turns her back on him, dressing. She slips into the brassiere, clips it behind her back. It is a peaceful scene, a semiconscious man draped in a chair, a well-made woman dressing. Lautrec. She puts on the blue cotton shirt, buttons it carefully. There is no clock. Time depends on nothing, it is divided into moments by the woman's breathing.

A sound behind her, a small zoo sound. The woman starts, turns. Jimmy G has come to the doorway. He has woken up and come to her. He has made the sound, a small sound, describable as half croon, half growl. A dark *chirr.* In itself, it is not remarkable, except that he has never uttered a sound, he barely miaows. Now he stands in the doorway to the bedroom, facing the man draped in the chair. His ears erect, his whiskers fanned straight out.

Jimmy G is traditionally soundless, expressionless. From the first day he walked into the house two years ago, he has rarely shown an emotion other than love.

The woman continues dressing, she pulls on a pair of jeans, low heels. There is a purse packed, she takes her car keys from the dresser, turns to leave the room.

Jimmy G has placed himself in front of her, sitting erect in the doorway. He is standing in her way. He is not staring at

Maude he is staring at Peter, his eyes stalk him, his tail switches like a wounded snake, hitting the doorframe, the floor, *thump, thump.*

Maude cannot walk past Jimmy G. It is phenomenal.

She backs away, watching him, fascinated, drops her purse on the bed, sits, amazed at the sight of Jimmy G, a small being she knows so well. He is glaring at Peter. His fur has bristled enlarging him, he stays rigid in the doorway, erect, straightened spine, occupying a small circle, his forepaws together, the Egyptian temple cat, Bastet, who kills the serpent that tries to stop the sun from revolving around the earth.

His eyes seem changed. The pupils have always been golden, a xanthosis. *Is there a greenish cast to them, a chrome green?*

The small croon followed by a chirring growl comes from him again, distinctly, the crooning growl. He is glowering. The gold green eyes have not wavered from the man in the chair, they are amazing. Something Maude does not understand is going on.

Is he trying to stop me? Maude feels that if she were to leave him alone in the house, he would climb up on Peter's shoulders and begin to gnaw through his neck, the way he would gnaw a rat's head off, and leave it as a treasure for Maude to find.

He is a nine-pound animal.

It's a cat. Am I taking orders from a cat?

As a cat, Jimmy G never considers death, as a cat, he subsists in the present tense. He does not make mistakes, of the few decisions he makes, he is positive of each one. All through last night and this morning, he has watched an intruder try to destroy the person he most admires in the world. Does he understand that?

Crap. Get your purse and get out of here. Interspecies displacement, parataxic distortion, none of it applies here. Go!

But Maude does not move, she cannot. She senses Jimmy G as a primordial being, she senses rage coming up through his small cat body, the pads of his feet, up through the floor, the decomposing rock beneath the small house. From aeons before our time. Jimmy G looks larger, it is his dormant power, his substance, his purity, his zonal belief, his mindless loyalty. His rules are natural, they come to him from a time long before our inventions.

When Jimmy G slipped into Maude's life, hadn't she felt then that he had been the perfect cat, come to her with a mission? He had simply appeared after Mason died, come to witness her suffering, divide her long nights, her cartons of milk. That first day, he had given her his forehead; *family*. She assumed his presence then and has ever since, she has slept with him hundreds of nights, she considers him to be her male side. Jimmy G has guarded her through her year in hell. And he has always shown her his need for food, love.

But this is different, it is something he would never want to show unless it was needed, it is from another nature. She has never seen this alien glare in any animal.

She does not know what Jimmy G is but she feels a sense of relief in his presence, as if a dreadful decision has been taken from her. She has been told from another source what she must do. It is all she needs.

"I'm supposed to do this." She turns to the man in the chair. "Am I psychotic? Oh, God, I hope not."

She shrugs, stands, goes to the wastebasket, reaches in, removes the balled-up latex gloves, straightens them, struggles to put them on, gives up, throws them away again, breaks the seal on a fresh pair.

She opens her maroon textbook, clips the pages with old paper clips stained on the page tops. She washes and dries her hands on paper towels. "I can't risk infection."

She is calm. It feels right.

"I just heard something snap in my head." She looks at Peter, "I think you've turned me into you." He is able to understand. Jimmy G has not moved from the doorway.

Again, Maude slips on the new gloves, up each finger,

snapping them taut each with a *clack*. She stares out the window at the small leaves catching the sun in patches. She pauses a long time, picks up the trocar and touches Peter's brow. Now Jimmy G jumps up on the bed, settles on the pillow, watches Maude's hands.

"I'm sorry for you, Peter, now, at this very moment, for what I am about to do to you."

Carefully, carefully, spring rises in her like the sun of a new day.

ACKNOWLEDGMENTS

With respect, thanks to Roger Jellinek, the good shepherd; Roger Donald, the champ.

To Mike Mattil, the good scout. And to Diane van Slyke, George McPheeters, Brian Madigan, Dura Temple. The Corner Cafe.

About the Author

GARDNER MCKAY published his first story at fifteen. His plays have been performed in every state and internationally. He has won three NEA grants and a Drama Critics Circle Award for playwriting. He has been a professional skipper, drama critic, sculptor, photographer, college teacher, actor, and has raised African lions. Each Sunday night he reads one of his stories on "Stories on the Wind," his program on Hawaiian Public Radio. He lives on Oahu with his wife and granddaughter, Cheyenne.